LAWRENCE:

BOOK ONE: GOLDWEAVING

BOOK TWO: ELABORYNTH

LAWRENCE:

BOOK ONE: GOLDWEAVING
BOOK TWO: ELABORYNTH

Rose Secrest

authorHOUSE®

AuthorHouse™
1663 Liberty Drive
Bloomington, IN 47403
www.authorhouse.com
Phone: 1-800-839-8640

First published by AuthorHouse   11/09/2011

ISBN: 978-1-4670-6653-2 (sc)
ISBN: 978-1-4670-6654-9 (ebk)

Library of Congress Control Number: 2011960098

Printed in the United States of America

Any people depicted in stock imagery provided by Thinkstock are models, and such images are being used for illustrative purposes only.
Certain stock imagery © Thinkstock.

This book is printed on acid-free paper.

PROLOGUE

"Innocents"   The experience first begins as an ache, centered in your front right eyetooth. The pain increases, throbbing acutely through your mouth, pulsating all over your head. Spasms wrack your body as the pain spreads, ripping your muscles from your bones. Your skin is roasted, hair being plucked out and brains being pulled out.

You twist upon the clay floor, a chain around your neck that allows you up to the cage bars and no further. A prisoner, full of frustration and anger. You have learned what cannot be done. Your captors dance far away to deep strains, feasting on your developing flesh.

Oppressors can meet their own desires so easily, for they deny yours. The hate within you seethes.

All through the experience presses the word "How?" How can I escape? You twirl on the nursery floor, flatten yourself on the satin sheets, drown your active mind in idleness or entertainment. You hunger or you are overfed. No law keeps the oppressors from having complete power over you, yet they do not appreciate this. They whine, losing control of themselves, hitting you again and again and again.

The mating season has come once more. You are the only female for a dozen males. You are in heat, crazed. They gang up on you, coming at you from all sides. Their need, the attack, the penetration.

You are not rational. You are innocent, free from cruelty, yet you learn their ways or are punished.

You tense, because now comes the fear, and you feel the pain of being dug into with a dull, dirty knife. You squeal at the slaughter. You feel the lash and snarl, only to have your teeth knocked out by a chain. You starve, locked in a closet. The yelling and beating then start, and the kind adult lifts your nightgown. The penetration lifts your buttocks from the bed and you feel like you're floating until the pain erases your buoyancy. Later, of course, you are blamed and beaten, for sin and crime is defined in terms of lack of control, not pain.

Suffering is infinite, and you scream.

You know what you desire: freedom. Responsibility. Power. No more compromises.

But the cage presses in on you, and you know it will always go on and on.

1

Chapter One

Silently the helibus glided over the snowcovered mountains, bringing the first wave of conventioneers. Though it was the first week of March, an ice storm had come to southern Appalachia, covering the trees with glitter in the bright winter sun.

Sitting in the overheated cabin, the passengers nervously kept silent, eyeing the hired pilot and the tearbringing scene outdoors.

Nicole coughed and put away her Hawk. Turning to the woman beside her, she asked, "Are we almost there?"

The pilot overheard her. He kept his eyes forward as his smooth bass answered, "As a matter of fact, yes. It's that mountain slightly to our right."

Nicole peered out and studied the mountainside. It took her a while, but, suddenly, as the helibus veered, giving her a better view, she caught sight of a few windows and a door set into the rocks gracing the upper part of the mountainside.

She frowned just as quickly. The mountains should be covered with trees. The heavy orange and brown rocks must be artificial.

Her question had started a murmur in the crowd, but none of it was directed at her. Even the woman beside her had turned away, laughing over her shoulder at someone in the back. Nicole strained her ears for suspicious whispers, wondering if the others were shy, jealous, or just fearful that she might portray them unjustly.

Nicole studied the faces of the thirty or so women around her. Most were animated, chatting easily. A few were quiet, but eagerly listening. *Maybe it's me. We all believe in the same things, but I'm here at this convention involuntarily. For that alone, they don't trust me.*

The helibus swerved gently, expelling steam to the left. Nicole watched the ice crystals splatter the window. *There might be a strong wind out there. I didn't bring any really warm clothing. I hope they rush us right in.*

They landed in a huge courtyard cleared of ice. Immediately the two wide gold and red wooden doors swung inward, before Nicole could fully grasp the intricate carved designs of each. Arabesque, she guessed, how ostentatious. The women climbed out of the helibus onto the large red cobblestones and stood well back to see it take off. Framed against a brilliant blue sky, the soft brown helibus shot up and away. Nicole turned to look inside the mansion.

3

One of the women, a tall, chunky brunette called Alma, grabbed the straps of her overalls and exclaimed, "Wow! Look at this place! Not like our last place at all! Now this is more like it!" She struck a pose. "Grace, beauty, and, most important of all, respect!" She silenced and stood, gazing with wonder at the magnificent entrance.

The crowd stood milling, not yet wanting to enter the almost verboten place. Nicole shifted, not sure if she should stalk ahead or wait. They might resent her lack of worshipful awe.

She after all did not have long to wait. Suzette entered, peeking around all the hidden corners as she pirouetted. When she turned to face the group, her look was as fiery as her hair.

"Remember that in this house we have only one friend," she whispered. "Lawrence."

"Lawrence . . ." The murmur hummed through the crowd. Several hands were clasped.

"We have more to thank Lawrence for than just letting us use her mansion," Alma claimed loudly, looking accusingly at Nicole for a second.

"Yeah! Like letting us be the first to participate in her newest experience!" someone shouted.

Everyone cheered.

Still, no one fully entered the mansion until Alma yelled, "Well, what are we waiting for? Let's go!"

The crowd streamed in.

The large anteroom dwarfed the group of thirty, who clustered together in one corner, as if frightened of dissipation if they scattered. Nicole stood apart and swiftly searched the room, wandering up a slope of stone that led to a cozy niche of burnished wood. The women, taking her initiative, began separate activities, some taking advantage of the side restrooms, others just standing around and talking. Nicole closed her ears. *I didn't come here to listen to them. I'm not on assignment. If I were a masochist, I'd call this a vacation.* An oriental woman paused near her, but all her nametag said was "Child Genius." *Humph. How weird. Obviously that's her lover next to her. Look at that outfit!* Nicole, never one to follow fashion, eyed the tall woman's skirt distastefully. *How old-fashioned. What kind of people are these, anyway?* Nicole looked up at a side door. *Now that Lawrence invited me, will she grant me an interview? Or is she really a hermit?*

The Child Genius' lover at one point lifted her skirt to straighten a stocking, and immediately Lawrence walked in from that side door, apparently by accident. Nicole jumped, gaping at the short, plump, shabbily dressed artist. Rapidly she took in the rosy cheeks, glasses, and long brown hair. Lawrence's sharp dark eyes blinked as, embarrassed, she began to cross the room, not looking at anyone. Avoiding everyone, however, was impossible. The crowd around her thickened as the women clamored for her attention. Nicole guessed Lawrence was panicking, so she approached her kindly.

Reaching through the mob, Nicole tapped Lawrence on the shoulder.

Lawrence whirled to look at her, and her eyes flew open wide. "Excuse me," she muttered and, as quickly as she could, fled the room.

Nicole stood in wonder, unknowingly bearing the glares of a few. *But she invited me, after I had already decided not to come to this convention.*

Her dismay was interrupted by a smooth male announcer's voice coming over a loudspeaker.

"Those wishing to participate in the new experience, please enter the auditoriums to the right." Nicole watched the black panels slide back to reveal three auditorium doors. "When the rest of the visitors have arrived, the experience will begin."

Needless to say, everyone began crowding the auditoriums immediately.

Lawrence stayed on the worn path so as to avoid touching the vines that hung from the trees. Completely familiar with each branch that protruded down to her height, she did not even disturb a leaf with her passing.

She aimed toward the pond, shielding her eyes from the intense light. She paused at the bank, hoping to linger, mesmerized by the gentle current and soft, moist air, but after several silent moments, she slowly moved on, soon to be cloaked by dark, draping pine branches, so that it seemed she disappeared into a place impenetrable by light. Now she had to grope in near total darkness until she found a stone wall. *At last!* she thought, wrenching a sturdy steel bar free from its clasp and stepping outside.

Snow peppered her face, causing her to blink. The weather inside had been mild; she had forgotten that there would be snow. Lawrence stepped out onto the open balcony after carefully sealing the door and stood until the cold had seeped into her soft, flannel, long-sleeved shirt and paint-stained jeans. Then she fell to her knees.

Again she waited, collecting snow on her hair and shoulders. Then suddenly she shuddered and roused herself. Grabbing a handful of snow, she pressed firmly and uniformly, forming a cylinder. Hurriedly she pressed more and more cylinders, her hands meticulously molding the snow, her nimble fingers gently caressing, never plunging. Soon she had a cluster of hard cylinders. The edges were not quite rounded, so she cupped it in her red, wet hands, melting away the parts that stood out until she had formed a sphere. She held it a while longer, then looked at it strangely, as if asking herself how it had come to be.

Lawrence rose and, to remind herself, leaned over the railing to look at the barn. With one hand holding her creation and the other wiping snow off the ledge in long, stroking motions, she thought of bloody mouths, teeth, and rain. Now she was ready.

Lawrence hummed softly to herself as she carried the snowball lightly back into the forest. At one point she paused, caught by a metallic glitter in the pristine woods. Lawrence approached slowly, feeling gently with her free hand. She yanked up a plastic bag to discover a panel of surveillance instruments. She stared at the dials. *Now this all might be useful.* Tucking the bag back around the gray block, she rose slowly, heading for the stand near the pond, stepping up to face the Hawks.

Lawrence spread apart the dogwood branches that covered the podium, curving them outward and leaving one small parting in the middle for her face to show through. As the Hawks fed her face's image and the Dogs fed her voice's sound to those in the three auditoriums, she bent her head and closed her eyes before her voice quavered.

"I wish to bless the beasts and the children. We all know that small domestic animals and one's own small children are perfect victims. Adult humans crave to take out their anger on the defenseless. It is so tempting for them to hurt little furry animals and tiny children. How luscious to the human temperament to hear them cry out!

"I'm sure you all have heard this a million times. Repetition deadens, not heightens, response, so I'll just remind you of my contributions to the humane organizations and of my support of any action taken against the perpetuation of the nuclear family structure." Lawrence unconsciously smiled at this point, and lifted her eyes to gaze cheerfully out at the audience she could not see. "Perhaps some of you remember my work entitled 'Innocents' and have learned how much I care." Lawrence lost her smile suddenly, for the Lions were feeding her laughter! Quickly she reviewed her words and found out why. She smiled again. *Of course* they remembered it! "Innocents" had been quite popular, probably due to the notion the critics and public had of her intent, not because anyone had actually enjoyed its sensations.

Lawrence gulped, pausing long after the laughter had died. *Please just let me go back to my laboratory,* she thought. *It's so much easier there!*

"I'd like today to familiarize you with a perhaps incomprehensible side of this problem. Animals and children can also be the only available outlet for love. I read in the paper last week about a person who was arrested for horrible sadistic crimes he had committed on several young females. Many of these women, most underage, were kept in boxes and, of course, raped several times. He randomly chose to beat them, and by a miracle he ended up killing none of them. Yet this person owned a total of seventeen pets he very obviously loved. He had a well-respected position as a business manager, and he was paid well. In turn, he lavished most of his paycheck on several humane organizations. It is completely possible that he was a loving person who had taken the easiest route society provides in showing his love. Obtaining a child or animal in order to love it is as common and sensible as obtaining it in order to harm it." Lawrence began to shake as her knees grew weak. She blushed and grasped the podium tightly. Her lips trembled and her eyes filled with tears. "I . . . I have a work tonight . . . It's incomplete, but suitable for group experience." Lawrence darted her eyes back and forth, as if she could actually see the audience's response. "Remember that no one here is required to see it. I must have voluntary cooperation." Here the audience laughed briefly before they all became quite silent. Lawrence waited in the silence a long time, then said, "Thank you."

Oh, god, oh, when Lawrence finally stepped back and I was hooked in . . . I couldn't believe it. I'd never experienced her before, you know. Just couldn't afford it. Sure, I wanted to see what it was like, but wow. Oh, the colors alone pressed me down and made my heart ache. My teeth ached, too. Hell, my whole brain, nerves, and ears ached, too. Here's how it was:

"Love Can Art" I am beside the creek, naked, vulnerable, then suddenly clothed. I fill the pottery and trace the lines on its sides. A goat wanders by, white and black against deep, dark green and the flavor is so intense on my tongue I rasp it against my wrist to calm it. But my heart is filled with so much . . . simple . . . love! Darkness creeps in overhead, and I am staring into the mists of the waterfall at a moonbow. Its three colors shine dimly, and I step into the creek but do not feel the wetness. My heart is faint with love. Who feels? We all feel? No, not yet. When I pass through the underground tunnel behind the waterfall, I begin to feel an emptiness, a complete absence of emotion that nevertheless sends me to shiver. It is so terrifying, being unable to love, that when warm darkness replaces the cool fluorescence, I am relieved, though there is no one. I need no one. Then above . . . there is a glowing face, and I almost burst out laughing, for, even to me, the face is familiar. The woman's chubby, wondering face with the cat-green eyes and blonde hair was Lawrence's icon. Why? Because Lawrence was once intrigued by her in a department store. It seemed silly, but the hookup was urging me to be hopeful, and so I became . . .

The hookup faded.

That's when the hunger began.

Lawrence's image reappeared. Her face was worried. She knelt, haphazard, near the podium where dripped the remains of her snowball and bit her lip.

"It's unfinished," she faltered, closing her eyes before fading out.

The crowds sat stunned, unmoving, unbelieving, and Lawrence was left alone in the woods with the knowledge that an incomplete masterpiece was the worst of all.

Chapter Two

Nicole gulped, lifting her hands to watch them shake. *What is this? I feel hurt, yet I want more!*

She jerked her attention to the front of the room. Several minutes had passed since Lawrence had faded out, and now a tall, heavyset man with crisp, short, curly black hair was dashing from the back, hands lifted high in placation.

"Okay, everybody, it's all right. Uh . . ." He paused to mop his face with a handkerchief. "I've just got through telling the other two rooms . . . it's all right. Lawrence has decided to show all of her experiences in here free of charge."

An appreciative murmur rose from the audience. Nicole caught herself before she joined in.

"For this room, we've decided to show 'Definitions.'" The audience stifled a groan. He blinked. "Thank you so much." Quickly he strode up the aisle right next to Nicole, so she was able to catch his frenzied medium blue eyes. He even wore a nametag: "Larry McKenzie, Manager."

"Definitions"   I had read the reviews of "Definitions," so I could understand the groans. The marketers released it reluctantly, quoted as saying that only intellectuals or English Ph.D.'s would like it, but it was very successful nonetheless. One released quote from Lawrence, borne by the committee, had her state that this was what the public needed. End of quote. Whatever that meant. Here is how it was:

I am born and grasp readily the basic words of my language, any language, then, just as rapidly, I lose this ability. But translations cannot be exact: I stare at the page of Greek in horror. At the climax, I learn the word is not the thing, that no relationship exists between the word's sound and what it represents. Fine; that's obvious. I stand next to him, and I am filled with longing. I see the sunset and am filled with awe. These words, though, these words! I cannot use these magical words to express my feelings. I cannot convey my experience. Appropriate words that would convey exactly my spirit and feeling cannot be found. I cannot name.

The experience ends cleverly. My conflict has brought together all language and this universe. I am accepting of language's limitations, yet I see that words can go beyond reality. A stream of beauty flows. Some things are not meant for words, but action, and expression. My nagging frustration bleeds from me. I leave Lawrence with a sense of clear unity and perfection.

When I leave, pleased after my first, incomplete experience to be satiated by the crystalline second one, my fragile membrane of joy that had scabbed over the pain is broken by hearing a member of the audience say, "Naw, I'm staying. The next one's got to be better. I just do this for orgasm."

"Just what did you think you were trying to prove?"

Lawrence stood up against the wall in the conference room meekly, mind blank, because, despite Alma's strident question, she never let Lawrence sneak in any words of explanation at all. Occasionally Lawrence let her eyes leap around the room. *Where's Nicole? Surely she didn't stay for an experience, did she?* Sudden panic filled her heart: *She left. Well, okay, that's good.* Lawrence smiled before she remembered that Nicole would have to request a helicopter through her before she could leave, unless . . . She hiked away from here! In the snow!

"It really was beautiful," Alma was finishing on a gentler note, "I'd like to see what you do with it." She turned away, toward the reception table, hand already outstretched for a tofu cookie, then spun back around. "Why don't you join Lesbians United? Then I could see more of you." Alma halted then, her self-confidence rapidly eroding, as if she were thinking: *Someone like me? Friends with Lawrence?* Stuffing a tofu cookie in her mouth, she waved goodbye and blended into the crowd.

Lawrence gulped. She was still nervous, but otherwise holding up pretty well. The Child Genius approached.

"It would really make a difference if you joined."

Lawrence quit gazing at the lovely face of the tall, slender Japanese woman and pointed at her convention badge. "Are you a member, too?"

"Certainly." Her gaze was friendly, even humble, Lawrence realized.

"I've heard a little bit about you. You're not a child anymore."

"No. But I'm still a genius."

Lawrence laughed. She was starting to feel quite comfortable with the Child Genius.

"It's a little cold in here," the Child Genius said, indicating her coat.

"Do you think so?" Lawrence frowned. She was burning up, but maybe that was because she was nervous. "It shouldn't be," she continued seriously. "The trees need warmth."

"Trees?" The Child Genius gaped, then quickly resumed her composed stare. "Oh yes, the dogwoods. Are there more?"

"Sure. I've got an entire forest growing in here."

"Wow."

Now why did I say that? I didn't want anybody to know about the forest. I didn't want them trampling around in it and messing it up. Of course, I'd let Nicole see it. Lawrence paused to examine her motives. *Is it this person's fame, or am I just infatuated with her?* She cleared her throat. "They've not been treating me too badly, considering."

"I think it's because they admire your talent."

Lawrence thrust back her bangs sharply. "No. That's exactly what they *shouldn't* be admiring."

The Child Genius stepped back and looked her up and down. "Why? Do you have something really admirable you've been hiding? Let's see it!"

"No, no," said Lawrence, blushing. "I'm just saying that I'm no different from anyone else."

The Child Genius cast her gaze over at the majestic marble staircase that filled the entire left wall, rising up toward the back of the passage that led to the auditoriums. "Indeed," she said dryly.

"So what have you been doing with your great genius?" Lawrence asked brightly.

"Same thing you've been doing with yours."

"Mine?" Lawrence laughed. "What little brains I got goes into creating experiences."

"I do that, too, sort of. I try to come up with alternate ways for people to live."

Lawrence looked up at the staircase. Nicole had just started walking down it. The handsome brown face above the turtleneck filled her with awe. Lawrence watched her arms swing with ease as she walked at a reasonable pace down the center of the stairs. *Wouldn't you know it? She doesn't need a handrail.*

"Is there someone else you're looking for?" The Child Genius asked politely.

"What? Oh, no, uh . . . Really? How do you create? Do you cover everything? Architecture? Family structure? Drugs? Fictive reality?"

The Child Genius sighed. "That and more. It really is an monumental project."

"Hmm. Your activity sounds fascinating. Do you design lives for people? Would you design one for me?"

The Child Genius studied her. Lawrence felt like a prospective sculpting model. "Would you want me to?"

"Probably not." Lawrence chuckled self-consciously. "I'd be curious, though, to see what you come up with."

"Maybe together it would work." The Child Genius spoke excitedly, as if she had just seen a breakthrough. "I don't usually do that, but I'd probably have to with you."

"Why?"

"Well, it makes sense, knowing you. You wouldn't let me dictate your actions. You'd work with me to adapt my suggestions to your life."

Lawrence seemed to have drifted off into thought. She nodded. "You're a hookie. Have you experienced all of me?"

"Of course!"

Then you know, Lawrence thought.

Nicole passed into the crowd, and was surprised to learn that the main topic of conversation was still whether or not Lawrence was justified in presenting an incomplete experience.

"I think it was just horrible! And unfair! And . . . unjust! I'm glad I left my intensifier at home!" Alma blurted.

Nicole pricked up her ears. "I thought those were illegal."

The small group of women laughed at her indignant look. Alma answered, "Honey, they're not illegal. It's claimed that Lawrence tried to prevent her marketers from selling them, but it didn't work, and that doesn't stop everyone else from doing it, does it?"

Suzette added softly, "I can remember when they used to sell pacifiers. They thought the new Lawrence experiences were too intense. They thought people would die."

"Yeah, then they found out that's what people wanted, so they produced intensifiers, even though Lawrence said no." Darla, a young, short, muscular woman spoke, tossing her tightly braided head.

"A *classic* intensifier, that's what I have!" boasted Alma.

Nicole, at a loss trying to figure out what "classic" could mean, decided anyway to argue, "Well, maybe Lawrence is right. Somebody *could* die, and who needs an intensifier, anyway?"

Alma opened her mouth in preparation for delivering a little sarcasm, then shut it and peered at Nicole's convention badge. "Hmph! Well, what do you know? A neube!"

"Not really." Nicole blushed.

"Well, you just wait. You will be. And when you get around to experiencing 'Goldweaving,' you'll want an intensifier, or else you'll end up sexually frustrated." Alma cackled gaily.

Nicole turned away and spotted Lawrence in a far away corner, then she faced Alma directly. "There's real life." Her voice came out a little harsher than she had tried to make it.

"Oh, yes, oh, yes, but it's not the same . . ." The woman smirked under her supposed acquiescence.

"Of course not," Nicole murmured, puzzled, her attention once more diverted as she looked for Lawrence. "Excuse me." She left the boisterous group and approached Lawrence, touching her arm very gently to get her attention.

Lawrence slightly jumped, eyes dilating in Nicole's presence, but her conversational skills did not slack; she was just as shy and incompetent as ever.

"Excuse me, Ms . . ."

"Oh, Lawrence, of course!" Lawrence interrupted immediately, smiling awkwardly. Nicole winced invisibly at her blunder. She had forgotten that Lawrence thought "Ms." was as out-of-date as any other title.

"Yes. Um, I'd like to ask you what you think about the danger involved in showing an incomplete experience."

Lawrence answered faintly and tiredly, "Well, they've been asking me that all morning. *I* think it was okay, but there *were* some neubes in the audience. Perhaps if there hadn't have been, I wouldn't feel so guilty, for two reasons: it was voluntary, and I think hookies should participate more in the experience."

Nicole was busily Dogging Lawrence's exact quotes surreptitiously, then stopped. Looking up from the tiny recording machine, she stammered, "Sorry. Reporter's instinct, you know."

Lawrence smiled warmly yet weakly. "Of course I know, darling. I . . . I mean . . ." She laughed. "I'm used to being around Jan! Such a bothersome habit!"

She faintly blushed.

Nicole hurried on, uncomfortable. "Many hookies say they're in it only for the sexual excitement. What do you think about that?"

"Oh, I don't know."

"Do you think that's why you're so popular?" Nicole persisted.

"Good grief, I don't know, but I suppose that would be a nice reason, better than some."

Nicole hesitated. "I didn't really, in the two I've experienced, feel that way. The feelings were intense, but not . . ."

"Hey, I won't be conservative and say sex is the more primitive emotion, but I can say that it's shallow if that's *all* they get out of it—and I don't think it is. Sex is just another feeling for me to expose. It's all right."

"What is 'Goldweaving'?"

Lawrence started to answer, then shook her head. "So that's it! You must have been talking to Alma, or the Child Genius, or somebody. Why don't you just experience it for yourself?"

"Oh, so you know—"

"Of course I know what turns people on. How could I not know?"

Nicole was about to Dog this too and then just leave, but then she hesitated. Too ambiguous, which was great, but *she* needed to know.

"How do you know?"

Lawrence sat back up against the wall and sighed, "Here I am, trying to mastermind, trying to come up with the right, no, not the right: good answers, for you or for the public, I don't know, and all I can say is that you're probably thinking I have some kind of deep, wise knowledge of what turns people on prior to working and that I conform to this idea. But no, I know because the promoters tell me, and then they tell me to aim for it, when that doesn't work, so I ignore them, and they're satisfied, I suppose because each work I do stimulates somebody somewhere, and they get money."

Nicole paused just long enough to have the conversation interrupted by the Child Genius.

"Lawrence, dear, I'm back again." She jerked her thumb over her shoulder. "Out on the floor we're having a lively conversation. I decided to ask you about whether it's dangerous to allow people to own pets or have children. You know, dangerous for the adult. Because it's allowing them to become festered in that love. Carmen seemed to agree with me . . ."

Lawrence interrupted sharply in turn. "First off, animals are never 'owned.' And the amount of danger from superficially innocuous sources for sane, mature *adults* in today's society is negligible."

The Child Genius appeared taken aback, and Nicole wondered. Any assertiveness on Lawrence's part didn't seem typical for her.

The Child Genius quickly recovered with a smug grin. "Ah, but who's sane and mature?"

Lawrence folded her arms. "Not too many people, in my opinion, not even me," she answered seriously. "But there are actually quite a few competents. They do all right."

"Not you?" Nicole butted in.

"No, not me." Lawrence gazed over to another corner of the room where a tall, fairly dark man with no nametag was approaching. "Because it's unfinished," she muttered out of the side of her mouth to Nicole.

"Is that Jan?" blurted the Child Genius.

Without another word Lawrence left.

Nicole almost put her Dog away, then left it out when she heard what Jan had to say.

"Sweetheart, I just came to tell you there's cheese —"

"Where?"

Jan fluttered a hand toward the wide cavern he had come through. "Back there. In Cave Six, I believe." His voice was tinged with what Nicole could only call wry pompousness, as if he still couldn't believe that he and his wife lived inside of a mountain. It was still exciting to him, yet it was just starting to be amusing, too. "Cave Six," indeed! "Nowhere else, just back where no one would suspect."

Lawrence's face flushed. "I won't have it! Who brought it? Oh, who cares who brought it? Just remove it from my house immediately!" She walked rapidly beside Jan, departing from whence he came.

Nicole shrugged and put away her Dog. She parted politely from the Child Genius and began to wander.

Chapter Three

After Lawrence's abrupt, if ridiculous, departure, Nicole walked about aimlessly, reading placards and notices, but not speaking to anyone. At one point she smacked her head and moaned. "Shit!" she muttered. "I forgot to ask Lawrence why she invited me!" She fumed for a while, until the printed announcements she had been staring at blindly came into focus. She read with false interest:

The New University: Any More Suggestions?

Fiction Writers' Workshop: Exclusionist Language and the Inclusion of Unimportant Characters. Readers Especially Welcome!

If You Are Chosen: How to Raise That Child Properly.

Cheese Lovers: Can We Now Reverse the Legacy?

Nicole's eyes kept going back to the second one. *It sounds interesting,* she mused. *But does it pertain to journalism? I suppose it could, but I don't think it pertains to radical journalism, which, if it lives up to its name, doesn't have any exclusionist language.* She contemplated. *No, I can't go. I know I don't have the necessary talent for such a thing as that. I get the message across directly, cleanly, and forcefully. That is my talent. But look at that political cartoonist.* Her eyes flashed up at a clipping pinned onto the wall. *He's lucky. He has important things to say, atrocities to protest, and when he completes his job, he has reached literally millions. Very few read my articles.* She paused, struck by a sudden thought. *Lawrence reaches millions. Is what she's saying worthy? I have a feeling it is, but I don't know what she's trying to say, or whether I believe in it. I need to find out.*

"Yellowstone" As I approach the auditorium, I am again flooded with desire. Yes, yes, my mind screams, go for it! I lurch backwards. Why not just ask Lawrence what she's trying to say? Why do I think I must sit through every experience to figure it out? I shrug. Lawrence probably isn't going to grant me an interview. Yeah, she allowed me to Dog her, but that doesn't mean she'll let me publish anything. My last lawsuit . . . I shudder. Okay. Sometimes the artist cannot begin to say what her message is. Like my interview with . . . oh, forget that jerk. Looks like I gotta experience Lawrence. Not "Goldweaving," though. Not yet.

The one they're showing concerns nature, typical for Lawrence. I find it hard to get lost in it, maybe because I'm getting used to it. Maybe hookies *know* her, so they can orient themselves inside of her rapidly. Or it's my fear of loss of control that's distancing me from the experience's effect. I admit, the geyser is overwhelming. It's breathless, yet full of power. I feel the pressures of columns of pure, cool liquid. How does she know how a geyser feels? And geysers aren't *cool*, but it works! About halfway through I remember Lawrence saying that people should participate more, and I try, but it's so easy to lie back and let it wash over me, for then I feel that all this is transitory, that it flows into me, through me, and way past me, and I need not fear its power.

When the lights return and the seats rotate back to their original positions, I imagine someone being aroused by the geyser image, perhaps a male more strongly. I for one feel nothing. Lawrence rarely has people in her, and when she does, there is fear. Perhaps once she would have been rated "G."

Jan cleared some papers off a tiny section of the lab table before squeezing into his chair. He put his bowl onto the table's cork surface, rapidly stirring as he looked down into his soup.

"You were so nice to cook today. You want me to tidy up a little?"

Jan looked up, shaking his head at Lawrence, who had grabbed a hammer near his glass of water before squatting beside him. "No, it's your laboratory. Do what you want. But—isn't this a bit rude?"

"What?" Lawrence started climbing the ladder that led to her banks of machinery, craftily perched on a cliff of dusty gray stone. She held a violin and a paint brush in her left hand.

Jan anxiously watched her progress. "Be careful. Oh, you know. Leaving the convention before it really started."

"Oh, that. Nope. I told them they could use my house. I didn't say I'd attend. Fuck 'em all."

Jan soothingly answered, "All right. Why don't you come down and eat something? You haven't had anything since . . . I don't know when, honestly." He shook his head.

Lawrence absentmindedly muttered, "Well, yeah, I gotta eat. Feed my brain, someday . . . I swear . . ." It seemed to Jan that she was tuning everything at once, turning the knobs on the encephalogram before whipping over to adjust the controls on the empathometer, so he bent down once more to his soup and waited.

"Shit!" Lawrence looked down at the paint brush she had dropped near his feet, then swung back down to retrieve it. "Not like I need it up there, anyway. I just found it . . ." Taking a deep breath, she shuddered. She looked beseechingly at her husband. "If only you hadn't arranged for Nicole to be here. What was that, some big surprise for our anniversary? Some surprise! I've been more nervous than I have been since . . . high school, I guess. I thought I was all over with that stupid adolescent jitteriness crap, too." She looked mournfully down at the miniature loom that graced a small table behind her, part of a velvet carpet only three inches wide still piled up at one end of it, then picked up her violin, playing a few notes sullenly, searching, always searching.

Jan broke the small loaf of wheat bread and nibbled. "It wasn't that weird a proposition. After all, she *is* a feminist and a humanist and humane and intelligent and . . ."

Lawrence sighed heavily, interrupting Jan with ". . . and a *neube*. Oh god. Oh shit. And beautiful and calm and brave and—" Determinedly she clicked on her Hawk and Dog, hesitated, then turned off the Hawk. She played a few more notes, this time obviously aiming for a tune, when Nicole came in, ducking her head under the stalactites and avoiding the dripping icicles. Lawrence, in a familiar pattern of concentration, murmured softly to her clear music and didn't notice Nicole until Jan stood up and waved, motioning for silence. Lawrence played yet more scratchily, then abruptly stopped, shutting off the Dog. She turned cool eyes toward Nicole and said sharply, "Thank you, though I suppose you know this grotto isn't a part of the convention."

At first Nicole was surprised at Lawrence's change from a shy, nervous individual to such an angry one, but then she reasoned that it was Lawrence's retreat she was invading. Disconcerted, she cleared her throat. "I saw you come down here and thought . . ." Eagerly she stepped forward, her curiosity overcoming her, making her feel even worse for intruding. "Do you play? I didn't hear any music in the experiences."

Relenting, Lawrence answered softly, "Most people don't the first couple of times. Don't worry about it."

"Why?"

Lawrence stood up to place her violin back in its case. "What *have* you experienced?" She asked, not looking at her.

Nicole hesitated, causing Lawrence to whip her gaze at her. "Well, mainly sights, emotion . . ." She shrugged. That was about it.

"You and millions of other people. There are a few gastronomes or . . . I don't know the word . . . people with strong senses of smell, and then I get the true sensitives, they feel *everything*, things I don't put in, like the strong sting of a mosquito biting. They're the best."

Nicole goggled, taking a few steps toward Lawrence. "Are you saying that all art is just for artists?" For a second, confused, she checked to see if her Dog was on. Of course it was. Around unpredictable Lawrence, she must always be prepared.

Lawrence took a deep breath and closed her eyes, slumping back on the stool. Almost immediately, though, she opened her eyes and looked at Jan. "I believe I'm about to starve. Jan, please . . ."

He stood. "What do you want?"

"Just soup and bread and water."

Jan left.

Lawrence glanced at Nicole, who said, "I just realized how famished I am. I forgot to feed at your banquets. I've been too busy, experiencing . . ." She broke off, confused by a slight twinge of guilt.

"Jan is thoughtful," reassured Lawrence. "He'll bring enough for three." She studied Nicole openly. "Why do you seek me?"

Nicole was ready. "It was *you* who invited *me.*"

Lawrence jumped, but answered slowly and calmly, "No. Jan invited you. I didn't."

Now it was Nicole's turn to jump as well as dart her glance at where Jan had been sitting. "Him? Why?"

"He's thoughtful, as I already said."

Nicole puzzled over that a while, then stepped back. "Okay, then why don't you just tell me to leave?"

Lawrence scooted back on her stool as if she were trying to hide herself. "I wouldn't do that, but if you want to leave, then . . ."

Nicole nodded, not showing her triumph. "Let me ask you something else. Why did you visit the first group, just walking through, like you were a queen begging for obeisance?"

Lawrence hesitated, then said, "Oh, that. The first time. I could tell you I didn't know that anybody was around yet, but . . ."

"I wouldn't believe you."

"Okay, so I'll say that it was a test to see if I'd panic. I thought I could handle it, but then I clammed up." Lawrence stared down meekly.

"But later you seemed perfectly normal."

Lawrence looked over at her eagerly. "Did I?"

"Yes," Nicole found herself answering reassuringly. She shifted her feet, then came forward. "Look, I've never been one to beat around the bush. Are you going to grant me an interview or not?"

Lawrence swiftly lifted her head, surprised, but with an even odder look of calculating revelation spread over her face.

"Don't be so shocked. I thought that it would be obvious . . . I'm a journalist. What did you expect?"

Lawrence seemed to be trying to choose another route. Nicole watched, puzzled, as her face registered amusement, sadness, and hope before finally settling on amusement. When her voice came out, though, it was rough. "Yeah, but you're doing the right thing. You're experiencing me. Keep on doing it. Let my art speak for itself. You don't need me to tell you."

"But, apparently, what were you saying?" *Damn.* Nicole thought. *She's good. Here come my questions again.* "You were implying I'd have to experience them over and over to pick up everything."

"Now I don't know that. But it seems to be true, from what I've heard. They don't hear the music at first, stuff like that." Lawrence looked humbly at her.

"I don't have time for that. If I'm going to learn anything that way, I need . . ." That reminded her. "What about intensifiers? Would they help?"

"No!" Lawrence yelled, swinging up off her stool and jutting her head out. "No way!" Now her jaw was clenched, the words just barely making it through. "That would just make it worse! I'm positive!"

Nicole stared. "But they're selling them," she answered calmly.

"I know that," Lawrence spoke quietly. Instantly her gaze shot up to her machinery banks. Nicole followed, seeing the quiet panels, the guitar, the driftwood tilting off one counter. Lawrence strode over to the ladder and climbed once more. From a drawer she yanked out a tiny, horned device. Turning to Nicole, she said, "A simple device, actually. All it does is increase the intensity by increasing the amplitude of the input. It's cheap. If you can afford experiences, you can afford this." She aimed it at Nicole. "Catch."

Nicole grabbed the lightly tossed intensifier.

"That's a classic intensifier. The first one ever made, and they haven't improved upon it. The new ones are a bit smaller, I believe . . ."

"I don't need this," murmured Nicole. "I just want to Hawk it."

"Go ahead."

Nicole turned on her Hawk and recorded an image of the device, then she put it down on the floor.

"Careful with that," warned Lawrence, practically coming down the ladder face forward. "I might trip on it if you leave it there. Why didn't you throw it back?"

"I'm curious. Why do you hate them so much?"

Lawrence paused at the base of the ladder. "I don't need them. I'm good enough," she answered gruffly, distractedly.

"Why do you have this one, then?"

"Aah, I don't know. I look at it sometimes. It's like a reminder. It makes me realize how much I'm dependent on technology." Lawrence bent down to pick up the intensifier.

Nicole aimed her Hawk at Lawrence as she held it.

"Not too subtle, are you?" Lawrence snapped. "No pictures."

Nicole kept the Hawk positioned on her. "Oh?"

"Yes, and I'm getting pretty sick of the questions, too." Lawrence grimaced, then, tucking the intensifier into her elbow, she shot her right hand out and pulled at the Hawk, shutting it off.

"Hey!"

"No pictures," Lawrence repeated.

"Ever?" Nicole asked hotly.

"That depends." Lawrence walked back to sit on the ladder. "I haven't given you permission to publish anything. Shit, I hate this." She peered over at Nicole. "How important is this story to you anyway?"

"Just that it's never been done. You've never let anyone come close. All the reports about you are obviously secondhand. Nobody's ever claimed they spoke to you, not one word. Of course I want the story." Nicole paused. Again Lawrence had an odd expression on her face.

"I didn't picture you as ambitious," Lawrence explained quietly.

"And what do you know about me?"

Lawrence blushed. "I've read everything by you. Not your stupid mainstream articles, I didn't know about those, but in all the radical publications. You got one fan letter out of me, and now you're here!" Awkwardly she stood, hunching her shoulders. "Obviously, you want some kind of story about me, and, judging from what I've read of yours, there's more to it than just exposing a celebrity. There's got to be. You never wrote the sort of crap that's in *Folks* magazine." Lawrence stopped pacing with a lurch, as if she hadn't been aware of it. "You've got something in mind, so I think I should . . . Let's strike a bargain."

Nicole nodded.

Lawrence came over to where she stood. Idly, yet gently, she reached out her hand and smoothed Nicole's cheek.

Nicole did not flinch.

Lawrence stepped back as she dropped her hand. "Thank you," she whispered. "For now," she continued more loudly, "I have no doubts. And you? Listen. This ain't nothing yet. I think I can promise you a good, I mean really good story about me. Heck, it might even win a prize, and you can be set. I don't care. But I need something in return. You want an interview. I want to finish my art. Let's make a deal. I talk, you listen. You can even Hawk me, I won't care." Lawrence at that moment looked as if she would care mightily. "But you have to grant me a favor. I need your complete cooperation. I need you to complete my art."

"Atmosphere of Stars" and "Summer Twilight"

After a simple but satisfying meal of bean soup, squash soup, multigrain bread, fruit and water in which nothing much is said, I leave, explaining that I had to think it over.

Jan had finally come back, and I didn't get the chance to ask Lawrence why she needs me. Odd isn't the right word. Absurd? Ludicrous? Yet she seemed so sure, and . . . I'd be crazy to pass up the interview. I must get her promise.

I head toward the auditorium, then stop myself. If I *don't* want to participate, then experiencing Lawrence wasn't the thing to do. I stand outside the door, urging myself to slow down. Now

I have to decide. If I go in there one more time, it'll mean that I was learning about Lawrence, doing my research, such as it is, and binding myself to her contract. If I *don't* go in there, I'll just have to leave. Yeah, I know it'd be a pain, but a smaller helicopter . . . Look, there's really no other great story here, I'm on vacation, and sometime soon, I should begin enjoying myself.

I take a step toward the auditorium. Whoa! Going in there *was* enjoying myself, but why? Was it addictive? Or was my desire to know Lawrence's message growing stronger?

Suddenly I throw away my doubts. Something was pushing me, it didn't matter what, so I supposed I should follow it, semiconsciously also following Lawrence's advice to let my senses guide me to happiness.

I am already settled in the room when I stand up, gripped with fear. Lawrence had never, in any spoken words whatsoever, given any such advice. Where had it come from?

But I am aware of people waving me down, so I hook up quickly, embarrassed. Before the experience grips me, I tell myself that perhaps, long ago, I had read about Lawrence's advice, maybe in that letter to me.

This one, "Atmosphere of Stars," is so powerful that I nearly rip out the hooks and run out, for I *can* hear the music, and feel the moisture of the clouds I pass through, and smell coldness and taste sweet cream. In the brief blanked moment before I hit the stars I wildly imagine I have an intensifier and try to rip it out. But then there are the stars, and cold, blue, moonlit clouds, and galaxy waves. The moon rises, and the stars like jewels glitter, pounding toward a crescendo. Within the intense tingling is the message: Ignore just the archaic symbolism of the sun's waxing and waning, for there is also a symbolism of the night. Each star has its path, its history, and the moon . . . My mind is overwhelmed with the knowledge of each intertwining into such a complexity that I cannot . . . but I can grasp it—it's simple! After drenching for what seems hours, the experience dies and is immediately replaced by "Summer Twilight." What is this? A double feature? Maybe. These are both short pieces. Yeah. So I swim in the strange light, revel in the sunset, abreast the clouds once more and drink the lightning bugs' light. I see objects so weirdly, and smell carrion and roses. When night comes, so gradually I recognize it for what it is and not a blackout, the experience is over.

When I come out of it, I see I am alone in the brightly lit room with Lawrence beside me.

She smiles softly and sweetly, and unbelievably, all I can feel is great tenderness for her. "Hello. We were worried about you. Most can't sit through two at once, and you're still a neube."

I shake my head. "No, I'm a hookie, forever. Did someone sneak in an intensifier?"
Lawrence looks startled.

Nicole rushed into the grotto, nearly sliding to her death on the slick floor before Jan caught her. She looked at him, dazed, and breathlessly asked, "Where's Lawrence?"

"She's resting," Jan automatically said.

"No, I'm not." A door hidden under the cliff swung open and Lawrence stepped out. "I'm in here fixing this horrible stretch of expostfilm." She left the door of her light room open as she approached Nicole.

Nicole blinked as she searched for deception in Lawrence's eyes, which were as clear as . . . as a sharp glide of creek water sliding through a narrow rocky passage . . . She faltered, feeling suddenly tired and light-headed. She groped for a place to sit.

Lawrence grabbed her arm and led her to a stool. "Do you need to lie down? I bet I know what it is. It's getting dark outside. You lost track of time . . . it's about ten or so, last time I looked. Some people get the time mixed up . . ."

Nicole stared at her, understanding none of the babble. "I just experienced 'Summer Twilight' and 'Atmosphere of Stars,' and . . ."

"Both at once?" Jan exclaimed, shooting a glance over at Lawrence as he did so.

Nicole tried to regain her composure. "Yes," she recited, as if it weren't that strange at all, kind of like the way her more famous interviewees dispassionately stated their foibles and mistakes. "I sat through two. Is it typical for hookies to do that sort of thing?"

"No." Lawrence shifted. "This is a special case. The way they do it usually is to only show one at a time, because that's all people have paid for, see? So, people recover, and go home."

Nicole frowned at Lawrence's obvious discomfort. "What about people who can afford more than one, or private sessions?"

"Such people are few. Not only that, but private sessions are more closely monitored." A ghost of a smile appeared on Lawrence's face.

"So?"

Lawrence answered openly, and again Nicole was amazed at how honest she looked, like nothing could faze her. "Buying a ticket publicly for a porno film allows you privacy in the dark with a crowd to do what you must. You could watch it in your own bedroom, except someone has to be there watching you—see?"

"Okay."

"Anyway, my auditorium is letting people sit as long as they want. That's at my request. You know, let them recover, let them savor it, but they're running them almost continuously." Lawrence stopped, then shrugged. "There's still not much to worry about. No one can sit there forever without having to eat or use the bathroom, so they're going to get up eventually."

"But," Nicole gulped. She had to tell. "I experienced you visiting me afterwards, but then I really woke up after that, and I realized that it was all just part of the same experience. Right? How did you personalize your conversation for everyone?"

Lawrence plopped down on the stool opposite her. "What?"

"And, before that," Nicole continued relentlessly, "I thought of some advice you never gave me. What was that?"

Lawrence shoved her face into her hands, causing her glasses to slip up into her bangs. "Hallucinations?" she muttered. "Nobody has ever reported that sort of thing." She leapt up and reached for the intercom. Slapping the on button, she yelped, "Mack?"

"Yes, Lawrence. What is it?" A faintly cheerful masculine voice came over the speaker.

"I'm sorry it's so late, but I know I can count on you. Listen. Shut down the auditorium for the night. As for tomorrow, uh, maybe you should show them less often. Um . . . I'll try to tell you about it later. Thanks." Lawrence turned off the intercom before Mack could respond.

Nicole watched in amazement as Lawrence turned a relatively calm face to her. "Maybe you should think about providing pacifiers in the future," she said dryly. "My experience this time was too intense."

"No," Lawrence blurted at once.

"Why won't you accept pacifiers? If it's dangerous . . ."

"I don't think it is, and I sure as hell don't want anything diminishing my art. That should go without saying." Before Nicole could interrupt, she continued in a whisper, "'The amount of danger for sane adults is negligible.'"

"What?" both Jan and Nicole asked.

"Nicole, what did you mean, they're too intense? What's that got to do with it? Wait. The advice I never gave, the comfort I never gave, yet maybe I did. Maybe you got all that from the experience, but I don't see how . . ."

"Where did it come from, then?"

"Could it be," Lawrence advanced cautiously, "that your mind participated more?"

Nicole did not speak at first. She passed a hand across her forehead. "I don't know, and at this point, I don't care. I doubt it. I mean, I was hooked up. I was lost in the experience. I think I can finally see that they are addictive. Each one leaves me craving more. I feel so helpless . . ." Suddenly overwhelmed with exhaustion, she stood. "It's been a long day. Let me rest, and we can talk about it tomorrow."

Lawrence stepped back.

"So you think experiencing is harming your thought processes?" Lawrence walked her to the door. "Maybe. But you know what I think? I think that, eventually, experiencing me will *free your thought.*"

Chapter Four

Jan the next morning at 6 a.m. arose without waking Lawrence and got to work. He dressed appropriately in long johns, jeans, boots, and heavy shirt and jacket. He left the gloves, hat, and scarf to be donned later. He checked his supplies of freeze-dried food and small equipment that he had packed the night before, then hefted an armload. Passing through the grotto with utmost silence, he crawled up the shaft in the back and went to his waiting helicopter on the rear launching pad. Two more identical trips, then, on his last trip down, he wondered whether he should eat breakfast first or just get going. Lawrence met him as he was entering the grotto.

"Hey, what is this?" She squinted at him a second. "Are you just going to take off without saying goodbye?"

Jan grimaced. "Well . . . Yeah!"

"But why?"

"Because I hate to ask again . . ."

Lawrence sighed. "It's my turn to cook, so come on into the kitchen and we'll discuss it." She opened her eyes a little wider and looked around. "I left my shoes down here, didn't I?"

Jan pulled them out from under the table.

"Thanks." She stooped to put them on, then eyed him. "Do you want the fan on or will you be okay?"

"I'll be okay. It's usually cold in here anyway."

They went into the small kitchen where Lawrence had already set out cereal and juice. She shrugged, "It's not much, but you were never one to plan enough time to eat."

Jan started eating his millet. "Neither are you," he pointed out.

"Oh, yeah," Lawrence muttered, not smiling. "You know," she said as she started on her grapefruit, "it's not your fault the grant didn't come through."

"It's not that I disdain taking your money, it's the headache involved in explaining where the money came from. And then having to sit through auditing. And then agreeing to forego the reimbursement. I'd rather just try to get along."

Lawrence tapped her spoon on his glass. "Oh, yeah? Compare that to telling your employees that they're not getting paid."

"I'll pay them no matter what happens."

"How? If you sit around waiting for the government to approve their wages . . . and I should know. I had to wait a lot for my wages in college." Lawrence stood. "So how much do you need?"

"As much as the grant was for," Jan answered firmly.

"I don't think that's enough—"

"All right, all right. Go ahead and give me the same amount you gave me last time." Lawrence grinned.

"And since you're here," Jan pointed, "help me load the last bit of equipment."

Lawrence walked over to the terminal and called up accounts. While she waited, she turned a friendly face over to Jan. "You always look so ridiculous in those clothes."

Jan looked woefully down at his tall, skinny body and shrugged. "It helps if the projects director blends in. Besides, where I'm going, I think I'll have to get rid of all these clothes." He pointed up the shaft and shuddered. "Just let me make it off this mountain without freezing, is all I ask."

Lawrence whipped her gaze over at her weather dials, looking at the outside readings. "It's not too bad," she murmured.

Once the finances were taken care of, Lawrence tossed a flannel shirt over her T-shirt, and the two gathered the last bundles and headed up the shaft.

"It's kind of steep," warned Jan, "but it's the most direct route up."

"That's okay," muttered Lawrence. "Our movement's kind of restricted anyway, because of the convention."

They reached the surface several minutes later and hiked in the thirty centimeters of snow to the helicopter, Lawrence following in Jan's footprints.

"At least it's not snowing. And the sky is so clear! No clouds to hinder your flight." Lawrence looked up over the mountain top and smiled. "How long are you going to be gone, anyway?"

Jan paused from inspecting the water exhaust pipe. "That's hard to say. A couple of days? I've got a lot of new employees to break in, but don't worry." He turned and smiled at Lawrence. "I'll be back for our anniversary."

Lawrence jumped over the bundles and hugged him.

"Climb on in before I leave."

Lawrence complied quickly.

Jan laughed. "Yeah, get in there where it's warm! What made you think twenty below was okay?"

"At least it's Centigrade."

Jan laughed.

"Why did you want me to get in?" Lawrence asked as he climbed in and shut the door. "Has anything changed?"

"You bet. Some animals were missing. Rumors say the upper echelons are eating meat. Some are managing to have children, too . . ."

24

Lawrence leaned forward and hissed. "And they can get away with it? Unbelievable!"

Jan shrugged. "Of course, there have been complaints from the lower echelons that promises aren't being kept."

"That goes without saying, but what can we do?"

Jan continued, "Even the trees—but that's my job."

"How many are you going to plant?"

"Well, my contract calls for 500 acres, but I'm going to double that."

"Jan!"

He looked up from adjusting the thermostat. "What?"

"My money! Won't you need twice as much?"

He chuckled. "No, honey. Even if you gave me the same amount as last year, I should have plenty. Remember how much I didn't use up?"

"Well, okay," she answered doubtfully. Lawrence squinted up at the sky and suddenly grabbed Jan's hand tightly.

"What is it?" he asked urgently.

"Oh, Jan! Your work has meaning, and is helping the Earth, while mine . . ."

Jan reached over and took up a few strands of her hair, idly lifting them to shine in the light from the platform signals. "Could be that it helps the human inhabitants of the Earth."

Lawrence said nothing.

"It's not over yet," Jan encouraged. "Remember, the environmentalists won and the depopulators won—Hence, my job. But there's the other side. Don't forget that the Westerners won and the pro-spacers won, and the anarchists lost."

Lawrence sighed. "I wish I could do more. Like those activists at this convention. They haven't stopped fighting. There's still hope."

"While we yet live, yes."

Lawrence smiled at him for a second, then said, "I have to go, darling."

"I know. I should have already been gone by now, but . . ."

They kissed.

Lawrence grabbed him for one last hug. "Oh, I'm going to miss you!"

"Just a few days . . ."

"Be back for our anniversary!"

"I will. And for your completed experience, too, I hope."

"Me too! Bye!"

"Bye!"

Lawrence leaped out and ran from the platform. Crouching in the wind, she waved until the tiny dot in the sky vanished, then she ran to the shaft and hurried down to the laboratory where her precious work waited.

And Mack. Lawrence came out of the shaft and stared at him blankly. After a few seconds, she moaned, "Mack! It's seven o'clock!"

He turned from her beverage machine and held out a cup. "Want some tea?"

Lawrence hurried over to peer at the controls. "Did you set it for coffee? The last time you did that—bleah! I had to get it cleaned."

Mack rolled his eyes. "I remember. It's okay."

Lawrence took a sip from the cup, then put it down. "I'm freezing. Let me go get a blanket."

When she returned, Mack was still standing patiently where she had left him, only mildly looking at the weather controls. Lawrence shook her head with a wry smile. He was a great manager, never poking his nose where it could get smacked.

He got right to the point. "What was that all about last night? And, even more shockingly, what are you doing up so early?"

Lawrence tucked the blanket around her as she sat down. She lifted the tea cup and drank before answering, "You know Jan requisitioned a helicopter for today."

"Yeah. Where's he going, anyway?"

"South America. I thought I'd call you and tell you not to show the experiences that often, because . . ." she hesitated. It was harder than she thought.

Mack didn't seem to notice her hesitation. "Speaking of those free experiences . . . What the hell? Showing that incomplete experience before we could approve it! I was lucky I didn't get lynched as I ran around, trying . . . You were supposed to present a new one, you know, not . . . And as for showing them less often, I'll be more than happy to do that. Free experiences? It's crazy. I'm sure by now everyone has seen each several times. The audiences are getting smaller. I guarantee by noon I can shut them off entirely."

"That would be okay," Lawrence murmured. "They have to get on with their convention somehow."

Mack plopped down across from her. "Lucky for me they're all hookies. They can't sue."

Lawrence shrugged, moodily staring down into her cup. "Why not?"

"They're registered, so they're legally bound from taking any action on us. But," here Mack took a heavy breath, "I checked the records. There was one neube in the audience. Nicole Garner. And she *can* sue us. Have you talked to her? I need to find her and somehow . . ."

"Yes, I have. That was what I was meaning to talk to you about. She's been experiencing right along with the others, and she came to me reporting a hallucination."

Mack leapt up. "All right, that does it. I'll . . ." He sat back down. "That's not supposed to happen. Or, at least, it never has."

"That you know of, you mean." Lawrence frowned. "Somebody could have just not reported one. But, it was so late . . . I keep thinking that it could have been many different things. Maybe she read a message in there. Maybe it was what she wanted to see. The experiences themselves could . . . Ah, I don't know."

Mack leaned back. "It's too early to talk to her, anyway. She needs to get a good night's sleep so she'll be a good mood when I see her."

Lawrence cleared her throat. "Do you want me to talk to her first?"

"No. Wait. Yes." Mack scratched his head. "If you think you can convince her . . . We'll pay for any treatment . . ." He stood. "Of course, that's my responsibility, but if you're on good terms with her . . ."

Lawrence smiled crookedly. "Well, I might have an easier time of it than you. Maybe." She stared up at him as he brushed his soft black curls off his forehead. "Is there something else you need to speak to me about?" Her voice came out gently, as if she anticipated what he was going to say.

Mack leaned up against the counter. "I came over to talk to you about your contract. It's up for renewal."

Lawrence nodded.

"You don't have much time, in other words. You've only got a few days to finish another experience."

"I know. I might be able to finish this one soon: soon enough for you."

"We don't want that one."

"Fuck! Why not?"

Mack patiently answered, "Because of the controversy over showing only part of it. Because we don't think it fits in with the others. We don't like it."

"How the fuck do you know? It's not finished! It was never previewed! Besides, you never said anywhere you told me what to create!" Lawrence threw the blanket off. Now that she was furious, it was superfluous.

Mack walked over to the terminal and called up her contract. He looked at her wryly. "I still can't get over this—no voice command." His face immediately became noncommittal. "Look. Here at the bottom." His finger tapped the screen. "It says here that your work must meet the approval of the committee. It's just that I have a feeling that, even if you do manage to finish it, it won't be approved. All I'm doing is advising you to start one you know will get approved, so you can fulfill your contract."

"Oh, thanks," she immediately said half-heartedly, then paused. "I don't know, though. If I change now, I bet you'll never have a hit again."

Mack chuckled. "That's a gentle threat. We've got your name. It'll sell, whether it's good or not."

"Only for a while."

"You don't know people."

"Yes, I do! My success proves it."

"Look, we're not dictating to you what to create. We're just asking you to come up with another one in time to fulfill your contract. Do whatever you want!"

Lawrence walked to the ladder and stared up at her banks of equipment. Suddenly she turned and folded her arms, looking down, and then finally into Mack's blue eyes. "Okay. I'll try. Thanks for the warning, Mack. Besides," she lowered her voice and dropped her gaze. "This one is so overpowering, maybe it'll be good for me to work on something else. I might need a vacation afterwards . . ."

"That's fine."

"Of course it is. You understand vacations."

Mack turned toward the tunnel. "Look, I'll just leave you alone to see what you come up with." He paused on the way out. "I think it would be in your best interest if I check back with you soon. Okay?"

Lawrence nodded, waving on her way back to bed.

Hell, I can't sleep, and I can't work until I hear from Nicole. Lawrence tossed the quilt off, then paused. *What do you mean? Nicole hasn't agreed to anything. Bah. I don't care. My mind's blank, and Mack . . .* She struggled back into her clothes and went to walk in the forest.

Again she stumbled over the spying equipment. She stared dully at them, then crouched down to watch the dials. "This 'Convention of Concerned Feminists' must scare somebody," she muttered to herself. "I guess it's not hard to see it as a front for a diverse group of revolutionaries." Then she snickered. That, at least, had been how Alma had described it in her scrambled request to Mack, asking in an all too timid manner if Lawrence would mind it being held in her house. She wrapped her arms tightly around her knees and sniffed. What had Alma expected? Of course Mack would alert his superiors, but, then again, how could she have reached Lawrence? And Lawrence had of course agreed to it, feeling oddly generous, while at the same time feeling like a traitor. She frowned down at the panels. Selecting at random a piece of a disc, she was not surprised to see and hear quite well a discussion going on somewhere in the convention. After a few seconds, however, she shut the disc off.

What do you think you're doing? And what do you hope to get out of it? Oh, I wish I could just go down there and participate, but I nearly died when I had hung around after the first showing. Yeah, I was brave, but that was just because I felt guilty. Lawrence looked up into the pines and gave herself a smirk. *And, once I knew Nicole was there and I had a fairly nice encounter with her, I forgot my fear and suddenly wanted to deluge her with contact and make some kind of great impression. Crazy, huh? Of course, now that she has come to me, I don't need to haunt the convention, waiting for her attention.* A wave of relief flooded her. Lawrence straightened, making an instant decision, and began playing the disc once more.

28

The Hawk zoomed in on a couple. Both were short, one a stout woman with black spiked hair, the other a thin man with nicely coiffured blond locks. "So," he whispered, "where'd you get the cows?"

"Not cows," his companion whispered back. "Aurochs. They don't produce much milk, but we don't dare breed them to become better milkers."

The man seemed impressed. "Doing good business?"

The woman looked smug. "You better believe it. Only the goat farmers do better."

"What made you do such a thing?" the man then asked in a slightly louder whisper. "I mean, you've never eaten cheese. How can you crave it?"

The woman chuckled. "Easy. I had knowledge of it, and after one taste . . . mmm. Besides, do you really think desire is inherent? Ha! You have to create it. Those in power do it all the time. First create the product, then foster the demand for it. They don't go out among the people and learn what they want, and then run back to their factories or legislatures and satisfy it." The woman leaned back, tensed, then huddled back to her partner. "Lawrence came around. I experienced her. Now I crave more. Just like the cheese. Maybe if I'd never heard of it, now . . ."

The man turned slightly and spoke loudly. "Have you seen 'Innocents' yet?"

The woman made a face, yet also turned slightly, opening the couple up to intruders now that the forbidden was past. "No, and I never will."

Lawrence froze the tape and studied the readout. *Last night, about nine o'clock. Setting: the large convention room to the east. They want to destroy power in different ways, but sometimes power accidentally does good, and frees. No, I'm not mad. Let me hear some more.*

"Autonomy"

Lawrence selected another disk. In the room to the west, the auditorium that held only a few hundred people, a small woman with short, chestnut brown hair stepped onto the stage. The Hawk zoomed to her convention badge: Sheila Rainbird. She smiled out at the audience and began: "I am very glad to see a number of people of color here. We are the majority in this room, at least. I am even glad to see so few of us here, for I feel that the discussion should be a discussion, not a speech. The issue is a difficult one. We prize freedom and independence so much, and some say that we have lost our free choice by submitting to reproductive restraint. I, however, see the fairness of the act. Since its induction, there has been no obvious selection of parents based on race or other irrelevant criteria. I think the procedure of species survival by controlled pregnancy works. What we question now is childrearing. I ask: Why is it necessary? Who shall do it? Who *is* doing it? And does it matter? Who wants to answer?" Sheila walked over and plunked down on the edge of the stage, shooting forth her elbows to put her chin on her knuckles.

The Child Genius spoke, and the Hawk swerved above the audience a short time before focusing on her. Lawrence nodded. Lack of editing. "Who's doing it? Practically everybody. A child gets born rarely, because of population control. That doesn't mean only a parent or two

29

takes care of it. No, a group of people who want to take some time raising a child participate. Who shall do it? Well, I think this way is best. That is how I was raised in Japan, back when they first started population control in China. I was not subject to one or two parents' idiosyncrasies. I was exposed to many different parents and I developed an open mind from having seen so many viewpoints."

Sheila nodded. "In many parts of our world, though, you must remember, the groupparents are not as diverse as they are now. All of your parents were Japanese, were they not?"

The Child Genius nodded. "But they were certainly diverse." She smiled reminiscently, then looked around her at the alert audience. "Aunt Kyoko, especially."

Alma cleared her throat as the Hawk flew to her. "I don't understand. Are you saying a child will be the same no matter who the groupparents are?"

Sheila nodded, thoughtful. "Now that's an idea. Who is enlightened? Can't someone break free of their upbringing?"

"And what did you mean by 'Is childrearing necessary'?" Alma continued. "Of course it is!"

"Is it? If we're speaking about the children as free individuals, then obviously why should they be raised at all?"

Everyone was silent for awhile, the Hawk hovering slightly above Sheila's head, then Lawrence heard Alma whisper, "'Autonomy.'"

Lawrence hit pause as she took in a deep breath. "Autonomy?" Why that all of a sudden? Lawrence remembered the short piece she had completed over a year ago. A flash of sparkly silver tips of ice on the trees, and a single achingly red tulip with a yellow and black center. Shaking her head, she released pause.

Sheila was once more speaking. "Last century, a lot of people were scorned and legislated because they wanted to raise their children differently from what the government thought was proper, yet over and over again the courts said that it was the biological parents' right to raise the child. Then, after abuse was noticed, the government stepped in to prevent it. Good."

"Not so good," replied Suzette. "At the same time they were against adoption and abortion. And they were mighty holy about it, too!" she said in a strong Georgian accent. "They didn't acknowledge what we would call an ethical individual. Give me a break! I want my child to be raised by a group of enlightened, intelligent, interesting, open-minded adults, not the goddamn government!" She lifted her fist, then sat down decorously.

Sheila chuckled, then spoke seriously. "Can anyone think of a better way to raise children than what we're doing now?"

"How about having them together and separate from us?" suggested a new face, a middle-aged woman with a tanned face and long black hair. A feather hung from her ear.

"Possibly," Sheila conceded. "If you're interested in peer theory."

Everybody groaned at the buzz words.

Lawrence noted the time as yesterday afternoon, three o'clock, then shut down the instruments. She sat a while, until a drop fell on her shoulder, causing her to look up into the trees, craving—what? *Time to get back to work.*

Lawrence entered the grotto to find Nicole already waiting for her. She lifted her cup. "I helped myself to some coffee. Do you mind?"

Lawrence instantly shook her head, then cautiously walked over to Nicole, studying her eyes.

"I'm okay," Nicole reassured her. "I slept very well, considering, but then I got up to experience 'Innocents.'" She swallowed some more coffee. "It was pretty gruesome. Maybe I should have experienced it earlier, before the sensations became so intense, but I was still miserable from the incomplete one that . . ." Nicole shut up. Shrugging, she continued, "I didn't feel so hot afterwards, so I sat through all of your short pieces." Nicole lifted her shoulders and sighed. "I still feel sick."

"But why?" Lawrence leaned across the table and touched her hand. "I mean, I thought for sure you would leave today, after what happened."

Nicole unobtrusively removed her hand and gave her an intense stare. "I intend to finish my story."

Lawrence stepped back as a thrill shot through her. "Okay. But you still have one more experience to go."

Nicole raised one eyebrow. "Indeed, but I came here to confirm that you will allow me to publish your interview. What do I need to do?"

"You will need to sign a contract, but first . . ."

"I know," Nicole conceded, astonished to find excitement building in her. "'Goldweaving.'" She sighed as she finished her coffee. "I might as well get it over with."

Lawrence laughed. "Oh, come on! It won't be as bad as 'Innocents,' I promise." Sobering, she came up close to Nicole as she stood. "Do you want to use my pod?"

"Your *what?*"

Lawrence explained patiently, "Where I go to test my experiences before I release them. It would be best for you if you could have a private session. That way, I could control how many you get, and you wouldn't have to be monitored. I don't want you . . ." She gestured helplessly.

Nicole nodded, completely calm. "That would be fine."

"Goldweaving"   Her best to date, according to everyone. And it might very well be also her strongest work, and it will be so intense! My heart flutters, yet the experience comes slowly.

I'm in the mountains, and it takes a very long time for me to get adjusted to merely the clean, crisp air. I breathe in its freshness through both my nose and mouth. Gradually I notice my surroundings. The scene is sharp. Appearing to my eyes clearly, each leaf glitters in its autumn flaring color. I snuggle cheerfully into my sweater against a sudden, brisk breeze. Sitting on a river bank, feet near the mud alive with worms and bugs, I listen for sounds, but the creek's noise is the only music I hear. Soon, however, I am aware of a creaking that I'm unable to place. I shift to bend down and touch the sparkling, beaded water. I drink a handful of the sweet, cold stream and rise. Placing my red, wet hand in my sweater to rest on my belly, I turn and begin to climb the hill.

The path is narrow and rocky; I pause several times to rest and admire the buttery, tinged leaves and the deep blue sky. I see brown and white birds dart about in play, and I stop to watch them. The pattern they make fascinates me, and I effortlessly begin to see black birds, dragonflies, red headed birds, jeweled bottle flies. My heart is so full, I begin to cry, but gently, so as to hear the swelling chords in the distance.

I smell hay, smoke, and leaves. I taste nuts, crisp grass, and sharp berries. I near the clearing, and as I approach the little shack, the creaking becomes more pronounced. I notice that its door is swinging back and forth without ever banging against the rail or frame. I watch in fascination, and come to know that there is a woman inside.

She comes to the door and greets me. I feel slowwitted, and do not immediately respond. My body seemingly drifts in a daze and I have no fear.

She smiles. I look at her fully, studying her face, and only gradually realize that I should be stunned, for she is beautiful! No, she is more than beautiful: she is what I have wished to be. She speaks gently.

"Hello. I've been waiting for so long."

I want to touch her, and . . . I do.

She laughs.

I kiss her. At first I am stunned by this development, which seems so natural. In the background, I sardonically think that this is what Alma was talking about.

I am overcome by memories, of riding in a canoe through the mountain stream, of walking softly in my moccasins through the woods, of gathering foods, and of being watchful.

The wind alights. I remember rising this morning, the wind cool on my nightgown, my eyes affording me only one admiring glance at my perfect, beautiful body before I head for the porch.

The morning begins. The air is golden, the sunrise so gorgeous I stare at only it until it is complete, for impressions come slowly in this world. On the fringes of my mind I feel the cloudy impingements of a dream.

She has come. A mare woman, a beautiful mare of the night. She has a light brown coat and spongy mane, blonde and gold. She climbs aboard my porch and kneels.

All alone on the mountaintop I am, and it is dark, and I am so afraid of the orange glows of the fires, the dry air . . . I strip off my nightgown and brush the mare's mane . . .

Oh, heaven, so like a forgotten dream, we make frolicking love, leaving the porch and spreading, until I feel that we're in each cranny, in each possible part of the Earth.

At one sharp point, separate from the dizzying dream, pulsing upon the forest floor which our frolicking has swept clean of leaves, I see, or am, a woman, or a horse, whose hair, streaked with gold, reddish tints, and a tiny bit of black, but mostly gold, rich, glowing gold, begins weaving, actually weaving into the forest mold, and the luster hidden in that brown, mingled with that rich, dark, deep soil, full of roots and loamy, stirs me, to almost, almost . . .

Come.

Chapter Five

"Simultaneity" Nicole emerged from the pod and fell into Lawrence's arms. Eyes closed, she hugged her tight, her mouth open, her face straining ever upward. In a pre-orgasmic mode, she felt Lawrence's arms slowly yet steadily come up, sliding across her buttocks, the warm hands pausing to take the waist on both sides. It felt so good, so nourishing. Then, unbelievably, she felt Lawrence pull away to tuck herself into her side, her arm sliding across her back to provide firm support.

"No," moaned Nicole. "Let me . . ."

But, helpless, she felt herself being led to a chair, and gently, almost freely, put down in it.

Still blind, she reached up to Lawrence, finding her T-shirt within arm's length, and yanked it. "Stay with me," she whispered fiercely, "I need . . ."

But Lawrence easily took her hand away, and Nicole felt it fall at her side. Her eyes flew open. The dream-like sensation was gone, replaced by a searing anger.

"Isn't this what you want?" she hissed, big black eyes flashing, not yet seeing what was in front of them.

Lawrence stood, arms hanging limply, waiting.

"Isn't it?"

"No," Lawrence said softly and sadly, causing Nicole to lean forward, peering at her.

"What? It would have been so easy to take me." Nicole froze, taking time to trace her desire, which had yet to leave her.

"I know. That's why, obviously." Lawrence pointed at the water cooler. "Do you want a drink?"

Nicole swallowed to calm a parched throat, remembering the fresh taste of a mountain spring, and shivered.

"Yes or no?" Lawrence asked sharply.

Nicole at first shook her head, but then the thirst overwhelmed her. "Oh, hell, yes!"

Lawrence was there with a cup of water a little too soon to her shot perceptions, but she gave no more thought to that and seized the cup.

It was so wet and luscious. She gulped it dry, letting the cup fall, and sighed, "Ah, that's so good! Does experiencing usually make people so thirsty?" She blushed slightly at her naive question.

Lawrence stooped to pick up the cup and paused to look up at her seriously. Nicole was again seized with desire, but this time all she wanted was a friendly caress. "The experience isn't real," Lawrence whispered. "One must fulfill the desire eventually."

For a second Nicole could feel the underside of her tongue twinge, and she recalled one of Lawrence's stranger short pieces: a very brief experience of all the seasons at once. She smiled at her suddenly, and Lawrence reached over to stroke her soft tufted hair, flattening it awkwardly, but Nicole didn't care. She began to feel an ache somewhere, daring to admit it might be her vulva.

Lawrence stood up and wrapped her arms about her tightly. "So. How did you like 'Goldweaving?'"

Nicole pulled herself back. Her rational mind all at once came back from its repression, so she found herself answering honestly, "I loved it."

Lawrence moved away to climb up the ladder to her laboratory. She methodically turned on a few Hawks and a Dog, focusing them on Nicole's corner, then she bent down to tweak the whiskers of the Cat with a pair of pliers.

"What are you doing?" Nicole asked idly.

"If you don't mind, I must record several images of you signing the contract. It's proof of consent."

Lawrence turned to go back down the ladder, still carrying the pliers.

Nicole shifted, then stood up, again in complete control of her movement. "Why are you being so formal about this contract, anyway?"

"I must hire you to be in my experience. I've never needed any help before, but my contract says that you must be considered my employee for the duration, and I must pay you accordingly." Lawrence looked at the pliers in her hand, shrugged, then threw them up the ladder.

"But we had an agreement: I help you and I get a story. That's all I need," Nicole said, feeling oddly like a charity case.

"Doesn't matter. Nobody's ever gotten a story out of me, but they'd have to sign a contract, too. You might as well go through me and sign one that contains both provisions." Lawrence climbed up to the kitchen sink and washed her hands. Taking a rosecovered towel off the rack, she walked down to a desk that had been stashed into the corner. Nicole stared at it oddly. She could swear she had never seen it there before. Lawrence dried her hands carefully, then pulled open a squeaky drawer. "Here it is."

Nicole wandered over and stared down at the glossy, thick piece of white parchment. "It's on paper!" she said, her voice full of surprise. She burst out laughing. "Listen to me!" Accepting the paper from Lawrence's hands, she read the plain typeface in one minute flat. "And it's readable, too." Nicole stole a look over at Lawrence's expressionless face. "That's your doing, I guess. I bet it's not half as complicated as your contract."

Lawrence turned to help herself at the water cooler. "No," she murmured. Then she leaned against the desk and sipped. "I'm a simple person, actually."

Nicole made a pretense of looking around. "Do you have a quill?"

Lawrence nodded, reaching into the desk to pull out a pen. "Here." Then she jumped up so suddenly she spilled some of her water. "Wait. I didn't mean that. Take this one." She pulled one out of her back jeans pocket and handed it to Nicole.

Nicole smoothed the parchment onto the rough surface of the desk and signed slowly yet firmly, noticing that the ink came out in a rich, black, thick stream. Leaning back to watch it dry, she asked, "What was that other pen?"

"This desk was where I had to sign my contract. The pen they gave me wrote in dark red ink."

Nicole shuddered as she looked at the dry, glossy ink.

"The committee loves symbols," Lawrence explained dryly. "All that when my fingerprints and a program are all that matters now. Oh, well. I wanted the paper so you don't get into their computers. A simple courtesy." She hopped down and went over to her weather controls. "You want to come with me? I want to go check my plants."

"Glassice"

What an understatement, thought Nicole as she crept out of the grotto and into the woods. Lawrence quickly outpaced her, but she stopped at an oak a few minutes later to let Nicole catch up with her. Ignoring her, she studied the bark and felt the branches that swooped down to her height.

Nicole took a seat on a nearby fallen pine log and unhooked her Dog. "I'd like to start on a more formal interview, if you don't mind."

"Sure," Lawrence tossed off. "I never gave one before. What's first? My youth? Boring."

"No. I want to start with 'Goldweaving.'"

Lawrence came over to sit beside her, hitching herself sideways on the log. She began carefully, "Okay. That piece was fantasy, not like the others, and for the first time it was based on a dream I had. I dreamed about the hair going into the loam."

"Now that I've experienced it, I'd still like to know what you think it is, what it is about it that made it an instant classic, and what made it turn all your other work into so-so beside it?"

Lawrence seemed not to hear her as she knit her brows. "Is that what *you* think?" came at last softly from her.

Nicole shrugged. "Like a lot of classics, it spoke to me. It seemed just made for me." She tapped her Dog. "But I'm here to listen to what you think. Don't ask me questions."

Lawrence laughed. "Okay. 'Goldweaving' was supposed to be sexual, because that was my dream. But then I thought . . . what's good for me isn't for everybody. I experimented with individuality. In my quest for audience participation, I left parts of it open. In some moments, you saw what you wanted to see, felt what you wanted to feel."

"Which parts?" Nicole asked suspiciously.

"I can't tell."

"Why not?" Nicole felt her anger rise.

"Because of the uncertainty involved. Like everything else, I can't be exact, because of the nature of the process. You know, like the Heisenberg Principle, all that shit." Lawrence turned to her excitedly. "Hey! Maybe *you* could tell *me* which parts you came up with."

Nicole ignored her. "You mean you don't know exactly what goes on in 'Goldweaving'?"

Lawrence's eyes drifted to the right as she chewed her lip. "I brought in the fall, and the mountain, but I could not dictate your lover. And there could be much more you added, I don't know." She waited, head dully lolling. Nicole watched her gulp, imagining that she felt the interview to be a form of mild torture.

"I guess you want to know what I saw . . ."

"No," interrupted Lawrence. "The plot means nothing to me. I wasn't being nosy. I just thought that you could . . . 'Goldweaving' might be a masterpiece, but it is a flawed one, because I could not help but influence what I touch."

But Nicole wasn't listening. Instead her ears were straining, listening for what she thought were soft chords and bells. The woods had darkened since they had come out, and Nicole felt chilled. In a flash she was again immersed in one of Lawrence's short pieces: again she stood in the cool, large, white brick building and gazed out of the huge orange hole that looked out onto the desert. The window is raised into place, and a black metal frame is sealed around it. The window is huge. A hammer and chisel make a tiny hole in the glass, cracking it everywhere. The surface is now frosted; the glass slivers like snow. The sun is now directly pouring into the tiny hole, alighting on a bug on a polished, golden pew. Nicole jerked away from the images, feeling as if any minute now she would hear a creaking or a sharp metal cry.

"What's wrong?" Lawrence's voice came softly, and Nicole felt her arm across her shoulder. Shrugging it off disgustedly, Nicole leaned forward.

"That's it!" she whispered, turning to Lawrence triumphantly. "You tell me you intentionally left 'Goldweaving' open."

Lawrence nodded, idly stroking a patch of moss behind Nicole.

"Well, doesn't that explain my hallucination? Maybe they're all like that." Now that she had discovered a plausible explanation, Nicole felt tension slough off her back.

"Could be," Lawrence commented briefly. "But that could have been due to my influence, not your participation." She shifted. "Even without an intensifier, I have a strong influence on whoever experiences me. But I see it like reading a book. For example: picture my courtyard."

Nicole frowned, curiosity guaranteeing her compliance. She closed her eyes. Yes, there were the big gold and red doors, and the gray flecked walls, and the flooring, which was red brick. It had been wide and open, swept clean of snow and ice, except for some flakes that were dusting over the walls and falling from the trees.

"Now, have you got it in your head? Exactly as you remember it?" came Lawrence's tight voice.

Nicole nodded.

"Does it have leaves?"

Nicole shook her head. "Why would it have leaves?"

"Leaves! Big brown leaves blowing about! And dust! And a late autumn orange sun!"

"Don't be ridiculous. You have mostly pines, and it's winter." Nicole shifted to face her, opening her eyes.

"But that is how I always see it," insisted Lawrence. "Stereotypes! The influence of static images by the unimaginative!"

Brusquely Lawrence stood, as if she could stay still no longer, and Nicole found herself following her over the rocks behind them into an open meadow. On the edge of the forest, Lawrence paused near a mimosa. Nicole stared at the ferny fronds blankly, then reached forward to caress them. After several strokes, the leaf began to curl, tucking itself in, away from the contact.

Lawrence's voice came calmly from beside her. "That's me."

Nicole glanced at her questioningly.

Lawrence grimaced. "In my youth, it was important for me to give my senses a try. Once I cracked open a peach seed and ate what was inside."

Nicole interrupted, "Clearly a bitter experience," she snickered.

Lawrence laughed. "Yes. I have eaten sour grass, wild onions and carrots, sour apples, unripe grapes, muscadines, raw hickory huts, even flowers."

Nicole listened to the litany, nodding. The source of much of Lawrence's ability.

"You know how sweetly they name those lifeless machines after the animal who has a greater talent in that area than humans, dog for hearing, hawk for seeing. Well, I like to think of me as being as sensitive as that mimosa leaf." She reached out to gather a fluffy pink and white blossom. "Not, of course, as beautiful as this."

Nicole said nothing, letting her memories cascade over the trance of "Goldweaving."

Lawrence continued, "That's why I became an artist; well, part of the reason. I wasn't much of a painter or musician, so I didn't know what to do. I studied in many fields, always searching, and then I got a lucky break."

"Which was?"

Lawrence looked at her strangely. "I thought you knew about that. The contest. I was in college, and I heard about the contest from NewTech Enterprises. I got to try out the new equipment in the university's lab because I had signed up for some dumb art class. I submitted 'Atmosphere of Stars' and won a contract from them to produce ten pieces of varying length in two years. The university still gets some royalties from that first one, because they sponsored it. Boy, do they love me now."

Nicole resumed walking around the scraggly meadow. "So how was college?"

"Don't ask! There I was, at the local university, and . . ."

"Which one?"

"Knoxville," Lawrence said briefly. "Anyway, there I was, majoring in physics . . ."

"Physics?!" Nicole halted to turn to her. "Whoa, back up."

Lawrence shrugged. "It feels like I've said all this a hundred times."

"But you haven't. I did my research and read your published interviews, the ones where they went through NewTech. None of them went into your personal life beyond a few obvious statistics, like age, marital status, stuff like that."

"Okay. You know what it's like doing something like that?"

"I know several female scientists, so yes, I've heard."

Lawrence gave her a big grin. "Good! Then you know all about the tampons and rubbers I kept finding here and there, taped on my desk, hanging out of my locker. Speaking of those lockers: One female student in biology who was squeamish got thrown in there, screaming, by a few boys. She had some kind of phobia about such places. I had to get her out. We were the only females in that advanced class, and they were wondering why she had so many troubles."

Lawrence gasped, and Nicole felt almost tempted to comfort her in some way. She had heard similar stories before. Lawrence continued, "Sometimes I felt that the requirements and teaching methods were conservative, but mainly I was worried about having enough money to finish . . ." She took a deep breath. "Well, as you know, I didn't. I started taking a wider variety of classes, as I said, and then I won the contest. Shit. The end."

Nicole nodded, pointing her head at all the trees around her. "And you came here, entrenching NewTech's corporate headquarters inside of this mountain. Why?"

"Hell," Lawrence spat. "They practically rode on my success. Might as well be as greatly attached to my person as possible. I needed a place to stay. This old scientific outpost was going to be abandoned unless the government came up with enough money to continue the research. And, of course, they didn't. Such perfect timing! And I knew all about it, of course, because I read everything I could find out about it. It fascinated me. NewTech was not necessarily open to it, but I paid for most of it. I could, you know."

"It fascinated you? Why?"

Lawrence caught herself up. "No big deal, I guess. I read a lot of science magazines."

Nicole also paused in her walking to notice they had made it halfway around the field. "No. You're not getting off that easy. When this project was first proposed in the late twentieth century, there had been a lot of controversy. Already there were large aquariums, zoos with artificial habitats, and laboratory false streams. Why this need to enclose something so that we can study it, when it's there outside, free and natural, no less available for study?"

Lawrence picked up a pebble and tossed it into the tall grass. "That was a long time ago," she answered quietly. "During *this* century, it was going to die unless something was done. I wasn't going to stand by and let that happen."

Nicole still stood straight and rather accusing, but inside she was confused. *Lawrence up to now seemed to be rather cold and indifferent, not at all concerned with other people's opinions or dangers.* "I suppose the unfinished experience is the tenth work," she began carefully.

"Yes. Good ol' Opus Ten."

"Opus Ten? Haven't you named it yet?"

"No. I never name them until I'm through."

Nicole felt intense curiosity. She had lived the images and had no idea what was to follow. "It might help me to help you if you gave me some idea what was in your mind as you created it. And you must have some sort of theme or preliminary title for Opus Ten."

Lawrence looked down at Nicole's Dog pointing at her, then she shrugged, resuming their walk. "I guess it doesn't matter. 'Love.'"

Nicole coughed. "That's it?"

"Yes. That's going to be its title, unless I come up with a better one."

They were quiet for awhile, walking at a steady pace back around the meadow. Nicole pushed her sluggish mind through their recent conversation. No, she couldn't think of any more questions. Besides, it was being recorded. She could listen to it and think about it hard before the next question.

Thunder cracked, and she jumped.

Lawrence laughed softly. "I guess that was just the last of the rain storm that watered the plants," she reassured Nicole. "They shouldn't be bringing more rain, though, unless something's wrong."

Nicole only half heard her. She was thinking about the experiences and how they seemed to lead nowhere. Especially "Goldweaving." If Lawrence didn't like intensifiers, was one supposed to leave "Goldweaving" feeling unsatisfied? Wasn't that how one always felt, not just with that unfinished one, either? Damn if she'd let that happen! If nothing else, it must be a marketing technique. They want you to feel frustrated, so you'll long for more and more, right? *But I can't help myself; I want more!*

"Lawrence," she began almost timidly, "there's one favor I must ask of you."

"Anything!"

"Let me experience 'Goldweaving' just one more time, and this time . . ." Nicole paused, wondering if she were really conquering anything or anybody, or if she was just horny. ". . . with an intensifier!"

"But . . . Nicole . . . I don't think you need one . . . you've . . ."

"Please." Nicole smarted. She hated to beg.

"Okay," Lawrence said grudgingly.

Nicole only heard the affirmative. *Oh, how you can love!*

Chapter Six

Lawrence scooted up to the table and sighed before she popped open the biology textbook. "DNA? Pretty corny. All I remember is the four bases. Oh, yeah. And how they're connected to each other with hydrogen bonds." Her finger traced the double helix up and down the glossy page. "I don't know. I don't seem to see much to it. Nothing's coming. Of course, it doesn't have to be just that. Maybe something else corny, like an egg. Naw . . ." She leapt up, shoved her hands into her pockets, and turned to pace toward the door when she saw Mack.

"Excuse me," he began politely.

"Man, doesn't anybody ring my glowing bell? You especially. Pull the rope. Or is it broken?" Lawrence ran through the tunnel that led to her private grotto to peer at the knotted braid at the side of its door. "What's wrong with it?"

"Nothing," Mack laughed. "It's just that you got sick of answering the door, so you said to come on in anytime it wasn't locked. You gonna change your mind?"

Lawrence walked slowly back to her chair. "Nicole wants to do a story about me."

Mack nodded. "I figured as much," he said calmly, then he slapped his forehead. "Wait a minute. This is great. The first interview! At this time! Perfect!"

Lawrence shook her head. "Why? I thought you'd be mad, seeing who she is."

"It doesn't matter who she is. She can sell it to anybody." Mack looked around. "Where's her contract? I need to read it."

Lawrence pointed. "It's in the drawer behind you."

Mack dashed over to the desk and yanked at the drawer. The paper flipped out, and he caught it clumsily. He read rapidly, then nodded. "Looks okay to me, but why on paper?"

"Oh, I guess I'm being old-fashioned," Lawrence shrugged.

"And, of course, we'll get to review her notes before she leaves?" Mack emphasized. "I don't see anything about that in this contract."

"Of course," Lawrence lied. "You never told me why you think now is a good time for an interview to appear."

Mack sat his butt down on the desk casually. "The marketers have loved the fact that you have hidden so carefully — well, as much as possible. Lots of celebrities do it. It's a great tradition, this mystery. The marketers think that it has helped your sales tremendously. And now, that your contract's up, what better time to break the secret? It's perfect."

Lawrence lifted her hand and let it fall. "Never mind. I still don't get it. I'm trying to develop a super gene," she announced.

Mack looked up. "Heh?"

"That's what I'm trying to do," Lawrence said gently, as if talking to a child.

"Oh. Oh." Mack shook his head. "I see. But that's like 'Definitions.' It'll never sell."

Lawrence remained silent.

"Oh," Mack conceded, "I know 'Definitions' sold, but it's not your biggest hit. 'Goldweaving' is."

Lawrence pointed out, "Well, if my name sells, what the fuck difference does it make what I do?"

"Yeah, you got me there." Mack rubbed his chin. "What do you know about genetics, anyway?"

"A whole lot more than you do, buddy," she muttered.

"So? How much do most people know about it? You got to think of your audience. What else have you come up with?" Mack asked, then pushed his hair off his forehead. "I know it's a little too early to be asking that, but you don't have much time."

Lawrence tightened her arms around her midriff and looked down. If he'd quit reminding her . . .

Mack looked at her almost playfully. "There is such a thing as meaningful silence."

Lawrence shrugged, then lifted her head to stare at him.

"You seem to be doing a good job so far, anticipating what the people want . . ."

"Hey, Mack. Shut up." Lawrence swung her arms out and started pacing. "You just gave me an idea."

Mack shut up, according to contract.

His presence didn't help, so after a few seconds she sighed. "Forget it. Go ahead with what you were saying."

"The committee of NewTech has a goal. They seek popular experiences. They know that what's popular is worthy of raw materials because it makes the most people happy."

Lawrence hummed brightly, clearly showing Mack how much she thought of *that* statement.

"Well? What was your great idea?" Mack asked somberly, undeterred.

Lawrence squatted. "How about no experience, or one that only causes people to react? You know, meaningful silence."

"Is that all?" Mack was appropriately scornful. "That's been done a lot already, especially in music."

"Yeah," Lawrence said softly. "That can't be all it is, I know. What I was trying to do is *make* them react, supply their own meanings . . ."

"Oh." Mack nodded slowly. "Symbolism. Simple. No big deal. You could have, I suppose . . . Naw. What am I saying? I'm out of my league here. Never mind."

Lawrence looked annoyed, but rose from her crouch and turned to the door of her light room, where Nicole was emerging.

Nicole had come out of the pod satisfied, but it was more than the afterglow of affection. She stretched languorously. It seemed to be complete. No more hankering for more experiences, and no more pain from the incomplete one. It all seemed childish now. Nicole shook her head. Even experiencing Lawrence seemed to be a bit too seeking. She strode from the light room and paused at the door to the grotto when she heard voices. It was hard to distinguish words, but she was certain that the tight voice and commanding attitude belonged to Larry McKenzie, Lawrence's manager. She stepped through impatiently.

"Hi, Nicole," Lawrence greeted her brightly. "This is Mack." She pointed at the man, who was studying Nicole warily. "How'd it go?"

"Yes, yes," Mack blustered effusively. "Are you feeling okay?"

Nicole stared at him haughtily. "Yes. I'm feeling much better, thanks."

Mack continued his boisterous speech. "Well, that's great. Lawrence here tells me you're going to do an interview. That's great. I just want you to know you have NewTech's full approval. I've glanced over your rather informal contract, and it's fine."

"Thank you," Nicole said tightly.

"It's very important to us that you never have any trouble with NewTech products. To what do you credit your present state of health?" Mack reeled off as Nicole stared in amazement.

She turned away from him to address Lawrence. "I was surprised not to find you in the pod. You were supposed to be monitoring me."

Lawrence nodded. "It's okay. I was there through most of it. It had automatic shut-off, too. I had to come back here to get a textbook."

"Lawrence is working on a new experience," Mack informed her.

"What? What about the one she's doing now? Are you just going to leave it unfinished?" Nicole looked back and forth, between the subdued Lawrence and the effusive Mack.

"We feel that it's in everybody's best interest to eject that one from our databanks."

"Who's we?" Nicole interrupted. "Look, I have an even better idea. Why don't you let Lawrence finish Opus Ten? I thought what was there was great. I experienced it, and I admit I felt hurt, but further experiences healed the pain. For the sake of everyone who has attended this convention, I think they should be given the complete Opus. Then they wouldn't be lacking anymore. They'd be fulfilled."

Mack glanced at her approvingly, then turned to Lawrence. "She might have something there. And she should know what she's talking about." Lawrence nodded briskly, keeping her eyes on Nicole, so he spun back to her and said, "I'll convey that to NewTech and see what they think. Now, if you'll just excuse me . . ."

"Wait!" Nicole lifted her hand to stop his passing. "I need to talk to you, and I need to talk to people from NewTech. I need background for my story." *There. That should show Lawrence. If she won't tell me her message, maybe her promoters can.*

"Nicole . . ." Lawrence began.

She ignored her as Mack took on a big grin. "I'm sure that can be arranged. Come with me."

Nicole followed him out the tunnel.

They entered that part of the mansion that least looked like it was inside of a mountain. Nicole studied the meticulously clean, shiny beige tiled floor, the straight, white ceiling, the ceramic tiled walls of soft blue. The corridor even had tall, thin, clean windows every three meters or so that were clear of ivy. The windows and the glowing panels overhead made the hall bright compared to Lawrence's tiny grotto. Tiny lighted arrows in the wall glowed greenly, and she pointed.

"Why are these flashing?"

Mack explained calmly. "Those are left over from the science outpost days. Back then, they got a lot of visitors that needed direction. These just happen to lead to my office."

They passed an identical hall on the left, and Nicole nodded. A veritable maze. "Is it okay to keep my Dog on?"

Mack nodded. "Yes, since you signed a contract. I doubt what we'll have to say will be restricted."

"How did you get here?" Nicole began.

"I was hired," Mack explained patiently and smoothly with no hesitation.

"Why you?"

"NewTech decided they needed a link to their artist. They advertised for a manager. I had experience in public relations, and, at the time, I was working a few wannabe-stars in Miami. My percentage with them was nothing, so I, like a hundred others, jumped at the chance of a bigger paycheck. NewTech selected me to be Lawrence's agent and she didn't reject me."

Nicole briefly mused: *I wonder why; he's so irritating.*

They came to his bland office and sat around his desk. Despite the lackluster, simple chair and desk, he did have a huge panoramic window facing due west. Nicole gazed admiringly at the view of the valley before nodding around. "Do you get many reporters in this office?"

Mack smiled briefly. "A few over the years. I wasn't here at the beginning, so I missed all the hoopla about the contest. The most reporters came at the advent of 'Goldweaving.' I suppose they thought it was time to break the silence."

"And?"

He shrugged. "Lawrence still refused to see any of them, so they came to me and got their information second-hand." Mack shrugged again. "It wasn't much. People have, of course, tried to bribe me occasionally, seeing as I have personal contact with Lawrence, but I have revealed nothing about my dealings with her."

Nicole nodded, her respect for him growing a smidgen. "What do you think it was about 'Goldweaving' that got everybody so interested?"

"It's a classic," Mack began heavily. "The classic is always a surprise. Analysts are always hard put to figure out what sells. Sometimes it's the most unlikely thing."

"No." Nicole tossed her head. "What do *you* think about 'Goldweaving'?"

"I have never experienced Lawrence. That's in my contract," Mack answered heavily.

Nicole leaned back, her mind racing. *What lunacy was behind that?*

Mack continued in a lighter tone, "However, from what I have heard concerning 'Goldweaving,' the reason for its popularity is clear: sex."

Nicole nodded. "Most likely," she said neutrally. Recovering herself, she asked, "Do you like your job?"

"Well, it pays more than any other I've had. It's okay."

"Do you like Lawrence?"

"She's okay." Mack chuckled. "I think you're better off asking her if she likes me. I've represented several temperamental artists in the past. She's not like that."

"Do you have security problems here?"

"Absolutely not. Lawrence is well-protected."

Nicole clicked off her Dog and stood. "I'd like to meet with representatives of NewTech, if you don't mind."

Mack nodded. "I've already sent them word." He looked at her with a mild sort of awe. "The whole upper committee is prepared to meet you, despite the inconvenience. This interview must excite them, too."

Nicole simply nodded, but inside she felt intense nausea.

Following the red arrows as Mack instructed, Nicole found herself counting the offices and side corridors as she passed. *Let's see: seventeen halls, forty-seven offices. Do they really need all this space?* Nicole paused to tap a door; no answer. She had passed no one in this corridor, and all the offices appeared to be vacant.

The hall stopped suddenly at a wide, featureless door, and the arrows stopped flashing. This must be the place, she reasoned. But to knock or just walk in? She grasped the knob firmly and opened the door.

The committee of five sat in identical chairs along a small table that faced the door. They sat calmly, practically motionless, as if that were their normal workday positions.

"We've been expecting you," came a authoritative voice from the woman at Nicole's far left. "Here at NewTech, our consumers' health is very important to us. We want our products to be risk-free, but we realize that individual quirks make that an ideal goal that is not always achievable. NewTech stands behind its products, however, and we want to make all of your experiences pleasant ones. At no cost to you, you have the option of a complete physical, including a wide range of psychiatric tests. Thank you for choosing NewTech."

Nicole blinked. *Did I just hear that?* She rubbed her Dog's "on" button. *Yep. It heard it, too.* Even though the words clearly came from one speaker, she couldn't shake off the impression that they had been spoken by everyone.

The woman continued, "Mr. McKenzie has informed us of your suggestion that we release Opus Ten in complete form. Could you clarify your arguments for this unprofitable course?"

"I doubt that it would be unprofitable. All of Lawrence's experiences have shown a profit, even 'Innocents.' I was thinking along the lines of how the incomplete experience made everyone feel." Nicole found herself arguing passionately, because not only she had suffered. "After I experienced it, I felt terrible, like somebody had jerked me away from an all-encompassing project. And unlike other times, when I could go back to what I was doing, I had nothing to turn to. Well, almost nothing. I turned to Lawrence's other experiences."

A small, slender oriental man who sat to the right interrupted. "Could you explain how these affected you?"

"That's not important," Nicole shot back hotly. "What is important is that you have about a thousand people who experienced Opus Ten, and they, if no one else, need the complete experience in order to feel fulfilled."

"Yet you implied that the other experiences were somewhat helpful," a young woman on the far right said calmly. "Could you tell us a little more about that, please?"

Nicole relented. "Yes. I found that, immediately after the showing of Opus Ten, I had a great desire to have more experiences. I went through all of them, and after they were all done, I felt released from the desire." She decided not to tell them about the intensifier.

The group looked disappointed, yet the first woman spoke neutrally. "Thank you for answering our questions. Now, do you have any to ask of us?"

"Yes, thank you. Have any of you ever experienced Lawrence?"

The woman shook her head.

Strange, thought Nicole. *You'd think they'd want to know what they're marketing!* "Okay, then, what is your procedure for previewing Lawrence?"

"We selected 113 previewers from the unemployed sector. We are proud to say that every single one of our experiences has met with their approval, and all have been marketed to resounding success. The system apparently must work. Whatever the previewers like, our audience of over one hundred million has liked," the woman said smugly.

"Are they unanimous is their approval?" Nicole asked.

"No, but what the majority likes has sold well."

"How does Lawrence present her work?"

"She is required to send us sketches periodically. Each skeleton becomes subsequently richer as she expands on her topic. All drafts must pass the previewing, and all of them have, except, of course, Opus Ten," the woman ended heavily.

"Why, then, did you release Opus Ten?" Nicole shifted her feet. It seemed impossible that they would have allowed such a thing.

"We didn't." Immediately Nicole saw angers flare across the board. "Lawrence did that all by her lonesome."

Nicole somehow controlled a snicker at the odd turn of phrase and turned her attention to the young man who sat next to the woman on the far left.

"Opus Ten was not previewed before that first showing. None of the other experiences just stopped like that," he said petulantly. "We have since previewed it, and after intense questioning of our previewers, we found that the content has potential, but the release of such an intense, yet stuttering piece before previewing it is unconscionable."

"Okay, then," Nicole said. "What then do you want Lawrence to come up with to replace Opus Ten?"

Each of the five laughed, and the woman who had not spoken up yet, the light brown, stocky one with soft white hair that inevitably reminded Nicole of her grandmother, said amiably, "Don't be silly. We want nothing. We would not presume to dictate what Lawrence should create."

"I see." Nicole shut off her Dog. "Well, I have no more questions. I'd like to speak with the previewers at your earliest convenience."

"At once."

Nicole was led to a large room similar to the auditoriums in which she had first experienced Lawrence. There sat the 113 previewers. Again Nicole got the impression that they had been sitting there all day in hopes that she would show up. She decided to mention this to the woman who had accompanied her.

"They are currently in residence here because Opus Ten is due out this week. We assembled them here at your request. Here is where they preview." Her pale, middle-aged face beneath the blonde page boy put forth a professional smile.

Nicole internally jerked. Lawrence had to have something ready by this week! Yet in all her contact with her she had never sensed any urgency about her. Focusing on a chubby, middle-aged man in the front row, she pointed at him. "What's your name?"

The man jumped. "Me? Jeff."

"Okay, Jeff, I'll start with you, but if anyone else wants to jump in, go ahead anytime. I'd like to ask you how you felt about experiencing Opus Ten."

Jeff didn't look exactly angry; it was more like disgusted. "I was disappointed, naturally."

"Did you feel some kind of loss, some kind of frustration?"

"Well, yeah," Jeff answered slowly. "I was mad, too. I wasn't expecting it just to end like that. I thought it would be complete."

Nicole's mind took a quantum leap to the ceiling. "You mean you thought you were experiencing a complete experience?"

"Well, no," he again spoke slowly. "We were warned beforehand that it wasn't finished, but I thought it was just a rough draft. I was expecting an outline."

Nicole nodded. "The upper committee has informed me of the nature of rough drafts. Now that you've experienced such an abrupt shock, would you like to see Opus Ten finished?" Nicole persisted.

Jeff reached up to rub his bald spot. "Yes," he said immediately, echoed by several in the room. "But wait." He looked anxiously over at the head of the committee. Sheepishly he continued, "I ain't too particular. Anything would be fine." He paused. "No, not just anything," he admitted. "Opus Ten is supposed to be like the others."

"In what way?" Nicole's probing antennae leaped.

He smiled reminiscently. "Pleasurable. Beautiful."

"What about 'Innocents'?"

Jeff laughed self-consciously. "Yeah, you got me there, but 'Innocents' as an exception isn't fair. We all knew what it was for, because Lawrence had said that her royalties were to go to the humane society. 'Innocents' was created as a public service message, as explained in Lawrence's contract."

"What if Opus Ten weren't at all like the others? Would you care?"

"It seemed to be a lot like the others. At least, the little we saw did. I guess if it were changed radically, that would be okay. I'd have to experience it . . . but it would have to be good," Jeff emphasized. "Or it won't sell."

"What if it were very different, but still it was the most beautiful and sold the most?" *Now this is crazy*, Nicole thought. *What am I saying? Of course they wouldn't mind that. What in the world am I basing my questions on?*

"That would be fine." Jeff looked at her strangely.

Nicole again seized possession of herself. "What I'm getting at here," she began lamely, "is that you, perhaps unconsciously, hope to have something that will top 'Goldweaving.'"

Jeff took a moment to think. "That's hard to say. 'Goldweaving' was the best. I would probably be happy so long as I got one as good as the others. But then again . . ."

Nicole waited. Idly studying the man, she wondered what he had seen in "Goldweaving." What had *he* felt?

Finally he answered, "I have to admit that I suppose I am hoping for something to top 'Goldweaving.' That seems impossible, though, so I don't want to hope too hard. Still —"

48

Nicole glanced at all 113 previewers. Each one was nodding slowly. She turned to the head of the committee questioningly.

"Of course that's what we want," she answered tightly. "Think of the public's disappointment if it were simply good. No, we can't risk a letdown now. We hope to ride the wave of success."

That's archaic, thought Nicole. "I'd like to ask one more question, if I may. What does Lawrence communicate?"

Jeff paused, apparently stymied, then turned to look about at the other previewers. "What do you all think?"

The group murmured. Nicole saw mostly puzzled glances. Finally a woman stood. "I'm Ona," she introduced herself. "I think that Lawrence sends us her feelings to be comprehended. It's how she feels things and sees things. We see the beauty of things from her viewpoint." She sat back down triumphantly.

"Thank you," said Nicole. She turned to the head of the committee. "Can I find out anytime soon about your decision? I still think completing the Opus Ten, at least for the ones who have already experienced it, would be best." Nicole frowned at her timid voice.

The head seemed to be looking at her pityingly. "Oh, *that.* We will inform Lawrence concerning our decision. Thank you for your suggestion."

Nicole snapped off her Dog and nodded to her. "I'm done with my questions." She tried to keep her voice neutral.

Instantly the professional smile was back. "We are glad to assist you with any answers you need. Please don't hesitate to contact us if you have further questions."

Nicole left gratefully.

After getting directions from the committee head, Nicole followed the flashing blue arrows in the corridor slowly, pausing every once in a while at the slender windows to peer out at the approaching night.

I should be exhausted. Nicole shifted her equipment back and forth over her shoulders. *But I think I need some more information, this time from her fans.*

She emerged on a balcony above the huge reception ballroom. Perfect! During the evening, most of the conventioneers converged here for food and discussion. She quickly found a spiral staircase and went down to meet them, running right smack into Alma.

"Well! Look who's finally back! Where have you been?" She turned and waved a Lion over to pick up Nicole's words.

Nicole grimaced. "I've been talking to Lawrence."

"Oooh." A crowd of people moaned and ran to gather quickly around Nicole, despite the Lion which roared her words clearly across the room.

"Why'd she let *you* see her?" Alma demanded hotly.

Nicole shrugged.

"Oh, I've been dying to see her!" moaned a small blonde woman. "I was just getting up the nerve to talk to her after the showing when she ran off."

"Yeah, what's her problem?" began a tall, dark man of what appeared to be of Indian descent. "I wasn't expecting a chance to see her personally, but why doesn't she at least come sit on our panels, or something?"

Nicole found herself saying, "She doesn't have time to participate in the convention because she's under a tight deadline. She's got to come up with another experience sometime this week."

Suzette was sharp. She poked her head around two others. "I don't understand. I thought she was just going to finish the one she's working on now."

"Well, her marketers would prefer she do something else. They're not pleased with this one. They want something to top 'Goldweaving.'" Nicole heard her voice go indignant.

"But this one—won't it?" Suzette asked.

The Child Genius smoothed her collar. "I have a feeling that it will."

"Yeah," whispered Alma. "I bet it would, if they'd just leave her alone and let her finish it. I'd hate to think they'd just destroy it and I'd never get to experience the whole thing."

"Oh, dear! Would they destroy it?" Suzette exclaimed.

"I don't think so," reassured Nicole. "But if it just lies around unfinished, though, I believe that to be about the same thing."

The group fell silent, then Alma blurted, "Let her finish it! We need it! If Lawrence were here right now, I'd tell her not to let herself get pushed around. Tell her marketers to stuff it. You go tell Lawrence I said so!"

Everyone laughed briefly, then stopped. Nicole watched them as they duplicated her own feeling of discomfort. "Okay," she finally said over the silence. "One final question: what does Lawrence communicate?" Alma looked at her haughtily. "I'd of thought by now you would have figured it out."

Nicole nodded, looking out over a hushed crowd. Some murmured briefly, hesitatingly, then again came silence. *Time to break up this party,* she thought. "Thank you very much," she found herself saying quietly, then she left them to go to her quarters.

Lawrence rose from her laboratory bench and clicked off the lamp. Taking a big sigh, she stretched mightily. *I made more progress than I expected. Maybe it won't be too bad, making another experience. But that's enough for tonight. I'm going upstairs and relax.* She rubbed her sore shoulders ruefully. *I didn't work that long, but I'm exhausted. Yeah. I'll take some tea, have some supper, read a book, go to bed, and never take my mind off of my project.* She headed toward the shaft back of the kitchen.

Humming, Lawrence popped open the door of her private quarters and adjusted the light. "Hi!"

She jumped back into the corridor to peer into the room's shadows. Groaning, she said, "Okay, Mack, what do you want?"

"Probably what you want. Something to eat."

"Shit," she muttered as she came back into the room. "Then go downstairs and get it. And remember to bring me up some."

Mack chuckled and adjusted the recliner so that he was sitting erect. "I already have." He sipped his drink.

"Huh?" Lawrence came over to the table he was sitting at and turned on the light above it. "Cute. Warm plates. Did you wake up the chef?"

"Yes. Now, help yourself."

"Mack," she moaned. "I'm tired. Why didn't you talk to me downstairs?"

"And get my head broke off? You know I can't disturb you when you're working, so I came up here. It's been nice, waiting." He pointed up at the sharp glass dome that formed the ceiling of the room. It glowed bluely in its rim lights, snowflakes occasionally adhering to the surface. "The snow's nice," he commented. "This room is very soothing."

"Mack, you're crazy. What could you have to say to me? It must be important, but not urgent."

He smiled at her angelically. "Oh, it's urgent, all right."

Lawrence felt her heart sink, even if she had no clue as to what he was talking about. She pulled up a chair across from him and grabbed a taquito, stuffing it into her mouth in what she hoped was her normal fashion.

"The committee rejected the neube's proposal to have you complete Opus Ten. They really could see no profit in exposing just a few private parties to it for healing purposes."

Lawrence nodded, only half-listening. "These taquitoes are good. Pass me that falafel. No, don't bother shoving it into some pita bread. I like them plain."

"Have you accomplished anything during your long hours in the lab?"

Lawrence stopped biting into her third crisp falafel ball to study his expression for irony. "I did some work on Opus Ten, and I fed the super gene into the banks, and I tried to prepare a template for the silent Opus."

"All losers." Mack finished his falafel sandwich and mopped up some tahini with half a pita bread.

"They might like the last one. You don't know."

"They won't if it's completely silent."

"It's not." Lawrence shifted forward eagerly. "I hate to hear you scream, but you might consider it abstract. There's just a suggestion here and there of melodious noise, other touches of sensory impressions, then people might just add what *they* think should be, and . . ."

Mack interrupted. "We want something to top 'Goldweaving,' not some weird participatory experience."

51

Lawrence nodded wearily, surprisingly not bursting out into invective.

"What's the matter? Aren't you going to yell at me?" Mack asked teasingly.

Lawrence leaned back with a banana. "I might once you give me something to argue about."

Mack opened his mouth, then paused to think. "You know something? I don't understand you. I don't understand why you accepted me and I don't know why you don't fire me. You're free to do so anytime."

Lawrence rolled her eyes. "Oh, Mack, use your tiny brain. I accepted you because I didn't want to make the committee mad, and I've kept you around because I like to argue. Besides," she stopped to frown, "your replacement could be lots worse."

"Yes, I know," Mack sighed. "Who will have my charming good looks?"

Lawrence threw her banana peel at him. Mack ducked and chuckled, then he became serious.

"I came to see you tonight to tell you what the committee has decided. They figured out that an incomplete experience would be a perfect finale for your contract. It seems that people would experience it, and then they'd be even more demanding to experience more than they are now, because of the feeling of incompleteness. What a wonderful way to ensure future sales!"

"Sheesh!" Lawrence stood up, grabbed her stomach, and walked over to the center of the room to stare up into the falling, sliding flakes. "Can I object?" she asked hopelessly.

"I doubt it," Mack said, amused.

Lawrence ran back over to the table and kicked her chair. "Listen to me out of your little capitalistic, democratic mind . . ."

"Leave out the politics, please . . ."

". . . it will hurt too many people . . ."

". . . and they'll pay for healing . . ."

". . . they'll probably suicide . . ."

". . . no one has. It seems unlikely . . ."

". . . sounds like original sin to me . . ."

". . . it would, I guess . . ."

". . . is there possibly another reason you want to do this besides profit?"

". . . what else is there?"

Lawrence finally gave him her worst stare. "I don't know, because I can't think like you, but I bet there's something."

Mack laughed.

Lawrence pointed at herself. "Look. I consider myself responsible for what I produce."

"That's your own, private stigma." He rose.

"Hey, Mack," she said so tensely he stared. "Do me a favor. When my contract's up, go into my pod and experience all of me."

Mack bent down to pick up his cup of coffee and stirred it awkwardly. "You know," he began softly, "I might just do that. I'm as curious as any poor person to know what it's like." He sipped and frowned. "I still don't know why that's in the contract."

Lawrence stood stunned at the expression on his face. He was flushed, and he was eyeing her almost friendly, with a curious interest in his gaze. She blushed. "I'm sure the committee has its reasons. Besides, you don't want to lose your job just to experience me."

"It's too late," he answered mournfully.

"What?"

"Isn't it obvious? The committee has accepted your Opus Ten. You're through. *We're* through."

Lawrence shook her head. "I don't understand. I can renew my contract."

"No. The committee was firm on that point. They're going to run another contest."

Lawrence simply nodded. "Another contest doesn't frighten me. They can sponsor two artists. What's the big deal?"

"They won't, though," Mack answered heavily. "I know them. They can't let you go unpunished."

Lawrence tucked her arms around herself and crouched. "I'll get along," she whispered. "If they're going to release Opus Ten as is, I'll have to go into hiding anyway." While she felt a great burden fall from her, she felt her chest tighten.

Mack stood up, and, still deep in mourning, she did, too. Idly she noticed Mack pulling something out of his pocket, but she didn't respond until he held it out. "Here."

Lawrence didn't even look, just shrugged away.

"Damn it. Here." Mack was shoving something into her hand. Sighing, she fumbled, feeling his soft, warm fingers around hers. She tried to grab onto it, but it fell. Both bent to pick it up, Mack rapidly, she more clumsily, hearing her right knee crack. They ended up crouched on the floor, nose to nose.

"They've locked you out of Opus Ten. Here's the key," whispered Mack. "Now get to work and finish the damn thing."

By the time Lawrence had leapt up, Mack had fled out the door.

Nicole mindlessly followed the tiny, flashing yellow arrows on the walls until they went out, leaving her in a dusky corridor.

"Oh, shit. What happened?" Nicole said aloud. She considered for a while. It was awfully late; Lawrence must have gone to bed. She sighed.

Suddenly her mind arrested upon the last part of her conversation at the convention. The way everyone had seemed together and laughing but then suddenly stopping was reminiscent of . . .

Of what?

Nicole wandered the hall, aiming for her rooms in a haphazard fashion. She puzzled. A flowing, then a sudden stop . . .

She figured it out.

Why, she thought, *it's just like Opus Ten. Here I was, coasting along, and then all at once I was ripped away. And since everybody here experienced it, too, they're . . . doing what? Reenacting it, trying to finish it, trying to push onward, but they can't?* Nicole frowned. *I guess it's like "Goldweaving," too, then. Will we be forced to continually replay the events until we go crazy? And what for? Where are we going?*

She straightened her shoulders. "Lawrence has done this. It's what *she* wants," she muttered out loud. Quickly she leaned up against the wall as a wave of nausea passed over her. It was followed by a sense of thrilling euphoria, like she was hooked up again. Rapturously she followed dream-like images, and everything was making sense . . .

Lawrence was leading her mind along a wild, tortuous journey full of mystery and wonder. "I will go now," she said, "with fresh hope, and accomplish that which I must." She strode forward. The mountain no longer seemed formidable. The vines enmeshed . . .

Nicole paused, hand on the panel that would slide open her room's door. *How'd I get here? Oh, hell, I must be tired. At least here's my room. Let me get a good night's rest, and tomorrow I'll be helping Lawrence meet her deadline.*

Chapter Seven

Lawrence awoke late the next morning in an optimistic mood. Excitement rose in her as she lay looking up at the clear blue sky through her dome. *Aw, fuck Mack and fuck the previewers and fuck the committee and fuck everyone even slightly connected to NewTech. They stupidly paved the way for me. I'm going to finish "Love," and, when I'm through, they won't want to market anything else. Fuck 'em all.*

Lawrence took a long shower and pulled on some clean clothes. Then, letting her hair drip, she headed for her laboratory.

"Hello." Nicole rose from her lotus position on the floor.

"What are you doing here?" growled Lawrence. "I'm busy."

Nicole answered calmly, "I'm willing to fulfill my obligation to my contract. What would you have me do to help you?"

Lawrence ignored her to open the door to the light room.

"You didn't tell me you had a deadline this week," Nicole accused. "My interview could have waited. I sensed no urgency about you."

Lawrence frowned. "Deadlines I meet. Always have. I have to work on what I want to work on. It's simple."

"So are you going to finish Opus Ten? 'Love'?" Nicole found herself conceding. "I spoke to the committee and . . ."

"Oh, yes. That. Thank you very much." Lawrence passed through the light room, making Nicole follow her before the door slammed.

"What? What is it?" Nicole surprised herself at her determination. If Lawrence didn't want her . . .

"They want to release Opus Ten as is. Apparently, you gave them the idea that it would cause intense craving to experience more of me, which would cause NewTech's profits to swell even more than they do now," Lawrence explained gruffly. "Now, I think I should finish it, shouldn't I?"

Nicole's jaw dropped. "Can't you make a substitute?"

"Unacceptable. My only route is to provide them with a complete Opus Ten. Either that, or destroy it as it is now, and I won't do that."

Nicole watched her as she slid open the door to the pod and pulled another lowback chair into the round chamber. "But what about me?"

"Aah," Lawrence shrugged as she crouched to connect the chairs to the basal hook.

"Why is this one so hard to finish? You get them all out so fast."

"I never rush them, except the short pieces. Each new experience seems to take longer. I know 'Goldweaving' took the longest. This one actually did start fairly quickly. I've spent about a month on it. It's just I'm stymied because . . ."

"Why?"

Lawrence clammed up. "You're my inspiration." She pointed at the chairs. "All this time you *have* helped me. You've talked to me. Oh, I know it has mostly been your questions and my measly answers, but it has helped. Now, though, I'd like to ask you to help me in a different way."

"How?" Nicole looked down at the chairs in the pod. "Are we going to hook up together?"

"Yes. We must learn of each other. To do that we . . ."

"Wait a minute!" Nicole choked, aware of an intense, flooding desire to hook up, this time with Lawrence directly, and she already knew that she wouldn't mind losing herself in her.

Lawrence continued mildly, "We can create an experience together. We might even meet in one."

Nicole shuddered. "That sounds weird!" She looked around. "Who will be monitoring us?"

"No one. What do you think, Nicole?" Lawrence said gently. "Do you think someone wastes their time monitoring me while I create?"

"Yeah, but you're used to going in there and creating images. I need practice. You might come out just fine, but I could get lost in there."

"Oh, no," reassured Lawrence. "Like I was saying, your bodily functions will warn you. I'll get up and turn you off if necessary. There's nothing to fear."

"Except you," she snapped.

Lawrence stepped back, startled.

"Oh, don't try the innocent act on me." Nicole snapped. "You have experience doing this, and you do it well. You could easily mess up my mind."

"But, Nicole, you're strong. You could easily mess up mine."

Nicole hesitated. "You think we're both at risk?"

"I do." Lawrence shrugged.

"Yet you don't want a monitor. Why?"

Lawrence nodded. "The same reason a lot of people don't like them. Privacy."

Nicole wasn't quite sure what to make of that. "I'm ready," was what she said.

Lawrence nodded, indicating the chair to the left. "I'll hook you up first, let you get oriented. Then I'll follow you."

Nicole nodded and stretched out. Oddly, she was calm. *It was inevitable,* she thought.

Nicole blinked. *Okay, now I'm hooked up with no stimulus from Lawrence's experiences. What do I see?* She looked around, noticing first that she was sitting in the same position as her physical body was sitting in the pod. She stood, dusting off her jeans. Gradually light appeared, and warmth, replacing the black Nicole only now recognized as the absence of color. *Where's Lawrence?* she wondered. *How long will it take before she hooks up?* Walking the sand dune that sloped downward, Nicole began taking inventory of what she felt. *I apparently must be clothed, and I must have something to walk on. These are things I must take for granted.* She shifted her knapsack. *Hey, what's this? Something else I take for granted?* She squatted and popped open the knapsack to examine its contents. Food, water, a tent, potty, other necessities. Nicole sighed. *If it's me creating all this, I'm pretty mundane.* She repacked the knapsack and continued walking. Ahead was a deep red line, so she aimed for it.

Quicker than she believed possible, she was at its edge. Removing her knapsack, Nicole sank down beside the current. Cautiously she touched it, expecting something dramatic, but only feeling sand. The current to her senses seemed to be red sand curling smokily through the air. *This is the most interesting thing I've created so far, so I'll honor it.*

Nicole was suddenly struck by a thought. What air? All around her was just undifferentiated yellow, and she wasn't breathing it. *I'm not sweating, either. I just feel nauseated, and my skin feels prickly.* As she watched the current fluctuate, gold sparks appeared here and there in the sand.

"That's because you kept saying 'current,' so your mind decided on electricity, my worst subject, I might add," came a soft, low voice without a trace of accent.

Nicole whipped around to find a tall, slender woman beside her. She studied the long golden curls and perfect cheekbones before glancing down at the shiny golden outfit that hugged long, sloping curves. Of course, the top of the slinky pantsuit showed ample breasts. She glared straight into the deep blue eyes. "Who are you?" she demanded.

It was the woman's turn to look puzzled. "Lawrence, of course! Did you think I'd just sneak someone else in here?" In her indignation, her accent had returned.

"But . . . but . . ." Nicole gestured. "Look at you!"

Lawrence looked down at the stream rushing by and sighed. "I kind of figured that would happen. Maybe I can change it." She looked down at her watery reflection and concentrated.

Nicole looked from her to the current and back again. "What do you see there . . . Lawrence?" She was unable to say the name without hesitation, though the woman's speech was clearly Lawrence's.

Lawrence glanced up amusedly. "A river stream. Quite boring, actually. Not like what you're experiencing, I bet."

"But I thought you could tell what I was experiencing because you explained why I saw sparks."

"Oh, that." Her brows knitted. "I can't see it, but I can think it."

"Are you reading my mind?" Nicole hastily tried not to think.

"I don't know. I just focused: where's Nicole? And I found you and know what you see."

"And why do you appear as you do? Am I doing that?" Nicole found herself gulping. Did she actually want some stereotypically beautiful white female?

"No," Lawrence said confidently. "I came up with this image years ago. I think I was eleven. I don't remember now, it's been so long." She glanced back over to the stream, then folded her arms firmly. "No, I guess I still look the same. You'll just have to get used to it."

"But . . . why?"

"Well, I suppose I like the fact that what I do excites people, and that all my experiences are beautiful, because . . ." Here Lawrence turned her tear-filled eyes away. "All around me I see the beauty of nature, and I so very much want to be a part of it!"

Nicole turned a sharp right angle away from her and waited until Lawrence had wiped her eyes. "Do I look the same to you?" she asked lowly.

Lawrence vigorously nodded.

"I wish I could have a mirror and see how I look to myself. I might be changed, too."

Lawrence reached over and pulled the knapsack over to her. She started digging through its contents.

"No, that's no good," Nicole hastily said, "I already looked."

But Lawrence was pulling out a small, ornate mirror. "Here."

"How did that mirror get in there?" Nicole demanded.

Lawrence came over and put her arms around her. "Don't you see?" she asked softly. "We can do anything here!"

Nicole pulled away and pointed at Lawrence. "Uh-uh. You didn't change the way you looked!"

Lawrence sobered. "I know. It takes a while."

Nicole now carefully took hold of the mirror and looked into it. Jerking, she dropped it. It did not break.

"Hey, what's the matter?" Lawrence bent to pick it up.

"That was that woman in 'Goldweaving'!"

"What woman?"

"Oh, you must know. You created it!"

Lawrence shook her head, then flashed the mirror at her.

"I don't want it." Nicole, idly feeling a need to escape, fled to bravely step into the current.

"Hey, that's neat," Lawrence said lowly. "You're not going into the water, but you're in the space relegated to the stream."

"Huh?"

Lawrence stepped into the stream.

"Yeah, I see what you mean. You're there, but you don't seem to be wading through dust."

Lawrence cleared her throat. "How about we try to see what the other is seeing, just for a minute."

Nicole kicked angrily. "How am I supposed to do that?" Still, she found herself mirroring Lawrence, closing her eyes and concentrating. She breathed deeply, focusing on the image of a mountain stream, one similar to the one she saw in "Love," then she opened her eyes.

Nothing. Still she stood in the sand, next to some Miss Universe Lawrence standing in her watery stream.

Sighing, she again closed her eyes, shifting her feet angrily, eager to be free of the stinging sand, then she suddenly choked as she slipped on the muddy bottom and swallowed water.

Lawrence strode through the waves of dust and picked her up.

Nicole spluttered, "How about us just stepping out of the stream and letting it be what it was before we looked at it?"

"But . . ." Lawrence silenced herself and helped her out of the stream, closing her eyes in an effort to concentrate, to not yank her too far.

Nicole climbed up the smooth, muddy bank and flopped down. "Hey, Lawrence . . ."

Before her stood a huge mirror. It covered the entire expanse of the sky, echoing the trees that draped the other bank.

Nicole stood slowly as Lawrence walked easily from the river, because to her it was still dust. Yes, in the mirror she was still the horse woman, and Lawrence was still, she hated to admit, breathtakingly beautiful, and not wet at all.

Nicole slicked her hair back, feeling the mud on her cheek as she did so. She could only watch Lawrence in the mirror, not wishing to tear her eyes away from that enchanting image.

Lawrence was staring at Nicole's reflection. "It worked! I see it!" she whispered excitedly. "Is that what you saw in 'Goldweaving'?" She stepped forward to touch the image, then stopped with a lurch to stare at Nicole. "And now you look like that to me!"

Nicole shrugged, trying to appear nonchalant as Lawrence approached her. "I still only see the creek," she commented disappointedly.

Lawrence nodded. "It's only what we make it."

"What *you* make it."

Lawrence only pointed at Nicole's reflection, then she reached over to take her hands. "You have some control in here, you just need to call up the skill. Look, you're wet and miserable. Start with something easy. Dry off."

Nicole kept her hands within Lawrence's, feeling superstitiously that it might help her ability. She drew up images of soft, scratchy clean blankets at her cousin's house, thirst, warm, dry air . . .

"Okay," came Lawrence's grunt. "How do you feel?"

Nicole opened her eyes. Loosening her hands, she brushed them up and down her arms. "Fine." She was quiet now, looking up the bank at the soft sunlight reflecting off the water. "It doesn't seem hard. Shall I begin?"

Lawrence materialized a dry log behind her legs and stooped to sit. "Go ahead."

Nicole joined her on the log and put her chin on her hands. Lawrence was quiet, letting her think.

What should I tell Lawrence? Must it be about love? No. She wants to see me. Yet it should be political, something far reaching yet coming from my small life. Yes, if I can do it in a way to make her see what she is.

Lawrence sat patiently, letting the river bank melt into a blank slate, then reform into a quiet, elegant African-American living room. Nicole as a teenager came into the front door, and Lawrence was amazed that she recognized her. Her hand of its own accord went to touch Nicole's, only to be slapped away.

"Leave me alone," she muttered. "I'm busy."

The teenaged Nicole went to the window, pausing only to touch the widescreen off. She looked out on the world from the tip of her pyramid, scanning her identical neighbors across the wide, smooth street. Car keys protruded from her hands, growing until they sealed off the scene. Lawrence blinked.

Nicole emerged from her dorm room, hauling out Goodall, Mead, and Boas and flinging them to the winds. Lawrence watched the textbooks, three and half years at Yale fly off as the younger Nicole entered Australia, a small salt map in the distance.

The pyramid was crumbling, in what seemed to be an unusual fashion. The top was metal and plastic, and it endured. Lawrence watched it glitter as it traipsed across the Australian desert. Meanwhile, back in Africa, the foundation, as well as China, India, all the small workers bound together, supporting the tiny, glittering tip, began wearing away, faster and faster, sliding into the river, whole chunks blasting off into space. Soon, the tip floated above a barren planet, zooming from Australia back to an older, enlightened ex-anthropology major joining up against the golden neighborhood, with its cars, TVs, and waste.

Lawrence saw a tired Nicole, home from her job washing dishes, stripping off her apron and entering the apartment she shared with three men and two women, sipping her everlasting coffee, slapping the naked lamp overhead, and typing yet another article on a screenless typer.

A pause. "Oh, shit," Nicole muttering, shifting on the log. "It's so boring. I've got to . . ."

Lawrence leaned forward immediately. "Do you want me to help you?"

"No! Shut up. Leave me alone." Nicole hunched forward, stretching her hand out, bleeding the colors of her heritage, the Osage, German, and, of course, the Afridi. Her image spread across the empty horizon, turning to face the distance. Lawrence watched her profile, wondering what she was seeing.

The Rapacious Age of a hundred years ago. Lawrence gulped at the wide legions of dark refugees passing over the ocean, grasping at straw, swallowing wheat, choking on white rice, readily chewing apples and only fingering idly the odd green pages with old heroes on them.

Now she felt Nicole's anger as the blocks of the old pyramid sealed overhead. Below, the shiny top was spreading, melting into a puddle of glowing miasma, and the elements of Nicole's consciousness grew.

The idols, beauty, wealth, and speed merged. Below, a man in soft brown overalls was hammering to a white billboard a life-size man in a business suit, and the millions knelt.

Nicole stood then. "Fuck it all!" She ineffectively thrust a lock of hair off her forehead, then seized her temples as the images locked and crazed, pumping out the blood and melodies, the images from the one, long, unending . . ."Unending," muttered Nicole . . . source.

"Whoa," cried Lawrence, grabbing her waist from behind and dragging her back. "It's time, love." She popped up, awake, leaping off the couch and running to unhook Nicole.

Nicole came around to the firm, warm fingers massaging her neck and shoulders as she sat crouched on the pod chair. "Damn," she whispered. It felt good, but her head was still pounding. Lawrence's hot palms fell onto her shoulder blades as she spoke, stopping the pressured fingers. "Why is it dark?"

Lawrence dropped her hands and stood. "Do you want light?"

"Of course I do! And some damn headremedy, while you're at it. Ugh." Her voice dropped to a whisper as the white light burned her sight.

Her hands faltered as she took the glass of water and vial from Lawrence. "You're killing me."

"You're just how I was the first time. It's hard to come up with such complex images. You'll get used to it."

Nicole glared at her. "It's not like I'm going to be doing any more. You got my best just now."

Lawrence turned away. "Can you get up?"

Nicole found herself wanting to rest and let those hot hands rub her whole back, but she thrust the desire down and stood. "Why? Are you going to go back and show me images? Maybe you want to refute some of what you just saw, huh?"

Lawrence laughed, and it seemed so genuine Nicole found herself smiling. "No. I mean, yes, I intend to take you back in for my turn, but you need to rest. Let's take a break. I think there's something in this mountain you would like to see, and now's as good a time as any other."

Nicole frowned. "Where is it? What is it?"

"Well, it's hidden way down in the basement, and it's locked. I doubt many people could find it. Besides, I've got the only key. Let me show you."

Nicole responded to the proud, yet begging tone. Shrugging, she said, "Okay."

Lawrence led her down to the central shaft, taking a wide staircase down amid white glowing panels.

Nicole pointed. "You call this a shaft? It's nicely kept, not damp and gloomy. Why, for a place that's never frequented?"

"I come down here often," Lawrence replied. "What is down here is considered precious by some people. Enough said." She hopped down from the last step and walked up to the sealed doors, reaching into her pocket as she did so.

"I hope you remembered to bring a key." Nicole leaned back to study the huge timbered door. Through her headache, she could not help but be amazed at what surprises the mansion gave her. "Look at this thing! It's so stereotypical! Huge beams, steel clasps. Does the key weigh a ton? Is it brass and filigree?"

Lawrence withdrew a slender white panel from her jeans pocket and pressed it to a recess in the left door until she heard a click. "I like this particular method of locking myself in. It's supposed to be foolproof." She swung the doors wide.

Nicole stepped into a cavernous room that lit up gradually as Lawrence flipped the switches behind her. "Oooooh."

She was in an enormous library. All she could see was shelves and shelves of volumes, shelves that reached up to a twenty foot ceiling. The telescoping view curved in a fairly dry, undisturbed cavern, so Nicole felt that the shelves went on for kilometers.

"Is this yours?"

Lawrence stepped away from the light switches and stood looking at the tiers wryly. "Might as well be." She turned to go to her right.

"Hey, wait. What do you want me to do?"

Lawrence gave her an honestly puzzled look. "Do whatever you like."

Nicole watched quietly as Lawrence slipped around a bookshelf and disappeared. Then, waving a hand in a belated, sarcastic farewell, she began to wander the shelves, pausing every once in a while to admire the taste of whoever had collected it. Lawrence had every seven meters or so a large recess that housed an ancient, yet perfectly functional electric steel elevator. Nicole found herself riding each one in succession, gaping in awe at the slimy paperbacks, the first editions, the tiny, white, moth-eaten special editions. Finally she made her selection and went in search of Lawrence.

It was eerie passing by the full shelves one by one, all of them perfectly silent. Whatever Lawrence was doing, she was being pretty quiet about it.

After her journey through about thirty shelves, she came to a small recess devoted to immaculate glass tables and a few comfortable futons, but no Lawrence. Nicole plopped herself down on the nearest futon and sighed. "Lawrence, if your goal was to give me some exercise, you've succeeded. Now, where the hell are you?"

She hissed. Somewhere unimaginably distant, she could hear something being scraped across the floor. It gave her the strangest feeling, as if she were doomed to stay locked in here forever, which wouldn't be too bad. Again she looked back admiringly at the shelves behind her. Just give her enough food to live on, and she'd be perfectly happy.

Nicole waited until she was rested, then rose to go once more in the same direction. "Lawrence!" she called. "Come on, shit!"

The shelves abruptly stopped about fifty tiers down, and Nicole found herself guiding her arm down the stone wall to find it fall through what could only be a door blasted into the rock.

Nicole stepped through the hole and halted.

With no acknowledgment of her arrival, Lawrence was walking up and down in a few colored lights, red, yellow, and green, with flashes of white light apparently coming from some device she held. Around her was what Nicole could only call a sculpture of thick wire. A few thin pieces of plywood held the wires up, forming an odd pink skeleton. Nicole blinked, then tightened her lips. It looked odd because it was seven oddly shaped sides that curved overhead, completely sealing off Lawrence, except for a gate to the left, where it was obvious the sculpture had been designed to be pulled apart to let the artist through. As she watched in amazement, Nicole saw Lawrence take a roll of wire off to the far left corner and proceed to strip it. Nicole lifted her hand to touch the odd pattern of wires that floated before her face.

"Hey! No touching!" Lawrence was there, pliers and wire cutters in hand. "Just admire it, will you?"

"What is it? A harp? So many wires!"

"Nothing much." Lawrence pointed down at the book she held. "What did you finally choose to read?"

"Poetry." Nicole showed her the title, but she didn't even look at it, just took her glasses off to clean them.

"Oh. Good choice."

"Why?" Somehow, Nicole could guess what she was going to say.

"It's meaningless." Lawrence reached up to stroke some of the wires that had been bent to form cat's whiskers, producing a surprisingly rich tone.

Nicole watched the golden light shine and sparkle on the moving strings. "Is this some sort of instrument? Is that why you're building it?" she persisted.

Lawrence looked disgusted as she frowned, then a smile reappeared on her face. "The interview, of course," she finally said softly. "Ask away, right? Yeah," she continued immediately. "I used to play with a lot of junk when I was a kid. Shaping wire was soothing at one point. I didn't think much of it, but when I found these leftover rolls down here, I couldn't resist. I could make a much bigger sculpture than I could ever have imagined. And here it is!" She stopped abruptly, embarrassed. "That's what you really wanted to know, isn't it? As to why, it's a hobby. When I work on it, my mind awakens. It requires some concentration, and having some focus helps me create other things."

"But then why do you hide it?"

Lawrence stood back in surprise, then grinned. "You've seen it. Hawk it all you want."

Obediently Nicole lifted her Hawk, then paused. "Does Mack know?" she blurted.

Lawrence dropped her wire cutters. "I—how strange you should ask. Yes, he does."

Nicole nodded, took one shot of the sculpture from where she stood, then walked around to the gate and let herself inside. Lawrence did not protest. She aimed her Hawk toward all seven sides of the sculpture, making sure to get an image of Lawrence standing within it at one point. "What did you think about my attempt?" she asked shyly.

Lawrence nodded, "Pretty good for the first time."

Nicole waited. "Is that all you can say? What about what I was trying to say?"

Lawrence shrugged. "Oh, I guess it was what you were always saying in your articles, you know, always ranting and raving about the disappearing of diversity, when, if you ask me, there's some good and some bad in equalizing, or Westernizing, as we like to call it."

"Oh, come on, who's we? I admit, I haven't done much except work for a few left journals, but, if you're sincere, what have you done?" Nicole shifted. "I mean, I'm nobody, but you've got money, position, there's so much you could be doing . . ."

"Such as?" Lawrence asked mildly. "You could ask where I got the junk to fool around with when I was a kid. I practically lived in a junk yard, that's how. Hell, I liked rules that kept kids like me from being born, rules that kept the woods where I scavenged other people's junk from being torn down." Lawrence watched as Nicole's face twisted. "If it'll make you feel any better, my contract's up. I now have time to see the world as it is, and, yes, your introduction was most edifying." A ghost of a smile appeared on Lawrence's face, and Nicole couldn't help but feel that showing Lawrence herself, as it were, had not been a good idea.

"So you have no problem with what has happened, the loss of other cultures, this Western need to worship ourselves, and the resultant making of the world in its image?" Nicole finally shouted, "What *you're* doing?"

Lawrence threw down her pliers and advanced. "Fuck it, now I know you're deluded. Your crazy theories about the damn world. What the fuck do *I* have to do with it?"

"Won't you admit that you're promoting your art all over the world?"

"I only reach 1% of my potential audience now."

"Which is?"

"Everyone, of course."

"Aha!"

"What?"

Nicole strode out of the sculpture and stepped up out of the crevice in which it sat. "Don't give me that bullshit innocent act! It's obvious that you want to reach everyone, no matter who they are, and make them conform to your ideas."

"What ideas? I consider my images and emotions to be universal. And don't give me any of that cultural purity crap. Look at what I'm doing. I don't inform. Entertainment is just another way to push useless information. I consider myself an entertainer. Those books back there." She waved a hand back at the shelves. "They're pretty dense. Advertisements, probably, have the densest information." She took a deep breath and sighed. "And, even if I'm ceremonial art, you can't convince me that a silly little pot had any meaning for the average primitive."

"Those hookies don't think so." Nicole eyes darted to a small writing table that stood in the corner. Scattered over its low surface were several sheets of paper. In the gloom behind the lights Nicole could only make out neat, printed handwriting in oddly straight, uniform lines. *It must be Lawrence's.*

"Really?" Lawrence said casually. "That's typical. It's only the audience that swoons. When they find something that relates to them, they take it to heart. Maybe they can find something in it, I don't really care."

But Nicole was stooping over the table, reading a top page: Lawrence Roberta Williams, her views, take it or cram it. Snickering, she asked, "How'd you get your name?"

"Damn! And people wonder why I don't give interviews." Lawrence's voice sounded light and genial, as if relieved at the change of subject. "Guess."

"Your parents wanted a boy."

"Hell no. Well, they probably did. Most families do. But I had three brothers to give the name to, and they didn't."

"It's a family name."

"No!"

"You had it changed legally."

"Nope. No more guesses. My mother liked the name, and so do I."

Nicole frowned. "What did your father have to say about that?"

"He was already dead before I was born, and I say good riddance." Lawrence stiffly walked out of the sculpture and turned to close the gate. Nicole watched her nimble fingers bring down two pieces of plywood and gently pull. Only then did she see the extraneous hook nailed to one board. She stared at the dull gray metal, watched as Lawrence slipped it into a hole nailed to the other piece of plywood. The hook seemed sad, out of place in the admittedly beautiful, light sculpture. Lawrence pointed at it. "This used to be on the bathroom door in our shack. I saved it after the door rotted through." She went over and flipped on the light over the table.

Nicole could now see a chair beside it. Lawrence sat down in it and gathered up the papers. "You want to read this garbage? You're welcome to it."

Nicole jumped forward, hand outspread. Lawrence laughed at her eager look.

"You must think that here is the answer, that my words are very important." Lawrence spoke tauntingly, but Nicole could see that her hands were shaking. "It's my off and on again diary. Some of it's new. Some of it is years old. Here it sits, out in the open in a locked room.

65

Make of it what you wish. Here." Lawrence stacked it all up neatly and handed it over before standing. "How's your headache?"

Nicole looked up from reading the first line. "Reader, I know you're out there . . ." "Oh, I can't see why you have to create anything for me."

"It's only fair," Lawrence said playfully.

Nicole heard an undertone of anxiety in her voice, and looked up to stare at her. Her curiosity was getting the best of her again. What would she come up with, in this custom-made experience made just for her? At the time, it seemed imperative to find out.

This time she awoke to a shining, glittery, sparkly sky, and spanning up and around and over the valley was a double helix shimmering in what seemed to be moonlight, except that it was too bright. Clustered around the unfinished portion were the bases. Above, far ahead, Nicole could see a worker building, and, faintly, she could hear:

"Helix, the cat! The wonderful, wonderful cat! When he runs out of his DNA, he reaches into his RNA!"

Nicole snickered, than called, "Hey!"

Lawrence turned. "Yeah?"

"I expected something more dramatic," she laughed as she started to climb, reaching Lawrence so fast that it seemed she traveled, too.

"*Traumatic*, you mean." Lawrence frowned critically down at the length of DNA. "You know, this is just symbolic. The *structure* of the experience will be double helix, not the *plot*." Lawrence pointed to the grass just below her feet. "Hey, hand me a cytosine."

Nicole reached down to dig through the brightly colored bases. "Here," she said, handing her a blue one.

"Thanks." Lawrence attached it with a screwdriver, then swung around to the other side to face Nicole.

"Hey! You look like yourself!"

"Oh, so you noticed," was all Lawrence said, leaving Nicole to wonder if she were somehow rejecting her. Spinning the strand of DNA, Lawrence bent down to yank up a rough woven rug from Appalachia.

Nicole grabbed the strand suddenly. "Don't do that, please. You're making me dizzy."

"Follow me." Lawrence grabbed the strand and spun it even harder.

They spun downward, faster and faster, twirling toward the valley bottom, and though Nicole could see no end to the double helix, she was soon off of it, somehow. She ended crouched in a meadow.

Recognizing it immediately, Nicole stood up and looked warily around. Yes, Lawrence had brought her to the beginning of "Love." The wildflowers clearly were from spring, and Nicole could now hear rushing water. *Does she want me to relive "Love"? Why?* Shrugging, she began to wander through the fresh, dewy morning flowers, quickly discovering a path, but it wasn't that wide, and it curved so much that eventually she stopped following it, reasoning that it must have just been caused by erosion. By chance, she had stopped near a little apple tree. She picked a hard, red-stained golden fruit without thinking and bit into it. *Wait a minute! Everywhere else it's spring, yet this tree thinks it's fall.* She chewed, cautiously studying the flavor. *I don't remember eating anything in the experiences. Boy, this is good! It doesn't even taste like an apple.* Slowly she finished it, savoring its rich, creamy flavor, so much like a sweet potato drenched in butter and allspice, closing her eyes for the full effect. When at last the apple was gone, Nicole opened her eyes to the tree in full, eerie golden blossom, her pants legs coated with beggar lice, and the vision of a young man laughing merrily.

Nicole froze. The young man approached, his buttery yellow skin glowing delightfully in the sunlight.

"Hello," he said, smiling with endearing dimples.

"Hello," she said dimly, aware only of the ringing in her ears and the pounding of her heart. "Is it spring or isn't it?"

"It's spring," he answered quietly and firmly, "but I wanted you to taste of my fruit first. Do you mind?" His voice was velvety and deep.

"I—No. Can you tell me who you are?"

"My name?"

"No, not that. Er, are you real?"

"Lawrence once said that she would sneak nobody else in here. Did you create me? Am I what you want?" Without waiting for an answer, the young man turned. "It is time to wash. Are you coming?"

Nicole followed him to the creek, where he stripped casually. Fascinated, Nicole admired his toned, youthful body. From his face, she had guessed him to be about twenty, but his body was fully mature, of that same glorious golden brown color as his face. The young man flexed and leaped, making a perfect dive to the still water below.

Nicole ran to the creek lankily, like a child, illogically fearing that he would strike bottom. When he quickly resurfaced, she relaxed.

"You know," he began softly, "we might be on the other side."

"Of the river?" she asked stupidly.

The young man frowned so that Nicole's heart cried out. "No. What I had in mind was the other side of her mountain, or the other side of winter. Autumn is Lawrence's favorite season." He swam toward her to rest his arms on the bank. "Won't you join me?" he asked so kindly and freshly that Nicole felt obliged.

"Sure!" Nicole pulled off her clothes and stepped into the water that swam over her skin like rich, warm milk. *Oh, my goodness.*

The kiss was flame that spluttered and dimmed, crackling as it took moths' and gnats' lives. Nicole looked out the wide French windows into the blackness, waiting for his return. As she wrapped her arms around him so that they wound and wound, pressing his warm, delicate moist flesh to hers.

They swam to the other bank, and Nicole lay in pale green grass softer and cleaner than any mattress. His dark, intense eyes drank in her beauty, and his lean, strong hands caressed her breasts, feeling like rose petals and cat's fur. Nicole was amazed beneath her passion at how gentle, yet arousing it was.

She ate the cold sand of the moon, danced near the ocean as heat waves drenched the nearby fields. A factory assembly line met her hands as she pressed against an asteroid. Little tiny wires met the clay as the ground beneath her turned to moss.

His lips upon her skin were no longer flame; she trembled from icicles and moist xylem. When she whirled to mount him, carefully enveloping him in dark juiciness, Nicole began mentally screaming, *If this ever ends, I'll die!*

Somehow he was rubbing her crotch and tasting deeply of her breasts. "Oh, Love, Love, anything, anything," she cried.

A prism of the universe, but whose colors mingled, a birth, a swollen cell upon a moist membrane. Effort, chance, but "Love!"

Exhausted, Nicole slowly slid to the ground, his last kiss gentle and lingering. She touched his black, only slightly kinked hair, and found herself enmeshed in moss, the earth swallowing her, until she saw orange magma streaking through the interior. She drank it, swimming through a darkness full of random sounds and music.

"You could call me 'Nick,' you know."

"No, that's all right." Nicole ate crystals and jewels. "Wow, so this is what quartz tastes like!" she said aloud, but he was no longer there.

She drank mercury. Again came the flame, but it grew red . . .

"Nicole . . ." A hiss.

"Yes?" Timidly.

But she swayed throughout the organism, swimming through sap and blood. Extending through leaves and epidermis. Pumping through vessels and hearts. Kissing flowers and soft pubic hair. Streaming through bark, fur, and his hair. "This is me," he whispered.

"I know," she whispered back. "I love you."

Now she was back in the field. An odd thought came to her: *I didn't go anywhere.*

"Nicole!"

She turned stultingly. Lawrence was there near the creek, waving.

"Over here!"

Nicole stumbled over.

"You've been in a long while," she explained. "I've come to take you back."

"Okay," Nicole answered thickly.

Lawrence disappeared, and she awoke.

Nicole stood, fresh and alert, headache long gone, waiting. *But for what?* Her quick eyes watched as Lawrence got up off her couch and shut the machinery off. In a daze that was nevertheless so observing, so alive, she followed Lawrence out of the light room and under the cliff in her laboratory.

Nicole felt much better after this experience. *Of course*, she thought. *I didn't create anything. Or did I?* She looked over at Lawrence suspiciously. The bringer of dreams calmly took a hazelnut butter and strawberry sandwich out of the small refrigerator near the table and climbed the ladder to her laboratory.

Nicole waited, watching as Lawrence began an activity she could only call "puttering." She went over and lifted a headset from a shelf and attached to the computer terminal. Then she nodded, switching on dials and turning every once in a while to engage a screen or two. But then she whipped her gaze over at the patient Nicole still standing at the table, and nodded. Lawrence stepped quietly up to the ledge, headset in hand. She, too, seemed to be waiting.

Nicole cleared her throat. That seemed to be the correct conversation opener.

"Thank you," was all Lawrence said.

"No," Nicole sighed, "I guess I should be the one to thank you. It was beautiful. I . . ." She looked away, overwhelmed with emotion, but then a nagging question leapt into her mind. "What was that about the double spiral being the structure? I was going to ask, but then . . . I got sidetracked."

"I build my experiences upon some sort of pattern. The plot usually clings to a structure of some sort." She flipped her hand, swinging the headset. "Never mind. It's kind of hard to explain."

Nicole felt a burst of inspiration. "What was the structure of 'Goldweaving'?"

Lawrence looked both embarrassed and proud at the same time. "Aw, that was easy. Positive feedback. You know, orgasm."

Nicole's heart sank, even though she had known all along what it was supposed to do. She still felt manipulated, somehow.

Lawrence twisted the cord of her headset, distorting images and sounds on its screen and in its speakers.

Nicole stared uneasily as Lawrence gave her a shaky smile.

"Well," she said softly. "Do you have any more questions? I'm really busy."

Nicole whipped out her Dog, pointing it at Lawrence. "Is this it?" she found herself demanding. "Do I finally have your message?"

Lawrence stared at the Dog and whispered, "I don't know. Do you?" *Does she?* She felt a thrill go through her. If only she did . . . *I gave her my all.*

69

"Well?"

Lawrence put down her headset and turned to come down the ladder. Nicole stood watching her curiously, feeling herself go oddly limp as Lawrence touched her arm.

"Call it 'Love Can Art' for what you gave me and for what you cannot see," Lawrence said mournfully, and Nicole could hear no trace of triumph in her voice.

"So . . . you created him?" Nicole whispered.

Lawrence shook her head. "No. I *was* him. I made love to you."

Chapter Eight

Lawrence tucked her Bird into a watertight bag and donned a hooded cape before venturing into the mist outside. It had stopped raining long before, but clouds still shrouded the mountain top, so that all she could see was white. Lawrence wiped moisture from her face and stared out. Only a few strips of snow were visible; most of the ground was rocky mud. She stepped forward gingerly, aiming for the barn that stood about a half mile down from her mountain top.

Kicking the mud off her hiking boots onto a plank that leaned into the barn door, Lawrence paused, noting woefully that the door had collapsed along with its frame, and she could no longer slide in under its slant. She took a few steps backward, then climbed up a slope to inspect the structure. To the side gaped a hole she could get through easily on hands and knees, so that is where she crawled.

A huge, sticky spider web slapped her face, but she was used to that. She didn't splutter, just calmly pulled it off her hair and continued. Once she could rise, she switched on her Lightning Bug and looked around at the wide, muddy floor of the storage barn. Hay still lay in places, and quite a few green plants had sprouted here and there, reaching for the sun that came in every so often where boards had fallen in. A few mice, no, rats, well, whatever they were, she couldn't tell, they moved so fast, zoomed back and forth, skimming her feet occasionally as she walked around quite calmly, looking for a place to sit.

She finally found a fairly dry spot and sat, putting the light beside her and sitting on her waterproof cape. As the mice finally settled back down into obscurity, Lawrence sat motionless, glancing around at the sky through the cracks, staring at the fog until she had to blink. She listened to it drip at random, and her mind was a complete blank. She scratched her nose and settled down, breathing softly. It was so simple. She sniffed the moisture as she squeezed her knees to her chest. Then it hit her and she leapt up.

"No!" she shouted. "I swear, I'll have this thing ripped down tomorrow! I should have done it long ago!"

The barn accepted her proclamation silently without menace. She stood studying the rotten pieces of wood and moaned. "Oh, I guess it's okay, as a reminder." She cracked a fallen board with her foot. "Besides, it will soon be completely gone."

A deep, forlorn melancholy gripped her, and she clutched at her heavy shirt. Fumbling, she reached down to straighten the cape, then she sat down, lifting her Bird.

At first she didn't even turn on the synthesizers. Treating it like a Dog, she spoke into it.

"That terrible background. Do you see? My art is just surface. Yes! Think of that! It has the potential of surface area to provide room, to absorb. It's as a plane, one that curves, never quite closing. It certainly avoids deep thought, right? You see, I'm not seeking to convey information, because I wonder just how much of it is empirical. Sometimes it's easy for me to believe that only what's insignificant is. What if no one had such great instruction from the parents, the teachers, that repeats itself so damn much and punishes so readily? I guess then everyone would merely be subject to what's really out there. And maybe that's me."

Lawrence turned on the entire Bird and sniffed. That might as well continue her diary. Now she had to achieve what she had come out here to do.

This song to Nicole has to be perfect, but I only got so far before it faded. So what if it's short? I can still make it beautiful. Quickly, then, she had waited long enough, it came out of her all at once. She recorded the voices, adding the music right along, softly, then she clicked off the machine and burst out crying.

Oh, god, it was horrible, huge, tearing sobs she wasn't quite sure how to handle. After all, as long as she could remember, even when she was a preschooler, she would be sad and go curl into a corner and leak a few tears where no one could see. Now here she was in a quite private corner getting her heart ripped out. *Oh, well, maybe it serves me right.*

The sobs tapered off almost immediately, so she went through the motions of freezing the disk and ejecting it, turning the Bird off and sealing everything back into the plastic pouch. Awkwardly she stood and dragged the cape around her. Using it to wipe her whole face down roughly, she stooped to crawl through the hole, muttering, "I've got to get back to work."

Mack stood patiently under his umbrella and waited in the clearing fog near the shaft for Lawrence. He pulled his gray raincoat a little tighter and shivered. *The things I do,* he thought ruefully. *Even when it's not my job, or even my business.* He shifted the umbrella to his left hand and sighed. "I'm going in," he announced, then, "No, wait. There she is now. She's just seen me, so is running."

Lawrence somehow managed to get to him quickly despite the mud, and breathless, she gasped, "What's wrong?"

Mack studied her concerned, almost frightened expression before answering mildly, "Nothing. Nothing new, anyway." It was only then he guessed she had been crying.

"Then why do you look so threatening?" She tossed her hand. "Oh, I guess that's the way you always look. What's up?" She slipped off her cape and tucked it underneath her arm.

Mack leaned over to offer her the umbrella, but she shook her head. "Yeah," he said almost tenderly, "I guess I should know better by now." He resisted patting her shoulder—damn awkward, comforting his boss—but he couldn't help but ask, "Is something wrong?" Immediately after he said it he wished he hadn't. He felt that any solicitousness on his part would be interpreted as proprietary.

Lawrence jerked and turned her face halfway. "No. Not anymore. What's up?"

Mack studied her flushed, rainstreaked face. "You got a message."

Lawrence shuffled her feet, frowning. "Is it important?" She shot her head up to smile. "Is it Jan?"

"No," said Mack, feeling only a twinge of embarrassment. It wasn't that he was jealous, exactly. He just sometimes irrationally wanted Lawrence to feel the same grudging admiration for him as he did for her. "It's the Child Genius, if you want to call her that."

"*Oh!*" Lawrence digested this, then looked curiously at him. "Is that all you needed to tell me?"

Mack took a deep breath. It was now or never. "No. I mean, uh . . ." He yanked his tie a little looser. "I trust you, that's all," he gulped.

Lawrence laughed. "I'm glad somebody does."

She stood awkwardly, until Mack said, "Hey, I don't know about you, but I can't stand out here all day. I'm freezing. Let's go inside."

Lawrence jumped. "Well, er, okay. You should have said something."

"I'm saying it now. Let's go."

Lawrence meekly helped him pull open the shaft door and followed him underground.

Lawrence washed her face and composed her features before entering her laboratory. *Mack is one thing, but I can't let anybody else see me blow my cool.* Immediately upon arrival she walked toward her weather instruments. "Give me a minute," she grumbled to the Child Genius. "I've got to check these today."

The readings looked off, so she ran the data from the last two years. From the corner of her eye she could see the Child Genius standing near the door in her pretty soft brown pantsuit. Her mien seemed to be one of quiet alertness, so calmly waiting, yet ever prepared. Lawrence swallowed a lump. *Not a bad person to get to know, to get to emulate.*

"Hmmm," she said out loud, hoping to bring the Child Genius into her sphere. "It looks like the forest needs still more rain. That's probably because of the convention. I guess I'll schedule more this morning." She fed the request to the water tanks and turned to go up the ladder. "What did you need to see me about?" she casually tossed over her shoulder.

The Child Genius smiled gently as she turned to face her. "Do I have to have a reason?"

Lawrence's cheeks flared. It would be a lot easier if the Child Genius did need something, because right now Lawrence wanted to ask a lot of her, and she wanted it to be even, or, at least, superficially even. "Uh, if you don't mind, that is, if the convention's not keeping you busy . . ." she began unevenly.

"It's winding down now," the Child Genius reassured her. "I said all I could. Now it's their turn."

Lawrence caught her breath.

The Child Genius turned a mildly curious face toward her. "Is something the matter?"

"No. Child Genius," Lawrence stuttered, "I hate to say this, but of all the people in the convention, you are the only one who shines strongly in my thoughts."

The Child Genius laughed widely, showing pretty white teeth. "So I get all this preferential treatment! Actually, though, we have a lot in common."

Lawrence frowned. "Huh? Like what?"

"We both get recognition for our talents, which are of course great," she said calmly.

"But not both of us are modest!" Lawrence pointed out immediately. "Look, I need to get out. Let's go somewhere special to talk."

The Child Genius acquiesced, and she followed as Lawrence took her into the back shaft. She turned apologetically.

"It's my shaft, and it's kind of tricky, as well as slippery," she warned.

The Child Genius pointed at her hiking boots. "I can handle it," she said casually. Lawrence swallowed a gulp. Not like her slippers she had on before. She must have guessed where I'd take her. Her admiration of the Child Genius rose even more.

The shafts went way down, then turned to go back up. The lanterns on the walls stopped, dim light shining from grated openings at each landing. At the first one, Lawrence paused to look down on the clouded forest. The Child Genius came up beside her and put her cheek close to hers to look out. She nodded down at the floor of the forest. Lawrence moved away first.

After eight flights, Lawrence beckoned her to the opening again, and together they gazed over the tree tops. The rain machines were going full tilt, wind sweeping up impressive, thick clouds of mist that showered down on the tall pines. Still, through the clouds they could see lights every so often among the trees.

"Pretty," The Child Genius commented as Lawrence stood there proudly.

Lawrence reached out to take her hand, watching as the forest darkened, feeling as if it were the first time she'd seen it. At first she quenched the giddiness, the sharp impressions, then she mentally kicked herself. *Damn it, this is feeling. Let it go.* So she let it gush, letting herself feel tenderness toward the quiet Child Genius, letting herself hope that her emotion was being returned.

Eventually she released the Child Genius' hand and pointed. "It's about ten more flights up."

A panel slid open to reveal a room at the top of the great waterfall that fed the forest's pond below.

"Wow," was all that the Child Genius could say. This might possibly be the most impressive room of them all.

The waterfall flowed from a hole in the ceiling to glaze an raw orange rock face before disappearing through the floor. The holes had been cut to an exact fit, so that the motion mesmerized. The Child Genius walked toward the falls, brushing back the limb of a fig tree to see better.

"Figs?" She looked around for Lawrence, finally spotting her stretching across a flat stone on the far side of the room, where she was reaching into the bushes for a strawberry.

Lawrence bit into the large, red fruit before answering. "No food in the forest. I grow my favorites up here."

The Child Genius walked over to peer down into the lettuce garden, then came back to sit next to Lawrence. "Thank you for taking me into your private home," she began humbly.

Lawrence shrugged. "Such as it is."

The Child Genius bent to take her hand and kissed it before bringing it to her cheek. "I experienced 'Goldweaving' this morning," she whispered huskily, coming to fall into a heap beside her outstretched form.

Lawrence felt like an actor who had forgotten all her lines; no, rather as if she had never been handed a script at all. Still, she reached over to stroke that shiny, smooth black cap of hair.

That was the Child Genius' cue, apparently. Her glazed eyes looked up at Lawrence as she whispered, "I need it now. Bring me into your exquisite world."

Lawrence shrugged, her vaguely amused dark blue eyes not being able to miss the determined look in the Child Genius' lovely black ones. She kissed her lightly on the lips, then more deeply on her cheek. "Do you even have a name?" she asked as she drew her hand up her thigh.

"Yes," murmured the Child Genius, allowing her head to be cushioned on Lawrence's arm.

Lawrence waited. "Well, what is it?"

"I only tell my lovers."

Lawrence mentally shrugged. That little requirement should be taken care of very shortly. As the Child Genius bent to unbutton her jeans, she managed to feel a slight twinge of guilt. If all this amorous attention was all due to "Goldweaving," maybe Lawrence should halt it right now. But, she hastily reasoned as the Child Genius' tongue came into position, that would be too cruel.

After it was over and they lay satiated in the soft, mealy grass next to the strawberry patch, Lawrence couldn't help but feel some kind of fuzzy euphoria. She reached over once more to caress the Child Genius' smooth golden breasts.

She accepted this readily enough, but Lawrence noticed that she seemed impatient. "Well," she said lightheartedly, "what's your name?"

"I only tell my lovers."

Lawrence burst out laughing and rolled up out of the grass to sit on the rock. "Ooh!" she cackled, sides painfully heaving. "Oh, that's a good one."

The Child Genius smiled condescendingly, waiting for her laughter to subside before asking, "Was it good?"

Lawrence blushed slightly. "I don't know. I never had anybody but Jan."

The Child Genius nodded slowly, apparently temporarily amazed by this bit of information. "I hope it was good," she said sincerely, "because I created it for you."

Lawrence dropped her head in her hands to take this in. She had clean forgotten the Child Genius' occupation. Still, she had to giggle. "Fictive reality? Is that what you're saying?"

"In a sense. It was both fun and challenging, taking what you contributed from 'Goldweaving' and adding what I thought up as satisfying."

Lawrence interrupted, "Believe me, it was satisfying." She pushed back her disappointment as she reached for her clothes. "I thank you, even if I'm a bit confused about remuneration."

The Child Genius looked insulted. "It is my gift."

Lawrence kissed her one last time, slowly and softly in farewell, then tossed her the crushed pantsuit. "Let's suit up. I want to talk."

The Child Genius slowly complied. "It still seems odd to me, that you're practically a virgin. A heterosexual couldn't have come up with 'Goldweaving.'"

"Who said I was heterosexual?" Lawrence protested. "Oh, if your definition of it is limited to who fucks whom, then I just got initiated into something else, didn't I? If you want to know my preferences, I'll take on anything. If there's anything I hate, it's limiting myself."

The Child Genius shivered deliciously. "But 'Goldweaving' was so real for me. How'd you do it?"

"Well, isn't homosexuality just beautiful?" Lawrence found herself gushing, but she couldn't help it. She had always been honest. "Maybe I just like the freedom of nonconformity, not to belittle your experiences, but . . ." She found herself hastily veering to the side of courtesy.

"Do you find me attractive?" the Child Genius demanded.

Lawrence blushed. "Of course."

"Why?"

Lawrence got up and started pacing, directing her words alternately to the Child Genius and the everlasting waterfall. "We are all unique, love," she began softly. "And each of us is a mystery to every other one of us, even ourselves. Love's duty is not just to look past our differences. It's found a new job in cherishing those differences."

"So you are attracted to other races?" the Child Genius said scornfully.

"Well, you see Jan, he's Hispanic, and Nicole, the African, and now you, pure Japanese, but you don't see it all." Lawrence stopped pacing, as if struck by a sudden thought, but she only said, "I said I didn't want to limit myself."

The Child Genius ventured, "Might it not be easier to love what you're familiar with?"

Lawrence hesitated. "Is that why you're a lesbian?"

"No, but that's the argument I use to support it," she snapped.

Lawrence successfully ignored her outburst. "Yet I love what I find myself learning about," she whispered wonderingly. She straightened. "Well, again, I want to thank you for helping me, but I need to get back to my laboratory. My deadline's nearing." She paused as she tried to calm that strange excitement that always came at a breakthrough. All of it was coming together nicely! She couldn't wait to get back to work.

The Child Genius sighed and stood. "I guess I'll head back to the convention now." She eyed Lawrence. "Aren't you ever going to be a part of it? We'd love to have you."

"As a matter of fact," Lawrence found herself promising rashly, "I'm hoping to be there right at the end, after I finish my work. I've still got a ways to go."

"With already being there," the Child Genius answered confidently.

Lawrence stood staring after she had left. Wasn't this all just giving as one got? And how did *she* know where Lawrence was? Shrugging, she headed down the shaft slowly, hearing the Child Genius clattering way ahead, but making no effort to catch up with her.

Nicole wrapped a piece of garlic nan around the scrumptious scrambled tofu provided from the kitchen downstairs and bit into it. "Mmmm," she murmured. Similar sandwiches had practically become her complete menu during the last couple of days, but at least Lawrence's chefs knew how to simulate nirvana. "Now, where was I?" She gathered the pages of Lawrence's diary and sighed. Did she really want to know? Was this really the end? She seethed, imagining Lawrence feeling all smug in her stupid grotto after she got what she wanted, but then she was overwhelmed by a flush of sweet fulfillment as she thought about how she was—not really tricked, or raped, just played with. "Oh, shit!" She leaned back, smoothing her long, strong hands down her thighs. *Yes, I must read. I've just seen Lawrence's great power.* Fingers trembling, she grabbed the papers.

Reader, I know you're out there, for you are me. There is no other. But I will speak to you. Wait.

What if someone were to read this? What if someone from my vast audience would actually be as me and come forward?

Naw, don't worry about it. There is only me down here. There is only me in the pod. It is only I who sees. I am it.

When people speak of energy that comes from nowhere, because less energy is added to the process than is taken out, I cringe, for that is me. These surges of ultrahuman thought come out of nowhere and they shall never be released. I will never fulfill construction. I am negative energy. A sink, not a source. I yet am a force strapped to that power. Power utilizes my energy, but I have the will to break free. I have fed the knowledge along straight, pure paths of simplicity. Perhaps now I see it is the only way!

Imagine totality! What little comes out of me goes into the experiences, but, alas, there is the grand desiccated blackness. My colors shine, ever shine, swallowed up by that damn black hole. Each effort spawns nothing. I speak of a cell of life, and, like life, it is indomitable. Life dominates. Life conquers. Life is power. Yet my creation is dead, swallowed by passivity, never eternal. I strive to become alive.

Fictive permanence. Life is change. I will not bend. I must change, for my art must simulate life. Life is drawn to me. I wish to make my life and actions art. Then in the complete mergence shall arise something changing, yet eternal.

I have a conjecture. Should life be eternal as it merely seems to be? Can someone actually change? I offer to you, my reader, who acts upon nothing and remains passive in awe of those glorious contradictions inside. Will someone or can someone change their ways? It is up to you, reader. Individuals are all there is. I repeat: separate, different individuals must be recognized. There will never be any mergers, but in the meantime keep in mind that there are no distinguishable boundaries. There is only one individual undifferentiated universe: I.

Nicole slowly let the papers flutter to the floor, then distractedly picked them up and smoothed them face down on the table to make a read pile. She shuddered. "A strange type of solipsism," she muttered before picking up the next sheet.

A man lives a life dedicated to maximum cruelty. Then, he falls in love, changing his ways forever. I ask, can it be possible to . . . Well, start at the beginning. I wish to achieve, but complete frustration has stopped me. So I in desperation conceive an impossible plan. I will give, no matter how much it hurts. Can one love the rapist? How about the breaking act that caused satisfaction? Complete participation might just free the background and bring it forth.

Nicole slapped the paper down onto the read pile and buried her face in her hands. "Damn," she moaned. "When did Lawrence write this? It's not dated. The paper looks a little yellowed, but that doesn't mean what she has written is old. All I know is that she wrote it long before she took me into her little fantasy experience." Nicole dropped her hands and sighed. "Come on, now. The next page."

Her doorbell softly chimed. Frowning, she leapt up, then remembered. She had asked Mack about contacting Jan. It must be him.

"Hello," he began cheerily. "Lawrence sent you this." He handed her the disk. "Something about her diary and final bequest, or something."

Was it her imagination or did she sense some kind of disappointment in Mack's eyes? "Thanks," she said briefly, taking the disk. "Do I Dog it?"

Mack nodded. "Yes. Lawrence told me it was only sound. I've got you hooked up to Jan now, if you want to take it."

Nicole pointed behind her shoulder. "I've never dealt with any of the recent vid models. Can you set me up?"

Mack came in, only slightly glancing at the sheets of paper before heading for the vid to turn it on. "He should be coming in with no difficulty. Ah, there he is. Hi, Jan." He waved down at the figure on the tiny screen before turning back to Nicole. "You shouldn't have any more trouble. Just shut it off here when you're done."

Nicole nodded sharply, feeling the anger that invariably swelled up when someone confused a slight discomfort for complete ignorance. "Thank you," she forced herself to say. As Mack left, she looked down at the screen, amazed to see Jan sharply against a fuzzy, differentiated gray. As she hesitated, she noticed a block of gray shift. Aha! She'd heard about this but never seen it. The satellite image was being censored, as if Jan's location and job were supposed to be so secret.

Jan smiled at her ruefully. "Sorry if I seem a little out of breath. I assumed it was Lawrence trying to reach me, so I ran over."

Nicole smiled at the skinny young man in khaki shorts and sunhat. "Does she do that often?"

"No, never." Jan shook his head. "Just for emergencies, we decided, so you can imagine . . ."

"I just needed to ask you a few questions for my interview of Lawrence," Nicole began.

Jan wiped his forehead with a blue bandanna. "Well, since you got me here, okay, but I'm returning tomorrow if you forget anything."

Nicole relaxed. His light, pleasant tone and courtesy were so refreshing. Lawrence had made such a good choice. "I'm seeking your point of view in your relationship with Lawrence. When and how did you meet?"

"Our second anniversary is tomorrow if that's any indication. We met shortly before that, in an environmental meeting. You know, one of those mandatory things. It was at the campus where she was going to school, and I was a recent graduate, so I went there. I felt more comfortable there than in the ones near my workplace."

"What was your first impression of her?"

"Quiet, except when she finally got motivated to speak, and, then, watch out!" Jan chuckled.

"Could you clarify that last statement, please?"

Jan paused in his laughter to peer at her. "Is there really any need to be this formal? You know her. She speaks forthrightly when she has something to say. She even spoke up at a few of those meetings. You know, they get so boring sometimes, like we all know everything and just want to get home, but, every once in a while, she'd put some liveliness in that audience." He whooped. "Aah, you should have been there, that's all."

"So what was behind your decision to get married?"

"Ah, an easy one! There we were . . . hang on a minute."

Nicole watched as Jan's image faded to the left and did not come back into focus. All she heard was a buzz, and all she could see was an undifferentiated gray screen, no sign of a jungle behind him at all. A few minutes passed, then he was back.

"Sorry about that. It was nothing, really. Juan here needed help with the bulldozer. He's new, and I like to help the new ones. Gives me something to do. Oh, yes, where was I? Yeah, we got married after the contest because we could afford it. Quite simple, don't you think?" Jan removed his hat to wipe his face again with the bandanna.

"Have you ever considered joining a group family?"

"No." Jan finally looked irritated. "Neither Lawrence nor I want to give up our privacy. Neither of us like people around us too much. And, of course, no children. Neither of us wants to be around them."

Nicole sensed a strong anger behind his last statement, but she couldn't trace it. Certainly under the new reproduction laws, no one was forcing him to assume fatherhood. Instead, she asked, "Have you ever been tested concerning your antisocial tendencies?"

Jan looked annoyed a second. "Yes, and it was no big deal. The concern faded after I was appointed manager. Now I have to deal with a lot of people, not just subordinates. When I'm off work, however, I'm perfectly happy alone with Lawrence." He shrugged. "We're newlyweds. Maybe even that could change." He sounded like he doubted it.

"Could you tell me a bit about your education and your job?"

"Well, it all began with the standard engineering curriculum. I wanted to be in a supervisory position because, as you can see," he stepped back, getting slightly fuzzy, and gestured toward his body, "I'm not a muscle man. I'm a bookworm. But I like my job. I have to feel as if I'm doing something for the world, and planting trees is an active, satisfying project. I mean, I can come here in a few years and point at this stretch and say, 'I did that.'" He nodded. "It's no big deal, nowadays, but I couldn't see myself sitting around inside of a mountain the rest of my life."

"Do you feel resentful toward Lawrence?"

"What for?" burst out of him. "People say she's a genius. Fine with me. It only shows what good taste I have."

"Have you experienced Lawrence?"

Jan sighed. "What an understatement! Of course she's constantly giving them to me, discussing their structure, their potential. She doesn't seek my approval, just my admiration."

Nicole rapidly studied his calm, yet proud expression. She couldn't explain her feeling at the moment, just that this young man had been let into something very precious, and she couldn't figure out why. What did Lawrence see in *him*? She finally nodded. "I'm finished with my questions, so I guess I'll let you go."

"How's Lawrence?" Jan shifted toward the front, becoming disproportionately large.

Nicole hesitated. "As far as I know, she's fine."

Jan nodded. "Just thought I'd ask." His image disappeared abruptly.

Nicole turned off the console quietly and put her Dog down beside it. When she turned back to the papers, she felt fresh courage. Maybe Lawrence wasn't that much of a nut after all. Her husband seemed perfectly normal.

Here is an analogy: the animals decide to segregate and create social boundaries. The game animals are honored. The farm animals are scorned. The pets, now illegal, are still around, and they are power. They are sterile. The rest of the animals are ignored. The Y chromosome will shrink even more. The sperm shall freeze and become dormant, yet the males shall live to be killed. Muscle's masculinity is meat. The females have the free energy. They shall be used as fuel. Food is female. Their eggs, a high energy insurer of future life, are removed. Their milk, a high energy nutrient for growing, active life is removed. It is fed to stagnant human life. Free energy: food obtained for nothing!

Impregnate the female from your small expenditure of sperm energy and out should come an infinite supply. You may now feed on embryos, placenta, menstrual blood, and the succulent newborn. No energy under the sun can be more efficient than this. Like the nut, seed, and sprout, burgeoning supplies those already stable and mature.

He licks his lips it feels so good the power and pumping masculinity feeds a fallow garden meanwhile she weakens and during the planting and the reaping and especially during the feeding her mind is calculating elsewhere as the energy dissipates creating nothing and death causes all to fade away.

How can I put this in an experience? A breast in iron. The smell of menstrual blood splattered on stomach.

Nicole stopped and rubbed her aching eyes. "This rounded handwriting looks so childish, so tidy, yet what it conveys is so dreadful. Can I go on? Yes." The next note was brief and was written in smaller letters.

Oh, shit. Power came to me the other day as I sat in the arch at sunset, saying you're young, twenty-two, there's still time! Oh my this concern over my health all of the sudden. We want you to become pregnant. What? Me? They appear to me as neutral, yet masculine, a glowing white cloud of air. I stutter. I'm already cleared for this life. I was chosen for sterility. That was before. Before what? Before we discovered your great talent. Bullshit. I had some worth before, even as a child with none of your money and smirking thrills. No. No you stupid assholes. I will not and you can't make me. A seed shall grow and I'll have nothing to do with it. No. It sometimes gets hard to breathe.

Nicole felt a brief excitement as some of the puzzle unraveled. That must have been what set Jan off when he mentioned children. And, it was a clue as to when some of this was written. Nicole stood up and wandered into the kitchen, taking up a Granny Smith and biting into it idly. *Lawrence is twenty-four. This must have happened right after she came here, maybe still a little unsure of her wealth, but she still fought them off. And she's been doing it ever since.* Nicole smiled softly. *She's brave, all right.* Nicole went back to reread the page. "What's all this about a seed? Did she write that back then, too?" She looked up at the smooth white ceiling. "Even back then she had some sort of plan for her art? What? Next page."

I felt once when I was younger a strong need to deliver the maximum joy to everyone, which I in my virginity (!) thought was sex. Deprivation of sex is the only pain? Maybe it's impossible anyway.

What is the nature of control anyway? The way they thrive on trivia. Now, child, you simply must draw your 8's and e's this way. Unimportant details fill their minds, so they miss the great, significant structure, the pain. And they are swallowed up in mindlessness.

Activate the populace!

"Good luck," was all that Nicole muttered, then, "Ah! Last page now."

The Specious Molecule: What it is, obviously, is that it is difficult to describe certain things. Hence, my need to create experiences. But I had a dream. You know, we have boyish women, girlish men. The strong horse-woman blankets the asexual. I thought if I could build a single molecule of truth that would be everything. Yes! A transmission of thought, or emotion, or, see, a physical explanation for everything. Whence comes the abstract? Lay it on there snugly: complete understanding of the physical universe would then yield the end of our quest. But then we would have chemical formulae of no meaning. But a physical molecule, now, preferably organic (DNA?) would do it. Explain everything. What would we do with it? Swallow it?

Nicole dropped the last page and stood and stretched. "Done," she said triumphantly, then shot a glance over at the vid where Mack had left Lawrence's disk. "Oh! I forgot the disk! Let me see that." She popped it into her Dog and listened, a little bemused, to the last diary entry. "Okay, thank you." A pause after the entry made her hesitate. Was there more? Yes. Lawrence's voice came on and said pompously, "Celestial Voices." Nicole listened as sweet synthesized music came softly, growing louder, then steady. She nodded. She was no music critic, but the melody was lovely. She could say that. After the short prelude, there came sweet female contraltos and male tenors that blended together particularly well, singing:

You know my secrets
You know my past
You know how I feel
    the moments of peace
    the valley's dear lights
    the wall's cold dampness

the smell of horror and misery

the subtle taste of a man and a woman

You know me

You know everything

The music played on a few more seconds, then abruptly quit. Nicole waited a while, but there was no other message.

"Hmph. Do I really know everything? Do I?" Nicole turned off her Dog and strode to the center of the room. "No," she sighed. "I still feel like there's something missing. Let's start at the beginning. What the hell is 'Love Can Art,' and what kind of title is that? Is it the resolution we've all been yearning for? Because everything, including 'Goldweaving,' all they ever did was arouse, cause tension, and frustrate us. Even though Lawrence said that the structure of 'Goldweaving' was positive feedback inducing orgasm, what's wrong with us all, that we need intensifiers?"

Nicole squatted. "I remember being told quite frequently, in math, in logic, in English, that I have a systematic way of looking at things. Why won't that help me now?" she moaned. "Lawrence is clearly aiming for something, but it's so unfocused. One minute, I'm ready to slap her because she's so smug and presumes so much, and in the next minute I'm ready to hug her because she seems so sincere and caring and not manipulative at all. I came here knowing that she was a celebrity mystery, and now I'm just as mystified . . . What? What is it about her? Like I said, she reaches so many people, and she seems so damn harmless—no, not harmless, just innocent. Damn."

Nicole took up the disk and stared at it, then slid her gaze over at the diary sheets. "Look," she sighed. "Lawrence's interview for the people is done. They'll be thrilled to learn anything after so much silence. If Lawrence is able to finish 'Love Can Art,' fine. I can experience it and learn what she has aimed to do for so long. My part in all of this is over. If she doesn't finish it . . ." Nicole paused as a wave of joy and disappointment filled her. "That's just as well. Life goes on."

Lawrence locked the grotto and opened the dumbwaiter, then she walked over to the computer to block all messages. When she finished she climbed the ladder and swung into her headset. "It's foolproof. I can sleep here, I can eat here, I can wash here, and I can think and talk and scream here, until I am quite insane. Mack won't let anyone through and he knows I'll be all right here, so long as I eat. Ha! I eat, so I must produce! To work!"

She sat down, then immediately leapt up to pace. "Let's see, the incomplete 'Love' was drawn from my life before the convention, so, obviously, 'Love Can Art' must be drawn solely from the events of the past four days. I've decided on abstract, fuck Mack, and I've taken a liking to that there DNA molecule. The whole gene, though, is what I'm after, the whole chromosome, one whole cell, an egg cell, to be fertilized, the birth of accomplishment, the growth of achievement. I need technology. It's a natural extension of human activity, so I'll lay it in really close. Maybe in the abstract part people can be reminded of machinery—whoops, human extensions. It's a helix structure, corny: one strand positive, one strand negative. No: one strand organic, one strand mechanical, and how the technology limits the procreation that drains. As for love, I've got to show its danger, its negative side, its obsessions, and then altruism, egoism, and, and . . . Oh, quit talking and get to work! You'll have something in no time!" Lawrence sat back down at her controls and slipped on the headset.

She worked all through that day, and well into the night. The last thing she remembered before falling asleep at the console was whether or not it should be allowed to expand out of control. Still hooked up inside of her headset that blared images and sounds, she had a dream.

Lawrence sank into the soft loam, deeper and deeper, stopping before she was completely buried. Softly and subtly a plant crossed over her tongue and emerged through her cheek to flower. The blossom swung over her nose so that she could see it clearly. It was an interesting specimen from the meadows of Tennessee. She used to see them in early summer. A large, orange center surrounded by a circle of long, purple honeysuckle-shaped flowers. It was a beautiful anamoly. There was a rock in her belly and the snow that fell were clearly water molecules. A squirrel climbed upon her to bury its acorn near her lung. She saw a full rainbow form over her head.

Lawrence spoke, her voice ringing out over the dream universe. "I don't want to limit myself. I want freedom of choice. Choices should be infinite, not just what they allow you to choose from. Though the Earth is finite, I can make it infinite by becoming an artist, thereby creating my choice.

"But all should be as free. All of us have the potential. All should be artists."

Chapter Nine

Jan opened the door and climbed out of the shaft. He pulled off his jacket and hat, then sat down to take off his boots. Sighing, he padded over in his thick crew socks to the kitchen to make a pot of tea. While waiting for the water to boil, he checked the computer for any messages and reported his location to his employer. He nodded around at the immaculate kitchen. Lawrence must be hard at work, any food she accepted being prepared by the chefs. Once the tea had steeped, he took a cup and headed for the dark laboratory.

"Hello?" he called softly.

No answer. He pressed the light on and entered. Above, hidden by a bank of computers, Lawrence still sat, head down, in front of a terminal. Jan put down his cup and climbed the ladder. It was eerie, even in the bright light, to crawl up to the cliff.

Shutting off the current, Jan removed the headset and shook Lawrence awake.

Lawrence looked up at him blearily. "Oh. Hi. Happy anniversary."

"Huh? What anniversary? I forgot all about it," Jan teased.

Lawrence took a deep breath and stood up to stretch.

"It's 8:42," he answered before he was asked.

Lawrence looked around at the weather monitors, then shrugged. "I have no idea," she whispered. "a.m. or p.m.?"

"Morning." Jan stepped back as she limped over to the ladder and stared down at it.

"Oh," she moaned. "Whose idea was it to build it this way?" Slowly she turned and headed down the ladder one step at a time, pausing every once in a while to rest her head against a rung.

Jan followed, then took her hand as he picked up his tea. "Come on," he said gently. "I bet you're hungry."

Lawrence growled, but meekly followed him up the shaft to their kitchen. "I need water," she explained, but then she walked over to the refrigerator and stared at it, apparently lost in thought.

Jan opened the refrigerator and got out her glass. "Here."

Lawrence took a deep swallow, then walked over to the corner, keeping her gaze to the floor.

Jan shrugged as he pulled out some tofu. Placing some pieces of bread on the flat scorcher, he started piling vegetables onto the chopping block. "How about scrambled tofu?" He turned to see her nod.

"Whatever. It's . . ."

Jan waited.

"It's done, isn't it?" Lawrence stuttered, then looked puzzledly at him. "I can't . . ."

"Look, don't worry about it until after you've eaten, okay?"

Lawrence nodded, attention caught by a spider as it dropped from the ceiling of rock. Jan watched as she used a towel to gently gather the spider off the table and carry it outside to the shaft. He shook his head, a wry grin on his face. Anyone else would have interpreted her gingerly motions, her wariness at keeping her head free of the web, as fear. But he knew it for what it was: respect, respect for the tiny insect's lifestyle.

Lawrence sat down across from him and, arms wrapped tightly around her, stared bleakly into the corner as he dished up the scrambled tofu and hot toast. When he set down the eternal grapefruit juice, however, she grabbed his arm.

He turned a mild gaze upon her, so that she was reminded of goats down at the petting zoo she had visited about twenty years ago, the last of its kind, now abandoned. Lawrence gulped, Jan looked at her fully, as he usually did if neither one was busy, and, as always, he was smiling, quite childishly, she had to admit. He wasn't afraid of directness, of intimacy.

Lawrence let go of his arm and took up her fork. During the meal she kept shrugging off Jan's feeble attempts at conversation, only sighing for answer until the rest of the meal could be had in silence. Yet she kept looking at his face and nodding.

That's what I like about him. No, not quite. It's really the way he's so quiet. Sometimes, I bet, he could go over twenty-four hours without speaking, and, damn it, it wouldn't bother him! I look at him and damned if I can tell what's going on inside his head. His mystery, the silence behind his eyes. I'm searching for him all the time. Lawrence snapped her teeth into her toast. *We are so much alike. We got the same beliefs, anyway. Why is it so easy to be with him and yet so hard to figure him out?* She shook her head and swallowed.

Lawrence took her last bite and finished her water. "Okay. Now what?"

Jan looked up at her and considered. Her voice now seemed cheerful and matter—of—fact, so he answered the same way. "Break time."

Lawrence nodded and headed back to the bath.

"You know, I've never seen you quite like this. I mean, I know you have a deadline, but . . ."

Lawrence turned to him and nodded. "I know, I shouldn't have fallen asleep in the lab like that, but . . ." She looked down, pensive, then shrugged with a smile. "Ah, what the hell? Let's have fun."

The mansion housed so much, offices, huge meeting rooms, auditoriums, and, of course, the forest, that Lawrence's and Jan's living quarters were just a tiny portion, and they were not that luxurious, except the bath.

Lawrence stepped into a glowing purple light and stripped. The curved walls enveloped a huge, warm pool of bubbling water. She stepped forward, the light shifting to soft green.

"Wait for me!" Jan said, struggling out of his pants.

Lawrence slipped smoothly under the surface while Jan turned on the hydropumps. He then jumped in, splashing green water up against the slick walls. Lawrence spluttered from the spray, then swam away from him to settle against the edge on the opposite side. "Ah! This feels so good!" She sighed deeply.

Jan pulled a chain, and a long horizontal rod dropped from the ceiling. He selected a tube and squeezed out some gel from the dispenser, then he used the rod to guide him over to Lawrence. "Here," he grunted.

Lawrence turned around and slid forward on the mound that rose from the surface of the water. Jan applied the gel to her neck and shoulders and sank his fingers in.

"Ow! I didn't know sleeping after rug placement could make me so sore."

Jan paused. "After *what*?"

"Well, I've got a rug in there, somewhere. I'll know later. Keep rubbing, though. I need it."

Lawrence soaped up half-heartedly, watching Jan as he efficiently scrubbed from the feet up and rinsed off, then he turned the hose on her as the tub drained.

"Thanks," Lawrence said briefly, then gathered the soft yellow towel around her. "I better go down and check on it, see if I can add more."

Jan yanked open the door to their bedroom. "How about coming in here and resting for a while?"

Lawrence peered into the cool blue. A bed! Suddenly every muscle in her body screamed with desire. Yes! To lie flat for a while. What a concept. "Okay," she admitted grudgingly, "but if I go to sleep, wake me up immediately."

Jan took her in his arms as her head fell against the pillow. She snuggled against him. Her head felt separated from her body, as if it were spinning away, so she jerked herself awake and muttered, "Don't let me . . ."

Jan held her until she went asleep, then left quietly.

At four she awoke.

Together Lawrence and Jan entered the grotto, Jan with a handy book in case of boredom, Lawrence secure with the knowledge that if the thing hadn't gotten completed last night, it damn sure was going to get finished now. She studied the records from last night. Yep. She had been held back at the top of the waterfall, right when an infatuation had to sneak in. Shit.

"Hey, fatty, what do you think?" She waved her hand over to Jan, who kept reading a few more seconds, then put the hardcover down and approached the ladder.

"What?" he asked brightly, so that Lawrence relaxed. Nobody could possibly get into her work like she did, so sometimes she hated to bother him.

"What do you think? Some kind of infatuation? Is that okay?" She blushed, because she could honestly say that she had never had a crush on Jan. Nope. They had been comfortable with each other right from the start.

Jan had been quiet, rubbing his chin, then letting his hand fall. Now he spoke in a high-pitched voice as he persuaded. "Why not? It's love, isn't it? Somebody's feeling love, right?"

Lawrence nodded thoughtfully. Yeah! Distractedly she turned to Jan, waving him away. "Oh, go back to what you were doing," she said gaily. "Love Can Art" was obviously a progression, not some finished, mature, static piece of shit. Yeah. All art evolved. Lawrence nodded, remembering a few of her crushes, most from high school. There hadn't been a bit of encouragement from the other to set her off. And, yes, she was wistful, if hopeless, and damn if they didn't . . . That guy, what was him name? David? Yeah. He and Lawrence had become friends. And that woman, Sheralyn . . . same thing. And even ol' Barry had written to her a while, and she considered that extraordinary, because of the openness in their letters. Lawrence shuddered. Compare that, I ask you, to all those girls you hung around with, whining about their honest-to-fuck boyfriends, when there probably wasn't any love around at all. Yeah, Lawrence affirmed, feeding the image just right in her computer banks.

"Jan . . ." When she turned to the table, she noticed that over an hour had passed.

Again he came over to the ladder and looked up, this time looking positively beatific.

"What about friendship?" She laughed.

Jan put his fists on his hips. "Now what the hell do you think we have?"

Friendship is love. It seemed so damn obvious now. Again she waved him away and plugged in an infinite loop. It was going to be all right.

Lawrence stood and came down the ladder. Jan rose and came to her, and she wrapped her arms around him. She spoke into his chest, "This is nothing. I just need to be alone in the woods a few minutes." She looked back up the cliff. "I think it's done," she mused, "but I might as well walk around a bit, see if I can come up with anything new." She gently pulled away from him, and he released her slowly, his long arms loosening gradually. Lawrence smiled.

Lawrence passed through the tunnel and almost ran over the Child Genius, who looked distracted and rushed. "It's Tama Yokamura," she whispered. "Bye." She walked hastily away, leaving Lawrence stunned.

Shrugging, Lawrence walked on, hands in her pockets, whistling. When she got to the forest, she nodded. The experience was finished. Tama had just proved it. All she was doing here was a small piece of unfinished business. She squatted down next to the instruments. "All right, you," she muttered, "what's their great big finale?"

She selected the big conference room and watched and listened.

"Our biggest challenge, we all admit, yet we must do something. That's our goal: raise the money, train a crew, and go up there and find out what's going on. It's been over five years now, five years of the Pro-Spacers constantly being put off. And it's not just regulations. Last year, I might as well go ahead and tell you, we found massive damage in our largest ships. If they can't control you with legalisms and bureaucratic tut-tutting, they'll resort to good ol' sabotage." The dark man wiped his face with a handkerchief. Lawrence studied him as waves of murmurs flooded the audience. "Well," he summed up, "I hope I have your full support in this. I'd like this year to be the year we go. Of course, I don't see any leeway with the authorities, but I'm not going to wait forever. I'm going, even if they blast me out of the sky!" Cheers accompanied his final "thank you."

Lawrence turned off the machine and stood. "No. Wait. Damn it, I forgot why I came down here." She then bent back down and slowly erased each disk. As the minutes flew by, she found herself nodding. The Great Eviction. Nicole's articles had introduced her to it; otherwise, she would have never known. It wasn't exactly popular knowledge, for obvious reasons. About a century ago, a decision was made to sterilize all adults in underdeveloped countries, and to take the children away to be trained. All fully educated children had then been sent up into space in satellites to collect data.

The Rapacious Age. One hundred nations starved to create Lawrence's world, according to Nicole. And the future?

Lawrence leapt up. "What can I do?" she asked aloud. "I'll release the complete 'Love Can Art,' but then what?" She pointed down at the machine. "I could go into space. Or try. That's one thing. Or I can stay here, in the mountain, and never create again . . . And yet . . ." She trailed off. To have finished "Love Can Art" was to finish it all, right? Besides, she was fired, sort of. Sure, she could evict all of NewTech and live here comfortably all of her life, but was that enough? What?

Lawrence entered the laboratory and saw Mack up on the cliff. She nodded to him, then asked, "Where's Jan?"

Mack looked around, puzzled. "Was he supposed to be in here? Maybe he went to the bathroom," he answered seriously.

Lawrence climbed up the ladder to join him. She sat down in the single chair before announcing, "I finished it this afternoon, between four and eight. I know I don't really have a deadline anymore, but I'd like to present the complete experience tonight at the convention. It's the least I can do." Lawrence slid Mack's key into the slot and waited. Nothing.

Mack squatted beside her and took her hand. She swatted him. Even Jan taking her hand when she was working was a distraction. "Hey. Leave me alone. What's wrong?"

Mack pulled out the key and asked, "Tell me what you're doing. Maybe I can help."

"Isn't it obvious?" Lawrence slammed both fists on the counter in frustration. "I finished the last part of the experience and now I want to slide it onto the first part." Lawrence pulled at a few controls, then dropped her hands.

Mack stood and said nothing until Lawrence looked at him. "That's still just your record," he explained. "Do you understand? The committee still has their copy of the incomplete experience, which they will promote. They'll easily ignore this one." He shrugged helplessly. "So, what's the use?"

Lawrence jumped up and pushed him back from her chair. Mack fell back a few steps, stumbling, almost falling back into the computer banks. "Shit!" she yelled, then she stared at him. She hadn't even noticed how much younger he looked, more like he was a boyish twenty-nine. He was no longer in his suit. He had on a soft brown sweatsuit and matching sneakers. "Oh, hell," she murmured, "I'm sorry. I . . . I didn't think I pushed that hard." Images of tough Amazons entered her head, then faded. She sure as hell had never been like that, pushy. "But what the fuck was that key, anyway?" she asked, still angry. "I thought it was supposed to let me into their records."

Mack looked woefully down at the patterned disc. "Yes, it would have," he answered, "but they no longer trust me. They caught you in there the last couple of nights, so they blocked my access, too. Then they fired me."

Lawrence folded her arms around herself and looked down, deep in thought.

"Can I say something?" Mack asked almost timidly.

Lawrence frowned, glancing up at him. "Of course you can."

"Well," he began with a grin on his face, "you were thinking, and I'm not supposed to interrupt you when . . ."

Lawrence roared with laughter, then ran over to him to hug him.

"Hey!" Mack wriggled free of her arms, which hadn't been aimed properly, anyway. "What I was going to say is that you could release your version independently. Nobody could stop you."

She felt a great sense of relief, then remembered the final speech of the convention: legalisms, sabotage, even censorship. Oh, they'd think of something. But she found herself saying, "Thanks, Mack." She turned to the terminal and sat, hooking the two pieces together on her file and spinning the disc out. She stood. "I'm ready."

Mack reached out to stroke her hair, lifting glinting strands of brown. "Gold," he commented.

"Of course."

Lawrence stepped out onto the balcony. Seeing her there, the crowds in the huge ballroom hushed.

"Hello, everybody. Uh, before you go, I'd like to tell you some good news. Opus Ten, "Love Can Art," is finished." She stepped back at the deafening cheers. "I want you all to experience it," she continued after they had quietened again. "If you please, return to the auditoriums and strap in. As before, no one is required to sit through it, but . . ." Here she clammed up. "I think it would be a good idea."

Somebody whistled, and Lawrence stood waiting as the crowd streamed out the eight doors, then she dimmed the lights.

After it was over, Lawrence grabbed Jan and ran through the woods. Popping open the door, they ran out onto the balcony and leaned out. In front of them stood the glaring lights of the helicopter pad as they glowed around the helibus, ready to take the first wave of conventioneers home. Above them was beautiful, clear sky, masked by the bright lights.

Lawrence felt herself sliding her hands over and over the balcony railing and smiling at the surface of wet gray concrete. It had stopped raining earlier, and the snow was almost all gone. It was still piercing cold, though. Soon, her hands were numb. "Jan," she murmured, "it's too slow. Change is just too damn slow. Whenever I study any history, damn it, all I see is the whole fucking society out there kind of mulling it over for decades. Who's got the time?" She ended up gazing up at the brilliant stars, losing herself in them as Jan tucked an arm around her. She almost didn't hear the door creak behind her.

Nicole stepped out from the forest and stood, feet apart. "I just came to tell you that I refused to experience 'Love Can Art.'" She paused, as if for reaction. "I want to think for myself."

Lawrence nodded. "You were always able to."

"I reject your gift."

"That's okay with me," Lawrence answered calmly. "Remember I'll always give it."

Nicole still stood, as if searching for something else to say. Lawrence felt her heart swell to fill her throat.

"You can keep your interview and publish it. The committee wanted to seize it. Go now while you have the chance."

Nicole stared at her, stunned.

"Hey," she choked past the lump, "it's what you taught me, what I teach you."

Nicole spun around and left, slamming the door shut so hard, that it popped back open the merest crack. Jan went toward it cautiously, checking to make sure it wasn't locked, then turned again toward the helicopter pad. Lawrence caught his arm and pulled him to her, snuggling against him, then she went back to peering out at the crowd assembled near the launching pad.

"Look!" She pointed. "Somebody's waving!" Relief shone in her voice. "It must be Mack. He said he'd wave if he could smuggle out my copy of 'Love Can Art.' The others can help him distribute it."

Jan and Lawrence continued to watch the exodus, wrapped together to stay warm. Lawrence couldn't help but smile at the contented faces of the enlightened, the way she had seen her audience emerge from the experience, too full to acknowledge her presence, yet content. Just for a second, she thought about what her future might hold. I must walk the Earth, she mused, but let my experiences get there for me, as me. When the last conventioneer (Nicole?) had entered the helicopter, they went inside.

Epilogue

"Love Can Art"
You stumble across a brief meadow and land beside the creek. You are naked, vulnerable as you gaze into the crystal glittery water, as clear as glass with a sandy bottom. Hot and sweaty, you drink, then plunge your head in. You decide to take a quick bath before rinsing and filling the pottery further upstream. As you trace the lines of its design, a goat wanders by, white and black against a deep, dark green, and the flavor is so intense on your tongue that you rasp it against your wrist to calm it. A little black cow with a wide strip of bandage wrapped around its middle calmly chews the grass, and your heart is filled with so much . . . simple . . . love. Your heart is faint with the love you feel. Who feels? We all feel? You stare into the mists of the waterfall at a moonbow; its three colors shine dimly. You step back into the creek but do not feel the wetness. You pass through the tunnel behind the waterfall, completely dull and emotionless. There is an emptiness that nevertheless sends you to shiver. It is so terrifying, the inability to love. I need no one, you affirm. Warm darkness replaces the cool fluorescence; along with it comes impressions. A musical tinge accompanied by the smell of freshly baked bread. Rough lace caresses your fingers; colors unimaginable pound against your eyelids. There is music, soft and gentle, and a harsh creaking of chain. You begin to realize that your love can never be simple. The sick feeling of being ignorant, of harmony through spoilage, of being so self-centered that you believe that what brings you happiness brings these aliens happiness. You spiral up towards the surface, seeking knowledge, seeking grace. Above, there is a glowing face — the green-eyed woman. You become hopeful, for she somehow stirs positive feelings in you after all that deadness. She helps you up, and points the way. Then you can, besides the tastes, smells, sights, and sounds that randomly came earlier, feel. You part the rough woven curtains of a huge tapestry, only briefly noting its design. Then you have all of eternity, it seems, to learn the design, for it stretches before you as a thick, dark rug. Impressions formed as you walk are of mountains, stones, cabins, wood smoke, corn shocks, and you realize the beautiful place from which the rug must have come. As you continue walking, you soon learn eternity would never be long enough to learn that pattern; it's too complex. You study it, becoming more and more immersed. Your hands are nervous. You want to manufacture, to participate in human creation. Your mouth is dry, so you swallow. What can you do? The breeze whispers

93

by; your hands try to capture it. You look into the rug as it builds, climbing and climbing, and you see the infinite possibilities of freedom, but you are somehow denied any outlet, any relief from your frustration. You want to remake the world, but you need the key and feel you cannot make it on your own. Crying now, forgetting that upwelling of hope that had been, after all, so weak, and so brief, you throw yourself onto the rug, ripping and screaming at the fabric. The pattern mocks you, so complex it's almost organic. There's no way any human could ever match its beauty. You claw, bite, and kick, but the rug rebounds still in dazzling wonder. Then there is a hand on your shoulder.

At first you think it is Lawrence, but the pattern shifts, and it is your first infatuation, ever so much more beautiful than you remember, but true. You kiss, and play, kicking the rug behind you, and rolling upon barren land. You are both naked, of course, and your frolicking leads you to a more lush land, and again you are alone.

You wander the land, until you are greeted by your one true love. The bonds grow thicker and thicker, you learn more and more, until at one point your perception has slightly but noticeably changed. You notice more, and everything is much more exaggerated, so that you can relish the bland and respect the ugly. You spiral onward, feeling that you have learned how everything feels, as the song confirms. Happily you touch your beloved, and you start to create.

But now there are all your loved ones, supporting you, as you hope to support them. You touch them, and shiver, for you are all reaching, striving to become, to create.

And the universe is twisted. People surround you; no one is clothed. You recognize everyone you have ever seen, heard, or otherwise experienced. People who brushed against you but whom you could not see are there—and you recognize them! Then, all around you, on the fringes, yet right beside you, are all the types of people you could possibly imagine, even those lost way up in space. You create, and spin, and build, and they have joined you already. They were there all along. You sweat, and tremble, for, after all, this is new, the first time . . .

But it's done. You look back upon the experience you yourself have created and swell with pride. Your sense of accomplishment is matched only by your sense of generosity as you thank everyone over and over, crying openly now out of joy and gratitude, and you are at the summit . . .

Then the Lawrence influence fades.

And you have finished that stage.

But the experience has only just begun . . .

The hope remains fresh.

BOOK TWO

ELABORYNTH

Lawrence hadn't shown up yet. Instead, the tree was all there was, and it was shimmering. As it fought to stabilize, seeking the present, it became a stump, green with moss and full of water and fleeting insects. No, it was a pine cone. The stump was its progenitor, safe on Earth. No, it was full grown, massive with five centuries' swelling, on a bleak garden satellite, and the cone was its eternal striving to yield offspring.

The pine added a ring, then another, responding habitually in a seasonless place. The patterns of light and dark made a day out of the year.

Forever became now for the tree, yet it once more swirled, losing control, expanding its rings of information. Myriad gene maps emerged: a flying squirrel, a shark, a sparrow, a lizard; a wheatgrass, a pansy, an alga, a liverwort. Queasily a jumble of rhythms joined them: erosion, death, dormancy, meals, and technology.

With human artifacts came human gene maps to proudly point at the architecture, the paintings, the chairs, the books, and claim ownership, if not responsibility of creation.

One human gene map stumbled and pulled away from the others. It and the mind witnessing all of this resonated, becoming Lawrence.

She raced to the center of the tree, the eye of the storm, the only area free and clear of chaos, and, taking a deep, shuddering breath, looked out over the field of her creation.

"Here I am! I'm really inside my Cube!" she exulted. She looked around eagerly, then frowned. "There's no action here. I have gene maps and natural forces, but they're not yet synchronous." Lawrence tilted her head back and forth. "Everything is still, not growing, but they sure were moving while I was out there." Sullenly she slumped, then shook herself.

"This won't do." She peered into the darkness and silence. "I need to be out there, in the middle of it all, to truly experience it. Clearly I can't just sit here and bask in my accomplishment." It struck her. "Apparently the Cube needs me to complete it and bring it all together." She sighed. "Okay." She stood, hesitated one more moment, then plunged forward to meet whatever might fling out of this hodgepodge of a crystalline Cube.

The nine prison guards tightened their orbit around her in the bright room, so that the trembling that Lawrence had tried so hard to control returned to join the sweat already soaking her shirt.

Thickly she spoke. "Please move away." Try as she might, it still came out tight, desperate, high-pitched.

"Shut up, prisoner 12-8-20-367-4," a male guard muttered tiredly, and a female guard reached out to firmly swat the back of Lawrence's head, pushing her face forward.

The first trigger.

Lawrence lay in the grass, shuddering from the blow. She could smell the brown, seared part near the roots and she could hear bugs crawling around the stems. Her eyes were closed. Somehow that was all right. Her face began to itch, though. She moved it back and forth, but the grass was not scratchy at all. The soothing, moist blades slithered against her skin so that she could feel their greenness. She flailed her arms up, up, scooting down the hill as she tried to wipe her eyes. Before she could hide the tears, someone brusquely pulled her up.

Lawrence sucked her arms around the wadded blankets, clutching them to her belly as she had once wanted to hold the cool earth. She buried her head further into the tear-soaked pillow, choking on the last feeble sobs she could muster.

"Gahh," she bubbled as she pushed her head up to look around.

She was in a prison cell of white walls, no window, and an old-fashioned door.

Lawrence slowly sat up, trembling fingers wiping her hot cheeks.

"It's over," she whispered, and heaved a sigh of relief.

The door beckoned. Calmly she strode over to its many coats of smooth ivory paint and tried the knob. It was locked.

Lawrence spun around. Now the bed was closer to the wall, and in the corner was a small desk, complete with screen.

She sat before it. It glowed gently, so she started typing: LET THE PSYCHCOMPUTERS AT IT, I DON'T CARE. LISTEN. YOU FOUND A PERIOD OF MY LIFE I DON'T LIKE. IT COULD HAVE BEEN A DREAM, IT HAPPENED SO LONG AGO. I WAS PART OF A FAMILY, AND THUS BEATEN, RAPED. I WAS TWO OR THREE. WHO CARES? I TOLD MARICELA ALL THIS ANYWAY, AND SHE'S A BETTER COMFORTER THAN YOU'LL EVER BE. SO GOODBYE NOW.

Lawrence again approached the door. Pretty, tinkling notes played at random came faintly now. She crammed her ear against the door. Now Lawrence could hear childish voices, laughter, bare feet running. Foolishly she grinned, giddy as she wiped her face and thighs over and over. Then she jumped onto the door, beating against it with her whole body, frantically clawing it, all in silence.

Lawrence sat on the floor practicing her xylophone. The other children milled around, making her nervous as they fluttered in and out of the light. Nervousness eventually led to irritation; Lawrence could see nothing to get excited about. *So we start low-tech school today*, she thought. *Big deal*. A nearby child was jostled and fell against Lawrence, who merely looked up, annoyed.

"Number Four."

Lawrence jumped up, gathered her stuff, and followed the woman who had called her into a small room where three people awaited her.

One of the men said brightly, "So you want to be called 'Lawrence,' right?"

She nodded, then looked down to put her xylophone on the floor. She rolled it around most of the time they spoke.

The pleasant man went to crouch beside her. "We'd like to test you, but first we need to know something."

He was just like the attendants in the nursery! Lawrence could feel her insides glow. "What?" she felt very comfortable asking. She even handed him the hammer so he could play.

The woman interposed then, but all she did was hand the man Lawrence's rhythm board. He stopped playing so he could cradle it before Lawrence's eyes. "Remember when the attendant asked to see this last week?"

Lawrence nodded.

"Well, she was so excited about it, she decided to let us see it. It certainly is a nice product. What do you call it?"

"A rhythm board," Lawrence replied casually.

The man repeated it softly. He was really friendly. Lawrence was beginning to hope he would be assigned to her class in low-tech. She knew she was smiling.

The man smiled at her and asked in such a clear, genuinely curious tone that Lawrence began to think he was just a big kid, "What's it for?"

"It relaxes you," Lawrence said matter-of-factly, because one of the attendants had said so. "How?"

That was a hard one. Lawrence looked up at him anxiously, but she couldn't help feeling that he wouldn't get mad, if she tried her very best. "Um . . . the wave function matches the nerves?" She wasn't clear now of the explanation.

"Why did you make it?" he immediately asked. His tone did not change, so she figured her answer had been all right.

Lawrence quickly glanced around. The two other people were frozen in stances of careful listening. That was odd. She had got the impression that they weren't listening at all. Maybe this was important. She began to get a little nervous, but right then the pleasant man started stroking her hair. It still seemed all right.

"I don't know," she finally stuttered. "They were teaching us music, and I got the idea." She fell silent, pondering, listening to her heart pound.

The woman shifted impatiently, but no, the pleasant man smiled and idly fiddled with the rhythm board. "Rhythm?" he murmured to the pair. "Music? Waves?"

"Not really," Lawrence supplied. "I just thought there was more. I wanted to do something against silence . . . no, I mean . . ." She looked at him, embarrassed.

"This has high-tech. Where did you learn that?" he pressed.

Lawrence was puzzled. She studied his face as he looked at her mildly. "The attendants showed me."

They seemed to want more, and the pleasant man shrugged at the pair. Lawrence felt sharp disappointment. Maybe if she worked on her vocabulary, she could express herself better and make the nice man happy.

Lawrence lay in her darkening cell, holding a rhythm board. She stroked it idly, watching the light panel above her dim.

"They—how absurd—they're slowly turning down the lights. Whoever 'they' are." Her voice came out sluggishly, due to the relaxing effect of the rhythm board. "Time to go to sleep," she sang.

"Yeah, that's me, back there, I mean." It felt perfectly natural speaking aloud. "Always wanting it all, always wanting to know it all. Like prison. I wondered what prison would be like." She waved her hand. "And here it is!"

She leaned her head back. "And the city, too. I couldn't wait to get to the city. And space. All the big unknowns. I couldn't stop. The biggest unknowns are still hidden from my sight. Like the personalities of my dearest. I sought to dig 'em all up. Vance. Kamela. Maricela. Jeffrey. Those are the big ones. Actually, I want them all. Everybody. So I'm here, sitting inside a blank Cube."

Finally the light was completely gone. Lawrence sat there a minute, blinked, then said, "Big deal."

Rick showed her the jaunty springs before he used them to hitch the door open. Lawrence fingered them with delight, liking the green that encircled the little black dots that somebody had painted in a row on each side of the spring's glossy wood. She watched him now, as, way up there, he cinched the clutch tight. It was hard to see, and the sunlight he brought in didn't help. Lawrence squinted before demanding, "How's it work?"

Rick's eyes crinkled. Lawrence watched them first, then casually slid her eyes down to his mouth to see a grin before she relaxed.

"It's not that hard. Look." He lifted her up, way up to the top of the door. Her heart leapt to be so tall. "See how it hooks there and stays because of the tension?"

Lawrence quit looking excitedly around and concentrated on the spring because she figured he'd get tired pretty fast. "Yes, I see." She yanked the spring crosswise.

"Not that way!" Rick shouted as the door swung into them. They wobbled a bit, then he was back, strong underneath her legs, to shove the door back to click into place. "No harm done." Without warning, he swung her off the piggyback and set her feet first on the floor. "Now why did you go and do that for?"

"I had to be fast, to find out how it worked. I thought pulling it that way would loosen it."

"And you were right!" He chuckled at the small, embarrassed figure rubbing her nose.

Lawrence smiled, then darted out into the sun. As she clattered down the steps, she heard Rick mutter, "Smart little booger!"

It was spring. She squeaked on the wet grass, only a little moist now in the sun, head down in thought. Again rubbing her nose, Lawrence remembered the words "Sometimes we goof." a second before a canvas ball socked her in the face, causing her to fall and forget all about the concerned faces grouped behind a door they forgot to shut.

"Hey, you reject! Can't you see?" Number One jeered.

Lawrence tossed away the ball as she jumped up. Number Five caught it deftly before turning away. Lawrence looked around. While Number One and Number Five were playing ball, grabbing it, tossing it, and stomping on each other, Number Two was working alone with the volumetric equipment again. Lawrence sighed; that left only Number Three to play with, and then only if he wanted to.

She found him in the compost pile.

"What're you doing?"

The pale boy continued digging a while, then murmured, "What did they say helped?"

"Humidity," Lawrence readily answered, saying the new word carefully.

Number Three said the word to himself.

"Everything rots really well here," Lawrence supplied cheerfully.

Number Three sighed and sat back. "You're such a big help, Lawrence. You know everything."

Lawrence remembered how he had panicked during a lights out. The rest of the children had run out giggling at once. Lawrence had stayed quietly in her corner, watching the attendants comfort him and not understanding.

"No, I don't," she finally said, but Number Three just sighed again.

"Call me Tom. I've decided."

Lawrence nodded.

He rubbed his forehead. "It certainly is hot for third month, isn't it?" His lip quivered.

Lawrence leaned to hear him, then she answered brightly, "No. It's barely 288. I looked."

"What's that?" His eyes seemed wary.

"The temperature, stupid. It just feels hot because we're not used to it yet."

"These tests weary me," he explained.

Lawrence kept quiet, thinking. Tests? Was that what they were? No . . . she had been tested. Nothing to it. Tom, though, had to keep going back, for something or other.

"It's good, though," he said faintly. "I know I'm limited."

"What's that?" Lawrence looked away to watch a blue jay alight amidst goldfinches.

"Isn't it obvious? I'm not smart like you. Intelligent."

"We all have intelligence." Lawrence straightened with a jerk, pleased at what she had said.

"I'm different," Tom said in the same dragging monotone, then he sprang up and ran toward the ball game. Lawrence chased him, trying to grab his braid. The yard spun as he swerved out of her way, or she would have run him down.

"Hey!" Number One shoved.

Lawrence grabbed the ball and ran. Rick was coming out, arms loaded with toys. She skidded in the worn depression at his feet.

"Whoa!" he yelled.

Number Two was there from somewhere. "Gimme that ball!"

But Lawrence was gone, flinging herself onto the ball atop the little hill near the woods. She started giggling, relishing the madness as she rolled into Number Two's tackle, not yet aware of her limitations.

Lawrence stumbled away from the machinery and bowed to vomit. A prison saint ran to steady her, handing her a damp towel.

Lawrence fumbled with the cloth until the p.s. took it back and wiped her face herself.

"There. It's all right. It's normal to feel nausea afterwards. You're not the first to throw up."

"What was it?" Lawrence shuddered, feeling again the clamps against her skull.

"We're reaping you," the p.s. said patiently.

Lawrence turned to look at her. "What?"

"We're reaping you." Same tone, but Lawrence noticed that her lips read "We're sowing you."

"Come again?"

The p.s. repeated it.

"What are you saying? Reap or sow?" Then it hit her. "I suppose it doesn't make any difference." She stepped into her own vomit and skidded.

Lawrence went in and there was a pink stuff all over the floor. It sure did stink. She stood there several minutes, then used the bathroom. As she washed she wrinkled her nose. At first it had smelled sweet. Now . . . Skirting to reach the door, she couldn't believe the relief fresh air afforded her.

Number Two was outside, waiting to go in. She beckoned him to the door. "Look." She pointed. "What is that stuff?"

"Oh, Number Five threw up. The janitor dumped some stuff on it and then she's going to come back and clean it up."

He didn't think it was odd, so Lawrence put it out of her mind and returned to class. Math kept her busy for a while, but she couldn't help but look up when Tom spoke.

"Back then there were no female doctors. Oh, I think there were a few. Why is that, Mentor? How come it wasn't even?"

After class the other kids crowded around him.

"Well, I don't know. After those tests they took me into this room and said they were going to make me smarter and would I like that? Of course! So they hooked me up and after a few days I had all this knowledge I didn't have before. It's great!"

"Wow!" said Number Two. "I wish I had that. I hate school. They could hook me up and I could learn everything up to high (tech) school and leave."

"I'm still in school," Tom pointed out.

"Yeah, but I'd tell them to give me everything."

Lawrence wandered away, vastly miserable. She was sure the nice man wasn't to blame. *Maybe . . .* she cheered up. *Maybe he liked me and asked them not to hurt me like they did Tom.* She felt flooded with gratitude, and vowed to study harder.

Another prison saint sat beside her so she could hold the fork Lawrence was using so clumsily. When she put it down, the p.s. raised a cup of water to her lips.

After she drank, Lawrence cleared her throat. "So. How come all you passive succors are female?"

The p.s. calmly picked up the fork again. "Women are different."

Lawrence grabbed the table and swung herself up. Whirling, she kicked the uncomfortable chair away.

The p.s. solemnly stared at the chair. "You are no longer five," she explained.

Lawrence stood outside on the stoop blinking. It was her first proud moment. She had been sent to woodshop with the others, and she had been scared of the tools. So were all the other kids, except Number Five. Her chair came out perfect. Lawrence had despaired at that, but she decided to try. What she had had in mind didn't really come out. What she had wanted to do was . . . but, never mind, she couldn't do it.

Mentor, though, must have seen inside her. She had praised Lawrence much more than Number Five. "While it's not perfect, it's different. It shows creativity." And she had patted her shoulder.

Lawrence walked slowly down the straight white corridor, head twisted away from the prison saint who walked quietly a step behind her. "Kamela?"

"Yes. She is a passive succor," the p.s. answered.

"Figures. Vance?"

"Our leader. Or, rather, the superintendent. Now that you are feeling better, you can learn a lot about what goes on here. It's not that bad." The p.s. crept closer. Lawrence eyed her. Her stilted speech was made up for by genuine warmth. Her kindliness kept Lawrence from strangling her.

"Yeah, but I don't get it. It's what I make of it. Isn't it? I kept trying to make a prison in my mind, and eventually I saw it as just another commune. A commune of misfits. Looked at that way, it sounded wonderful. I began to seek it, crave it."

"When?"

"I . . . don't know. It was after the artists, I'm pretty sure, because it would have been them, this misfit commune, and I didn't want to have anything to do with them. So it was . . . maybe right before I got my lab. Yeah. Not that the responsible position they gave me solved all of my problems, understand. It's just that I became too busy to think about it much anymore. I kept planning it, coming to my place, seeing Vance, all those people. Hmmpf. *Even* the ones who wouldn't be there, like Maricela. That is strange. She was with me at the time. Why did I think I'd see her again, after so long, to start anew, someplace different? I — "

Lawrence stopped. Slyly she glanced over at the prison saint, who had disappeared.

Huh?

Lawrence started running, and the corridor started curving. She chased it as the lights began dimming behind her and almost slammed into the wall of windows that led outside.

Hungrily Lawrence drank in the sight of bright light, pale sky, and desert that was before her. She pushed open a glass door and ran outside, pausing to turn and see what kind of building had housed her, except there wasn't any. Only a tired, wooden door was buried into an incline of sand.

Lawrence shrugged, walking over the dunes. Nevada. Whatever that was. She looked idly up at the cloudless sky and tripped, stubbing her toes.

"What the — ?" She looked down to find some rocks, sticks. She bent down. "They seem fashioned."

Lawrence sat down and fitted a stone to her hand. It conformed nicely. She scratched with it, leaving her name in the sand. Then she lifted a stick. A string was attached to it, making a bow.

She pulled it as hard as she could, then threw it down, dislodging a small bowl. She watched it roll down the hill.

"These are tools. I'm too far along now. I can't go back. Childhood. The beginning." She pushed her hair back and started, surprised. A bright yellow maple leaf had intruded, drifting widely in her field of vision.

The Mentor came into the classroom and naturally everyone shut up. Lawrence wriggled, wishing she could talk, but never did in class, and, besides, she didn't want to call attention to herself. Deeply she wished someone would talk, but no, they all sat and watched that Mentor go to his desk. Lawrence pointedly studied her monitor. Yesterday she had found something new: architecture. She had begun quickly, learning to plan and build simulations, and it was easy to lose herself once more that way, yet the back of her mind was waiting not too calmly. Finally the Mentor spoke.

"Today's lesson is a bit different. If you would clear your screens . . ."

Lawrence waited while he tested his bank.

"Lawrence."

Again she waited. A few snickered, so that she turned red, but she did not look up from her screen.

"Please clear your screen."

Still she waited. Everyone laughed.

"Mentor," spluttered Number One. "Lawrence doesn't *talk*."

"Oh."

She looked at him. He waited maybe twenty seconds.

"Okay. Let me discuss it first." He came around the desk and strode before the class. He smiled and spread his hands. Lawrence noticed his hesitation and wondered. "You have to tell me what is wrong with your education." He looked around. Lawrence had begun to stare at him, but she looked away when he saw her. "Is everybody willing to do it?"

Number Two roared, "That's crazy, Mentor. How do we know?"

Several nodded.

"I can't think of anything," said Number Five.

Lawrence quit listening and started wondering about the vocabulary test she was going to give herself later.

"Well, just start working at your screens and see if you can think up any complaints. Start with the good things first," he suggested.

Lawrence went back to architecture. After a while, Mentor came up to see what she was working on. No Mentor had ever done that before! Lawrence panicked.

"Hey," he said quietly. "Why?"

Lawrence still could not look at him. "What is your name?" she whispered chokingly.

He hesitated. "Mentor."

She shook her head. "No."

He moved to sit beside her. Lawrence directed her attention out the window at the maple. Rain streaked down the pane, but she could still see a bright yellow blur. Looking out there made her feel quite alone and safe.

"Vance."

Instantly their gazes locked, hers wild with interest.

"Okay, Vance," she began slowly. "It's ludicrous."

"What?"

"It's *ludicrous!*"

Vance stood up. "Do you want to tell me why?" he asked loudly.

Lawrence stood, trembling, aware that all were staring, but she didn't care. She closed her eyes and rapidly composed her answer, because she felt a burning choking that told her this was important. She spoke slowly, carefully, in a bleak tone.

"Why should I waste my precious time doing something useless? It won't even be read, much less implemented." Her lips slid over the new word she wasn't sure how to pronounce. "They just want you to think you have some control, but you don't!" The low tone became a screech at the end. Lawrence stumbled out of the room in tears.

She spent maybe a half hour or so out there in the hall, scrunched up into a little sobbing ball. Then she felt a hand on her arm, urging her up, and she wiped her eyes to see Vance's gentle smile.

"Come with me."

She followed him to his office. Immediately she went to the window. There was the corn.

Vance addressed the back of her head. "Uh, have a seat."

"Corn likes rain."

"And so do I." He brought a chair over to the window and pointed at it. She looked around at him, then gingerly sat on the edge. Vance turned his chair to her, then sat. For several seconds he pulled his fingers through his hair. "Look, uh, suppose I told you that I asked for complaints so that I might effect some improvements. Would you believe me?"

Lawrence watched him until their eyes met. He sure sounded sincere, if preoccupied. "I am trusting," she said simply.

"Would you then write for me a list of complaints?"

She shrugged. "I guess so. But maybe I shouldn't. I mean, maybe I should watch you a while. You will probably be a lot different from the past Mentor."

Vance watched her. "I wouldn't call that trusting, but okay. That seems fair."

Lawrence heard his strange accents. She had never seen, close up, anybody from outside the commune before. "Where did you come from?"

"Let me ask the questions."

Lawrence straightened. This was new! Or was it? Sharply she remembered the nice man. He had asked a lot of questions. Usually, though, she was taught, it was the children who were supposed to do the asking.

She put up a faint protest. "But you are the adult."

"So? Adults don't know everything. Especially one who's new around here." He smiled at her, but his eyes were distant and vaguely sad.

Lawrence wanted to see them sparkle. "I'm sorry I yelled at you."

He did cheer up a little. "No, that's good. I'm surprised no one asked your opinion before. You might have some good ideas on how to run things." He chuckled. "By the way, you must have had some complaints before I came. What were they?"

Lawrence shrugged. "I don't know. I'm always left alone to learn what I want. I like it." She looked down then and rubbed her hand on her corduroy jeans. "I'd like to, though," she began shyly, "know more. You could tell me what's outside the commune."

Vance paused. "And for me?"

Lawrence darted her eyes to his, completely nonplussed. "What?"

"If I help you, what will you do for me?"

She frowned. As a child, she was used to everyone being solicitous to her in everything—food, pain, knowledge. To give him—she puzzled over it deliciously. "Well—"

Vance stood. "Take your time. Anyway, one thing I was going to ask you was whether you had ever been sowed, or, forcelearned."

Lawrence shuddered. That was Tom. "No." As she said it she began to wonder for the first time if everyone eventually did. Maybe she should have said "yes."

"Good. Still, you speak so well, I wondered . . ."

"Oh, yes," Lawrence blathered. "I constantly work on my vocabulary."

"Why?"

"Because . . ." Then she blushed.

Vance scratched his head. "Well, that's good. Keep working at it." He was all Mentor now. "Maybe you'd better run along. I don't know your schedule, but I'm sure you have to be somewhere else."

"Okay." Lawrence jumped up and left.

"Too late," Lawrence muttered. "By the time I was three or four, I was already learning, and school, especially Vance, clinched it. I can't go back to before I was . . . acting like myself. That six-year-old is almost too familiar." She clinked the stones together and looked out across the desert.

Here came Vance, wiping the knife onto his gray pants, leaving a brown smudge. Lawrence watched dispassionately, remembering the tendril of blood Kamela bore from love of doctors. It had to be human blood, the only kind she'd seen. Come to think of it, it was probably hers.

Vance grinned and sat beside her, tossing the knife in with the bows. "I thought you'd catch up with me eventually."

Lawrence touched his hair. It was still pure black.

"Don't trust your memories, Lawrence. Even if, knowing you, you remember well, they'll still be distorted. What Tom got was a messed-up mind. Even our cultural memories aren't perfect."

"Why is that?" Lawrence hurriedly swallowed. Here she was, not thinking, asking the all-knowing adult.

"Look at it this way. You are all ages here, like the tree, but really, out there in the real world, you are twenty. Your adult mind will color your memories. You'll fill in the wordlessness. You'll interpret it. You won't just let it be."

Lawrence looked down at the stones. The rings chattered as they theorized: those stones are clearly representative of the Olduwan, no, the Acheulean, method. She shook her head.

Vance smiled crookedly. "See? They don't know. Nobody does."

Lawrence this time chose to watch Vance come in, and listen this time while watching him. The professional Mentors were usually good. They didn't come into class all preoccupied or grouchy. No, Vance came in and smiled at everyone, and she could not help smiling back.

"I read your complaints last night. I must admit that I'm disappointed. Surely there must be more around here to complain about. Screens."

The students prepared their screens for note-taking, except Lawrence. She never did that. All she did was memorize everything after "screens." Vance did not point her out.

"Let me explain yesterday's assignment. I can't believe everything here is perfect for everybody, even if I only have to teach five, and even if this commune is small. There must be some things that are wrong, that irritate you. Do not hesitate to complain if something doesn't seem right. Also, I get to complain, too. You have been told that you are equally responsible for your education. I expect improvement from you, too. Fair?"

Everybody was so used to being deemed responsible that the last slid right in. Even Lawrence nodded with everyone else, though she was using Vance's pause to discard her mental notes. Vance still seemed disturbed as he glanced at each in turn. He seemed to be thinking hard, planning what he would next say.

"A smooth pond is a dead pond. If you're completely satisfied, you cannot live and flourish. If you have no dissatisfaction, I must find something to rile you away from contentment. You must always be hungry. End screens."

Lawrence suddenly had a thought. She switched on the screen to record it. QUALITY. IT IS NOT RARE; IT IS . . . SCORNED FOR THAT WHICH HAS MORE VALUE.

"What good did it do, Vance? Why fight? I calmed down, cooperated with everyone, and I was given everything I needed to complete my project. Well . . ." She grimaced. "I admit they got a little nervous there toward the end. They certainly didn't want me going up into space. Yeah, I had to finagle something there. *But*, in everything else, the general principle was sound: do what they say, cooperate, and you'll be rewarded."

Lawrence turned to look at Vance, who wasn't there.

She leapt up. "What is it with this place? First the prison saint, then the prison, and now you! Oh, Vance!" She frowned. His presence, however much she hated to admit it, had been comforting.

When she sat now on the island, the water flowed on one side only. The western current had over the years filled up with leaves, dirt, crayfish shells, sticks, and other debris. Lawrence listened to the single stream, then jumped up.

She scratched her side as she paced. "I must want this. I must want them all to leave me alone. Yes. The need to reach was a false desire. I really like blocking everybody out."

Lawrence awoke on a cot in the common room. She lifted her head and looked around. The four other beds looked like still evening, for they were untouched. Now that it was warm again the children thought nothing of sleeping outside. Still, all four? Then Lawrence remembered. Tom always slept in his bed. He must have got up early, to teach games. His bed was made up because he always made it up upon rising. Tom was weird, but quiet. Lawrence figured he was okay.

She lay there awhile, watching the leaves flutter as shadows on the wall. The light was soft. Tom hadn't pulled down the blackout screen. That was nice of him. Lawrence liked to sleep nearest the window and see the trees when she awoke. Tom was nearest the door; maybe that was why he didn't mind.

Once awake, Lawrence was immediately alert, but today she chose to linger under the light blanket, thinking about Mentor.

When she went to breakfast, she might see her age mates. She might see the older children. She would see the adults. One of them would cook for her if she asked him. Sometimes she saw the new baby.

Vance was different from those at breakfast. Lawrence stirred, trying to put a finger on why. The cook smiled at her, just like Vance. She smiled back at Vance, though. School was exciting now, thanks to him; to wait until afternoon was always excruciating, and . . .

She had been meaning to ask if her screens were tidy, if they fit his scheme.

Lawrence wriggled. It was no longer possible to lie in bed! The thought of fruit and grain nauseated her, but she could wait and eat later. It was probably still early.

Yes, she had to go look! She jumped out of bed and tugged on the coveralls that were practically a uniform among her age mates and ran to look out the window. She gasped.

A tiny black kitten was on the porch. It was looking at her. It didn't turn to look at her; it was already looking at her, as if it had known she would look out. But she didn't know it was there to be seen by her. She stared at the kitten, mind feebly striving to grasp the concept. Eventually she shook herself, and she ran to comb her hair and open the door before the kitten moved.

Lawrence opened the door gently and actually remembered to shut it behind her before inching around the corner to the porch. The kitten was still there. She came up close to it in some kind of wonder. The kitten continued to watch with mild interest, then suddenly stopped to lick itself. It stretched and hopped off the porch.

Lawrence followed it idly for a moment, then veered down a path that led into the woods. She kept her eyes to the ground so she wouldn't miss the turnoff. Just because she had never been lost didn't mean . . . *Let's see, here's the big orange rock which has a tiny gully around its point, and here's the dogwood. Got it! Now I think I usually go through this cedar and this whatever it is to get to the meadow.* Finally she disappeared into the pale green leaves.

Lawrence stomped determinedly in the right direction, mind deep within becoming a blank, so contemplative was it. She got to the meadow quickly and sat, looking around at new buds and blossoms. She looked down at a patch of violets and breathed deeply through her nose. *Smell it out here. How strong it smells! Last year I remembered I got to smell the violets. I kept looking forward to that, without even realizing it.* She fiddled with grass stems as she realized the passing of seasons gloomily.

When she looked up at the sun, she tried to recall her feelings earlier and put them into words. Vance . . . that kitten . . . Lawrence jumped. There was the kitten, going into a hollow the kudzu vines had made. It had followed her, and she had not been aware. Lawrence straightened. Now here was something she could control. She had already thought herself observant, as she worked the screens. She went out and memorized certain qualitative features over the years, the fact that the maple's leaves were earlier than most, for example, just long enough to transfer the information onto the screen, but that must not be enough.

Every day Vance asked her minor incursive questions about her life in the commune, and she would know sometimes, or thought she knew, but there was so much she hadn't noticed, or couldn't remember. This would help.

She wasn't sure how to begin. Eyes followed movement; hers watched the birds passing overhead in clumps. She should watch, keep her eyes open, listen, keep her ears open, but that wasn't enough. She could sense, that came naturally, but this was more than that. It was knowing the presence of the kitten. It was therefore being the kitten.

I must reach. Forget me, because otherwise that's all it will ever be. I need to . . . She took a deep breath. *Be aware now, don't miss anything.* She concentrated, breathing faster, heart pounding. She lifted her head off the ground an inch or so, until she became dizzy and let it drop back down. *Most of all, don't think! Feel! Sense!*

Lawrence stretched out her arms into the grass, physically reaching what her mind could not. She coursed: needles, grass, pebbles, a few brittle leaves. She tried to listen better. She could certainly hear the birds, but wasn't that a squirrel chattering far off?

She stuck her tongue out to taste the air. Noises. A few crunchings. No. Several hard, loud crunchings. Someone walking nearby. Who? If she could reach, know, or if she could really listen and interpret what she heard. She shook her head, scrunching up her closed eyes. She would have to go look.

Lawrence jumped up and ran toward the footsteps. They stopped once she had hit the woods and started crunching herself, then they started again. Lawrence followed, but she must have walked too fast; she ran into Vance at the creek. Quickly hiding behind a rock, she was certain he hadn't seen her.

"Okay, Lawrence," Vance immediately said fairly loudly with disgust. "What do you want?"

Huh? He's got it, too? Or has he really *got it? Oh, boy!* She couldn't help herself. She poked her nose around the rock. He could teach her this, too.

Vance was sitting on the bank holding the kitten on his lap. "Well?"

Sheepishly Lawrence emerged and stood, squinting in the darkness of the evergreens. "And . . ."

"No."

"Huh?"

"Don't start with 'and.'"

"Oh." Lawrence scratched her side. "How did you know it was me?"

"Who else comes out here?"

Lawrence grinned. "So you know."

He shook his head. "What do you mean?"

But Lawrence was satisfied. He knew, she was sure of it. She vowed to work harder at it. Who knows? Maybe when she got to be Vance's age, she could . . ."Can I go now?"

Vance's eyes widened. "No. Have a seat. I would like to talk to you."

Lawrence sat down slowly, several feet away.

"Lawrence, you are an enigma. I can't figure you out."

"Enigma? I am what?"

Vance paused. "I'm sorry. I keep forgetting. Let me explain. You speak so well I thought for sure you had been sowed. I checked your records. You never were."

She interrupted. "Will I be?"

"No. They don't do that to intelligent children, or children with special abilities." He laughed. "Look at your face! You must have really worried about it. I thought it was strange that your records were open. You should have been reaped long ago. You had the tests everyone else had when they were four. You tested high, of course. They should have sent for you, but somehow you slipped through. Their memories must have had a defect and lost you. You're lucky."

Lawrence went through his speech over and over. It was hard to make sense out of it. "Vance," she began timidly, "what does 'reap' mean?"

"It's something dangerous. The people I've met who have been reaped are . . . But they would have taken you away."

The adult, with his nervousness alone, not his vague intimations of danger, conveyed to Lawrence a sense of fear.

"When will they find out?"

"Never, I hope. I'll change your records to bright, but nothing special, okay?"

"Okay." Lawrence felt relief and gratitude. She superimposed Vance upon the image of the nice man protecting her against those savage elements, the hard, crafty looks and the slaps. Still, she couldn't help wondering what might have happened. She leapt up. "Follow me." Lawrence started walking rapidly away from the creek.

Vance ran to catch up. "What is it?"

"Something I want to show you." She stuck her finger out. "Up here." She started climbing. They went past a huge fallen oak and began paralleling one of the several washes that ran into the creek.

"Here." Lawrence pointed, then dove under a tree and crossed a stream to fall upon a wide, pointed oval. "Look at this little island. Isn't it great?" The stream split at its head and roared past roots to meet again at its bottom. "I've never seen a real island before. Look."

Vance sat beside her. "Boy, that water is loud. Do you know about white noise?"

Lawrence shook her head.

"Well, listen. It masks. Can you hear the birds as well here?"

Lawrence listened. "No." She shifted. "Look. If you lie in the center, you can hear both streams equally."

Vance did this. His gaze grew peaceful as he stared up at the green rarely pierced by blue. He mildly said, "You know, this will dry up soon."

"Will it?" Lawrence asked, then she remembered. Of course. She had never seen the water before, and she had crawled up and down the dry washes for years without figuring out what had made them. She wasn't allowed out in the woods during rain storms.

"I've got to give you better assignments," Vance mused. "What would you like to do?"

Lawrence shrugged.

"Now, wait," Vance laughed. "I've got it. You're already doing what you want to do. What I've got to do is find out what, supplement it, correct it if I have to, and approve it. That's simple enough."

Lawrence this time was quick. "But that means I don't have to go to school," she answered slowly, though secretly she triumphed. All school did was interrupt her projects, and now she had so much more to do, with this new thing she had discovered.

"No, I think you should stay in school."

Lawrence frowned.

"Now what's wrong with that? I'll use that time to check up on you. Besides, it will make you look more normal."

Lawrence didn't understand. "I need to look normal?"

"Of course you do! Now, did you eat breakfast?"

Lawrence thought. "No." Then it hit her. "I'm starving." She jumped to look for the sun. "It's late," she said when she found it.

"Well, come with me and share mine."

Lawrence followed him eagerly.

"That was the beginning, I remember. I was eight years old, and I woke up with an impression. Then I saw the kitten. All that morning, I remember, I was confused, but that was the first hint of the Cube. What I set out to do—I don't know if I ever had any idea. Maybe everyone kept putting names to it and they were all wrong, but if they were to ask me, I wouldn't have been able to tell them, either. I know I'm here to experience . . . something else. Whatever the others can give me. I . . ." Lawrence hushed and looked down as a movement caught her attention.

Her gene map spasmed and started to unfold against the mottled gray background. The egg donor's face appeared separately from the sperm donor.

"Look, I'm not interested in my own history!" Lawrence spluttered.

Drat. Nevertheless, Lawrence found herself studying the donors' faces. *Wow. Those two gave me my genetic tendencies.* But Lawrence had been taught well, or, she had figured it out to her own satisfaction well. "History is not important," she yelled at the gene map, bunching up apologetically now. "That's genetic determinism, and I'm responsible for what I am, not two people selected at random whose sperm and egg made me. I've never met them, so shut up." She stalked past the gene map to the other side of the tree.

A little bubble coalesced into her vision. She smiled at it because it was green. "Here they are!" she triumphed. She bent down and peered into the glass. The tiny plants wriggled. "Yeah, I'm looking at you!"

Lawrence stepped back so that the bubble could become larger. She had to walk backwards, climbing upwards in soft rooty dirt. The glass bubble expanded rapidly to greater than her height, so she stopped.

She smiled welcomingly. "Now: let me in."

But as she approached, it shrank once more, and no door appeared to tear the precious atmosphere free.

111

Delores handed her the tray of glass and smiled. Her voice was tender as she said, "Don't drop the tray, Lawrence. I'm counting on you."

Proudly Lawrence carried the tray to the other children and set it on the floor. Each with great trepidation selected their own jar, Lawrence waiting until last. *That wasn't hard. They always make a big deal when I do something easy.*

"Now, kids, don't play in the dirt just yet. First you gotta put rocks in." Rick hastily pulled digging fingers free and pointed at the rocks they had gathered yesterday. Lawrence remembered Peaches had warned them not to pick pretty ones, but a few quartz glittered from the pile.

Nobody praised me for coming up with this idea in the first place, sulked Lawrence. "Hey!" she said loudly. "Why do we put rocks in?"

"Geology lesson," Rick answered. He watched as the children dutifully dropped their rocks to pay attention. "Unofficial, of course," he quickly said. "Go ahead and get your rocks. You've got to have drainage, or the plants won't grow. What we're doing, see, is simulating what's outdoors. Soil isn't packed out there, and the water drains so the roots don't get waterlogged. End of lesson."

Quietly the children worked, then it was time to select seeds.

"Which ones do you want? Flowers or food?" Delores spread the bags out to show their labels.

Lawrence looked at them seriously. "Only this many?"

"These are the ones that grow best under these conditions," explained Delores.

Practically, Lawrence selected the one labeled *Daucus carota*. She could already envision the fluffy carrot tops peeking from her soil. The other kids hadn't been as studious in learning the Language of Science; they asked what each one was several times before they chose.

"I saw a snake in the woods yesterday," Lawrence chattered carelessly as they planted. Inside she muttered, an *Elaphe obsoleta obsoleta*, to be exact.

"What did it look like?" Number One had buried her seed too deeply, and was digging it out.

"Ooh. It was big, and black. It was just lying there, too, looking like turds, bloopy ones."

"Snake," murmured Tom, eyes distant.

Lawrence waited, but he didn't continue. She dug quietly herself, remembering the woods that day. It had worn her out, but she had finally walked far enough that there was no longer any sign of the commune. She had seen the snake, but, although she had searched every hollow, she'd only seen the birds and squirrels that played nearer the commune. She wondered if they were tame.

"Okay, kids, time to wash up for lunch." Lawrence stood last in line to the sink. Rick inspected the hands before he let them go, so it took a while. Soon she was up there, scrubbing.

"Rick, the doctor told me once about germs. She said they were like little organisms." (She pronounced it "organ-(pause)-isms.")

"Yes. The way you kids handle your food, we like to see your hands clean." He inspected hers, then gave her a towel.

"But—food comes from the ground. It's just dirt, today." Lawrence wiped vigorously against the coarse cotton cloth.

"Aren't we killing them?" she blurted when Rick said nothing.

He looked at her seriously. "It's important that your hands be clean."

Lawrence threw down the towel and stalked out. It was just like Rick to answer her as if she were like the other kids! She went to look for Vance.

There was a piano, and a whole wall full of books. Lawrence got up to study the titles. "Haydn," the rings whispered as the piano began to play by itself. Lawrence whipped around at the sound, then shrugged when she saw no one at the keys. The instrument was probably a machine. She turned back to the books, trying to shut her ears, but the rings probably would have continued the melody anyway, quite like the way titles appeared before her eyes as memories freshened. "I read that one!" an eager voice flickered.

Lawrence finally pulled out a book and flipped through it. She saw only blank pages. Words would come weakly only now and then. Memory was poor; the "history" of the braindead was given little significance.

Vance took the book away from her and smiled until his eyes crinkled. "True art is transitory, as a revolution must be. It fills the need, then disappears."

Lawrence walked into the office and stood next to Vance's chair. His screen was open, but she politely kept her gaze from it. He continued working a short time, then sighed. "I know, I know," he muttered. "My office has no door for a purpose. What do you need?"

Lawrence waited until he cleared the screen. "Nothing. I thought you wanted to talk to me."

"Lawrence, this happens every time. Are you sure you don't want anything?"

"No, I have plenty to do." She pointedly looked out the window at the summer day.

"Explain it, then. I admit, sometimes I have something I'd like to tell you, and you always seem to know and show up here. It's uncanny."

Lawrence glanced at him quickly, solemnly, but said nothing.

"Have you been learning government?" His tone sounded casual, but maybe this was what he wanted to know.

"Sociology," she corrected. "You know I have."

"Do you know why?"

113

Lawrence thought. The days were spent oddly past the crafts, science, and music. She had to spend her free study time with the machines, scanning for culture. She even got wafts of history doing that, and it made her tremble. But Vance insisted. She wasn't sure it was right. She had to learn how people were cooperating at the Center, and what kind of people existed. She was to learn what was true. She was supposed to look around her for ideals manifest. She was also supposed to interpret what was unsaid but just as true. For example, what they thought was important, not just what they said was important. When she encountered the commonplace or what she already knew, she was not to abandon it at once. Rather, she should see if she could incorporate it into the new knowledge. All in all, it was a tiresome, unending project that failed to enlighten her one bit. "No," she finally answered.

Vance laughed. "Let me guess. You have ten ideas as to why, and you want me to tell you which ones are right. Okay. Remember our fight about giving, answering questions?"

"Fight?" Lawrence was so confused, she sat down with a plunk.

"Well, okay, it wasn't a fight. Maybe I just sensed your stubbornness. Learning this stuff prepares you for when I ask you to give me something."

Immediately Lawrence asked, "When?"

"When you're ready."

"Now?"

"No." Vance walked over to the windowsill. "I wanted to show you something." He picked up a thick brown object and brought it to her. "Here," he said, holding it out.

Lawrence looked at it mildly. "What is it?"

"It's a book."

Lawrence shook her head, meaning "you didn't answer me."

"Well, look at it." He thrust it at her. "Take it."

She took it carefully and felt the cover. "What is this stuff?"

"Leather." Vance paused. "The skin of a cow, an extinct animal."

Lawrence laughed. "No! It doesn't feel like—"

"Yes. They scraped its—fur off."

Lawrence felt safe. It was probably just plastic. There was no way they could take skin and . . . She opened it. "Oh, it has words in paragraphs. No diagrams, though. What are these little things?" She showed the page to Vance, pointing.

"Those are quotation marks, to show somebody speaking. Don't read it. It's fiction."

Lawrence thought. No, she hadn't been warned about any dangers associated with fiction. "Why not?"

"It's like the side effects of a learning machine."

Still, Lawrence did not scream or fling the book away. She obediently ignored the words and studied how the book was made. Vance had always given her time to think. The only problem with that was that eventually there was going to be a lot of long pauses.

"Why wasn't I warned?" She handed the book back calmly.

"You don't know of their existence." Vance closed the drawer firmly on the volume. "That's better than letting you find out and then denying you them."

"I see." Lawrence thrilled at how mature those two words sounded. "Why, then, did *you* give it to me and then tell me not to read it?" she asked haughtily. Lawrence did not rebuke him here; she was merely curious.

Vance looked away from her. "You need to see what can be done."

"Do I? What is it?" Lawrence liked his answer, though it seemed irrelevant. She gestured vaguely at the book within the drawer. "Am I to do that?"

Vance didn't seem to understand, which was odd, since he started it. "Specifically?"

"No!" Lawrence waved her hands in frustration. "Generally. I mean . . ."

"Yes. What is that called?"

Suspiciously Lawrence glared at him. "I'm asking you."

"What would you call it?"

This time it came through, much more clearly than it had ever done before. Empirical experiences. Lawrence took a deep breath and turned to sit at the screen. She lifted her hands and waited. No, there need be no more preparation. Begin.

Her fingers caressed the keys. Vance ran over to hit 2D. At an angle the teacher/student screens diverged, so that at her side he could read what she fed into it:

I WAS WONDERING IF THERE WERE NOT MORE. THEY WERE TEACHING US MUSIC, AND I THOUGHT IT WAS EFFORT AGAINST IMPOSING SILENCE. IF I HAD DONE NOTHING IT WOULD HAVE CRUSHED ME.

Here she lifted her fingers. "It was becoming my rhythm board," she explained to Vance. "You probably don't know about that."

"It's in your record," he murmured.

Lawrence turned back to the machine. This particular section still beckoned.

BUT THE MUSIC IS COALESCING OUT OF THAT AND IT'S FIGHTING BACK. IT'S POWERLESS, THOUGH. AND I WANTED TO DO SOMETHING ELSE, FREE UP SOME SPACE. I SAW THE CHAIR AS ENDLESS VARIATIONS.

"Ah, yes, the chair," murmured Vance. "I hadn't thought it important."

Lawrence sat slumped, staring at the screen. It just flowed into another branch of her existence. She saw then, in a flash, that her life might possibly be a logical construct of cause and effect, and she might be dependent upon factors that hindered her. While it was true that the chair was yet another effort similar to that which produced a rhythm board, her future efforts might transcend the terrarium and the abuse. Yeah, that. Oh, well, might as well finish it.

I TRIED TO BRING FORTH SOMETHING I'D NEVER SEEN BEFORE. IT SHOWED CREATIVITY. THAT IS GOOD, OR REWARDED.

Lawrence, still seized, forced herself to stop, pulling her fingers up, but not letting them relax.

"You seem to have the idea."

Idea? Lawrence turned to him before she realized she had her eyes closed. "Reaping," she said, opening them. "Isn't that just giving them what I have?"

Vance shook his head. "No. That is purging. Reaping involves them taking." He waited a little bit, then said, "It is called art. You are an artist."

Lawrence neither accepted nor rejected this. "What does an artist do?"

Vance seemed to be struggling for words. "That's an ancient question. One of those with too many answers."

Lawrence got up and walked over to the book. She had her left hand on the cover before she remembered. "Oh. Wait a minute." She went back to the screen to erase it.

But Vance was already saving it, locking up. He looked at her, eyebrows raised. "What were you going to do?"

"Erase it. Move. Let me do it."

Vance stood in her way. "You're not supposed to know how to erase it. We need everything you've done, and even then we'll probably not get everything."

"Why not?" Lawrence studied the situation, ever ready to jump and hit the proper key sequence.

"Because little kids don't think to put down everything, and when they do, it's not spontaneous."

Lawrence took the opportunity to thrust her hand around him and hit the keyboard. He grabbed her arm.

"It's too late. You don't know how to erase after lock anyway."

Lawrence stilled and tried to calm her breathing. He was right; besides, it didn't matter. Feigning indifference, she went over to the book. "That's not really animal skin, is it?" Her voice trembled.

Vance studied her expression, which she tried to keep calm. Strangely, she was not on the verge of crying, so it was not that hard. Finally he shrugged. "Sure."

Lawrence comforted herself with disbelief and skirted around him to leave. Purging sounded interesting; maybe that's what she was doing when she fed the machines. Maybe it was a good idea to stop erasing so much of it.

The wind whipped her face as she flung herself down the rocky slope. A path did exist, albeit winding and narrow, but the storm had made it a stream. Still, Lawrence triumphed, it's the fastest way to get there. Her boots scraped their soles against the tiny gravel that nicely coated the humps to the side of the stream. Intent on watching her feet so as to keep her step, Lawrence kept pushing her hair out of her eyes.

The clouds were full, had been for days, but at the moment no rain fell.

"Good," muttered Lawrence. "That'd be just one more thing to worry about."

Thunder cracked, and she gulped. She pulled the blanket tighter around her stooped form. It was very cold, and all she had on was a half-shirt. Only now to her Southern mind did it connect: there might be snow.

Lawrence entered past the larches of the valley. Hail stones greeted her. A small one chose to lodge in the tread of her boot, causing her to fall quite hard on her butt.

"Ugh!" she grunted. "Worse than gravel. Better than having them falling from the sky, though, I guess." She tugged at the hailstone, contorting herself so she could blow on it. Eventually it loosened, slipping out of her hands.

A movement caught her attention. Near a decaying gray building on the flatlands something walked. It seemed to be coming toward her, so Lawrence peered closer. Tingles crawled up her back; she recognized fear.

The woman's eyes were very bright; Lawrence stared at her face a long time, her own rapidly ranging from fear to friendliness to worry to, finally, impassivity, before she managed to calmly say, "Hello."

Those eyes! The lightning, white and wide behind them in the sky, could not compare. As they stared blankly, Lawrence was at last able to see them as blue, the rare color her own eyes took, but their glare, their paleness.

Lawrence stood and hobbled over to her. The woman nodded and turned, heading back to the buildings. Lawrence now saw two of them, one smaller and not so decrepit.

They paused at the larger. Lawrence let her continue to the fields and stayed to study the barn. It *was* similar to those that stored grain, beans, peanuts. It certainly wasn't meant to be lived in. The walls were not insulated to conserve energy. It was just for storage.

The woman herded several animals toward the barn from the field, and Lawrence moved from the door to let her by. The animals were interesting. She watched the woman pat the large black and white creatures and was tempted to do the same. They seemed so meek.

Now the woman was squatted beside the female, and Lawrence saw fresh milk squirt out. Sickened, she turned and left for the other building.

It too was uninsulated. Lawrence marveled at the thin cracks shining through the tar paper. A huge, smelly fire burned in the kitchen. Lawrence coughed and wiped her stinging eyes, yet she was drawn to its warmth. She crouched beside it and stuck her fingers in close to the flame.

Ouch! Lawrence yanked her scorched fingers back just when the woman entered and, like her, came near the fire and huddled. Lawrence watched her face openly, yet the woman merely stared into the fire, not responding at all. The flame in those bright eyes dimmed them.

Finally the woman stood, and Lawrence imitated her. From the oven she brought a steaming mound of cornbread in a black pan. She placed this on the small, chunky table, along with the beast's milk and a piece of flesh. Without looking at Lawrence again, she sat and started to break bread.

Lawrence eagerly accepted the crumbly, thick slice of cornbread and gulped the yellow, rich globs. It was not quite hot enough to burn her, but, still, after a few bites, she had to stop. It tasted odd. She choked on its moistness.

During her pause, the storm hit. The woman's lantern held steady while the world roared outside. Lawrence glanced around, and, seeing no window, tried to imagine what it must look like. She sipped the white, foamy stuff to clear her throat, and again choked. The meat she left alone.

The woman calmly continued eating, not looking up once. Lawrence sat mealless, searching for the source of her disquiet. Closing her eyes, she found it: the woman.

I hope it stays put. Gotta plow down there tomorrow. Barn'll probably blow. Then where will I be? Can she stay? Can she work? Seemed a bit scared there, unsure. Got to make her feel welcome. There's no one else. Stay alive. Work hard. Keep it going.

These were not words. The woman had no words. No language. No one, ever.

Lawrence went over and lay down on the bed the woman screened from hers. Lawrence, before those bright eyes, for the first time did not jerk off her clothes as if at last free. She even lay with her boots on, heart heavy with sobs unreleased.

The morning will come, and I'm nervous. Why? Lawrence thought. *Something's going to happen. If I relive it all, I'll know myself. That will eliminate me from the unknown and I'll finally have objective reality. Okay.*

The day was large. It was the first day different from the other days. The students filed in, eager to convey, though not so eager to admit adulthood. Only Lawrence could not share their concentrative bliss. The day was different, all right, but she could only dread it. They had known a long time that they would be asked, so they were ready. Lawrence watched them wriggle joyously with light envy. She chose to sit impassively, waiting for Vance's question calmly, confident he'd let her sneak through.

Number Five had spent all of yesterday morning working on the solar energy cells perched on the main building's roof, so she said she was going to be an engineer. Number Two had carved a table over months; he wanted to be a carpenter. Number One had counted the water bugs; she said marine biologist. Tom had cleaned the bed pans and dispensed medicine: certainly a nurse!

Then it was Lawrence's turn. When she stood before the class, she was at first too preoccupied with wondering why she was last. She tilted her gaze up and stammered, "Uh—I haven't decided yet."

The children snickered.

Vance dismissed class, as he was required to do, and waited quietly until everyone else had run out into the hall. He went to shut the door while Lawrence went and sat down. She watched him come back, terrified by his expression. It wasn't encouraging at all. She fiddled with her hands, flattened her hair, waited.

He sat beside her in Tom's desk, but didn't say anything for a minute. Then he turned to face her, smiling wryly, as if they were in on a joke alone. "It sounds silly, but I'm supposed to ask you to reveal yourself."

Lawrence nodded, waving her hand out languidly. "The aptitude tests. My records."

Vance shook his head and touched her arm. "No, that's not good enough. That's not what they want." He waited for her to look at him before he repeated, "Reveal yourself."

Lawrence didn't know what to do, so she chose the easiest. She pointed out the window. "That is me. All that out there is me." She got up and walked over to stare out at the warm spring day. Vance got up after a while, too, and joined her. They both stared, standing about a foot apart.

"You could be right," he murmured.

Lawrence glanced at him sharply, then started slinking toward the door.

"Not so fast. I want to show you something." Vance went over and moved his desk over to the window, clearing the raised platform. "Look." He climbed up on his dais and began, looking oddly to the opposite corner. His voice got stronger. "It is what we must do, Cinda. We agreed to this." He walked to his chair and sat down, hands covering his face. "Oh, Vance. I can't. I can't face the children. You're good, but I can't be the one to implement my theories."

Vance jumped up and ran to his original position. He taunted, "Oh, but you can every time there's a confrontation. You blaze then, all right." He ran back to the chair and again sat, only to leap up immediately to shout, "That's right, and if you don't like me being tough, then jump on it!"

"Wait! What are you doing? And don't ask me to tell you." Lawrence dashed over to him.

"I'm acting."

Lawrence stood up straight and alert. "Now *that* I've heard of."

"Yes." He smiled.

"What were you doing?" Her eyes darted back and forth, reliving the scene. "Is it evil?"

"I was acting out a play my wife and I wrote."

Lawrence tried to picture it. "Wife? What's that?"

"Well, she wasn't my wife, okay? She was my sole companion."

Lawrence had to step back then, ending her slow jaunt to the stage. This newcomer (and she persisted in calling him that, because everyone else had always been there) was truly stranger than she had thought.

"If you love somebody, Lawrence, and can't get along with others as well as with them, you sort of have to stick with it."

"How long?" She had wanted to say we get along, don't we, or something else, maybe about love. Instead, her mind had convulsed, so she stuck to a more permissible curiosity.

"Six years."

"Wow." She sneezed. Whose turn had it been last time to clean the schoolroom? It was dusty. She wiped her face and kept going. "Why are you showing me this?"

"I'm going to teach you how to act."

"What does that involve?" She felt worried, yet excited, that she could touch the forbidden.

"Well, not exactly act, but to not be yourself. To hide what you feel. To show what you don't feel. It will help you, believe me."

But Vance had given himself away. She could see him better now. Craft had won her early. She had learned to keep her mouth shut and watch the hurtful others. She had learned the necessary stratagems and was able to avoid pain, sometimes. Later, she had watched interesting people, Vance most of all. Still, she did not know who he was, and now she knew why.

Lawrence froze her hands in place. Relax for now. Think about it later. Don't get nervous or cry now that you're unsure. "I don't want to do that. I want to be myself." There. That sounded right. She had sounded very firm and determined.

Vance, however, again looked at her with that odd smile. He seemed to be saying you know now. We both know. Lawrence shuddered without knowing why.

"Lawrence." His voice was silkily seductive, subtly suggestive. She began to imagine that it had always been so. "Haven't you been doing it all along?"

Lawrence for the first time sought out the nearer rings. "Look: Does anyone here know anything at all about Vance? Who is he? Why did he act the way he did?"

She heard a gene map snicker: "'Act!' Get it? Tee-hee!"

A woman came forward, black hair all gnarled, that she was trying to braid. "I can clear up some of your confusion. Vance was braindead."

"No!" Lawrence looked suspiciously at her flat black eyes. "Who are you?"

She shrugged. "Does it matter?"

"Yes, because I can't believe you without proof."

"Ah, but you don't want to believe me. I know. I led him there myself. He wanted so much to be a Mentor." She sounded wistful, eyes drifting, then they shot back to Lawrence. "It makes sense, doesn't it? He knew so much history, even little traditions, like a prison. He used to like to hold books, though I never saw him read them." The woman cheerfully talked, drawing closer. Lawrence watched the attempt at intimacy with distaste.

"Bah!" She stalked off, into the woods.

Lawrence had held the computer screens too long, seized by a thought. The machine bleated, so she stopped the memory entirely. "Oh, yeah?" she muttered. "You ain't going to be forcing me on, faster and faster. I can stop whenever I want to, or whenever I need to. So there!"

Comfortable now in the empty pause, she returned to her thought. *Ever since Career Day, everyone seems to keep asking me what I'm going to be giving. I don't know, and they're just making me nervous. I've got years to decide.*

Lawrence felt a little better, so she released the frozen screen and raised her fingers again. The whirring outside had ceased to exist. It was just the farm truck, anyway. Now in the quiet she could easily concentrate on her studies. Math awaits! She switched from Diary to classwork. Her request wouldn't go through. She hit the requisite key pattern again, heart racing. Nothing. Maybe her freezing of the screen had broken it.

She looked at the panel with relief. A flashing light told her that a message needed to get through, that's all. She accepted it to read: MEET ME UP ON THE HILL. Lawrence instantly hit erase, practically before the words were through tracing, then took a deep breath. Reluctance weighed her down at first, but she knew she'd go eventually. He had probably just now entered the message, so he was, at best, just now leaving. She was determined not to get there first, even if the last eight times had seen her going to him for help. Now that he had asked her, instead of merely assuming she would come to him, she'd go, and pretend that she hadn't been ignoring him lately. This method she'd thought up to get his attention must have worked, for he had stooped to sending a traceable message.

It was good that he'd been there quite a while before she made it. "About time," he muttered after he stopped throwing pebbles off the cliff.

Lawrence stood for a while admiring the view. Though everyone called it the hill, it was really a massive rock thrust out of the ground, complete with cave at the bottom, crevices and strata in the middle, and pines on top. "I erased your message."

"Wasn't necessary. I meant it to dissolve in two seconds. Don't tell me you're faster than two seconds."

Lawrence shrugged, pleased. "Okay. I extended it."

Vance paused. "I don't believe you," he said in a strained voice.

"Go ahead and panic. All you did was tell me to come up here." Lawrence kept looking out over the mountains. If she didn't directly observe him in his rare states of openness, she learned more.

"Why did you make me send it? Why didn't you just come, like you used to?" he pleaded.

Lawrence kept silent. If there was one thing she detested, it was stupid questions.

"Okay, forget it." He sighed and pulled out a piece of paper. "I'm just jumpy, because I got a letter today."

Lawrence couldn't help it. Her eyes darted to the strange material. "Is that a letter?"

"Yes. From my wife. Imagine. A letter after all this time." He was feasting his eyes on it, ignoring her completely.

"Where is your wife?" she asked automatically, but not enthusiastically.

"She is in prison."

Lawrence's eyes darted to his triumphantly. "There are no prisons."

"There is one. I don't know who gets sent there. They took her a long time ago and didn't take me. Meanwhile, I study what it takes to go to prison, and what it takes to survive there. Your creeks with their white noise, for example," he ended cryptically, then stared at her, as if asking her for help.

Lawrence turned away, uncomfortable, and thought before asking, "What is a prison, exactly?"

"Yes. I need to know that, too. I have her letter. I might soon know." He looked at her pathetically. "I haven't seen you in a while."

She shrugged.

"What have you been doing lately?" His tone became almost conversational as he refolded the letter and stuffed it back into his pocket. Lawrence watched it disappear disappointedly. He looked up at her and grinned. "Wait. I know. You're eleven. You're supposed to be figuring out what you're going to do."

Lawrence's heart sank. No matter how she tried to avoid it, there it was. People expecting her to . . ."I'm not, though. I'm just working on my studies. Maybe then I'll become more capable, more worthy in their eyes."

Vance vigorously laughed at this, so that she frowned.

"Why did you call me here?" she asked sharply.

Vance sobered immediately. "You are my only friend here."

Lawrence could feel her heart pound. It was blinding. She could not speak.

"Have you figured me out yet?" he asked gently.

Now that was a strange question! She stared at his desperate look. "I don't understand," she whispered. Or did she? Maybe Vance had the same problem she did. She watched his expression smooth and she knew she had it. He even nodded, encouraging her. She could begin immediately.

"There was a smooth concavity here before you came. Then you, a point, sadly above the curve. It spread. You disrupted us. But that's okay. I can't see why it can't be like that." She moved her hands out and over, then pointed up above the level her hands had made. "To be there, beside you, or down there. What difference does it make?"

Vance looked impatient all through her speech as he nodded briskly, nervously. "No, Lawrence. That's you. Not surprisingly, you've got us mixed up." He sat down on a rock. Lawrence did likewise.

Like she always did, she changed the subject rapidly. "What is it when you worry about people's motives, or you figure you're being —"

"Baited."

"Is that what it's called?"

"No. That's the word you were wanting to complete your sentence. I think you are thinking of paranoid." He fingered his letter once more.

Leather. And now, baited, paranoid. Words that weren't in the big word memories. How did Vance know them?

Again he took out his letter, and that was all right. Why should he bother with her little problem at a time like this? He mused, "She must have learned to write, if it is hers."

"I can write," Lawrence supplied, then stopped, waiting for him to ask her what had motivated her into using her hands to imitate letters that glowed on the screen. Tom had helped her, of course.

"Yes." was all he said. "It might become useful again someday. Let me try to help you here. I think you are probably seeing yourself as a passive succor. But you won't be bound to that route. You'll fight it."

"But if that is what I am . . ." She wasn't even sure what he was talking about; she just wanted to argue.

Vance laughed. "Lawrence, don't pretend you understand when you don't. Passive succors work at the prison."

Lawrence frowned. She had thought he meant something more general.

"But I was speaking more generally. Active succors change society to make it better; passive succors just tend the hurt."

"I don't want to be paranoid," she blurted.

"Now wait a minute. If I recall correctly, you yelled at me when I first met you. You've always been rebellious." He had that look again, and she hated it. It was like he was telling her which mold to fit in to make him happy.

"I didn't yell out against your stupid society. I yelled at everyone who wasn't listening to me!" Lawrence caught herself blubbering, and tried to stop it.

"No, you weren't," he laughed. "You were yelling at me." Vance sobered and quickly looked away.

"Yeah." She was quieter. "I figured you wouldn't do anything. You were just fake friendly, like the others, like that man."

"What man?" Mentor foremost, Vance listened for any sign of earlier sexual abuse from this man.

Lawrence shifted. "Oh, it seems silly now. A man came to ask me about my rhythm board."

"Oh. During the tests, I presume. They usually bring along a child psychologist. What did you expect?"

Lawrence's voice hardened. "I didn't *expect* anything. I was only four."

Vance awkwardly put his hand on her shoulder. "I don't know, Lawrence. I wouldn't worry too much about this career thing. Lots of kids change their minds, or don't pass the tests."

"But I don't even have a decision to later change." Lawrence held herself still so he would think she liked being touched.

"So what? You've got a few years before I demand that you choose something. And when that time comes, pick something, anything, and keep as you were." He pocketed his letter and stood.

Lawrence got up, too. "I thought you wanted me for that project today," she said clumsily, not sure what to call it. "Something important."

"What? Oh, that. No. You'll know when the time comes. If you never know, that's just as well. We will have failed, and that's fine, because I don't expect much anymore."

Lawrence watched him.

"I wouldn't . . ." he began after a while, when Lawrence's attention had wavered.

She again looked at him, easily, calmly.

"I would like to see you around," he stumbled.

"Sure." She smartly turned and headed down the hill.

At the bottom of the hill Lawrence found the tree, or what was left of it. A huge stump, freshly cut, filled the path.

"Oh, no! Now how am I ever going to get back?" She looked around. That was the tree all right, though the shining silver root next to it looked new.

"This isn't the garden ship, though. It's—" She turned around, expecting to see the rock and Vance. "Well, I thought it was . . ." She turned back to the stump. "Still, the tree has been cut. That must mean *something*."

Lawrence pulled out the Elaborynth and smoothed it out upon the stump. It fluttered quite a bit up there, clear of trees so the wind could blow, so she again reached into her pockets to get pins and fastened it carefully all around. This simple task took all of her concentration. Only when she was done could she really look at it.

Lawrence found herself nodding. It was exactly as she remembered it. "Here it is. The humans' world, just one tiny bit of history, just one tiny bit of the Cube." She walked around to the other side, eyeing it all the while. Once she stumbled against that slender root and had to catch herself, balancing a palm on "prison." "Really, though, it's Vance's world. My world is the Cube, and it's much better." Still, she had made this one, too, and having it before her now made her feel more like a real person, a full one.

"It's as if I need to be defined by what I've made. I feel that way because, at every turn, they wanted to see what I had done. They kept records of everything. Sometimes, though, on a cool, pleasant day, I'd do nothing. I'd just enjoy the not-self. Is this human? I thought being human was to play with the elements." She looked down at the tawdry Elaborynth. "The Cube is not a facsimile. It's like a brain. The least I can do when I get out of here is tell everybody what I've experienced, tell them what the Cube is."

Lawrence strode into the tall, wet grass, solid stick ready. The smooth bark against her hands, the midafternoon sun after a brief storm, and Vance's single hut before her combined to give her strength. She banged the door firmly with the stick.

He answered rapidly. "How many times do I have to tell you? I hit the wrong key just now."

Lawrence dropped the stick and glared. "You know vast and well these doors are too thick for my delicate hands."

Vance waved her inside. "I'm grading screens, but that can wait. What do you want?"

"I need you to do something for me. It will save my brain, I promise. Listen." She paced back and forth, open, excited, hands gesturing. "They're short on the farm. Say I'm sixteen."

"Now wait a minute. Don't you think everyone around here *knows* you're twelve?"

"Oh, Vance, of course they do, but they don't care. They're desperate. All I need is to be put on the records as sixteen." She blushed. It still seemed too much to ask.

Vance went over to the window where he could just see the corner of the fields. "I don't see why not. Except, why? What's so glamorous about farmwork?"

Lawrence shrugged. "It'll get me out of school. That's all I care about."

"And what's wrong with my school?" Vance mocked anger, horror, and humor.

"Ah, I don't know." Lawrence walked over to the wall and bounced her foot against it. "It irritates me to get in there with the others and . . . sometimes I wish I were stupid. Then I wouldn't have to fool with—" She fluttered her hand. "Whatever."

"Have you talked with the farmers yet?"

"Uh, no. I talked with the man who runs things. He said they could use another worker."

"What's his name? Charles?"

"I don't know. I didn't ask, naturally. What do I care?" Lawrence glanced at him to see how he took that.

He smiled. "I know Charles. He's okay. A bit argumentative, but fair. But what are you going to do about schoolwork?"

Lawrence fumed. "I can learn on my own."

"And high-tech? When it comes?"

"I'll be running machines on the farm." She lifted her chin.

Vance went over to the screen. "If you're sixteen, I have to put down what you want to be. Shall I put down artist?"

Lawrence walked over and kicked her stick. "That again! I don't understand. You try to explain it to me, and I can't see it as anything but an extension of myself. I said as much once. High-tech is a part of the adults they can't separate out when they train us. I mean, they can't be children again, right? That's how I feel about art. We do it all the time in class. It comes out in torrents—" She stopped, struck by an idea. She shuffled over to him. "Why'd you bring it up now, of all times?"

"Those farmers like to call themselves artists, so I wondered."

"Charles?"

"Yes. So, why? Is it just a coincidence?"

Lawrence lowered her brows. "I think you're making too much of this. I just want—"

Vance drew nearer and said, "Look at me."

She looked straight into his rich brown eyes.

"First you have to do something for me. Remember?"

Lawrence balked, then paused to reach deeply inside herself. There was something there, a feeling she got right before she did something that got the teachers all excited. She itched to create. Repressing this, she sighed. "No. It'd take too long. I'm hungry. I'm too excited," she muttered, withdrawing.

Vance looked away and down. "All right." From where he stood, he easily reached over and ran his fingers through her hair, dislodging a leaf.

Lawrence stiffened.

"You don't like that, do you?" he murmured, almost in her ear.

"Yes. I prefer to remain alone, if you don't mind."

Vance kept his hand there, gracing her shoulder.

Eventually she relaxed. As long as it stayed there . . ."Besides, you didn't keep up your end of the bargain. I didn't learn everything."

"I taught you everything I knew. Of course that's not everything." He pulled his hand away and walked over to a drawer. From it he drew a massive, thick sheet of paper. He put it on the table and smoothed it down. Then he pulled up a chair. "Sit here. Give it all to me." Vance forced the words out in a blur.

Lawrence still hesitated. It would feel so good to fill up that sheet with ink. She moved toward it, then yanked herself away from the odd temptation.

Vance shrugged fully. "You will, or else you'll still be twelve."

Lawrence decided then to run. It wasn't worth it, really. She could stay in school. But she needed it as badly as he did. She found herself walking over to the paper and sitting down. He handed her a tool, and she began to draw.

What she drew was the culmination of all she could find out. What she drew was her extrapolation and guesses about what had been, is, and will be. She drew the structure of the communes, the occupations, the relationships. She drew the city and its history, speculating on what had caused it to be raised. She drew the prison, faintly, because she still wasn't sure it existed. She drew the communication vortex, and the future. She wasn't even aware how she came up with all this as she detailed motives and fluctuations. She could eventually distance herself so that her mind could rationalize and explain that this was all guesswork. Vance had started cooking immediately upon her attempt, and she ate haphazardly, at random, whatever he put in front of her, continuing to draw. After three hours Vance slammed the cutting board across it.

"Break time," he said shortly.

Lawrence shivered, gazing up at him blindly. "Maybe you don't know me. What's a break?"

Vance merely lifted her out of the chair and walked her to the door. She was pulled around the building a couple of times before she could think to move for herself. Still seized by the diagrams, unconsciously she wandered a bit into the woods, and she suddenly found herself alone, fingering a beggar lice flower. She turned to speak to Vance, but he had gone back inside, so instead she muttered to herself, "I wonder what grows elsewhere, that's all." Some time passed somehow, she had no idea how much, and she was leaning against the cabin watching the sun near the horizon when Vance came out and got her. Lawrence's mind centered then, and she happily walked briskly to the unfinished project.

When she got back in, though, she was given a fresh sheet of paper. "Hey!"

But Vance was ready, for he quickly intoned, "A fresh start, fresh ideas."

Lawrence grumbled and began again. She drew and drew and still could not bring herself into the equation. "All the artists do is one word," she said once. Later she muttered, "Where's the center?"

Here was a deep, cold mug of water. She drank, watching Vance as at a distance in the dusk quietly tidying up her scribbled sheets. He must have handed her a lot; she hadn't noticed. Lawrence spread her fingers wide on cloth, while accepting the cedar twig Vance brought her.

"Oh, I meant to ask. How did you get the paper?" But then she knew, so he didn't answer.

Once several hours later she stood and suddenly became aware. The door to the back step was open. A mild breeze blew in, wrapping itself around her. Lawrence became aware of the heavy, dark clouds, the dust on the floor boards, the star above the great pines that were always stolid against a solid blue sky, Vance coming from the kitchen with the last of the food. She accepted a hot potato, gnawing it abstractedly.

"I'm not in it yet. I can't draw myself in," she told him.

Vance sat down to face the door, brightening the light panel as he did so. "Maybe that's good." He sounded more tired than she felt.

"No." Lawrence cracked her neck back and forth to relieve the strain. "I've got to be in it. But how?" She rubbed her right arm. "I probably should come up with something, shouldn't I?" She looked at him shyly.

He only shrugged. "It's your life."

Again Lawrence sat down to draw. Almost immediately she said, "Here's you."

Vance jumped up to grab the sheet, then paused, stepping back. "No, not myself. I don't want to know."

You'll find out anyway, stupid, when I'm done. I'm not crossing anything out, Lawrence thought viciously.

Lawrence was finally through. She titled the final sheet ELABORYNTH and stood sulkily, actually dully, tiredly. "Okay. Here it is." She stared into the corner with eyes too dry to cry. "Am I sixteen?"

"Yes." Vance was standing, stretching.

Lawrence looked down to rub her hand against the table. "Well, don't study it too closely. It's only the best I could do. If you ever see me in the picture, maybe we'll meet again." It was odd. She honestly could not remember a thing she had drawn. "When you experience me as an adult, maybe then." Lawrence went outside and walked to the corner of the hut. She had a hard time finding that star now, but there it was. It was still showing, though clouds covered a third of the sky.

Vance came up beside her. She waited for him to say something, but he kept looking at the stars, smiling a very small smile.

"I'll miss you," she said, then she headed for the children's room.

Lawrence wheeled herself out to the prison yard, then allowed the guard to take over. He pushed her to a shaded corner and handed her pen and paper. She fumbled with it.

"Here." He stooped to help her.

"Vance?" she asked weakly. "Thank goodness you're back. I need to ask *you* why, not your wife or whoever she was."

"It's okay," he said gently. "Whatever you want to do."

The stump returned to her memory. "Vance, I saw it just now! The Elaborynth!" She grinned up at him, delirious.

He grimaced. "I lost the Elaborynth years ago."

"Did it ever change? I mean—"

"It was just a piece of paper. It couldn't change by itself."

"Oh." She approached it from the other side. "Was it accurate?"

"Yeah, I guess so, as far as it went. Here's the prison after all."

"And I saw your wife," mused Lawrence.

"What happened?" they asked simultaneously.

Vance answered first, shrugging. "I ended up here. It's not too bad."

"No. I mean, why were you so paranoid? I hear from the rings that in the past they tried to suppress artists, but not art. Something to do with worshipping celebrities. They had great wealth and power. But now they're farmers." She tried to look him in the eye. "Harmless."

Vance laughed shortly. "I had good reason to be paranoid. I ended up here, didn't I?"

"Yeah. I guess what I'm asking is . . ." She stood up, firmly planting her legs, wheelchair forgotten. Her hands felt the muscles on the sides of her thighs while Vance watched. "What I'm asking is, why did you have to go fuck with *my* mind? What were you trying to do?"

Vance looked away. "You're right. First your body, then your mind, correct?" He turned back to her, unrepentant. "What happened? Was your life ruined?"

Lawrence spun away from him and paced. Was it? Did Vance actually help her by giving her the frame on which she designed the Cube? Should she forgive him? No, never. But . . . she did go on to better things. And Vance's warning proved true. There *were* a lot of nasty people, people who were a lot nastier than he. Okay. All right.

"No," she finally answered, and smiled at the memory of Maricela.

When they told her to report to work after dark, Lawrence got suspicious. When they told her to bring her pieces, all of them, it started to come back to her. The agricultural center was a haven for artists. She almost backed out, but then she told herself that not every one of them could be an artist. It wasn't like they could hold a monopoly on farmwork. Some people liked to do it, some people were assigned to do it, and during the busy times of the year everybody did it. Lawrence decided to disguise herself as a hard physical laborer bored of school routine and all-out ready for the great outdoors. She could do it; Vance had taught her that acting stupid was her best disguise. Acting ignorant, really, was even better, but she had to act stupid first, or nobody would ever believe she was ignorant. Vance had said stupid people were the safest, which, of course, made his sort of sense. Lawrence was willing to try it.

She entered the storage building, practically empty now, and joined the others sitting on low benches, the kind they used for low hand labor, like picking strawberries, when they didn't crouch to sit on the benches but rather lay on them on their stomachs to snatch at the small red balls. She sat, trying to adjust her knees to the height, which was too close to the floor. Eventually, out of courtesy as more farmers filed in and the belief she'd never get comfortable that way, she gratefully took the softer dirt floor. Unnecessary chairs weren't allowed; Lawrence was surprised they had improvised, since there weren't enough to go around, anyway.

After she was settled, Lawrence took time to casually look around at the others grouped together, speaking in low voices. The small number ignored her, and more coming in did the same. She studied their bearing as the benches quickly filled and several joined her on the floor. What was it? Pride?

Finally Charles arrived. Lawrence suspected that he always planned to enter last. She therefore became determined to always enter first.

He walked over calmly, not strutting, to the one last clear bench opposite Lawrence. She remembered it being occupied, so maybe all of them had planned that, too.

Charles scanned the crowd. "We got a new worker the other day." He gestured. "Stand up, Lawrence."

She did so immediately, though she'd never been in a room with so many other people before. He head spun as she tried to breathe.

"Can you pull your own weight?"

Lawrence thought rapidly. She was already over a hundred pounds and taller than others her age. Could she pull one hundred pounds? And what for? "Yes." She decided to answer that to show she was used to hard labor.

Charles smiled dimly. "We'll see. Did you bring your opera?"

Lawrence stumbled in an indistinct, partially confused tone, "I wasn't sure what you meant by that. My school records?"

Many burst out laughing. Charles hooted. "You're not braindead. Vance told us about you. You're not stupid, either, so cut the acting. It wouldn't have worked, anyway."

Lawrence felt vaguely disappointed. If her acting wasn't any good . . .

Charles went over to the supply screen and began pressing buttons. "It's in here," he muttered. "Just be patient. Ah!" He smiled. "Got it! Stupid machine." He beckoned Lawrence, who meekly went over to stand beside the supply screen. "I've got it all ready to show." He projected the screen in a way different from 2D, which Lawrence had seen Mentor use daily. She stared with interest. Now everybody could clearly see the contents of the screen on the far wall.

The group could then see her star and weather charts, her growth data and seasonal records. They saw the class assignments in music, drawing, and screen feeding. They even saw her old rhythm board and sculptures. Then there were Vance's recordings of conversations, edited to fit his whim, and what she had entered as Diary. Lawrence watched it, too, and breathed a sigh of relief to learn that there was nothing there that came directly from herself for the reason of no choice.

Charles reversed, moving closer to the screen so that he could stop it precisely when he found what he was looking for. "Here's an interesting observation." He turned to look at Lawrence. "Why do you tilt the light panels?"

Charles' voice seemed to come from far away. Lawrence had been steeped in her work; experiencing it backwards had been unnerving. The resonance . . . Finally she shook herself and murmured, "The light bothers my eyes."

Charles destroyed the screen. Lawrence blinked. "Sensitive," he muttered. "Could be."

Lawrence waited. He kept his head down a long time. She glanced back and forth, wondering if she was supposed to do something. Some looked bored. Some were nodding. A redheaded man smiled at her.

Charles lifted his head and eyed her. "We don't accept just anyone. You have vision. We just can't see where it's going. It's best for you to hang around with us and learn, because we can't afford to waste you." He tossed his long, loose, straight black hair back.

Lawrence interrupted. "You think you speak for all?" she asked incredulously.

A few hooted, and Charles hesitated. Lawrence could already tell that this was rare for him. "It's your choice," he darkly said and went to sit down.

Lawrence blushed, but said nothing as she again sat on the floor. Someone tossed her a plaid flannel shirt. She knew what it was: the badge of outdoor farm work. She was surprised she had gotten it so readily.

Immediately upon sitting down the conversations began. Lawrence couldn't help but think, *This is what it is like to belong. Everybody ignores you.*

"I have an opus," a young woman began. "It's in the basement. I didn't want to show it tonight because I'd rather wait and show it in the city."

A young man interrupted. "But, Antem, what for? So far, we've been your best critics."

She pushed her short, curly bangs aside and answered, "I don't know. I still don't think it's very good." Antem passed her hand down her overalls. "I'm in a rut. The same patterns over and over."

"But where did you start? On the machines?" Charles accused.

She nodded.

"Well, what did you expect? I don't truck those things. They've got their own rhythms that interfere with your own. That's probably what it is."

Lawrence couldn't help it. "You mean there's a template? I didn't know that." It seemed easy, just blurting out like that.

"There's always a template," said the young man. "By the way, my name is Entov. The language, for instance. We never really do anything that's new."

"I don't know about that! Hi, I'm Celeste." She smiled briefly at Lawrence and then turned sharply back to Entov. "We're not braindead. It's not as if we have influences."

"The machines," Charles insisted.

Celeste chuckled, a knowing look on her face. "Yes, Charles, keep ranting about the screens." She sounded as if she were quite tired of it.

Antem spoke next. "The question is always, 'Who are we?' Do we know?"

The group brooded. Lawrence, who was wondering the same thing herself, pondered.

Antem continued, "Back to what I originally brought up, if you please. Does excellence depend on approval?"

"We exist, despite being ignored," Charles pointed out.

Entov complained, "What is art without an audience?" His tiny body shook with pride at this loud statement.

"Are we even artists?" queried Celeste.

Lawrence knew all about it, of course, but it made her jump to hear it spoken aloud by a stranger. Artist. She shifted eagerly.

Charles changed the subject, though not really. "Who gets reaped, ever? And how? 'Cause I betcha those force-learning machines reap."

"But that doesn't make sense," insisted Celeste. "They sow stuff. They don't yank it out."

Entov yelled while yanking his hand back the way Lawrence had seen farmers drive a tractor. "Put it into reverse! Yeah!"

Everyone chuckled, even Lawrence.

"We're supposed to be different," Antem said quietly. She lifted her head to look at everybody. Her words came out harshly. "It's ironic. Here we are, dying in our uniformity. I'd rather be reaped, because then I'd never know." She leaned her head on Entov's shoulder and managed to look melancholy.

Lawrence looked around. Practically everyone now had similar expressions. Her heart pounded. Reaping is craved?

"Reaped. That's my dream. Yeah." Celeste confirmed her suspicion.

Several seconds of silence followed while Lawrence rapidly analyzed what she had heard. Maybe her admittance was their attempt at diversity. They had chosen well.

A redheaded man who had not yet spoken started another topic in a friendly voice. "I'm going to get some bananas soon." He looked shyly over at Lawrence. "I'm Scott." He stopped then, abruptly, and blushed.

Charles snorted. "Wrong direction, pal!"

Scott looked genuinely puzzled. In his soft voice he asked, "Why not? I don't have to go to the city to accomplish something. I figure heading south is best now."

Charles shrugged. "Hey, if you need bananas, go ahead and go." He looked over at Lawrence. "It's late, and we're to start planting tomorrow. I think you should show up at dawn the first day. There's a lot to learn."

Lawrence nodded, automatically assimilating the simple knowledge while wondering where bananas came from. But there was more to it than that. What the heck did bananas look like as they grew? What plant was it from? Did it grow wild?

She got up bravely and lingered near the supply screen. Charles came over, eyebrows raised. "What do you want?"

"Do you need somebody on the egg trucks?" He had told her to call them that.

Charles' eyes were startled; the rest of him remained grim. "Oh, no, you don't. They're our greatest power. You've got to prove yourself first. Maybe in a couple of years you'll go."

Lawrence shrugged, trying not to look disappointed. Someone tapped her on the shoulder: Antem asked her to follow her to the sleep building, and she complied.

Lawrence lay in her cell. She kept ticking her fingers five, but it always came back again. How long had she been in this darkness? Five times one billion. Or she could add five more fingers to make ten; maybe then the time could go twice as fast. Both hands now ticked on, and she breathed deeper, finally sitting up.

Lawrence saw a prison saint standing impassively, waiting for her to acknowledge the tray of food.

"Kamela?"

It was hard to tell. She looked so old. She studied the strange gold-gray hair pulled tightly back. The right hand, beginning to shake from having to hold the tray so long, was red with bite marks.

"Here." Lawrence took the tray and put it aside. "Is this a . . ." She felt a waft of knowledge slide over from the rings of the braindead conglomerate. "Mental institution?" She used her own word next. "You're a psychcomputer?"

Kamela looked at her; her flat brown eyes were deader than ever.

Lawrence tentatively put her arms around her. She was stiff in Lawrence's arms.

"Maybe I did it all so I could get to see you again," whispered Lawrence as she held her. Absurd, untrue, but it opened Kamela up.

"I'm not supposed to see you, but I came anyway." Her voice was soft, forgiving.

Lawrence's mouth searched, and her hand came to cradle Kamela's right gently. Kamela bent her head to expose her neck and let Lawrence's left hand come up to loosen the cowl. Her mouth followed deeply into the cleavage, and Kamela stayed silent, did not moan.

Lawrence then lifted Kamela's hand and pulled her face away, cowed and made cautious by her too willing silence. Her eyes questioned Kamela about the hand, and she looked down at it unwillingly and sadly. "That's the feeding hand. They give me the biters."

Lawrence entered the library. It was hard not to turn and smile, because she still expected Vance to be there, as he had always been on the rare evenings she had chosen the library as a quiet place to learn. They had almost invariably been alone, so it was odd for Lawrence now to see one other person in the room. Just like old times. Lawrence openly took a glance. A girl about her age, doing her homework. Lawrence watched a long time, perverse to her original intent, because she knew the girl would not look up. Finally, though, she'd seen all she needed to see and turned to her own work.

Lawrence didn't turn on the screen right away because she wasn't sure what to do. Guilt had led her to consider spanning an opus, and Charles' hatred of the screens made her want to try them as a medium, but when she tried upon a cleared screen, her fingers would not move. She gave up at last and selected electronics, because she hated it and needed some review.

Lawrence yawned. She should probably only study about two hours tonight so she could get to bed early. She still wasn't used to her new schedule, but it made sense to work during daylight.

Diurnal. The idea seized her. She cleared the screen and selected biology. She was following migration patterns in her search for animal sleeping patterns when she sensed the movement of the girl. Lawrence simultaneously listened for her movements while she watched the screen shift. At the girl's third step she had trailed into the opus. Nothing worth hailing about, like, look, Charles, this is something, but it did bring together elements of herself that she hadn't thought of before. At the fifth step she had too many connections. And at the eighth: *If I learn everything, and form a pattern out of selected elements, will I have succeeded with my opus?* Lawrence stopped at the eleventh step, using her proven method of pausing the floating screens. This gave the girl a chance to butt in. She stepped forward shyly.

"Hi," she said, smiling brightly. "My name is Kamela."

Lawrence was nonplussed. She gave her a disturbed look. "Hello," she said lowly.

Kamela burst out laughing. "Aren't you going to say your name?"

"It's Lawrence," she said readily, gritting her teeth at the ridiculous custom.

Kamela looked politely at her screen. "What are you doing?"

"Homework," Lawrence shifted, amazed at how much questions bothered her. Just Vance had ever . . .

"But you don't go to school. I would have seen you there."

Lawrence looked at her suspiciously. "Yeah, so? I can still learn."

"What do you do?" Kamela corrected herself immediately. "I mean, what are you going to be?"

"I'm sixteen," Lawrence contradicted.

Kamela laughed, seemingly at ease. "No, you're not."

Lawrence shrugged.

Kamela pressed on. "You're probably about my age. Why aren't you in school?"

"I work on the farm."

Kamela sympathized. "That must be very hard work." She looked lingeringly at her own screen, which was now blank to conserve electricity. "I work hard, too, in a different way. I'm here every night. I have to study hard to get into medical school. I'm not brilliant or anything. It doesn't just come to me." Kamela allowed herself a brief jealous glance. "You sure do zip through those screens fast."

Lawrence casually said, "It's not hard, especially if you know most of it already."

Kamela really looked envious now, or unbelieving. "I came here because of your fantastic medical lab. Of course, the city will be much better. I wonder . . ." Here she looked at Lawrence slyly, though she was already confiding more than Lawrence would ever care to know. "I think I should get force-learning. I want so much to be accepted! Have you . . . have you . . ."

"No!"

Kamela jumped, wide-eyed. "Well, there's no need to yell! You're so smart."

"Some people are born that way, I guess," Lawrence said sharply, her memory choosing to forego any recall of vast amounts of effort made when young. "Why, you like those inlaid people?" (She was careful not to say "braindead.")

"It does seem to help, doesn't it? All the ones I've met, anyway. They . . ."

"Help what?" Lawrence suddenly became eagerly interested. Maybe Vance was wrong. Maybe the artists were wrong. Maybe there was really nothing to worry about.

"Oh, you know. It won't make you smarter, but you'll know more."

"Oh," Lawrence said, disappointed. She couldn't for the life of her understand why knowledge was so great. She was thinking maybe force-learning could do more, make her create, come up with something. But wait! Wouldn't it help give her elements to work with? She needed that, right?

Kamela finally sat down beside her. Lawrence sat uncomfortably, staring at the frozen screen while Kamela studied her. "I've seen you sometimes, and you're not with the farmers all the time. You're off a lot on your own. I think," she said timidly but forthrightly, "no matter what, no matter who you're with, you're always alone."

Lawrence, acting gears well-oiled, glanced calmly at her. "I can imagine worse things," she said dryly, heart pounding. An insightful person, all right. It came to Lawrence in a flash. "Do you want to join the psychcomputers?"

There was a long silence. Lawrence waited, then glanced over at Kamela, who sat, hands to temples, looking pensive.

"Hey," she found herself saying softly. "What's wrong with that?"

Kamela stood suddenly. "Let's go outside." She walked back to her screen.

Lawrence turned off her own screen and stood, surprised at how eager she had become.

Outside, Kamela offered her some pecans. Lawrence took the local produce readily enough, but she wondered how she could reciprocate. Bananas?

Kamela swiftly touched her arm; Lawrence jerked it away. "I know I talk a lot," Kamela whispered, "but I do that when I'm around people who don't say too much. I hope you don't mind."

Lawrence almost caught herself saying that she wouldn't be sitting there in the dark on a cold, gray stone bench in the extracurricular circle if she minded, but she held herself in, keeping herself to merely shrugging.

"Let's talk about something else," said a brisk, efficient voice that emanated from Kamela's mouth. "What do you do in the woods?"

Lawrence had just come to realize that it would either be Kamela asking questions, or herself asking questions, and she couldn't figure out which was worse. "Lots of things. What's it like where you come from?"

"Oh, pretty much the same, I guess." She looked pointedly at the rounded buildings that surrounded them.

"I've never been anyplace else," Lawrence moaned, then she straightened. "There's a cave in the woods about ten miles from here. It's the farthest I've ever gone."

"Oh!" Kamela whipped her head around, eyes dilated. "Will you show me?"

Lawrence turned to look at her fully.

"Oh!" Kamela breathed again. "I never noticed your eyes before. What a strange color!"

Lawrence flinched, blinking her eyes at Kamela's smooth, pecan-colored skin. Some people were pale, blue-eyed, after all. She stood. "I gotta go."

"Where?"

"To bed."

"This early?"

"Yes. I have to get up early to plant." She strode to the edge of the muddy circle.

Kamela trotted after her. "Goodbye, then."

Lawrence turned halfway, careful not to look at her. "Bye," she answered. "See you later." Inside, she added, *Not really*.

To the fields she notched yet another actor, yet another one who played nice, for who knows what motive, what new device to beg for Lawrence to give?

"Bleah!" She shook her shoulders and walked faster, past the peanuts in the crumbling red dirt.

The weaving shop was empty, the looms silent. Lawrence went past them into the cool, dark interior. Though the cotton was picked, cleaned, and carded, none were there to spin it. She sank her fingers deep into the rich, fluffy whiteness. Ah, it felt good!

The dye rooms lay silent, too. Lawrence opened up some of the tins to feast her eyes on the dark colors, then pounded them shut. She opened the door to the sewing room.

Immediately she could hear someone swathing the fabric onto bolts. She went inside quietly, shutting the door cautiously. Still, the worker paused at her sound.

"Hey, Scott! Need some help?"

"You bet! Where is everybody?" He grinned at her through a scraggly beard.

It was as she expected. Scott would be the same everywhere. It fazed her a bit, though. She turned to look at the door. "Nobody in there," she murmured.

"Yeah, and this is a two-person job, at least." He took a green length then, and folded it in half.

"You're supposed to be sewing, right?" Tentatively Lawrence felt around the situation. How old was she supposed to be?

Scott nodded. "But these were in a mess when I got here. I need to wrap them up, put them in order." He grabbed a bolt. "Here. Let's start this one."

Lawrence held up the end as he wrapped neatly. It was winter cloth, heavier than she expected. Her arms tired quickly. Scott waited patiently during her first break. She luxuriated in rest until he glanced at her to silently say, "Begin?"

"So you brought the work upon yourself," she surmised.

"Somebody's got to do it." He shrugged, even as he wound. "Besides." He stopped to look at her, as always smiling. "You showed up."

Lawrence came in from the cotton fields and rinsed off at the pump. Picking cotton by hand, as if it were an initiation. Still, she had the feel of it now, the firmness of the correct boll. She couldn't say she hated the work. The sun had beat into her head, and the bugs bit, but she felt like she was doing something. Tractors stuck you way up in the air; you couldn't even smell the soil.

Sharon joined her at the pump, swarthy skin flushed. She splashed, then stood dripping to ask, "You got a medium picked out?"

"Not yet," Lawrence answered pleasantly.

Sharon was not satisfied. "What do you need?"

"I'm not sure yet."

Sharon shifted impatiently. "We usually like to talk about our work in progress. It helps the project a lot. We're good critics. We know what to do. Of course, you don't have to talk about it constantly if you don't want to. Are you going to wait until it's finished before we see it?"

Lawrence saw Scott coming from the fields. When he saw her looking at him, he smiled. "I think that would be best," she murmured. These people hadn't wanted her to be too different, after all. Keeping her promise should be easy. She hadn't even started thinking of an opus; the creation process might take years.

Scott came up to them. Sharon moved back. "Hello, Lawrence."

Lawrence couldn't remember a time when someone was so glad to see her, and, unlike Kamela, it seemed so genuine. She couldn't help smiling back. "Hello."

Scott was silent as he splashed. Sharon left without saying another word. Despite her impatience, Lawrence liked her because she didn't fool with greetings and signoffs. She said they were meaningless.

"It's good, isn't it, sometimes?" Scott burbled through the water.

Lawrence thought she knew what he meant. "Yes."

He eyed her, shutting off the pump with a jerk. He probably wasn't used to people answering him so readily. "I meant," he stumbled, "the farm work. It's not too bad. It's got to be done. Sometimes, though, I get real joy out of it. Like today. I was in the flax, and the orchard. It seems right, to take the ripe foods to eat, to take the fibers to wear. I'm seeing the source." His mouth slammed shut as he blushed.

But Lawrence understood. "Yes. It's different from studying the woods. It's more active."

"It's going into my work," he said shyly, dripping. "The other artists, some of them, anyway," he shrugged, "got some strange ideas about what should constitute themselves, when really . . ." He stopped to look at her and swallow. "Anything will do, Lawrence," he said lowly.

She looked up at him, amazed. "What if I wanted to make everything?"

"Hey, if you want to do it, go ahead." He laughed, then looked disturbed. "Beats me why they won't give us towels," he muttered.

"What do you need a towel for?" Lawrence was already hot again.

He looked at her a long time, making her nervous. "Never mind," he said quietly. "Let's go eat."

The new artist was already there, serving up the lentils. She moved gracefully, as if attuned to the cooking assignment everyone got every two weeks. Lawrence watched her smile, flick her hair back, and she knew she was obsessed with newcomers. This one was rare; she was from the south.

Lawrence gathered up the lentils, rice, and water and started heading toward her usual spot in the corner.

"Don't eat there!" Scott interposed gently, blocking her way. "Come sit with us at the main table."

Lawrence shrugged and did so, not wanting to call attention to herself, especially in front of the new one. Charles smirked as she sat down.

"Got us anything yet?" he asked nastily.

Lawrence jumped. Charles wasn't even going to try to be nice, ever. She decided she hated him.

"Leave her alone, Charles," blurted Scott. "She's young."

Charles gave him a hard, long look that baffled Lawrence. "Yeah, she's young, all right." He turned back to his meal.

Celeste started. "We wanted to talk about whether art was communication. Sharon suggested it."

"Oh, no, not that again!" moaned Entov. "Let me eat."

"Go ahead and eat," Antem said gently, caressing his arm. Some snickered.

"Isn't art giving of oneself?" asked the new artist.

Lawrence's heart leapt. Vance had said . . . Ah, fuck Vance, she thought, reveling in her newfound ancient word. She stared hungrily at the new person. "What's your name?" she was dying to ask. No, not that. Just "who are you?" would do.

"I'm changing my name again," Entov supplied, grinning. "I think I'll be Spot, or Rover."

Everybody ignored him, though Lawrence thought it was interesting, to say the least. She had selected her own name after much thought eight or nine years ago, and she was still satisfied with it. Entov had taken her aside once and argued that since you were only going to be a number anyway, specifically, 12-8-20-367-4 [Region, Area, Commune, Year, Birth Order], so why not change your name at will? Lawrence now saw it as only futile protest. Better to be named.

"When you give of yourself," continued the new artist, "what does that mean?"

"It means you've communicated what's important about yourself," said Celeste.

"No," said the new artist intensely, persisting. "All this time I've tried to give myself, and never did. I told everybody to create something, as long as it was about me. And nothing was. Not really." She sighed. "Art communicates nothing."

Again a sense of melancholy pervaded the air. Lawrence glanced back and forth. What was she supposed to do, leave the fields and forests and assume sadness among friends? Vaguely she considered it a coverup of a plot whose goal was to encourage her to burst out with something. That was Vance paranoid thinking, though. Lawrence decided to only accept it, not dwell upon it.

Charles' eyes met hers as she gazed around at the glum faces. "You don't talk much, do you?"

Strange! Lots of people weren't talking. Lawrence looked down at her empty plate.

"I don't know why all artists have to be such blabbermouths," Scott interceded sternly. "Leave her alone."

"Hey!" Charles aimed his fork. "*You* leave her alone!"

"Charles!" Antem yelled. "Shut up!"

He grumbled and shoveled some radish salad into his mouth. "It's my duty as boss to keep an eye out for everybody," he muttered.

"Don't talk with food in your mouth. I'm taking care of her," Antem said mysteriously.

Lawrence uncomfortably swallowed the rest of her food and rose to go before anyone else had finished. She went directly to the door.

Scott half rose. "Where are you going?"

"To the library," she tossed casually over her shoulder.

"That braindead going to be there?"

Lawrence turned to look solemnly at Charles. "She's not braindead."

"Same as," he chuckled.

Lawrence just left.

Out of habit, Lawrence strode to the nearest cactus, fumbling at her belt for the sampler. "Oh, Jeffrey," she said happily. "I saw a bug back there. Check to see if you've got it." She stood waiting at the cactus for his reply.

"We have that," she heard Jeffrey say.

Lawrence nodded and jabbed her right hand onto the cactus needles. As the pain plunged deeply into her arm, she blinked tears back to see a kangaroo rat hop around the cactus to stare at her. It was so cute. Lawrence could now see the pen, the cage, the fence, the laboratory. Little black eyes in rows peered from the sterile white traps. It wouldn't hurt, would it, to pick one up, and pet it?

Lawrence yanked back her hand and licked off the blood as the kangaroo rat scampered away. "These are Kamela thoughts. Go away."

"Hey! Come over here! Look at this!" Lawrence frantically gestured to Kamela with her right hand, her left hand pointing at the earth. "See it?"

Kamela came over from smelling a fringed iris and bent down to see. "Ooooooh," she breathed. "What is it?"

"I don't know. I counted its legs. It's not a spider." Lawrence smiled benevolently down at her gray-gold head, hair glistening in the sunlight, and with great difficulty kept herself from touching it.

"Well. Should we collect it?" Kamela asked in a business-like tone.

"What for?" Lawrence was greatly disturbed, almost feeling an urge to wring her hands. Pick up the thing? Displace it?

"To see what it is," Kamela answered patiently.

"But . . . I'll look it up when we get back." Lawrence stood on the alert, ready to jerk Kamela away if she tried to touch it.

"I don't know," she mused. "We might wonder if it really had a yellow dot on its belly." Kamela stood up and shook her pants at the knee.

"But it does." Lawrence was confused.

"But it might be something else we forget," persisted Kamela.

"I don't forget." Lawrence said this calmly. "I've been doing this for years."

Kamela looked down at the bug. "It is frustrating, not to record what we see."

"I see a lot," Lawrence said nonsequitorially.

Kamela was quiet. Lawrence decided to cheer her up.

"You want to see the cave?"

"Oh. Is it far?" she asked vaguely.

Lawrence looked disgusted, because she'd already told her how far it was. "Ten miles."

"Oh, I don't think so. Not today, anyway. You got anything closer?"

Lawrence tilted her head. "Yeah. Right behind you. See that trunk? And the leaves — over here. They're sour. Taste one." She stripped a stem and handed the green, sticky froth to her.

Kamela rubbed her thumb over the bark. "How strange. Like skin."

"Skin?" Kamela was full of surprises. She constantly saw things in a way different from Lawrence's.

"Well, not the texture, exactly. The wrinkles."

Skin didn't have wrinkles! Not many, anyway. Then Lawrence remembered that Kamela worked in the geriatrics ward. She lifted the leaves as a reminder.

Kamela came over, mouth open, lips seeking the tender leaves.

Lawrence fed her, watching the closed eyes, the lips that curled, the biting teeth, the seeking tongue. She could watch that all day. A smile came to her as something inside her stirred.

Lawrence could not remember a day in which she had been so happy. The questing mouth, so red, was like the days before her shot. No, it wasn't that. What was it, though? She pictured Entov, now Rover, and Antem. Was it that?

It sure seemed to be. Kamela wanting to be with her, wading through the fields and seeing the flowers. Spring at its height, the sun warm, but not too warm. Her hand steadying Kamela's arm as she stumbled on a burrow, probably abandoned, though she had waited eagerly enough with Kamela to see.

The mouth was done, the swallowing completed. Lawrence found herself breathing hard, tongue out, firmly questing.

Kamela opened her eyes. They looked exquisite, as if Kamela had just woken up from a sensual dream. She laughed self-consciously. "I didn't leave any for you."

"That's okay," Lawrence said lowly, voice rough. She coughed.

While Lawrence stared, firmly in her spell, Kamela spoke. "You want to go with me to the doctor's today? You said you would."

Lawrence started, shaking herself from a daze. "Oh, yeah," she murmured. "It's time for my shot, anyway." She had been putting it off, even if not doing it wasn't allowed, because she wondered what would happen if she did start the bleeding for once. It would be something new. Something else to share with Kamela.

They climbed back slowly up a big hill, with Lawrence pausing every so often for her to catch up. At the top, Kamela stopped to sit on the orange square of soil to rest.

"Ah, come on, Kamela," coaxed Lawrence, pointing down at the cluster of buildings far away. "It's all downhill from now on."

Kamela glared at her. "I'm resting."

Lawrence compromised by crouching beside her, not sitting. "Look." She gestured upward. "It's going to rain."

Kamela squinted up at the clouds. "It's doubtful."

Lawrence stood up and walked over to a corner of the square. There was a flat, thick, upright rock there, and she kicked it. "I wish berry time would hurry up and get here."

"Me, too. I'm *thirsty*!"

Lawrence glanced at her, amused. "Well, they're not going to show up anytime too soon. Besides, the rain'll take care of that."

"I don't think it will rain."

The downpour caught them in the middle of the field just before the doctor's. Lawrence grabbed for the screeching Kamela's hand and ran for it. That time, she kept up pretty well.

They arrived breathless, Lawrence slamming the door. Though she knew she was giggling, she couldn't stop grinning at Kamela's beaded face. She shook the rain from her hair, then she squeezed it tightly to a rope, letting it pour and splatter. The wood floor absorbed it; she watched it glisten from the outdoor light. Then she glanced up, out at the rain. Still on the farm, she wondered if it would be enough, or whether the seedlings would be washed away. Her eyes, in search of a connection, timidly went to the inner door. Inside was the plastic, the sterile severity.

Lawrence stepped away from Kamela and began to slowly pull off her clothes to trade them for the green cotton gown Kamela had fetched.

The doctor poked her head in then. She frowned, directing her gaze to the source of her anger. "That floor won't last forever."

Lawrence stroked deliciously her accent. If you want to meet different people, get sick. Kamela had taught her this. Trouble was, Lawrence was hardly ever sick. There was plenty of time before "birth" to abort if any difficulties were detected. There were plenty of other eggs and sperm to choose from. So, it was just checkups every other year, and the antimens shot.

The doctor was from Region 3, way up the big river. She had once lived on a great lake. But she had come way down here, like Kamela, to learn the ways of our medical lab.

"Yes," Lawrence smiled sweetly, watching the doctor look her up and down as she listened to Lawrence slip into the easy smart-aleck tone. "Nothing does."

The doctor snorted and left, leaving the door open, a mocking invitation.

Lawrence briefly saddened. She had wanted to hear her gripe or argue, wanted to hear that delicious accent she could never capture. She even tried to imagine her own lips forming the words, but couldn't. She continued slewing water from herself, then accepted the gown from Kamela.

Lawrence went into the doctor's and climbed up on the high bed. The doctor swung the machine over her middle, then she prepared the shot. She gave Lawrence minimal touches, knowing her ways, though she had never consulted the psychcomputers. Kamela busied herself in the corner with the medical screens. Lawrence kept a mild eye on her throughout.

"Your eggs are fine," the doctor was saying. "But you'll still have to wait until you're twenty to be tested." She hoisted the machine and swung it aside on its arm until it clicked into place. "I wish it didn't have to be that way, but . . ."

"Why?"

"Because they're healthy now," the doctor said patiently. "It would be best, in my opinion, to seize every viable egg, to be safe, but they would rather just start you late and take it from there."

"Oh." Lawrence lost interest. It was obviously better to wait; the world was crowded enough as it was.

The doctor continued, probably for Kamela's benefit. "The backlog is enormous."

Kamela came forward, eagerly curious. "Why is that? Are there still so many viable eggs?"

The doctor shrugged. "Sometimes nature second-guesses us."

Lawrence watched the interplay, thoughtful. Her egg and Kamela's egg? What was so fun about that? She shook her head, pretending not to notice the two women lined up in front of her, the younger awestruck beside the older, solemn one.

"Okay, Lawrence, you can go. No problems, as usual," the doctor said briskly, turning away. Kamela half-turned to follow her.

Lawrence stood up and looked questioningly over at Kamela.

"I'm staying," she announced. "That is, at least until the shower's over. You must admit we can't look at much in the rain."

Lawrence actually felt charmed. "That's okay," she said brightly, and went to get dressed.

"Don't forget to look up that bug!" Kamela yelled after her.

Lawrence left with a grin, but she couldn't help but center on her dream of heading for the cave with Kamela, getting hit by the storm on the way over, and relishing the comforting dryness and cozy smell of the shallow cave.

Lawrence awoke naked and turned to find Maricela by her side. At first she only thought it unusual to awaken first, but then she focused her attention on Maricela, who lay under a green/blue blanket, breathing softly, eyes incredibly smooth, arm beneath her head. Her black, kinked hair was tangled in a few branches, and her cheek was smudged.

Above her were faint stars in a medium blue sky. Lawrence frowned. Stars didn't look like that. Gently she raised herself on one elbow to look about. It was definitely odd. They lay on a smooth, silver tray surrounded by deciduous forest in a bleak winter, yet she was not cold. She left the blanket tucked firmly around Maricela and went to untangle her hair. Luckily the branch could bear no menace. It lay mostly on the hair, not through it, so Lawrence was able to get it free and toss it aside without waking Maricela.

At last she was chilled. She shivered, but there was only the blanket for cover, and it seemed to have shrunk, for it covered Maricela amply, but that was all.

Lawrence started to curse, then her attention jumped outward. "These trees . . . they're poplars in this circle." She crouched next to Maricela, feeling warmer as her feet accepted the heat the tray gave. "I'd hate to wake you, but I'd like to talk to you." She put her hand out to touch the cheek. Maricela did not respond. Lawrence felt guilt: Let her sleep. "This tray, though, and you. What is it?"

Lawrence resumed her sleeping position, pulling the blanket around her. "Now it fits!" she murmured. The heat soothed her, making her drowsy. She jerked alert. "No. I want to be awake when Maricela opens those eyes to this world. I've got to stay awake."

She drifted, seeing a row of punchouts on a sheet of paper. Her job was to make a thousand more of the rows. She sighed.

Lawrence entered the food granting area. She grabbed a granny smith and bit into it.

"Hey," said a voice in her ear.

She jumped, spinning around to see Scott behind the apple barrel. He was grinning.

"Only one apple apiece today," he warned softly. "These came from the north."

Lawrence frowned. "I'm no greed, but, Scott, I'm hungry! And these are so good! I'm losing weight, too. Doctor said so."

He nodded. "Charles once complained that the farmers should be allowed more food because we work so hard. And the quota was increased. It still might not be enough, especially for you, because you're still growing." Scott looked down at her with an amused grin. "Yep. Pretty short. Here, why don't you have mine?" He selected a big, shiny, green apple and held it out to her.

Lawrence shook her head. "I'm 163. That's not short." She took another bite of her apple. "I found things to eat in the woods. If I get desperate, I can do it again."

Scott looked mildly at the kitchen. "I wonder if we really can make do with less. Maybe we're supposed to be skinny in the natural state."

Lawrence swallowed rapidly so she could reply. "I see a lot of fat birds and squirrels. Not fat—big!"

He smiled and said, "I came for a late supper. Have you eaten?"

Lawrence shook her head, intent on finishing the apple. She bit off the top and the bottom, leaving only a skeleton surrounding seeds, which she then sucked.

"Want to join me?"

Lawrence shrugged, completely indifferent. They went over to the grains.

"How'd you like the peanuts?"

Lawrence remembered the clods of dirt clinging to the nutty legumes that she shook. "It sure beats picking cotton."

Scott was searching the cooler. "Those greeds. Not a single leftover. We'll have to cook." He looked over at her before she could make a move toward the pans. "I can do it."

Lawrence looked at him wide-eyed. "Aren't you tired?"

"I had pecans," was his answer, as if hauling baskets of the wry striped nuts was much easier than shaking peanuts. "Go ahead, try me. You'll be pleasantly surprised."

Lawrence smiled, figuring he must care, what with his fresh herbs that he grew himself in his own tiny plot. Many mornings she'd see him crouched beside the small green plants with a trowel.

She went over to the table and began to fiddle with a solitaire she found lying there until he came over with the salad.

Lawrence put aside the game and studied the salad. "What's that brown stuff?"

"Sumac. My secret ingredient. Shh." He moved aside the solitaire, then joined Lawrence in eating the salad. He pointed with his fork. "Who invented that? Do you know?"

Lawrence shook her head. "I just found it lying there myself. Did they sign it?" she asked when he picked it up.

"That's what I'm looking for. No." He put it back down. He sounded exasperated. "I hate that. People ought to be proud of their work."

"I never signed anything," Lawrence offered. She remembered her shock at learning that artists could write. They couldn't, though. They were just able to put their names, dates, communes, symbols, whatever they thought of significance, onto their opera.

"That's because you were subtly trained not to." Scott sighed.

"No, I still won't, because I know I did it." Choosing between convention and the artists was easy, especially if they were going to be snooty about it.

Scott asked abruptly, "Do you want to ride on the egg trucks? I can take you. But first you have to tell me why."

Lawrence lifted her face, composed it, then reached for the salad bowl. She ate all of it before answering in a sated, tired voice. "I don't know why. I just have to see. I feel that there's more, somewhere." She ended awkwardly, looking at him beseechingly, for a second forgetting who he was, what he asked, and how his dark eyes shone.

Scott lifted his eyes and stared into hers. His expression changed, going beyond his usual friendly, yet neutral visage. "Like velvet . . ." he murmured. Lawrence returned to self-consciousness to see him blush and swallow, his left hand rising to fumble in his shirt pocket. "There is, sort of." He licked his lips and blinked. "Here." He placed a tiny silver tray on the table.

"What's that?" Lawrence asked brightly, refraining from saying, "It's so cute!"

Scott froze, stumbling. "How old are you?" he asked through stiff lips.

"Thirteen."

He looked down, mouth open, so that Lawrence imagined that something had just dropped inside of his skull. "Now I know what Charles meant." He glanced at her. "I'm on the road a lot, by choice. I don't get too much of what's going on. Nobody told me. I assumed you were seventeen." He laughed. "It's hard to deny accepted opinion, even if reality is obviously something different. I mean, now I can look at you, and say, yeah, she's a kid, but since you can't work here until you're sixteen, I assumed . . ."

"I'm sorry," Lawrence said sincerely, still not sure what he had lost.

Scott got up and pulled the stew off the heat plate. "Nearly fried," he muttered. He selected a clean spoon and tasted, grunting. "It's done," he announced. "Pretty good, too, if I do say so myself." He picked up the ladle to serve Lawrence. "What are you doing here?" Scott humphed in an unnaturally casual tone. "Back when I was twelve you couldn't have gotten me to work. It's the artists, though, isn't it?"

Lawrence was already shaking her head. "I can't tell you why I'm here. I'm thinking about pulling out." Lawrence sat back, surprised. That had just came out, without any intention.

"Really? Why? All the artists hang on, harvest after harvest."

"That's their problem." Lawrence was suddenly firm in her decision to scorn, perhaps leave, them.

"Yeah, many of us have admitted as much. Look at me. I can't stand to hang around here too long." He fumbled with the tray, trying to put it back into his pocket, but he dropped it. As he bent to pick it up, he muttered, "I keep coming back, though. Maybe someday I won't."

Lawrence waited until he had sat back down and caught up with her stew-wise before she leaned forward. "What's out there that isn't here?"

Scott answered readily. "I don't know. Maybe nothing. I just like to keep moving."

Lawrence went back to eating. It wasn't long before they were done. Maybe Scott was right: farmers got short rations.

"Lawrence!" someone yelled.

She spun around to see Charles' nastily smiling face at the door.

"Your little friend is here." He stepped back to let Kamela through.

Scott stumbled up out of his chair and went toward the door. "Hey, Charles, wait up! I've got something to say to you!" He pushed past Kamela and slammed the door.

Lawrence stood awkwardly, bowl in hand. "Hello," she said lowly, as if this were the first time they had met.

Kamela smiled a tiny smile. Lawrence thought her standing there was the most beautiful thing she had ever seen. "I want you to come with me."

Lawrence waited a few seconds, feeling that bliss wash over her, then murmured, "Let me get the plates cleaned up, to please the cook."

"Okay."

Lawrence gathered up the dishes, put them in the sink, then wiped the table. Kamela followed her to the stove, hitching herself up near the sink to watch Lawrence scrub Scott's pan.

"It'll be fun when we get to high (tech) school, though I think it's silly to call it that. Haven't we been learning it all along?"

Now Lawrence knew why she had blurted to Scott that she was leaving; Kamela had been gradually wearing her down. While in her presence, it was easy to gratify her by appearing to want to go to back to school. On the other hand, when away from Kamela, it would be the last thing to cross her mind. This was power, she was sure of it. "Yeah," she said, hoping to sound convincing. "It's pretty stupid. I think they should say science school, or something."

"We've been doing that, too," Kamela pointed out. "We won't just be learning science, either. There's language, as always. How is it different?"

Lawrence noticed the switch in tense. Kamela was already there in her mind. "We get more Mentors," she supplied. "It's kind of like the caretakers. We went from a nursery where they had a lot of 'em, to a 'family' which was small, then back to the nursery. We had a bunch of teachers in nursery, then one, and now several."

146

Kamela was quiet. "That's how they did it where I come from, too. I never thought of it as strange. Now all I can say is, 'why?'"

Lawrence rinsed thoughtfully. "I don't know. The Mentor I had in low (tech) school seemed to me to be a little much. It seemed he had too much power."

"Where is he? I haven't met him."

"I don't know."

Kamela hesitated, so that Lawrence began to wonder if she should have said "He went to prison!" but she didn't know! "My Mentor was okay," was all that Kamela chose to say.

Lawrence dried her hands. "What did you want to show me?"

Kamela looked pleased as she hopped off her perch. "Come on."

Lawrence tripped to catch up.

Outside they encountered soft dusk. Lawrence saw Charles and Scott murmuring in the shadows near the showers building, but she valiantly ignored them. At a corner before they reached the fields Lawrence tugged Kamela's arm. "Wait. I have to give you something." She went into the sleeping building, leaving the door open. Kamela hovered at the threshold while Lawrence rummaged through a drawer. "Here. Put this on." She tossed the plaid flannel shirt at her, and Kamela put it on. It enveloped her tall, spare body.

Lawrence leaned back to take a look.

"It's so big!" giggled Kamela.

"Yeah," Lawrence said, then coughed. It was amazing how rough her voice had gotten.

Kamela led her out past the fields and up into the mountains. They climbed only a short distance to arrive at a circle of poplars. Lawrence waited far back on the eroded dirt path for Kamela to enter the trees. Once she reached them, Lawrence duplicated her movements and walked to the rim. During that time, Kamela went to the center and spun to face her. Lawrence nonchalantly paused, leaning against her favorite tree, the one displaced slightly from the circle.

"I found this," Kamela said smugly.

Lawrence nodded. She saw no need to explain that she had found it years ago. Kamela was trying to please her, and that always resonated.

"I wonder what made it?" Her hushed voice hearkened back to the time when Lawrence had thought it must have been magic that did it.

"It's probably artificial. This might have been farmland once, maybe when the commune was new," Lawrence guessed, because past the slight hill was plenty of flat land, complete with rock piles from ancient farmers clearing the soil.

"Why would they plant trees in the fields?" persisted Kamela.

"Imagine it. A pretty lawn, dinner among the trees. When they're shorter, the leaves wouldn't be way up there. They'd be down here, surrounding a banquet. The smell of the fresh fields blowing through." She squashed through the yellow October leaves to touch Kamela's face.

Her lips were wet, moving with no sound. Lawrence remembered the mouth eating leaves. She touched the throat; she bent to kiss the long collar bone. Kamela stood strongly, giving in just a little. That was good. Lawrence wondered why Kamela seemed to be breathing so loudly, then she knew it was because she herself had forgotten to breathe.

Lawrence dropped her hand to lightly caress the tiny breast, then turned to sit down in the leaves. Kamela joined her. The two glanced at each other, then immediately lay down. Lawrence inched over to place her body next to hers. Kamela began stroking her thigh.

"My mouth," Lawrence began. "My mouth wants to hold you."

Kamela pulled the string of her own shirt. "Let it."

The breasts looked pale in the starlight, but that just made them more tempting. Lawrence licked. After a while, Kamela had pulled her shirt off to do the same.

But Lawrence wanted more. She had already pressed her lips over most of the tender, moist flesh, so she pulled on the buttons of the trousers until they gave.

Here were sweet folds to feed on. When her tongue touched the softness, a shock passed through her. Kamela jerked, letting a faint moan escape her throat. Encouraged, Lawrence with both hands seized her hips and brought them to her mouth, burying her tongue deeply into the hole. Kamela clutched her blindly, almost pushing her out, then she calmed as the tongue chose to stay there. Then Lawrence moved, seeking the network's center. The little knob fluttered as she kissed it. She locked it into her mouth and gave her tongue free play. Kamela thrust eagerly, juice onto Lawrence's cheeks. The sheath spread, the little point of flesh swelling and shooting out to Kamela's throaty screech, banging Lawrence's head deep into the leaves as she came, shuddering. Lawrence felt the hard flesh subside, so she cradled it gently, and she figured ruefully that a woman of that strength would find a way to survive anything.

Lawrence put down her paintbrush and smirked. Beautiful work! Such neat lettering! REALITY OR BUST. *I like it.*

"I like it," a voice said, echoing her thought.

Lawrence focused, moving her sign away. The androgynous sycophant winked back.

The androgyne lovingly caressed her/his bright, rough shirt. "Why did you build the Cube?"

Lawrence silently pulled away, feeling a pure attraction for her/him and not wanting to show it. "That's easy. I wanted to experience everything . . ." Lawrence quickly said brightly.

"Hold the world in your hand, hmm?" The androgyne sighed. "To know the world, or to have it know you?"

"To know the world, of course! The stupid artists, with their search for fame. I don't want the Cube to show me at all, but I'm in here, all alone, an individual." Lawrence accepted her/his hand casually, deep in thought.

"Wonderful! And you're thinking, too. Even better." The androgyne clapped her/his hands, pulling free from Lawrence's grasp, making her jump and blush. "But your world was once created. You didn't do anything new."

Lawrence strode away, but the androgyne stood in front of her. "So you got kicked out. It's their fault if they can't appreciate you?"

"Move," Lawrence muttered, bending to scrape the pieces of bark out of the grass.

"Maybe you should have listened to Kamela instead of just lusting after her." The androgyne stroked her head gently.

Lawrence moved away, fumbling over the pieces of bark so that the breeze set them aflutter. They flew into the sun.

"Gotta get them," Lawrence grunted, "before someone becomes the recipient."

She scrambled after them, but they had disappeared. "Lost 'em," she muttered.

That evening no one would look at her, not even Scott. Lawrence tried to read them as she had Kamela, except Kamela was easy: she wanted Lawrence's talents to be easily available. Looking at the dispirited crowd, Lawrence had to imagine they wanted pretty much the same thing.

Charles came in last as always and sat. He took a long time to stare at Lawrence. She couldn't stand it, she wanted to slap him, but she stared back until he looked away.

"Here is our business tonight, and I shall keep it short. Screens."

Someone near the supply screen slipped Lawrence's Square in and hit display.

Everyone leaned forward to study the new data. Lawrence was quite embarrassed. In two years she had not done much. The farm work had exhausted her; she craved to once again have time to fill it.

Charles did not think a detailed study was necessary. He nodded to the one near the screens, and they were shut off. Scott took it upon himself to retrieve Lawrence's Square and return it to her, his lips aquiver with pity. Lawrence looked at him completely emotionless.

"No opus," announced Charles.

Lawrence out of the corner of her eye saw Scott hang his head with a sigh. She faced Charles determinedly, however. Inside, though, she felt oddly surprised, as well as guilty. Maybe she had been hoping that a miracle would happen, and that what she was would undoubtedly be seen by an astute observer as artist. The only thing she had left out were some love poems about Kamela. She had written them on beech bark with a twig as a pencil, saved them for a while, then buried them out in the cave. Charles wouldn't have wanted those silly things, anyway.

"And how was this decision determined?" Her voice came out brittle, harsh.

Charles achieved smugness; it did not sit well on his face. "We voted."

"Pardon?" A new word!

"All of us reviewed your record and unanimously agreed that there was no opus. We then decided that we must let you go."

"Is that voting?" It didn't sound unusual.

"Yes. A majority of us—you are aware of what a majority is, don't you? Consider your numbers, oh scientist. More of us thought it best that you not continue, so that became our decision."

Mastering her emotions, Lawrence spoke clearly. "What kind of nonsense is this?"

"It is how we work. It is how we must work."

It came to Lawrence in a flash. Charles was *boss*, another unfamiliar concept, so that she had just thought of him as a Mentor. And now this . . . among artists.

"You all are hypocrites." She stood, gathered her bags, threw away the shirt, and left.

Lawrence smiled at the little dove maneuvering her beak past the bar to nibble the grain. It seemed a bit silly, to actually feel so gentle toward the aggressive bird, but the smile stayed.

Lawrence chewed a piece of corn herself. Now that she came near the trees she was alone. Not only that, though. Lonely. She choked on a sob and lay on her stomach. *It's not too bad. I've just got to go on living. Fill my Square. Yeah.* She scooted forward to look over the crumbling cliff into the misted valley.

Ledarius went over to shake Vance's hand. No. He was walking to her to shake her hand. No. Kamela was standing on their shoulders, smiling. Yeah.

Someone tapped Lawrence on the shoulder. She shrugged irritably, figuring it had to be Kamela, but she finally turned at the second tap to see Jeffrey.

"Maricela wanted you to come to the party. It's over now."

"Is it?" she asked stupidly, then she waved her hand out over the valley. "I thought it was right here, all along."

Lawrence climbed the path from her night in the wet woods and headed for the school. Her head felt heavy from crying, but she would cry no more. It made her lose sleep, and sleep was a nice gesture when trying to forget.

Kamela met her above the laundry. "Hi! Where are you going?"

Lawrence slid her hand across her forehead. Even now, when there was no hope left, she hesitated. "Got a minute?" she asked timidly.

"Sure! I wanted to see you, anyway, about going to high (tech) school, and seeing Ledarius. She's the science Mentor." Kamela gave her this brilliant smile; it was all right.

"Yeah, that's why I'm here. I decided to go to back to school." Lawrence's voice sounded plodding, but she could feel that idiotic, bright, meaningless smile fill her face. It made her sick, but she couldn't help it.

Kamela pointed. "She's over there in her office. I'll take you there. You got your Square?"

Lawrence nodded, then got into that slow, casual gait alongside her. Soon they reached the Mentors' building, and Kamela began walking faster, once they were inside. Lawrence was just the opposite, and let herself be practically dragged to Ledarius' office.

The small, dark woman was immersed in screens. It didn't seem possible that the yell to enter had emanated from her. Lawrence looked at her curiously while her attention was occupied. She could read nothing.

Kamela had no qualms and began easily, "Ledarius, here's Lawrence. She's decided to come back to school." She entered the room, all the way up to the desk.

Ledarius looked impatiently at Lawrence just standing there. "Come in, come in. Don't stand in the door. And shut it, too." Ledarius gestured with both hands sharply.

Lawrence did as she was told, awkwardly, hands in pockets through most of it. Her bag, on wrist, clunked against her thigh.

Ledarius held out her hand. "Your Square, please," she said briskly. "Oh, Kamela, this is confidential." Her gaze was sweet for a moment. Lawrence's eyes widened. Kamela nodded happily and quietly sneaked out. "Now." Ledarius inserted the Square and rapidly went through the screens. Lawrence thought she was showing off.

Eventually she had to slow down. Lawrence shifted her feet impatiently and yawned.

"I can't understand this," she finally muttered. "You say you're fourteen and want to leave the farm, yet your records show you're a dull eighteen with no future. Which is true?" She pointed at the screen. "Looking at this, I see the first one is."

Lawrence nodded, remembering Scott saying that he had acted on his assumptions. She wanted to become one person again and erase Vance's influence off her record.

Ledarius was watching her with large black eyes. "Should I test you?"

Lawrence used to love taking tests, witnessing her mind pull out the right answers, filling the neat little spaces. Still, her heart leapt, though now she knew they were futile. "I don't think so," she answered softly. "I have to go to school anyway."

"Yes. Whose idea was it to start you on the farm early?"

"It was mine," Lawrence said helpfully.

Ledarius shook her head. "Crazy. Unbelievable." She shrugged, eyes wide. "Just what did you expect?"

Lawrence uncomfortably watched her eyes narrow. She decided to act the casual, bored, intelligent student. "Nothing. I just thought I was ready for high (tech) school and nobody would let me go on."

Ledarius suddenly seemed to understand. "Yes," she whispered slowly. "That's it." She turned back to the screens, and Lawrence watched her face transform to a beatific, satisfied, friendly look. "Your old Mentor could have done something, but . . ." She pointed at Lawrence's records. "Get off that tractor! Though you may change your mind later or reject it right now, my decision is to start you in botany. You've got the ability, of course. Chances are, let me say without doubt you'll make it to the city in two years. Wouldn't that be great!" Triumphantly she hit release and gathered up Lawrence's Square.

Lawrence knew she didn't expect an answer, because her eyes were full of contemplating the star student, *her* star student, but she answered anyway, dutifully, as she took back her Square, "Yes, Ledarius."

Lawrence's brain was having a feast. High (tech) school was both more interesting and challenging than she thought it would be. It seemed like everything she had ever done was all on the curriculum. Nothing existed for her inquiring mind beyond it. She worked hard, mostly aiming to lessen her casualness and become more accurate, since her work was now graded, not just a hobby.

Lawrence's brain was not as happy as could be expected, because the threat of Kamela—Just what is she planning?—melted through just enough to bother her. Ledarius, at least, she could fathom. These Mentors, all alike.

Lawrence awoke in the very faint light the farmers called dawn. She was lying on her back, so her eyes opened wide onto the ceiling. She stayed staring a long time, until she was forced to blink, then she closed them for about a minute. They flew open again, and she did not stir.

This was the twist in that continuous ring. Lawrence had been merely herself, and now she was all. But this condition could not be separated from herself, who had always been there.

She had been dreaming, but the dream couldn't be disconnected from the day before, or the month before, or whenever it was it had first come to her, whether in the woods at the sight of a possum, or at the crux experienced from Kamela's tongue on her, or much earlier, except that it had probably always been there, to distinguish it from that which was always fading, not dead as rock, but alive, at least for a time.

It was all clear now. To be ecstatic forever, on one trembling edge, so that she could just start grabbing it all, eyes in the mind's universe.

Something weighed upon her chest, on her hypothalamus, on her chest, and she breathed deeply, calmly, logically lined up the dots, to try to free it. Lawrence was tired, having waited a long time for something, just what she was not sure. It must be merely a puzzling aftereffect of the dream, when a sigh had awakened, a union of cells had created her, in a warm, organic bath surrounded by sterile glass.

She could not move; it was not worth moving. The patterns weren't up above, in the beams. They were in her head. Everything was in her head. She had to get it out and shape it into something physically real, maybe lines in a Square, as she had been taught in school. But, no, that would mess it all up, put it back at the beginning, no, she needed to cram it all into her head. Her hands/thoughts leapt occasionally, but she willed herself not to jump out of bed, but to lie and think, or just diffuse and be, plan this opus of creation that only now decided to burst forth, that only now decided to come together. She traced its patterns, wondered what material she would need, wondered at its strange makeup, so like her and yet distant.

The feast was not yet over.

Lawrence wiped the sweat out of her eyes and coughed, accepting the dipper of cold water the wide-eyed boy handed her.

"That's good," she grunted when she was done.

The boy too drank, and sat beside the crushed rock Lawrence had built up, seemingly forever.

"Boss say you work too hard."

Lawrence looked at his black eyes. "Yeah?"

"Boss say no muscle."

Lawrence rolled up the soaked blue cotton sleeve and studied her biceps. "You're right," she murmured. "The brain is not a muscle."

"Boss say don't need no more rock. The job's done."

Lawrence stepped back and considered. "Seems I just started."

Lawrence stood firmly between the two. "I won't."

"But, Lawrence!" Ledarius smiled. "What could possibly hurt you? You don't need to study as hard as you've been doing. The tests aren't that hard, not for someone like you."

Lawrence forced herself to stare at Ledarius. She must be finding it awfully hard to coax like that, instead of getting bossy. It made Lawrence nauseated.

Ledarius continued, "It would be good for you to study less, interact more."

Lawrence scowled. "I've been interacting all my life. My psychcomputer social scores are normal." She returned her countenance to a solemn, distant stare.

Kamela couldn't take it anymore. She leapt up from her quiet position next to Ledarius and screeched, "You're cruel! You're working for nothing! You don't even want to go to the city! Not as much as I do!" She started bawling, right there. Lawrence from her deep perspective looked on, amazed.

"But I do," she answered in a voice that sounded as if she were stating the obvious.

This was news to Kamela. She stopped crying and stared at Lawrence wild-eyed.

Lawrence continued silkily, "What do I get for tutoring you? You make it a fair bargain, and I'll change my mind."

Kamela stomped, enraged, about the room. "I gave!"

"It was false," answered Lawrence's exquisitely cool voice.

Kamela stomped, stomped and wailed, until she stomped right out of the room.

Lawrence watched Ledarius shut the door and took note of her sad expression. Maybe that was because Kamela had wanted to be a doctor, even though that couldn't be all there was to it. As Lawrence watched Kamela shine up to Mentor in class, she puzzled why that obsequious behavior was favored over the ability to do schoolwork well. Tom, inching along in a required basic syllabus, muttered to her that Kamela was what used to be a "Teacher's Pet," and they were always favored over merely competent students.

Ledarius sighed when she sat back down. She glanced at Lawrence, apparently with a timid reconciliation. "Don't worry about it, okay? She probably wouldn't have passed even if you had helped her. Those tests will probably be way beyond her. Still . . ." She shook her head. "It's just that I've never seen a more devoted student. I had hopes for her."

And now you're stuck with just me, thought Lawrence. She was going to say that Kamela wants to hold a person in her hand, to have the power of giving, but she kept quiet. Sometimes it was better that way.

"Oh, you're good, all right," she now heard Ledarius say, "but not devoted enough. I kept trying to bring out the spark of desire, but it looks like you found it yourself." Ledarius looked her over. "A sudden transition to intense devotion, looks like. Why?"

Lawrence couldn't even begin to explain what had seized her, even if she had wanted to, so she said, "I want to be a scientist."

Ledarius clapped her hands. "Good! It suits you. You're on the right track. Listen, just for a minute, though. I can't see it in your records. Maybe it's not even there, but it fits what I've seen. You're always overcompensating. I don't understand it. You've got to believe in yourself."

Lawrence almost laughed, hugging her discovery to her, knowing that it must be kept a secret. Of course the schoolwork wasn't challenging, but she had to work hard for what lay ahead of her, not the city or what it might give her. Accomplishing what had seized her would not be a simple task.

Ledarius was waiting. What Lawrence had to say next was so ridiculous, one of those statements that should go without saying, so a person could go on to more important things.

Lawrence looked her straight in the eye and said it easily. "I believe in myself."

Ledarius seemed satisfied.

Lawrence sat humbly in the cathedral, head bowed, heart thumping.

The Man of Cloth burst in, flinging his placard labeled HISTORY onto the nearest pew.

"Whew!" he gushed. "It's a mess out there! All a realm of guesses, faded memories, most only wanting to start afresh, and that's what got them into this trouble in the first place."

Lawrence ignored this, sniffing back the tears.

"Well, time to get started in here, right?"

He squatted near the altar across from her.

"Go away," Lawrence snarled.

"It's obvious that you came here in need. What happened?" His voice suddenly became gentle, like Scott's.

Lawrence shifted, wiping the little globules of tears away immediately as they formed. "Isn't it obvious? I didn't like being nasty, but I was so sick of her being false. Of course I could have helped her, losing nothing, except . . ."

"Hasn't anyone ever been true?" He did not look at her.

"Well, yeah, I guess so. I never accused them of anything. What I was going to say just occurred to me. What if I had helped her, and she kept herself free, unsowed, and she still flunked? She would have killed me! Maybe it was better to be nasty."

"No. Never."

Lawrence tilted her head. That authority coupled with the guise of hospitality. "You remind me of the Shawicc."

"If it makes you comfortable, I am she."

"Yes." Lawrence nodded vigorously. "It does. I know her."

The man's expression went from a pleasant, considerate mask to a horrid smile. It was worse than Charles on a bad day. Lawrence leapt up, shuddering. A clock could now be heard, faintly bonging. She took a ragged breath.

"When you came up with the Cube, did you get assistance?" He had now bent his head down, hands to temples, shifting. The floor was moving. Lawrence was still able to stand, bringing her feet up each new inch.

"No. That was later. I had no one. Then, I had zoologists, doctors, botanists, plasma engineers. I accede to that." Lawrence flung up her hands in a world that was blurred, like glass in a storm.

In a flash all was clear. The Shawicc now stood before her. Lawrence smiled, taking her hands and kneeling before her.

The Shawicc stroked her hands. "But, Lawrence, the Cube was based on Squares. You built on what was there before. You can't just blot earlier works from your choices."

Lawrence frowned. "Well, maybe. I'm not an artist. Scientific knowledge remained intact, and, yes, I did build on that. What do you think, my love, that I'm going to strut away from all this and scream 'worship me!'? I'm only doing this to find out. Laurels will all be tossed aside. What happened with Kamela was not my lording my superiority over her. I had to escape her cloying comforts." Lawrence paused. She could feel a premonition, a message from the ephemeral Shawicc, crossing to her mind. "What are you going to tell me? Just say it. I'm not going to start sharing now."

The Shawicc tilted her head. "There are those who are quite a bit more impatient than you. They will seek you out, for your power and to overpower you."

"My power? What power?" Lawrence got up off her knees and confronted her.

"Do I tell you? Don't you know?"

Lawrence rapidly stroked her legs through the tall grass Ton had been forbidden to cut. She carried in her left hand the little clock Kamela had left for her with a note: THREE MORE DAYS TO GO!

Lawrence had erased the screen, and almost broke the clock by throwing it around the room. It had rung once, she remembered. When at last she had calmed down, she went over, picked it up, and felt the hard case. Oddly, it did not hum. It ticked. That caused her to tear it open to study the interior.

Many hours had passed since a doctor had come from the hospital concerning Kamela. Lawrence impassively took the message, hiding the clock in her pocket. After the doctor left, it was hard to return to studying. She kept to the screens, however, until dusk, when she decided she had better go.

Lawrence leaned against the hospital door, which for once felt light. She creaked onto the floor, keeping the light off, her eyes already accustomed to the southern bright nights.

The attendant was still there, back in the kitchen, eating, but ready to go any minute. Kamela must not be in too much danger, if no one was to stay the night. It was Delores, a woman Lawrence remembered from the nursery, where all the attendants had been kind and encouraging. It was therefore appropriate, though to see her staring was unnerving.

Delores looked at her accusingly. "She's been asking for you. Why did you wait?"

Lawrence had to figure out a good answer to that. "Why should you care? Because you're soon leaving?"

Delores was smarter than Lawrence remembered her being. "Maybe."

Lawrence ignored her and went to stand over Kamela, asleep, eyes still. Behind her, the attendant turned off the kitchen light and went toward the back. Lawrence heard the door close.

It's words, Lawrence suddenly thought, *that bind, and what I'm going to do will, too. It's the last refuge, one I'm going to break and replace.*

She ran her fingers over the pillow until they lightly touched Kamela's cheek.

At the human touch, her eyes opened a merest bit, and she slurred, "Steak. Crack. Democracy. TV. The equations aren't . . ."

And they had sat side by side in high (tech) school for two years. For over a year, there had been no words. No more touching, either. It was just that Kamela would come in last, and that would be the only empty chair.

"Hey," she hissed, but Kamela couldn't listen; she stared with wide eyes blankly, head pressed hard into the pillow.

"I can't see them. The tests . . . the tests," Kamela moaned, loud and mournful. "I can't remember," she muttered.

Lawrence turned and sat at the window, composing her explanation in her mind: *It's out there. I've got it all. You needn't have worried. Even if I could give myself, it would only always be me. What was I supposed to do, reap me and feed me to others? Look, you go right ahead. Feed on those ancestors of yours, lost from our history and our genes. I'm going to be pushing it all aside, or bringing it back. In about two days I will sit with you and take the tests. I will see it as a competition. Braindead versus Child Genius. Then you'll see.*

Lawrence pulled out the clock and threw it across the room.

"See what I think of you?" she yelled at Kamela. "I do not care. I will never care. Because I don't need people like you, people always wanting things. I'll pass, go to the city, and you . . ." Lawrence pulled her hands out of the air and calmed down. "Ah, who cares?"

She stalked from the room.

Lawrence paused in her journey to look down. In a dry spot under an encompassing hollow log, on the clean, leafy mound, a mother cat nursed. You had groundlings; Jeffrey had told her so.

Beyond the log in the meadow was a hollow. She wasn't sure if they should be there, but the nest was presented to her, nevertheless. Enclasped by dry yellow stalks of taller grasses, the duck fed her young. Lawrence watched the baby birds a while, then went back to the log. The mother cat now was nursing from an older female cat, who was alleviating her burden by taking two kittens as her own. The ones that had been born two days ago had died. Lawrence saw the two little bodies; beyond lay four more, deformed, as a hungry mouth lay atremble in the bushes.

Now at the log the older cat suckled a young mother, bereft of young. When Lawrence crossed her eyes, she saw the entire chain of them, making a circle. She went back to the birds.

The duck leapt at her, wriggling its tail. The little brown babies were entering the pond. As they swam, their bills dug into the spring mud, heads asquirm to dislodge the tightly bound food. Heads and tails both wriggle.

Lawrence took her clothing, her few personal items, and her Square, not even full, and packed it all into a bag. She had to take the Square so that she could continue her work, but she was certain no one would ask to see it. She had passed the tests; that was all they cared about. Cramming the bundle under her arm, she walked out into the bright morning fog, aiming for the wide road.

Charles stopped her near the fields. She allowed him, thinking he was about to tell her that the truck had broken down, so she'd better walk.

He eyed her solemnly. "So you're going."

"Yeah." Lawrence shrugged. It wasn't like it was a big deal. She thought Kamela was the only one dead set on going.

Charles reached out to tap her head. "You must be braindead, I figure, if you passed their tests."

Lawrence jerked back, and her whole demeanor changed. She watched Charles' face register shock. "Tom didn't," she tightly informed him. "Neither did Kamela. And she tried."

Charles snickered. "What about your little friend, Lawrence? You gonna train her to follow you about? What about your brand new tray?"

Thinking fast was becoming an advantage at last. "Uh, Charles," she began sweetly, "while it is true my luscious self got a nice, shiny tray for my sixteenth birthday, you'll never see it. Besides, it looks too much like yours, from lack of use. I suggest that, if you need it, go pump yourself over the water. Feed the fish."

Charles reared back at that one. "When I see your tally years from now, I'll make you swallow . . . your present words. Think about it."

As if she ever wanted to see him again! Lawrence smiled brightly and continued on her way. "Big city. Lots of folks." she tossed over her shoulder, but inside her heart was loose. So many people. And her having to go alone. Wrong direction, pal, indeed.

The road beckoned into the forest. As she expected, the truck was not there yet, so she sat down in the wet grass to wait. The stupid truck should have left at dawn. Now she'd be lucky to get to the city in two days.

Lawrence glared impatiently back at the farm buildings. A moving human figure in the fog caught her attention. She stood and straightened, assuming it had come to tell her to meet the truck elsewhere.

"Hey," Scott said softly. "How're you doing?"

Lawrence relaxed and kicked her bag. "Okay."

"Nervous?" Scott tried to smile, but he only ended up looking woeful.

"Of course." Lawrence laughed.

Almost on top of her oft-used phrase Scott blurted, "You could have come with me. Even later."

Lawrence looked away, embarrassed. "Naw, that's okay. I think the way it turned out will be better."

Scott watched her. "Too bad about Kamela."

"Not really. It was her choice. Time I started making a few of my own." The way she was now, she didn't care what Scott thought.

"Seems like you've been doing that for quite some time," he said slowly. "I hate to see you go without knowing why. Do you have an opus? I mean . . ."

Lawrence smiled thinly. "I . . . I have something you wouldn't recognize as an Opus. It's . . ."

Scott whooped. "Fantastic!"

Lawrence found herself grinning with him. It was so easy. Her voice this time was less hesitant. "It's something I have to go to the City to complete. When it gets done, I'll let you know. You'll be the first to see it."

He nodded happily.

The egg truck started, and began to pull slowly toward the road. Lawrence grabbed her bag, even though she had plenty of time.

"I'll see you." Over the years she had polished that bright tone, dulled it to realistic. It worked.

"Goodbye." Scott stepped back far enough to make Lawrence feel alone.

She watched the truck inch up the road, and her thoughts came fast and thick through sheer panic: Wasn't any reason to have eyes and ears anymore, if she always knew. She would always know her way about. She could bluff and chant with all the rest, and none would know the difference. All that mattered was the flow, getting by.

The truck stopped; its door whooshed open. "A student!" the driver crowed.

If this is reality . . . her thoughts fled. All there was was that big, gaping door, ready to swallow her up. No time to look around just once more. She had to go now, and she did, intent on entering gracefully with pack under arm. The door slammed shut. Lawrence timidly looked around.

"Stay up here near the front," the driver ordered. "I need company."

Lawrence obediently sat on the white plastic chair in the front. She eagerly looked to both sides of her, then glanced at the driver.

She began fairly easily, "They never let you know until you're there that there's going to be a student. Ain't that something?"

Lawrence peered up ahead, then glanced back and forth again. "Why don't they?"

"Beats me. I lose a lot of tonnage I didn't plan on losing. And some students get on my nerves. Thank goodness it only happens once a year."

"About how fast are we going?" Lawrence asked rapidly.

"It's about two days from here," she said tiredly.

That didn't answer her question! That was telling her something she already knew! Lawrence felt the anger rise, but she controlled it. Instead, she considered asking the driver if it would be that different up there. They'd warned her about snow. That was about it. She tried to test the truck's movement. It was certainly faster than she walked, but how much faster? Lawrence watched a tree go past and timed the length to another outstanding one. Two days! She reckoned the time she had to walk and estimated. Seventy kilometers an hour? Twelve hours a day? Hmm. Fifteen hundred kilometers? Such a vast distance, and still temperate!

It couldn't last long. Her eager watching that yielded trees, more trees, ever more trees, not even farmland, tired her rapidly. She shifted, resting her feet on her little bundle, and sighed.

The driver noticed and laughed softly. "Not that exciting, huh?"

Lawrence became alert. She nodded, glad now for the talk. "I thought riding the egg trucks would be exciting. Now I just feel sorry for the drivers." She stretched her arms out and yawned. "I shoulda stayed home, except . . ."

"Except what? I've never had any artists posing as students."

"I'm not an artist. I just picked up a few words, that's all."

The driver shrugged. "So? Fine with me. Scott said to watch after you. Huh! What's he, your nurse or something?"

"Don't be ridiculous," Lawrence snapped, blushing, grateful that the driver never took her eyes from the road.

"Could have these egg trucks automated, if you ask me," she muttered. In a brighter tone, she continued, "You never did answer my question—Except what?"

Lawrence tried to read her. She sensed that she must be shy, since driving couldn't be that hard. Just a single, unending road with no other traffic didn't need her full attention. Maybe she was shy like Scott. Maybe all drivers were.

That couldn't be, though. They got to see people outside of the commune all the time. Constant interaction, Lawrence saw it. But maybe they craved the driving, almost always alone, with the new things they could quietly contemplate. Maybe being a driver was her kind of job after all.

"I don't know," Lawrence said, eyes on a glint of a puddle in the crushed stone, fascinated by its shimmer. "I want to see new stuff. I'm working on a project and . . ."

"Aha! Most students I get are so blamed uppity! Why're you going to the city? 'Cause they want me, 'cause I'm good. Bleah! At least you're going with something in mind. An idea, maybe, to strip the city of any lousy thing you can. You're not going with any yearning, I take it, to give them anything." The driver nodded, smiling.

But I am! Lawrence thought, then it hit her. What she was doing, everything she chose to do, she was doing for herself.

The first stop was still in Region 12. No student. Lawrence got out to stretch and walk, rubbing her butt ruefully as the driver laughed. She helped the farmers load up some crates before getting back on board. Looking up at the sun, she sighed. It wasn't even noon. The driver had smiled at her as she placed the crates. No one had bothered her at all.

The next stop, still in Region 12. They were in mountainous country. At least, there they were, to the right. The road was still straight and true. Lawrence studied the mountains, wondering if they had more boulders and creeks than she was used to seeing. They fogged, even now. The driver warned about impending rain.

The student at this stop didn't help to load. Lawrence ignored him. At one point, deep in the truck pulling in the corn to make room for the nuts, the driver chuckled, "Yep. Typical student out there. Standing proudly, screaming, I was chosen, I was chosen, look at me, except he knows farmers don't care, and you're one of him. He'll wonder about you helping. He might even speak to you. But me—forget it! He'd rather eat lead."

Lawrence studied her face in the sunlight, the comfortable wrinkles, and decided she wasn't hurt. Instead, her face shone only amusement.

They got back on board and set off again. The student climbed awkwardly on last, distaste showing in his face. He hesitated over the seating arrangement, but he chose to settle in across from Lawrence. A timid smile came upon his features, and he ventured politely, "What's your major?"

Lawrence feigned mild surprise, then idly said, "I haven't decided yet."

That blew his mind sufficiently to silence him a few minutes, but he came back readily enough. "I'm physics."

Lawrence nodded. *It figured.* She could feel the driver's pent-up expectation, and she decided for her sake not to read him. He wasn't dangerous enough, anyway. Lawrence guessed she already knew his weaknesses, his tender vulnerabilities, and they were laughable.

The fourth stop was in Region 11. No student. Lawrence despaired. Night was coming on, so they had to stop. She hadn't realized until that fateful dip into the valley of the commune that she had been aching for student companionship. She had been thinking that they would be just like her, young, intelligent, aware, and she would open up and drink of them. She had pictured groups sitting around and discussing deep concepts until her mind whirled. So far, all she had was the stiff oak shoot sitting there, silent, and, later, moody.

The three pulled out their bundles simultaneously and headed for the showers. Guests were rare anywhere you went, and they went confidently from shower to food granting, where someone graciously offered to cook for the weary travelers, to bed. Lawrence's heart trembled at the crowds of new people, so at one point she volunteered to go to the supply shed for enough garlic. All three loved garlic, Lawrence was surprised to learn. Even though all she had done was sit all day, the bed felt wondrous. She was already half-asleep when the physics showed her his tray. She struggled awake.

"No, thank you," she said clearly, smiling gently at him. Anybody who loved garlic couldn't be all that bad. "I'm very tired. We need sleep much more tonight."

He left amiably, and Lawrence remembered the driver's request over dinner to join once more the farmers. She couldn't see the difference.

The next day brought two more students, both female, who chatted to each other much more readily than to the others, but Lawrence was glad. She eased her mind free of the gab, remembering only to be alert when the driver spoke, just because the others had all snubbed her. The boring ride had softened her anxiety. She began to feel that the city wouldn't be that frightening after all.

Darkness came before they crossed the border of mountains into Region 10. The four were heart-achingly silent as the driver brightened the exterior lights. Now that the darkness hid them, the students didn't offer up any more of themselves, knowing anonymity only existed in the commune. Lawrence had listened for accents, for wide-awake assertions, and was satisfied with nothing. While it was true she had divulged nothing, either, she had a good, strong reason.

When the driver pulled over to let them get out and stretch, no commune back there for several hours, Lawrence leaped out into the comforting darkness and strode onto the road. She had felt trapped there for a minute, inside that vehicle, and she couldn't quench the images of nasty, hard looks she had tried to outwit, or, better, outrun. She needed to get out and breathe the last waft of wild roses and pine, halt this rebirth now that she was in control.

One of the students had followed her. "Hey!" she whispered.

Lawrence jumped. Vaguely she recalled the smirk of the artist/driver, and wondered if maybe all students were braindead. "Yeah?" she whispered back.

The student came closer. "Are you all right?"

"Yeah." Lawrence wiped her eyes.

"Just a little nervous?"

"Yeah," Lawrence lied. In her seizure of tricky smiles and strong hands, she had forgotten all about the stupid city. She followed the student back to the egg truck.

"Hey." The driver addressed her, and her alone. In the minor light, Lawrence studied to see if this had an effect on the others. It did.

She walked over to the door, where the driver's head was poking out. "Yeah?"

"You want to eat before we get to the city? It might be better for you not to have to worry about food when you first get there."

Lawrence glanced at the others. Everyone associated the egg trucks with food, anyway, and they had no idea what, if anything, the city could offer them, so she nodded to the driver.

The little kitchen could only hold one at a time, so the driver gave directions so that they all ate the same things but each made a different thing.

Lawrence nibbled the last of the watermelon and gazed up at the tiny quarter moon up above. Home seemed years away, yet she wasn't worried. Not now. She felt calm, peaceful, almost light-headed with ease.

"Why not walk the rest of the way?" she giggled. "How far is it?"

But the driver still would not answer, though what did it matter now? "Pretty far. Let's clean up and get going."

In less than ten minutes the egg truck parked onto the ridge overlooking the city. Unlike communes, it glittered at night. Only Lawrence gasped. She told herself that they were only lights, that it was only buildings crowding a valley, that trees and such were richer and daily visitors, but she could only see the scene of night clouds, stars, and city lights as magical.

"Okay, kiddies, hop out. Goodbye." The driver's voice was light and soft.

The four started. Lawrence stared around at the others, understanding that they all probably wore the same expression as she. Startled and frightened, they blinked at the city beseechingly, looking like baby birds just leaving the nest. Lawrence turned to farewell the driver, who was idle, looking down at the truck floorboard, twisting a gray-black lock. Yes. A fitting mother bird, all right.

Lawrence put her right foot forward and stepped off the printed "START." And so the maze unfolded. She walked on a little white road that was bordered on both sides with black ink.

Behind her she left a thin gray pencil line. She stepped confidently. A child could do, should do, had done this simple maze. The yellow-green printed trees zoomed into view. Hideous and frightening to one only used to the real thing, the blobs held away from Lawrence, who chose to stay on the road. Ahead was a house.

It stood on the corner, surrounded by tidy bushes. When Lawrence tilted her head so that it hovered off the path, she saw a real-life image of an inviting, shady sidewalk leading up to the house. It all looked familiar. Lawrence pulled back her head, returned to just the drawing of the house, and thought.

It is a domicile. I recognize it as something I could live in. Yet I have never seen the like before.

Lawrence took one more second to look at the simple maze she trod on, then she leapt, leaving behind a smudge where the pencil's lead tip had snapped.

Here she was, in a charming neighborhood, circa . . . 1957. *Huh?* Lawrence concentrated on reaching the rings. *What does that mean? I was born 367. Are you saying that this is the future? Wow, 1590 years!* Lawrence struggled to grasp the immensity. *It sure is crowded, like a city.* All the rings could answer was that it was long ago.

Lawrence watched a little boy run by with a baseball glove. Taken up so much with the odd object—leather again—she almost tripped over a little girl playing marbles on the sidewalk. This was even more interesting. While the little girl glared up at her, Lawrence ignored her anger and studied the odd clothes she was wearing. It was all of a piece, pink, and fluffy. A careful inspection confirmed what Lawrence had only thought she'd seen: it had no legs!

"Get outta my light!" came a small, determined voice.

Lawrence jumped and looked behind her. Sure enough, the sun was behind her. Immediately she moved to one side. With no sign of gratitude, the little girl returned to her game.

Lawrence walked a little further. It got harder. The maze of sidewalks took her over hills and under bridges. There were a lot of gardens. She paused at an aster bush to finger the little purple stars.

"I don't remember this one," she murmured to Jeffrey.

In the yard sat a smiling young man staring at her through dark glasses. A cat sat on his stomach. Casually he reached over to turn down his—"radio." Lawrence smiled back. He did look adult, with long chestnut hair and beard and brightly colored clothes. He could almost enter into Lawrence's world without anybody noticing him, except that he was firmly enmeshed in a suburban home.

Suddenly an older man came into view, dressed much more strangely, face red with effort.

"I told you to cut the grass, you lazy bum!" The cat zoomed away from under his nose. "Not sit here and flirt with sleazy passersby!"

Lawrence ducked and reached out to the cat, but it ignored her to slink through the fence and head the opposite way down the sidewalk. She turned to go forward, the rings filling her in on the details: 1967. A teenager, like her, a son. Parental authority. *Cut the grass? Like Tom had wanted to do! Cut perfectly healthy, rare grass!*

Lawrence ran now. She found this history much too disturbing. And the maze flexed with her. It grew more complex. Data banks, frozen with the load of more people, more planning, more dispute. Swamps and forests lush with life that she must push herself through, slide herself across, until she sank down, exhausted, in the middle of nowhere.

Lawrence looked around. Halls in separate directions. "Frap!" she said aloud. "The woods and all were okay. I thought I was making progress. Now I'm lost."

A chill shot through her as she panicked. "I'm scared, I'm scared," she moaned, then she forced herself to shut up. She stood and took a deep breath.

Quickly her mind came to a conclusion: here you cannot retrace your steps. Decisions, decisions, yet you cannot make a logical choice based on the past. The best thing to do would be to select a path, and get going.

Lawrence nodded and simply went forward. Time heightened. Years passed without care, without thought. She came to the road and walked south, entering her place of birth almost instantaneously. Eagerly she picked up her step. She went past the fields and crossed to the nearest hut.

Scott opened the door. He looked at her expectantly. "What have you done?"

Lawrence was suddenly very tired. At twenty, she had returned to the commune from . . . nothing. She had done nothing.

No, wait, it welled inside her, fleshing into real memory. She had spent years creating her opus. No, she was *going* to spend years creating her opus. No, it was done. She could rest. No, she . . .

Lawrence straightened. "Sorry, Scott, but I've got to be going. I've got a lot to do."

Lawrence awoke that morning in a strange bed. Keeping her eyes closed, she tucked her travel-worn body deeper under the covers and buried her ears to avoid the sound of bells gonging somewhere. Someone tugged her blanket nonetheless, and she awoke straight into amused brown eyes.

"Time to get up," their owner whispered. "I think."

Lawrence stared at the fresh face before her. She couldn't place it, but she could believe she had never seen anyone so *alive* before.

She couldn't even begin a response; even now a man appeared at the door of the long sleep room. Twenty! Lawrence kept her eyes away from him and recounted the number of students in that room. It made her dizzy.

"The sun has risen," the man announced. "I'm sorry, but we have to get you up early for testing. Come down to breakfast now." He turned and left immediately, leaving the door open.

Twenty pairs of eyes flicked back and forth before twenty mouths started talking. Twenty selected youths almost simultaneously tossed away the covers and began to dig out probably their last clean outfit of homespun cotton.

The woman of the dark brown eyes remained smiling close to Lawrence. "I'm from the West, Region 27," she chattered. "I arrived yesterday afternoon."

Lawrence ignored her as she checked the faces around her once more. She failed to spot her three traveling companions. Idly she tried to picture the city as it was now, in the early dawn's light, but all she could see was the breathtakingly glittery night city.

"Where're you from?" came a bright voice, destroying the image.

Lawrence jerked her attention back to the woman. The western accent was odd, probably hard to imitate, but interesting, as they all were. "Region 12," she said shortly. "South."

The woman smiled encouragingly, as if Lawrence's answer had been the most beautiful encounter in the world. "And your name?"

Lawrence yanked on her yellow shirt angrily. What was she supposed to do, say it all day? *Give me a nametag, I guess.* "Lawrence."

"I'm Maricela Rose." She tugged on her shoes and sat waiting for Lawrence to finish.

Lawrence had run it together as one word: "maricelarose" because she had never met anyone with two names before. She found herself smiling at the bright face as she laced her shoes.

"Come on over here." Maricela stood up and started walking across the room, pointing. "Here's Jeffrey, over here. Say hi."

Lawrence found herself smoothly gliding after her, evading dressing students with no trouble. What with all the jerking arms and legs, it had to be sheer luck. A dark boy with curly black hair was her destination. She was stunned to see that his eyes were dark green. She had been beginning to believe that only she didn't have brown eyes.

"Hi," Jeffrey smiled. Lawrence relaxed.

"Let's get some breakfast," suggested Maricela, and it didn't sound stupid or forced at all.

The cafeteria was huge, with hundreds of chairs just sitting there waiting to be filled. Maricela calmly strode in with several others, then turned around.

"What's the matter? Come on." Impatiently she waved at them to follow her.

Lawrence and Jeffrey, wide-eyed, eventually complied. The clatter!

When they were once more with Maricela, she shrugged. "Better get used to it. This is how we will always eat." She pointed at the end of the short line. "Get your plates and line up." She smiled at an attendant who paused near them. "We've got it. Go attend those who need it."

The attendant nodded and went to a quivering bunch near the door.

"We have to line up," informed Maricela, "to most efficiently get through." She reached for a grapefruit.

Lawrence tapped her shoulder. "How much should we take, so everyone has enough?"

"Oh, Lawrence! Take your normal rations, of course." Maricela could say anything without really sounding mad.

"Oh. Okay," answered Jeffrey, who selected a peach. "Mmm. Not too many of these where I come from."

"Where's that?" Lawrence found herself asking.

"Region 3. North." He moved forward and got a piece of toast.

"Wow. We got all sorts of things. Lots of peaches. In the summer, they're all over the place." She paused to get the butt of the loaf, amazingly crunchy through and through. "Picking them is a pain, the fuzz, you know. They're good, though. What's the matter?" She looked at the two, who stood before her, eyes wide.

"You picked the peaches?" Maricela finally asked.

"Sure." Lawrence shrugged. "Everybody has to help during harvest."

Maricela shook her head. "We're holding up the line."

They sat and ate quickly, quietly, much too eager to consider the food, more curious as to what would come next. At one point during the noisy meal Lawrence found herself straining to hear the answer to one of Jeffrey's questions.

"Maricela, how do you know so much about this place?"

"I've been here before." was the mind-blowing answer. "Several people in my commune were students, and they told me all about it. Once they brought me here because it was obvious just talking about it wasn't enough."

"I know what you mean," Jeffrey readily said. "They told me about a lot, but I'm still nervous."

"Nobody told me anything," Lawrence blathered. "Not really. I just figured on there being lots more people. I didn't know it'd be like this."

"Yeah, probably all of us envisioned a commune on a larger scale: certainly more spread out." Maricela picked up her tray. "You two done? Let's get going."

The three started walking right down the middle of a paved street. Only a few people were about, and Lawrence eagerly looked at each face, disappointed when it turned out to be a stranger. Eventually she made herself stop looking and directed her gaze strictly in front of her, eyeing the Center.

Bells at the Center started ringing, and Lawrence shook her head. "Loud," she commented.

"We're just in time," Maricela announced. "They have to be loud to call everybody in. Do you two have your Squares?"

Both Lawrence and Jeffrey readily pulled theirs out from an outer pocket. Maricela laughed.

"Just checking, but let's go ahead and leave them out. Show them we're ready."

They joined a group at the front of the massive building. Almost immediately upon their arrival five people emerged from the front double doors and hooked them back. They went out and began lining students up. Remembering the cafeteria, most were intent on forming a neat, straight line.

"No, no," a little man chirped. "You're supposed to go in formation. A star-like."

Lawrence knew full well that stars were spheroid, yet many of the crowd caught on immediately. Her watchful eyes selected the few that were not braindead.

Maricela and Jeffrey cooperatively moved under direction to their places as Lawrence watched. The little man noticed her hesitation.

"You there!" He jumped to assist her. And he touched her.

Lawrence dropped her Square and froze, blind to Maricela bending down and retrieving her Square from the spotless white concrete.

The man came away and quietly, even kindly, said, "Just move ten over, you know."

Lawrence accepted her Square from Maricela and looked down at her feet. Ten centimeters. Like so.

"Perfect!" the little man crowed. He ran up to the door. "Now, everybody, let's go inside!" He gestured with both hands, then disappeared into the darkness.

Lawrence saw the pattern before her feet started shuffling, and as the students marched, she was amazed that it did not waver. She looked back down at her feet. Keeping the pattern in its relation to her in her mind, she was able to move approximately two centimeters out of line.

They were told "sit" in the huge antechamber, and they did so, on the floor. All were strangely silent, even after numbers filled the air and individual students rose to go. Lawrence herself felt an aching anticlimax.

Eventually her number was called. She was led into a wild maze of halls. Nervous, she unthinkingly kept her eyes on the attendant's back the whole way, adjusting to the small room's light with a sudden start.

Three people sat in the small room. Lawrence looked directly at each face in turn as the question was asked.

"Have you ever been sown?"

"No," Lawrence said firmly. She had practiced and practiced so that she would not sound proud of it, but she could not sound doubtful: That could be interpreted as desiring it. They seemed satisfied.

"Then you shall accompany me to another room." The middle figure stood and passed Lawrence as she went to the open door. "Come."

They went immediately to the red room, a room as starkly white as the next, but with a garish red painting of birds on the wall. Lawrence glanced at it, then decided that it was designed to draw attention. She successfully ignored it thereafter.

The one who had accompanied her held out her hand. "Your Square, please."

Lawrence handed it over quickly. Nodding, the woman slipped it into the slot. She frowned, fingers running over keys. "What is this?" she murmured.

Lawrence swallowed a tremor down. She almost wished she didn't have to yield her Square.

"Sit down," she sharply said, herself pulling a chair over to the screens. "Hmm."

Lawrence watched her meekly as she flashed page after page before their eyes.

Several minutes passed before she shut off the screens. "I'm sorry. Please wait a minute." She left the room and returned with two new attendants, who immediately went to look at the Square.

"Let me explain," she addressed Lawrence. "Linear circuits can teach the young, but two dimensions, that's different. There is just so much more room. Just one Square can run this whole city." She gestured at the machine. "Yours is full."

Lawrence struggled to appear calm. Inside, though, she quailed as her mind raced. Impossible! She had last checked the Square's memories just three days ago, right before she had left her commune, and it had had plenty of memory left. Well, actually, it had not been quite full, but still Lawrence had felt disappointed because she thought it was supposed to be full. Now she knew that a Square was for the millions, things way beyond her mere existence, her commune. How did it get filled up on the way to the city? Something inside her twisted.

All three were looking at her in awe. Lawrence cleared her throat.

One of the new ones gestured helplessly. "What goes beyond a Square?"

"A Cube!" Lawrence blurted.

The three glanced at each other. "We have no Cube," the first one said.

The man added, "But it looks like you'll need one. Your memories are growing."

That explained it! Sort of. "How do memories grow?" asked Lawrence.

"We're hoping you can tell us," he answered.

"And how can I get a Cube, if one doesn't exist?" she continued.

"Looks like you'll have to invent one," he said cheerily. "Look, let us keep your Square a few days to let us study it. You can have a clean one to start college with, okay?"

Lawrence smiled. "Yes. Thank you." She was so grateful to get a new one so readily in order to continue her work that she didn't bother worrying about the fate of her first one.

One of the attendants came forward. "Please accompany me. I will show you where you all will be tested."

Again they went through many undecorated halls and up several flights of stairs. Once they stood aside to let others pass. It was then that Lawrence realized that she had no idea how to get out of the place. Such a huge, confusing building—maybe everyone got lost. Worse, maybe no one did. She could only picture herself wandering the halls in complete darkness; she thought no one stayed at night.

"Here we are." The attendant led her into a small room. Lawrence saw the familiar set-up of a psychcomputer. Of course! She had already passed their knowledge/intelligence tests. Meekly she sat down and fumbled with the controls.

"I didn't expect you to be able to hook yourself up," the attendant brightly remarked. She helped Lawrence get adjusted. "There. I'll be back when you're done."

The machine registered a Five.

"So I started calling my opus the Cube. Even then, when I thought all it needed was a second Square," Lawrence informed the questing public.

Wake up! These people so intent upon you aren't curious!

"They aren't?" Lawrence moved a little closer to the audience. "What are they then?" She peered into the darkness. "Get me some light to see them with."

Slowly the theater brightened.

Don't turn away from them now. Keep watching.

Lawrence scowled but kept her eye trained on the crowd.

It was not that long before she could easily distinguish their features. She found herself shivering.

They were not pleased. They were not frightened. They were not angry. They were . . . nothing.

"Now, brainddead I have seen, but this!" Lawrence spoke too loudly.

Nobody blinked. Nobody cared. Nobody thought.

"I'm planning all of this artifice," Lawrence said firmly. "I always know what will be."

The pillbox remained as before, each pellet staring blandly forward. Lawrence turned away.

There in the middle of the forest floor was the white, chalky face, smudged a bit with the red clay she had scraped away with a stone. Now she threw away the stone and wiped her sweaty forehead with her arm. Squatting down, she gently, patiently covered it with leaves, bits of bark, and nut shells. Then it rained.

Lawrence opened the door onto a tiny cotroom. She paused a moment to put the empty Square next to the screen and then went to the window.

"At least there's a window," she murmured, staring down at the scene four levels below. It made her dizzy, yet exhilarated. To be so tall! She turned back to the bed to see Maricela at the door.

"You like it?"

Lawrence shook her head.

"Why not?"

"I requested a single, but now I don't like it."

"Why did you request it, then?"

Lawrence felt uncomfortable under her direct gaze, but she answered soon enough. "At the time, I thought I would need time alone to study."

"And now?"

Lawrence blushed slightly. "I don't know. I just don't feel as if I *need* a single."

"Things changed for me, too. I asked them to switch my roommate, and it was no problem. They know people are going to see different, more desirable people once they get here." Maricela came on into the room, followed by Jeffrey. "If you don't mind, Jeffrey had a good idea."

Again Jeffrey seemed pleased to see her. Lawrence smiled at his serious, dark face. He closed the door.

"I thought we three should hold a meeting here, since it's quieter, and discuss what happened today, or whatever." He looked a little apologetic, since it wasn't his room, Lawrence guessed.

"Sounds good to me. Have a seat on the bed." Lawrence waited for them to practically crawl around the desk to get to the bed, then pulled her screen chair over toward them. Sitting, she continued, "What's a Five mean?"

"I got a One," offered Maricela.

"Me, too," Jeffrey said. Both of them looked curiously at Lawrence.

"Well, what does it mean? That I'll get sent back?" Lawrence could feel her torso sink.

"Ah, don't worry about it. They told me they were more lenient if you were never sowed." Maricela came close to patting her hand, then sat back, as if she figured out that Lawrence wouldn't like it. Lawrence pretended not to notice.

Lawrence straightened instantly. "Yeah. I've never been sowed. And I guessed you two haven't, either."

"That's one thing I wanted to bring up: Let's all stick together. We're not inlaid." Jeffrey spoke deeply, yet intensely.

Maricela shifted uncomfortably, causing Lawrence to reach near her legs to smooth the blanket she had forgotten to pull off the bed and store underneath it. "It's not that we should avoid them. I mean, they're not that bad. I think, though, we should stick together because we're attracted to one another, and because we're in a strange place. It has nothing to do with the —"

"Braindead. That's what the farmers called 'em," answered Lawrence eagerly, once more forgetting to cautiously think about the effect of what she chose to say before blurting it out.

Maricela jumped up and pointed. "That's what I wanted to ask you about! You were once a farmer. Why?"

Lawrence shrugged. "Vance told me it was because I was an artist."

Maricela and Jeffrey exchanged glances. The latter asked, "Who's Vance?"

"My Mentor in low-tech school. I joined the farmers because it was the only way I could get out of school. It was so boring it was driving me crazy." Lawrence spoke nonchalantly, hoping to casually steer the conversation away from the artists.

"Imagine someone of your intelligence on a farm. I never thought it possible." Maricela looked at Lawrence with respect. "But what's this about artists?" She scratched her nose briefly. "And braindead! Those naughty farmers! How dare they! It's not like inlaid people are completely hopeless."

"I'm sorry if I offended you," Lawrence felt obliged to say.

"Oh, no, that's all right," Maricela hastened to say, as if it were very important to be polite to Lawrence.

Lawrence nodded and looked at both of them in turn. "Did they make a big deal out of your Square?"

"Uh, no," Maricela answered while Jeffrey shook his head. "They gave it back to me after a couple of hours. Told me to fill it up in the next four years. I hope I can."

"Well, mine was already full. I got a new one here." She reached over and picked it up, practically leaning over Jeffrey's lap to reach it. "On my old one I've got all my old schoolwork and what the artists call an opus. Look upon it as a scientific project. I thought I'd transfer all my schoolwork onto this one and leave the other free for my project. I'll have as much trouble as either of you filling up my schoolwork Square in four years. The project, however, as they told me, requires more than one Square. Essentially, they asked me to create a Cube to house it."

Maricela and Jeffrey were staring at her, excitement evident as they breathed hard.

"Oh, what is it?" squealed Jeffrey. "What is your project?"

Lawrence groaned. "It's a little hard to explain."

"No, no, you're got to try! shouted Maricela, wriggling. "Something bigger than a Square! Wow!"

"I'm trying to make a physical model of everything that is important in the universe, everything that is alive and has consciousness. Basically, I'm creating Biota on a small scale. I'm—"

"You'll need gene maps, won't you?" Jeffrey interrupted.

"Wait a minute. Tell me you've already got the gene maps. How else could it fill up the Square?" Maricela demanded.

"No. I think I will need gene maps soon. What few we have. What's on my Square are the relationships I've discovered. Maybe my observations. Still, it's—"

"And it still filled a Square?" Maricela persisted.

Lawrence nodded. "I think it's growing, or infinite. You see, you start a model, and it's not going to be static. Events will occur. The situation will change . . ."

"Oh, Lawrence!" groaned Jeffrey. "We know all about dynamics, and cause and effect."

"Listen!" shouted Maricela. "Listen to me," she said more quietly. "What's your major?"

"Botany," answered Lawrence. "Why?"

"Shh! Jeffrey?"

"Zoology." He looked as puzzled as Lawrence felt.

171

"And mine is medical research. What luck! Do you see?" She did not wait for them to answer, though the light was dawning in their eyes. "We've got all of Biota right here in this room!"

Lawrence stood up by scooping over the chair sideways and pushing it tightly under the desk. "It's my project. Not that you two wouldn't be welcome, but you're got better things to do than live my dream." She spoke quietly.

Maricela calmed down and considered what she was saying. "Yes. Not only that, but it might fail. Still—"

"Still we could help you with your gene maps. College is rough," continued Jeffrey. "I'll let you get enmeshed in the Cube project all by yourself, Lawrence, while I study. But every once in a while I could supply you with gene maps of Fauna."

"My task is a lot easier," moped Maricela. "We have all the human maps already. Well," she brightened. "Maybe I could do something else."

"This will probably take years," mourned Lawrence. "I've got to keep up my studies, too, you know."

"But just think. Ooh, I can't. It's so *big*!" Jeffrey's eyes, unfocused, stared beyond Lawrence so wildly that she almost spun around to see what was there.

"Well, this meeting turned out to be a lot more exciting that I thought it would be!" said Maricela. She looked at Lawrence with so much respect it was embarrassing. "And someday you'll have to tell me about those artists of yours." She stood, so that Lawrence had to back up into the window sill to let her by.

Lawrence nodded eagerly, grinning, blushing, as Jeffrey pulled open the door just barely enough to get through.

"Oh, wait." Mareicela paused at the door. "We should plan another time to meet."

"We can't until we've adjusted to our schedules," explained Lawrence. "When that's done, leave me a message on my screen."

"Oh, that!" Maricela tossed aside the whole system with a gesture. "I'll just come by, okay?"

Lawrence nodded. "Okay."

Lawrence was in control, riding the reins, reaching those places she'd never seen, doing things she would never be able to do. Everything should move quickly now. She nodded at the gene maps surrounding her. They were known.

"All I am, I suppose, is my gene map."

She fell off the mount, off the pinnacle, head first into the sand.

She shook herself free. "Phooey! Now why'd I go and say a thing like that for?" She spit the sand off her tongue and walked forward.

The African woman came to her, hand out. Lawrence was confused. "Shawicc?"

The woman shook her head. "I am from the past, the beginning of the human tree. I come from the bush." She came forward silently to touch Lawrence's calluses. "There is no doubt you have worked hard," she said, murmuring so that her lips barely moved. "But come. I have something to show you." She paused a moment, and Lawrence turned around, lifting her shirt as she did so. The woman touched her scars with a feathery stroke, but then it was time to move on.

They crossed the sands to the bush, hand in hand, Lawrnce feeling that life stirring in her as before, not that long ago.

"Here." The African woman parted the branches and pointed. "What do you see?"

An old African man stood, a cloth about his loins, bowl in hands. It was an interesting bowl, orange-brown and elaborately carved. Immediately he began to tilt it so that the water dripped very, very slowly. At that rate, it should take several hours to empty, yet he stood patiently. Lawrence's vision sometimes jarred, seeing the bowl spin completely over backwards while in actuality it remained slightly tilted,. Many times as she watched it flipped when it really was as stationary, as sturdy as . . .

She blinked, and the scene changed.

Lawrence saw Maricela walking, eyes straight ahead, feet continually fading into the soft black underfoot. She swallowed tears.

"Maricela," she muttered. "I'm sorry if I did hurt you."

Lawrence yelled, "Come in!" but did not move from her window seat.

Maricela popped her head inside, then barged in, as best as she could around the door, indignant. "Oh, look at you!" she began impatiently. "You're just sitting there! I thought you'd be busy."

Lawrence frowned. "I am never busy, but I am not doing nothing."

Maricela surveyed the room. "What are you doing then?"

"I'm watching." Lawrence pointed out the window.

Delicately Maricela stepped over to the window, faintly curious. A single glance made her exclaim, "There's nothing out there!" Then she leaned further and squinted. "Nope. No nude workers I can see. No delightfully cool young man passing by in his loincloth, either."

Lawrence rolled her eyes, trying to remain indifferent. "There's a lot out there," she explained patiently. "I'm studying the patterns of people, just like I studied the patterns of nature."

"Speaking of studying —" Maricela paused to fall face down on Lawrence's cot, moan, and then roll over onto her side, propping her head up on her elbow and grinning. "Don't you ever?"

Lawrence pbbbttfd and stood. "Sometimes I usually rely on my foundation, so I don't waste time."

"Your *what*?"

Lawrence flicked her hair out of her face impatiently. "You know. My foundation of knowledge I extrapolate from. I've found it better to select a guess than wait for someone to show me. I'm usually right."

Maricela rolled her eyes. "You and Jeffrey. The perfect pair."

Lawrence considered. "What's that mean?"

Maricela rolled over and sat up. "Forget I said it. You two are actually quite different."

Lawrence scratched her head.

"I'm not about to explain it, either. You always want an explanation." Maricela pointed at the work table Lawrence had squeezed in somehow next to her screen. "How's the Cube coming?"

"It's hard for me to see the human variation," Lawrence answered, diversifying the subject a bit.

Maricela studied her a minute, frowning, then she brightened. "Oh, I get it. About us all being different. Jeffrey was just complaining about the inlaids. All they do is study, study, study. They say they have to catch up. I can . . . sort of see why he thinks they're all alike." Maricela looked over at Lawrence, who was fingering a rhythm board she had enigmatically placed in the middle of the fragmented Squares on her work table. "I've got one of those," she offered. "They're weird, aren't they?"

Lawrence looked solemnly at her. "I invented it."

Maricela laughed. "I've had it so long. You couldn't have."

Lawrence shrugged. "I was four. I've stopped working on the Cube because I really don't know enough about computer plasma. So, in the meantime, I started adjusting the basic mechanism of this thing," here she waved the rhythm board, "for human sensory emphasis, like the way we observe Biota."

Maricela leaned forward, suddenly interested. "Is that necessary?"

"Oh, don't ask me that now. I haven't done enough to say. It's probably going to take me off the right path and waste me a lot of time to fool around with this rhythm board. Anyway, I mean, still, I have an idea that it's what I did in my youth that's important. Like I have to start there. And who knows? Maybe I'm right." Awkwardly Lawrence rubbed her hand down her thigh.

Maricela did not ridicule her, however. She merely looked thoughtful.

Lawrence sighed as she picked up a series of Squares. "Sometimes I think I need a break." She meant a trip from the room that she stayed in every moment she wasn't in class. She looked shyly over at Maricela and gulped. Would she go with her if she asked casually enough?

Maricela said brightly, "We are given some vacation time, you know. Whenever we want it. I'm going next week, to see my family."

Lawrence was about to chuckle, "Leaving so soon?" but the last word terrified her. She forgot all about acting casual as she stuttered, "You, you stayed with your family?"

Maricela nodded. "Oh, I know it's not required after school, and I didn't live with them anymore. Still, I feel loyal to them."

It was hard for Lawrence to hold back the tears at this confession. She struggled to swallow a lump in her throat. "Maricela . . ."

Maricela looked at her with clear, innocent eyes, confusing Lawrence. How could someone be so alive, so joyous, and so ignorant? "What's wrong?"

Lawrence gently put down the series of Squares and almost turned toward the bed. She couldn't, however, and merely went back to the window.

Maricela withdrew her tray and placed it on the work table. She placed a tiny scalpel and a needle on it and eyed Lawrence, who didn't notice as she closed her eyes, head against the cool, soothing window glass.

"Come here," commanded Maricela softly.

Lawrence found herself obeying, blindly stretching out her hands. Maricela gathered them in hers and rubbed the backs with her thumbs, her fingers gracing the rims. "Calluses," she murmured. She cupped the palms in hers, then massaged the heels. Then it was time to raise them to her lips.

Lawrence yanked her hands away and went back to the window, where she could faintly hear the musical tone of repair workers.

Maricela, still gentle, came up behind her. "What's the matter? Are you scared?"

"No." Lawrence puzzled over how to convince her that this wasn't a lie.

That proved impossible, because Maricela murmured, "It's all right."

Lawrence despaired, because what happened next was just as she expected.

"Why did you start then?" Maricela asked hotly.

"Oh, Maricela." Lawrence turned and stuck a knee up on the bed. "I don't have any experience with the tray. It's nothing personal."

"That's strange," Maricela murmured. "I was thinking you were more experienced than I."

"Really?" Lawrence considered. "I can't imagine why," she said dryly.

"I don't know," Maricela said honestly. "You seem so *mature*."

Lawrence didn't say anything.

"You stand out."

Sharply Lawrence turned to her. "I do?" She remembered Vance telling her how important it was for her to blend in.

"Yes," Maricela said in a low, serious voice, sounding quite like Jeffrey. "Your presence is commanding. The way you look . . . at things."

Lawrence tried to digest this new piece of information while Maricela waited patiently. Living was a memory lately. Each new, exciting thing could be treasured only later. Like with the hands. That had been nice.

Maricela packed the tray and sighed. "It's not right, now, what I'm feeling."

175

"I'm sorry." Lawrence almost explained her reluctance upon seeing that bent head.

"That's okay," Maricela said, not looking at her. "Because you're not experienced."

"I said I didn't have any experience with *trays*," Lawrence corrected.

Maricela got it. She swung away from the door and gawked, whooping, "Oh, right! Our childhood sex games! I had forgotten. They just don't seem official, without the tray, but oh! I guess that explains your maturity, somewhat." She slid up to the hips through the door, then tossed over her shoulder, "Maybe some other time, okay?"

"Sure," Lawrence answered loudly, cheerily, then waited for the door to close. Once alone, she went back over to the rhythm board and gathered it up. *Come on, Lawrence, get to work.* She berated herself. *You've got to do it now. You've got to do something.* She sniffed and wiped her eyes. "I've got to do it for *her*, and make her happy."

The gong came crisply since she was not occupied. She put down the rhythm board, took time to rinse her face in the shower spigot that had to serve as her sink, and went down for the evening meal.

Lawrence entered the psychcomputer room and sat in the nearer of the two seats.

The female behind the desk smiled at her choice of seating. "You're improving. Closer, less fearful of contact with those of authority."

Lawrence interrupted. "No, just hard of hearing."

"You wanted to know what a Five meant," she answered calmly.

Lawrence had to give her a little credit; nothing fazed her. "Assuming you'll tell me the truth. How could my best friends be so different from me?"

"It's not necessarily a bad sign, in their case. A One shows high intelligence, coherence, a goal-oriented personality, self-confidence, leadership ability, cooperativeness, rather like an ideal successful person," the psychcomputer began.

"Excuse me while I go throw up," Lawrence said without a trace of exasperation.

"You have a sense of humor. That's fine." The psychcomputer again smiled at her classification that narrowed her perspective of the human personality. "I'll continue. In your case, Lawrence . . ."

"Insert personal name every few sentences," interrupted Lawrence, reading from the psychcomputer manual. "This works wonders against the intractable patient."

"A Five indicates . . ." Finally the psychcomputer paused, wincing. "Well, an essential uncooperativeness. It's hard to explain because many factors are involved. Your intelligence, of course, but other things as well. You've never been sowed. You always sought beyond authority, never accepting anything. You always studied on your own. Now that all that mess of closed and falsified records of yours has been straightened out, we see a lot of inexplicable behavior and thoughts. For instance, your record shows that you were even a farmer at one point."

Lawrence flapped her right arm up in a fluttering arc before slamming it against the arm of the chair, because it was starting to get to where she already knew what she was being told. "Get to the point."

"We always seem to have trouble with Fives. You're different, because you have a goal, but even now we see the Cube as a dangerous construct. It will have to be placed under our control from here on. Maybe you cannot understand the concern, but . . ."

That did it. Lawrence listened to the slow, methodical tones and saw the careful, calm face and rapidly kicked it. Kicked it several times. "You nasty people!" (kick) The woman changed to an older man, so Lawrence kicked harder. "It's because I was so sweet (kick) and cooperative (kick) that I ended up in this mess. (kick) Gotta go now (kick) and save Maricela." (kick kick)

Lawrence ran out of the room and coursed away from the seething humans and entered Fauna. There was Buddy, and a pair of eyes that gazed, unafraid, into hers. The squirrel blinked, a chattering sound coming from the wriggling tail. A deer chewed, its large eyes full, deep, and again unafraid.

Lawrence looked down. Ants were crawling across her feet. She stepped out of their path.

The rain had stopped, so Jeffrey came over to ask her to join him, as planned. "Today's good for me. How about you?"

Lawrence turned to see him rattling the door latch, grinning with a fresh, open face. "Sure. Give me a few minutes to save what I have here."

Jeffrey peered over at her screen. "Ooh, pictures! What for?"

"It's for the Cube. These are representations of everything as we see them."

"Yeah, that 3D, fractal stuff," Jeffrey said offhandedly. "You're going to make an . . . ?" He looked at her. "I don't get it."

"It's going to be a device where you can actually enter it. It's got to be. It's not going to be just data banks isolated from experience." Lawrence entered another equation and waited for it to clear.

"But pictures?" Jeffrey scratched his head. "We're going to view your project?"

Lawrence grinned. His funny Northern accent always helped. "No. That's surface." Then she regretted letting that artist remark through.

"What about the gene maps? We're supposed to study them, too? I get enough of that in class." Jeffrey sounded like he was honestly trying to understand, but Lawrence couldn't explain.

"Look." Lawrence ran the screen up and pointed. "I think the gene here is wrong. Their records could have measured a mutant."

Jeffrey bent and peered at the screen. "What's that one?"

"*Anastatica hierochuntica.* A flowering specimen of the East/North continent."

"Someone could check it, I guess. How many Squares is it now?"

"Seven. Of course, most of it is just those genetic maps. It's not like it's actually anything yet." She gazed up at Jeffrey.

"If that's all it is, a representation of the Earth," he began.

Lawrence followed the glance of his deep green eyes. "No. That isn't all it is. That's just surface."

"What's that mean? You said that's what it was. A collection of gene maps." His eyes were puzzled.

"It's just the beginning," substituted Lawrence.

"Ah, that makes sense." His eyes gazed friendily on her. "It really does. You'll see."

Lawrence turned off the screen and stood.

"You ready to go?"

"Sure."

They went down to the temporary pens. "Be quiet, now," Jeffrey warned. "His cage is way back here."

Lawrence passed the cages warily, walking carefully down the wide, grassy aisle and not looking too closely at any of the inhabitants.

"Here it is." Jeffrey pointed to a cage labeled *Cerdocyon thous*, then approached it cautiously. "Here, Buddy. It's me." He placed his hands flat and low on the cage, and Buddy licked his right one. "Yeah!"

Lawrence stood to the side and slid open the door at Jeffrey's gesture. He reached in and stroked Buddy's throat, then he cradled his arm around the belly and lifted.

"I'm supposed to check his saliva," he explained to Lawrence.

Lawrence shut the cage's door and climbed back down, eyeing the little fox.

"He won't hurt you."

Lawrence found herself explaining, "I'm afraid of hurting *him*."

Jeffrey's eyes changed, and he stood straighter. "I'm not going to hurt him."

Lawrence stared, startled. "I didn't say you were going to."

Jeffrey turned abruptly and marched over to the lab, clutching Buddy gently. Lawrence followed awkwardly, wondering if she had hurt Jeffrey in some way.

She waited in the cool anteroom while Jeffrey withdrew a specimen. He read it, then turned apologetically to Lawrence.

"It looks like I'm going to have to draw blood. Would you hold him?"

Lawrence sterilized and entered the lab. She took her place beside Jeffrey and reached for Buddy. Her hands went automatically to the right places, ignoring the tempting fur and holding firmly the limbs.

Jeffrey read his sample, then fed all of the data to his Square. "Come on, Buddy," he said, stroking the little fox's head. "I'll take you out for some exercise."

Buddy leapt off the table and trotted after him to the door. Jeffrey slid it open to let the little fox canter onto the grass in the fenced yard. He turned back to Lawrence. "Come on outside." He gestured. "Here's a place where we can sit down."

The two went and sat in the corner most coated with leaves.

"It sure is warm today," Jeffrey commented.

Lawrence nodded. "Yeah. They kept warning me about how bad the winters are up here, but there's not that much difference."

"Naw. This is nothing. Go up to Region 3. Brr!" His eyes went to the fox. "I'm going to miss him when he takes off for the West/South continent tomorrow."

"In the egg trucks?"

Jeffrey laughed. "The farm trucks, yes. How else? Why do you call them egg trucks?" He shook his head. "Listen to me. Egg?"

"The farmers call them that."

"What eggs?" Jeffrey splurted, exasperated. "Oh!" He blushed. "But they carry sperm, too. And that so rarely, anyway. No wonder I didn't get it." He looked at her, recovered now, still bemused. "Your farmers are crazy."

Lawrence watched the fox sniff a few red flowers on the gate. Damn. There was a specimen she didn't recognize, and it was practically in her backyard! Time not to hang around in her room anymore. "I never saw any animals on them," she mused.

They sat for a while, each lost in their own thoughts, then Jeffrey stirred.

"Look. I made Buddy a ball." He showed her the soft sphere made out of what looked to be brown denim before he tossed it. Buddy ran, caught it, and threw it down at Jeffrey's feet.

Lawrence laughed.

"I'm grateful you came over today. I like to show somebody the animals," Jeffrey said lowly, looking away as he tossed the ball again.

"Well, I like them," Lawrence said unevenly.

"Yeah, but you're a botanist." Before Lawrence could protest, he raised his hand in peace. "I know, don't tell me. You're interested in everything. I kind of feel the same thing myself. It was tough, choosing a major."

Lawrence murmured agreeably.

"I finally decided on this one, though. I couldn't go just part way on this. I want to work with animals, but you know something? It feels strange. Not too many people are in our fields. I kind of feel out of place."

"That's stupid," Lawrence said firmly. "Who cares what other people do?"

"You're right. Sometimes, though, I look at those eyes and wonder what they're thinking. I try to be kind, but . . . how can I know what I'm doing?"

Lawrence was quiet a long time, thinking back over the thrill of meeting Buddy, holding him. Starting from an easy point, she finally asked, "Are you going to keep this major?"

Jeffrey shifted and looked disgusted, as if sick of this question. "Yeah. I've thought it through and decided there are no answers. I want to do this. Besides, I'm shy. People are just too—I don't know, jumpy for me. I'd rather stay with the animals." Jeffrey faced her, to touch her cheek. "Even Maricela. But you're different, Lawrence. I don't know why. Maybe it's because you're calm, quiet, especially when you need to be. You'd be good with the animals."

But Lawrence was already shaking her head, though she found it hard to keep from laughing. Imagine! Jeffrey as shy! No way! "No. I couldn't."

Jeffrey nodded. "Yeah. I can see that. It's a tough decision, to swallow all your questions, your guilt, even, and accept the job. Besides, there's your project. Hey!"

Lawrence rapidly glanced at Buddy to see if he was in danger. "He's all right." She smiled at him pulling on a rag that hung from the wall. She squinted. The rag looked like the piece of brown denim Jeffrey had used to make Buddy's ball, though why it was tacked up outside she couldn't fathom.

But Jeffrey didn't hear her. "Hey!" he said more quietly. "Your project would let us actually experience the being of their lives?" He grabbed her hand and squeezed. "Could it?"

"I don't know," Lawrence blathered, feeling her heart pound and sparks shoot through her. "It might someday. That's my hope." She clutched, startled, when Jeffrey hugged her.

"Your hope, my dream!" he exulted.

Lucky for Lawrence he calmed down before she really needed that next breath. He let her go and turned.

"Come here, Buddy."

The fox came and hopped on his lap.

"I'll get you some water, and you can stay out here a little longer. I've got to see to the other animals." He stood and dusted off his butt. Lawrence watched as he filled a small wooden bowl and left it on the porch. He glanced back at Lawrence, and his voice came out respectfully and silkily. "The others aren't quite so tame, naturally. Think you can watch?"

Lawrence wriggled a foot that had fallen asleep and stretched upward, limping slightly to meet him. "I believe I can."

"Not like it worked. Why doesn't it work? I haven't yet popped into anything's life's experiences. I think it's because I haven't completely abandoned the world from which I came. It's because I haven't totally lost myself within the Cube. But I can't do that, anyway. If I lose myself, I won't be able to observe; I won't be able to react like a human. I won't be able to tell what's going on. It would be consciousness without intellect. I'd never get out of here, either! Eek!" She lifted another dab of mortar and splatted it onto her sculpture of a tidal pool.

"Hey, look out!" Another art student angrily wiped the glob off of her face and returned to her sketches of wallabies playing dulcimers.

"Sorry," Lawrence muttered. "I didn't know you were there."

"Lawrence." A hushed voice called her urgently.

Lawrence wiped her hands and went over to the instructor.

"Please come with me. I'd like to talk to you."

Meekly she followed Scott out of the room, into a meadow.

"How are you doing?" he began.

Lawrence bent down to look at the saw grass. "Okay. Get to the point, Scott. You were always too polite."

"I hesitate because what I have to tell you might not help you," he said tensely.

"I don't care. Go ahead. I'll take anything. I'd hate to go back to Jeffrey as a failure." She shifted her squat, but her foot caught in a hollow so she plunked down. A bird squawked out of a clump of grass. Together they watched it fly off.

"The reason you can't do what you set out to do, starting at the age of eight, am I right about that?"

"Yeah, I guess so." Lawrence tried to think back. "It happened so recently. Anyway, keep going."

"The reason is that it can't be you in here. It's got to be somebody else. This is a work of art, and everything in here is a product of your mind. You made the decisions as to just what would come out."

Lawrence squinted up at him wryly. "So you're saying it's tainted?"

Scott took a deep breath. "No. I'm just saying you're in control. I don't have to appear in this role. You could make my face green, my hand abusive . . ."

"Scott!" Lawrence moaned. "The gene maps created you."

"Listen to you. That's predeterminism, and you know it. The environment you created is acting on my gene map. It can diverge, you know." He stepped back. "Do you really think *I* have any power?"

"Yes, but never mind. Go back to your classroom. Teach. Program the students. Set up a lesson plan they can live with. As if anybody has anything to learn. And one more thing: don't expect anybody to come up with something other than what you designated as the right answer." Lawrence touched the chaff around the saw grass seeds, catching the fluff on her fingers.

One day after class Lawrence went out into the soft autumn sunlight and headed past the dorms to the city. Maricela had told her that a new shipment had arrived. It felt weird, not to even take part in the planting, and yet partake of the food. In less agricultural regions than hers, though, that was the norm.

The stores were full, with those who were not students making their selections from the stalls. Lawrence smelled the rich flavors appreciatively, but avoided the foods. She had thought to pick up a few snacks, like the broccoli sprouts she had come to crave, but now she'd shop for other things.

She stopped in front of the furniture store. Maricela had shown it to her when she went to get a work table to match Lawrence's.

First she peered into the window and jumped when she saw her dark image peering back. That was one of Celeste's mirrors, she had no doubt. You couldn't miss one of those. Lawrence found herself all at once eager to enter.

Without a moment's loss she went over and studied the mirror. Celeste had developed a refractive surface that glowed within a slight concavity. Then she had framed the device with soft, feathery offshoots. Lawrence admired it a long time, then went to find the trunk.

The seed design carved into the trunk's wood had enchanted her, but she couldn't really use it. It wouldn't have fitted into her room anyway. She supposed some of the school's linens would go into it eventually. An individual would be too reluctant to take on such an immensity, she guessed, though the college with its vast staff could always use more storage.

Over against the wall were racks of clothes. Lawrence admired a burgundy shirt made of cotton from the islands off the coast, but she knew her clothes were holding up. She returned to study the mirror, wondering who would get it.

Another face appeared in the mirror, distorted in the angle its height presented. Lawrence gave it as serious a study as she had the mirror itself, noting the pulled features as merely an interesting optical phenomenon, so it was several seconds before she recognized him. The new beard didn't help.

"Hello," Scott said quietly.

Lawrence continued to stare at him in the mirror, mystified by her rapid heartbeat. "When did your beard start?"

Scott seemed uncomfortable. "I've had it forever, it seems. Probably two years." He smiled down, assuming an awkward angle so he could face her in the mirror. "Maybe. Or maybe I'm just saying that because I haven't seen you for that long."

Lawrence moved away to sit in a rocking chair, unsuccessfully trying to hide her blush.

"When you left," Scott mumbled as he crouched to sit on the trunk set next to the wide-bottomed chair, "I thought I'd see you again quickly. You students have regular vacation times. But you never came home."

"Why should I?"

Scott grinned, fingering the burgundy shirt. "Oh, I don't know. There was some cotton that needed picking."

Lawrence pursed her lips in an attempt to look disgusted. "I don't need to go there. I spent sixteen years living there and nowhere else. Why would I need to go back? Ain't nothing there new to see, is there?"

Scott looked out the window, where the view of the road was blocked by the immense Center. "You actually like it here?"

Lawrence shrugged. "It's okay. It's not much different."

"Not much different?! How can that be? Look how many people are crammed into one spot. There must be—I don't know—twenty thousand?!" Scott waved his hand toward the window, where the bare clearing belied his demonstration. He glared at the Center and folded his arms.

"The commune was the same way. It had a large number of people living close together in one clearing. It wasn't like you wanted to hang around there all the time, anyway," Lawrence asserted. "Besides, I think in this city people leave me alone more." No, that wasn't what she wanted to say. "I—"

"Do you even have an opus?" He was picking rather obsessively at a thread in his jeans, as if he knew what Lawrence was going to say next, that certain people here treated her better than she could have imagined back home.

Lawrence hesitated. "For you, Scott, I'll talk about it." Her voice was gentle. There had been *one* like that at home, she remembered. "I just can't be bothered with that artist frap right now." She hurried on so he couldn't interrupt. "I'm working on something now."

"The way you talk—has it all these years been just one project? You keep telling me, I have a project, and I've never seen one . . . Maybe you don't want to show them to me. Well, that's okay—"

"Scott. Please." She rolled her eyes. "It's big. Chit. It's been in my head for ten years. I've been trying to bring it out here, in college. It's nowhere near done. I don't know how long it's gonna take."

"How big is it?" Scott asked hastily.

"It's eleven Squares now. Those that are full, that is. I've got lots of partial Squares I'm using to build its case. I wasn't kidding when I said it was big."

"But . . . but . . . *what* is it?" Scott blurted, then paused. "If you want to tell me."

"I'll try. It's hard to explain. Right now, I'm mapping the genes of the world." Now that sounded absurd, not quite it.

"Is that all?" Scott leaned forward. "The scientists do gene maps. What are you doing? Collecting them? Big—"

"Yes," Lawrence interrupted. "Big deal."

"I'm sorry, but—"

"It's more than that. I must build its house, its environment. Then, I've got the idea to represent how humans perceive the world. Then, I'll let it run, interact . . ."

"Sounds like virtual reality to me. I don't see *you* in it, Lawrence. It's not art." He sounded disappointed.

183

"I'm in there, certainly. I don't know what you mean," Lawrence lied, not willing to start mouthing off about how she didn't *want* herself in there. "Anyway, most of my vacations are spent mapping. It's great. An entire month just to work on my project!"

Reluctantly Scott answered, "If you'd stayed with us, you would have been given times like that. I spent three months on my last opus."

Lawrence looked away to consider. Could she have stayed? Built up their trust? But high technology was a part of her she could not relinquish. She stood and went back over to the mirror. Celeste had to find some way to make that mirror curve the right way, didn't she? "You forget, Scott," she said dryly. "The artists kicked me out. They deemed, and now apparently you deem, me not to be an artist."

"I didn't say that!" Scott jumped up. "Uh, look, please, I don't want to argue. Um." He pointed at the mirror. "It's beautiful. I've got one she made. Makes me looks taller."

Lawrence snickered. "Was that your idea, or was she just playing a joke?"

Scott looked honestly at her. "You don't need one, though."

Lawrence frowned, not wanting to tell him that the school didn't think so, either; her room had none.

Scott continued, "I mean, not height, just looks. You . . . look a little happier, or something."

"I don't know about that, but perhaps it's because I've found my place." She looked at him just as openly, but was distracted by a movement at the window.

Maricela passed by, stopped, backed up, peered in, and then, finally, chose to enter.

"Hello, Lawrence," she said shyly. "I saw the mirror from outside."

Lawrence leaned back so she could take in the whole thing, while Scott jumped to the side.

Maricela impassionately absorbed its structure. "It's odd," she finally announced. "What makes it do that?"

"Its focal length. Plus, of course, it's concave." Lawrence's voice came out low and gentle, though she wondered why Maricela couldn't simply grasp the applied physics as she had.

Maricela wavered in front of it, then turned sideways to look at her profile. "It accentuates my glow," she announced.

"What glow?" Lawrence demanded.

Maricela tossed her head. "The glow that charms, certainly, not that you'll ever see it." She came close to look at the frame. "What strange stuff. What is it?" Her fingers strayed lightly above it, not deigning to touch it yet.

Lawrence told her, "Roots. Leaf veins. Offshoots. Anything feathery, soft." She couldn't say this without wondering what Maricela saw that was similar in her prairie region.

Maricela glanced casually at her from under lowered eyelids, sidelong at Scott, then let her hand drop. "It looks softer than it feels." She strode past both of them and stood at the window with fists on her hips. "I was expecting Jeffrey, not you, at market day. I wonder where he went." Instantly she was back at the mirror, pointing distractedly. "I've got to have this mirror! Do you think they'll let me have it?" she asked Scott, who merely looked addled.

"I ain't even got a mirror, Maricela. We ought to be able to finagle something with rationing, where I get it for you. You don't even have to trade me the one you got now," came a meek, overawed voice as Lawrence pictured ruefully their sumptuous double room, which could easily support two mirrors, while hers . . .

Maricela looked for a second into Lawrence's drenched eyes, and allowed a delicate smile to shine upon her face. "I'd like that." She went over to the trunk, Lawrence following right along, to sit. Maricela haughtily glanced at Scott as she trailed her hand into Lawrence's and touched gently the inner cracks of her fingers. "Everything should be made like that, beautiful, unique." She still stared at Scott defiantly.

"That's what they teach us," Scott said, red-faced.

Lawrence nodded, successfully appearing nonchalant at Maricela's touch. "Make it good, or don't make it at all."

"I don't know, though," Maricela said softly. "If I had just made something that lovely, I'd keep it."

Lawrence cleared her throat. "What if you don't think it's beautiful, and someone else does?"

Before Maricela could even think, Scott asked smoothly, "Ah, but what if only you can see the beauty?"

Both women turned and looked at Scott.

"I don't think that ever happens," answered Maricela finally. "Besides, we have to share. If I had made a hundred mirrors, I'd have to share. Still," she sighed, gazing at the opaque shine. "I'd have to keep that one."

Lawrence blanched. Ownership of the Cube? Still, she wondered if maybe Celeste missed her mirror. On second thought . . . she whipped her glance away from Scott's feeble smile to wonder if he had something else in mind when he said that. Aha! No, he couldn't, but . . .

Scott stood. "I better get going," he said heavily. He looked at Lawrence beseechingly, so that she unlaced her hand from Maricela's and stood.

She nodded. "I'll go with you."

Maricela ungracefully climbed up and faced Lawrence. "I'm going to go find Jeffrey. Meet me at lunch, if you can."

Lawrence, already in step with Scott, shrugged over her shoulder. "Okay."

On the way to his truck, Scott trudged, mainly, looking at his feet. Eventually, he asked, "Who's Jeffrey? Her lover?"

"Probably. They're roommates."

Scott sighed, glanced sharply at her, then away. "And you?" he choked.

"I have my own room," she answered, surprised.

Scott stopped and took her arm. "You know what I mean."

Lawrence turned to face him, so that she ended up snuggling against his chest. Out of the corner of her eye she could see Maricela turned back, watching. "We stick together," she said shortly. "Beats me as to why."

He released her, then went down alone to the truck. Lawrence trailed behind him uneagerly, wanting to get it over with.

Scott took hold of the handle and pulled himself into the open door. "Lawrence. I wish you well." was all he said before he hopped into the driver's seat.

Lawrence stepped back when the engine started. That time, it sounded like he never wanted to see her again. She shrugged, then went back to the furniture store.

She wasn't really looking where she was going, so the presence of Maricela lingering at the door startled her. She gave her a smirk and a casual glance before going in to arrange transfer. Maricela held the door open for her when she came out, holding the mirror delicately from its back hook.

"That was fast! I guess you could have had a mirror all along, if you'd asked. Are you sure you don't want mine?" Maricela immediately forgot she said this as she reached out. "Oh, don't drop it. Here. I have to help you carry it." She went from fluttering with anxiety to sensibly grabbing the base and firmly pulling it level. She looked wryly at Lawrence with a superior grin. "He looks a little old to be the one you fooled around with."

Lawrence laughed. "Who said there was only one?"

Maricela didn't drop her precious mirror at that, but she didn't speak to Lawrence the rest of the day . . . or any of the next.

Lawrence was under a hot, bright sun in downtown Atlanta. Without fear she garnered the unusual name from the braindead rings, in which the sap had started to flow, refreshing the memories.

Lawrence held flowers for sale as . . . cars flowed by. "Goddamn, it's hot! It's too bright!" How easily the words came, how normal it was to reach into her jeans pocket and pull out some sunglasses. "Ah, that's better. Neat invention." Except she had always had them, just a different style. She walked back and forth, back and forth, she could see the cars stop, flow, stop, flow, it repeated fairly consistently, all wanted to turn left, turn right, go straight, go north, go south, go east, go west, whoops, make a U-turn, it could be the same one hundred cars, for all the difference it made, going, going around, and around.

Lawrence looked at her watch. An hour. One lousy hour. No sale. Of course not. In that stream, though the lights conditioned a pause at the glimmer of red, who could stop, see, work for food? Yeah, we all do, artists most of all, where I come from, way back there. Shit, it's hot.

Lawrence watched her feet. Yeah, the same, pretty much the same, back and forth, back and forth, a little lopsided circle. Tired of standing here. The production line's slow today. Education. Requirements. Face it. I ache. I'm *bored*. It is work. We do work.

"The best I've seen," whispered one of the braindead, "that is, it's the best because I've seen it referred to the most, is the metaphor of the lion in its cage, pacing back and forth."

"Hey, listen!" Lawrence threw down the flowers. "Fuck your metaphor! I'm human, and I've had enough!" She stepped into and through the flowing traffic, to the hills beyond. Immediately she felt alone, loose, and free, in a cool, overflowing river. She sighed, sinking deeply into the pulsating echoes.

Maricela came in and saw a hot, flustered, angry student thrown across her cot. Window open, light off.

"Hey, what's wrong?" She alighted on Lawrence's stool.

Almost without letting her ask the question, Lawrence moaned, "I can't breathe. I'm going crazy."

Maricela looked at the equipment scattered everywhere, especially the wide Cube Lawrence must leap over to go to the bathroom. "Go for a walk," she suggested brightly.

"I did. That didn't help." Lawrence closed her eyes.

"Well," began Maricela, then her eyes saw Lawrence's screen flashing. "Hey! You've got a message from the board!"

"Yeah, so?" She didn't move.

"Answer it!" Maricela almost wrung her hands, but managed to keep her voice strong.

Lawrence peeked her eyes open a little bit. "I never answer those things. I erase them."

"You can't do that! I can't even imagine it! Not responding to the board! I'd better answer it!" Maricela leaned over to hit "acknowledge."

"That's your weakness, I suppose." Lawrence sat up, all serious now. "What did they do to you, Maricela?"

"What do you mean? Shh." She typed in, after entering her personal identification code: MY FRIEND IS INDISPOSED. MESSAGE? She turned to Lawrence. "They need to see you at the Center."

"They want to see me, they can come here and see me. *You* do," she pointed out. "Hey, Maricela, are you scared?" She scooted over and touched her arm.

"No, I'm mad at you. You want to be kicked out of school?" Maricela brushed her hand away.

"Oh, yeah." Lawrence pretended to just remember something. "I did put in a request recently. I wonder if they got it? Anyway," she said brightly, "I can't go over there if I'm indisposed, now can I?" She grinned.

"I give up!" murmured Maricela. "Sometimes you . . ."

Jeffrey fell into the door, breathing hard. "We got it! We got it!"

Maricela suddenly understood. "Oh! *That* request! Both of you?" she asked Jeffrey as he gasped for breath.

He nodded blissfully.

Lawrence reached over and pulled a few Squares away from the desk after Jeffrey brushed against them to sit on the bed. "Please be careful with these."

"And . . ." Jeffrey managed to begin.

"Aren't you excited?" Maricela jumped on Lawrence.

"No," she said quite honestly.

"I am!" Jeffrey breathed. "And guess what? Lawrence's going—"

Maricela ignored him to continue berating Lawrence. "I can't believe this! So soon you get this, and you . . ."

"Shh! Shh!" Jeffrey motioned. "Yes, we got our three-month research leave, but not only that, but they accepted Lawrence's simulations. The biggest problem was with the rhythm board, until some old guy said he had been there talking to her when she had invented it."

Lawrence jumped up. "What guy?"

"Oh, you know. One of the child psychologists they dragged along during tests. Funny that they didn't use a psychcomputer. It would remember better, you know. Anyway, once that got cleared up, they decided your idea was legitimate, and that you could accelerate to laboratory manager." Jeffrey laughed. "Isn't it great?"

"So what does that mean? I'm going to miss you two, but I think I'll be on vacation through some of your trip. Don't worry about me." Maricela drooped.

Jeffrey wagged a finger at Lawrence. "Be polite, now. Tell Maricela you're sorry that she can't come."

"Oh, I don't want to come," Maricela hastily reassured, straightening. "You can both have a fine time in the rain forest without me coming along, thank you!" She sniffed before breaking out into a grin. "I can't help it! I'm so happy for you two!"

"What it means is, to answer your question, is that I'll have space, my bed in an empty room!" Lawrence got up and twirled in the sole empty circle near the bathroom. "That lab's got plasma, room. I'll be so grateful for that lab, I'll live in it!" She crouched near the Cube. "Come on, baby, you're going to grow!" She hugged all 73 Squares.

"They found a pilot, did I tell you? We won't have to learn to fly or nothing," Jeffrey said as Maricela laughed.

"Look at her now! So excited!" She clapped her hands, apparently forgetting Lawrence's disobedience.

"I still can't believe it," said Jeffrey. "Three months of genetic mapping in the richest section of the planet!" He sighed, hugging himself.

Lawrence refused to share his enthusiasm. She figured she'd die of boredom in three months, but somebody had to do the plants, and the board had said that it must be her. All she wanted to do right now was move straight into that laboratory and get to work. Her mouth watered at how much more efficient she would instantly become, and as for creativity . . . just you wait! But no, she had to chafe down in the West/South continent until she was free again to work on the part of the Cube that really mattered.

Maricela was standing over her, looking worried. "When I see you again, Lawrence, maybe I can make you see."

Lawrence sobered, though she couldn't understand why she was making a big deal out of it. "Anything to help you, Maricela."

Lawrence sat in the cleared circle and waved buzzing insects out of her face. All around her sat Yanomamo.

She bent her head, then stood. Slowly she spun, stepping widely in the dirt, until she had viewed each member of the tribe.

The leader waved. "Sit down."

Lawrence meekly sat down and studied the one who spoke. He did sit in a special place. She frowned.

"I must talk to you."

She nodded. "I have been to this place before. It is the West/South continent."

He inclined his head. "Yes. And we are the local ancestors of those few in the satellites."

Lawrence started. "I did not think it was possible to speak to ancestors. I do not have your gene maps."

He waved his hand again. "Anything is possible here. Listen."

Lawrence acquiesced, already surreptitiously studying them again. *So this is how they were before they interbred.*

"The rain forests of your time contain no humans. If you will allow us, we will settle here, and rebuild our traditional life."

Lawrence listened. His voice sounded confident. His bearing was superb. "I do not understand. You don't need my permission."

"It is your Cube," he pointed out.

"Yes," Lawrence immediately agreed. That was the one sure thing.

"God stands behind you," he said cryptically. "Do you believe it is all fiction?"

Lawrence stretched her leg out and kicked a few pebbles. "I'm not sure what you mean by God, but I think you do exist, in a sense. After all, I'm talking to you." She crossed her eyes, straining to speak.

"When you created the Cube, you sought all life on Earth. All life was not on Earth, so you sought the satellites. You could not catalog all life, but since it is all on Earth, except a few humans, easily catalogued, you could complete it."

Lawrence tilted her head down. Before her a beetle scampered. "I don't think so. I'm afraid that's a bit too mystical for me. There will be gaps."

"Due to?"

Lawrence gave up. "What are you getting at?"

"Are you beginning to see yourself?" he persisted. "Your people are robots, created from the past, as we all are, yet specifically from human desires of what you should be, not from nature's forces—the simple genes. You have no history. You know this, but think of the forest. You traveled, you even came here, but you don't go anywhere. The paths are already there—you didn't make them. And if you do—"

"I end up following a routine. I see." Lawrence closed her eyes tightly.

"Long ago, your people learned to cooperate with one another. They did so in order to survive. Now it is not so simple. You have forgotten, while it has never left us. Now you are given another chance."

Lawrence lifted her head and opened her eyes. Cooperation? Wasn't that like—?

The leader nodded. "We can help. We will create the Cube for you, and help you regain your lost Earth."

"Who's the pilot?" Lawrence asked as they lugged the first load of equipment out to the open field.

"Some guy named Scott," Jeffrey shrugged.

Uh-oh, Lawrence thought.

"Have you ever wondered why the farmers have to transport us everywhere?" Jeffrey shivered. "I still remember the first time I traveled in a truck. And each time, I dread it, but what can I do? I can't walk home."

"They might as well drive the egg trucks, don't you think? As for flying vehicles, I don't know." Lawrence squinted toward the craft in the field, seeing a blazing red head waving, nearing them.

"You need help carrying that?" he offered when he was closer.

"No," Lawrence said sternly. "We brought exactly as much as we could carry. You can help on the subsequent loads."

Jeffrey snickered, watching Scott's helpless face turn bright red.

"I've never flown students—er, scientists before," he began as he trailed them to the craft.

"Who would you fly?" Lawrence frowned.

Jeffrey interrupted, "What do you call one of these things?" He had hastily tossed his gear onto the ground near the cargo door and was now excitedly inspecting the craft.

Scott looked down disgustedly at the gear and opened the door. "The braindead like to call it an aeroplane. They sing it, too. Go ahead, Lawrence." He moved over to let her place her equipment in cargo, then bent to pick up Jeffrey's.

Jeffrey looked haughtily at his bent head. "What is it really called?"

Scott didn't look up. "Call it what you like," he muttered.

Looking at his bent head, Lawrence was reminded of picking green beans, with the pickers and the gatherers working in tandem, one above and erect, the other crouched and heavy. She stepped forward to almost come between them, giving Scott a warning look before gazing disapprovingly at Jeffrey. "If there's one thing I can't stand, it's someone who won't do his share of the work. Show some common courtesy."

Jeffrey looked at both of them in sequence rapidly, blinking. "Okay. I guess I was excited."

"It's called a floater," Scott said.

"Maricela said not to call them braindead," he answered cheerfully.

"Who the cratch is Maricela?" sputtered Scott.

Lawrence despaired. "Never mind, Scott," she finally said gently. "They bother him as much as they bother you."

They returned to get the rest of their luggage, Scott easily carrying twice their maximum load. "This is nothing. One more trip, and we're on our way."

They flew what seemed like forever before new, untemperate land appeared beneath them, but it was hard to see it well. Variegated greens, uniform, smooth expanses of trees, a river. Lawrence in the seat beside Scott while Jeffrey sat sulking in the cramped back seat, twisted and peeked, trying to look all about her.

Finally, Scott laid a hand across her knee. "Lawrence, I'm trying to be careful."

She tossed her head. "How'm I supposed to *see*?"

He grinned. "We could have driven, you know. Take about a month, but you'd see more."

Again, Lawrence asked, "How far?"

"Six hours."

Since it was Scott, she asked, "How come you drivers always measure distance with time?"

He looked mildly surprised. "When I'm traveling, I'm worried about how long it's going to take to get me there. Why would distance matter?"

Lawrence thought a minute. *I guess it matters to someone trying to center, trying to reconstruct this planet in her mind.* Sure, there was geography, but just zipping up the maps did no good. She needed to capture the movement, the exhaustion.

"You seen Kamela lately?"

Lawrence jumped. "No," she said slowly, looking at him oddly.

Scott shrugged. "Me either. When she left, I thought she had gone to the city."

Not much else was discussed until close to landing. "There it is." Scott pointed.

191

Both Lawrence and Jeffrey peered out the window. Veering below them was a platform with a tiny hut to the side. Scott landed with ease in the cleared space. He sat for a while after landing, so Lawrence and Jeffrey hesitated, wondering if it were safe to get out.

"It's different here, all right," Scott intoned solemnly. "Let's get out and I'll orient you."

They scrambled out. Lawrence chose to immediately run to the edge of the platform and look out on that endless plain. "Wow!"

Jeffrey passed by Scott uneasily, than ran to join her. Scott set out the cells to recharge, wrestling with their mass, then he stood with arms folded until the two effervescent explorers meekly returned.

"Like I said, things are going to be different down here," Scott began. He pulled out a heavy yet flexible sheet of plastic from his chest on board. "This is a map. There are no screens down here, so you'll have to rely on this to get around. If it'll help, hold it in front of your eyes before you get used to laying it flat on the ground."

"Does it move?" Jeffrey looked eagerly at the piece, expecting a great new device like the digital writing pad he had pasted to his door back at the dorm.

"No. It's not a screen that can direct you. You must read it. Here is our agricultural station." He pointed at an orange X at the upper right corner of the map. "You can contact us if there's any trouble." Scott answered as if by rote.

"How?" Jeffrey began.

Lawrence at that moment plopped down and held her head. Immediately Scott was beside her, Jeffrey reluctantly having to second him.

"You all right?" Scott took her shoulder with care.

"Yes. I guess the flight made me dizzy." Lawrence opened her eyes and focused. Closing them had only made the vertigo worse.

"Just dizziness? No nausea? Can I get you anything?" Scott made for the water jug.

"No. Keep telling us more of what we need to know." She smiled faintly.

Scott unwillingly returned to the kit and pulled out the repellers. Solemnly he held them. "Do your best with these." They knew what he meant. No killing, of course, but no constant use, either. They were difficult to recharge. "Your activity should keep them away."

Jeffrey came forward and accepted the stunner gingerly.

"It's very simple to use," Scott informed him. "Just point and press here underneath. Like this." He aimed the one he had.

Jeffrey imitated him, nodding. He eyed Lawrence. "It's not the animals I'm afraid of; it's the plants. We'll probably die from a poisonous plant, if I know Lawrence. She'll want to eat everything."

"But you won't," she protested weakly, feeling quite content that the banter was supposed to keep her mind off her nausea.

"Hey, you cook it, I'll eat it. I'll probably love it, too." His voice was easy.

Scott sniffed and lay down the repeller to withdraw a single device from the kit. "This is a signaller. You need one because there's no screens. Use this to contact the station. You'll be hearing from me when I return. Answer immediately. I need to know you're okay." He spoke quite calmly, as if unaware of their intimacy. "Finally: don't stray too far. You have your compass, but . . ."

Lawrence lifted her head. "Scott, we have to find new species. We have to go far."

Jeffrey spurted, "Yeah, we're . . ." He shut up at Scott's look.

"Not babies," Lawrence finished for him gently.

Scott nodded with a jerk and went over to unload the floater. Jeffrey went to help, and Lawrence after a while stood normally and followed. Together they quietly removed everything to the hut, then replaced the cells onto the floater. Scott left abruptly, nodding his farewell.

Jeffrey whooped when he was gone. "Three months! Three months of bugs, bugs, bugs!"

Lawrence joined in his laughter. Three months of seeing different vegetation! Inside, her excitement boiled. Maybe this was enough. Maybe it could be all she ever wanted.

Lawrence got off the bank and started walking on the huge gray rocks that stood in midstream. At the largest, she flopped down on her stomach.

A flash of red caught her attention. There it was! The shirt was caught on a collection of sticks. Using a tree branch, she pulled it out of the water.

"Damn! It's all muddy now." Lawrence looked at it disdainfully, wrung it, then spread it to dry.

She stretched out again so that she peered over the edge of the rock into the pool. "The deepest part," she murmured. "I've ever seen," she said slowly, as if an afterthought.

She could see the bottom of the creek clearly. Silt-covered rocks, mostly. One portion, however, fairly close to her, was dark. She pointed. "There's where it's the deepest!"

Lawrence again seized the tree branch that was as tall as a lowlying shrub and shoved it into the water.

"Wow." She pushed the stick down. "This water sure is hard to get into. There. I *think* it hit bottom."

She yanked it out and threw it onto the rocks. Bending down, she estimated the length of the wet portion by using both hands. "Three meters! Okay."

Quickly she jumped off the rock and teetered down into the water.

Things shifted. Lawrence was completely immersed without needing to breathe. Above her in the muted sunlight she could see—no, that wasn't the right word—sense the water bugs darting above her, using their middle feet to stroke, leaving cut concentric circles behind them. They seemed undisturbed by her presence. Below her feet the algae teemed. Nearby, a mudpuppy was safe in its matrix of sandy soil.

Something was missing. No. No gaps. The world was suddenly *there*. And Lawrence wasn't.

Yes, she was. She needed air, so she swam upward, bursting out and taking a jagged breath of fetid atmosphere.

On the bank stood a girl and a boy, both about ten years old. Lawrence immediately checked herself to see if she were ten. No, she had pubic hair, full breasts.

The girl spoke first, coming down concernedly on one bent knee. "You are me? I don't understand."

Lawrence stared into those puzzled eyes a moment before answering softly, "No, you are my dear Maricela."

The boy scooped up to sit on a horizontal tree. "If the Cube is to grow it must be fed."

Lawrence looked over at him. "Jeffrey."

Lawrence lay next to Jeffrey in the hut, listening to the rain pour outside. She knew it must be light, but it didn't matter. They wouldn't be able to do much until the storm abated. She shifted so that her face was alit from the window and slowly opened her eyes. It was bright out there, and the streams of rain glittered silver in constant motion. Lawrence had never seen such beautiful water, except for the misty waterfall she and Jeffrey had discovered, oh, was it five weeks ago? It was hard to keep track.

Jeffrey stirred and murmured. She turned to see wide open eyes darkly glistening at her. Staring at him silently, she pinpointed the cause of her recent dissatisfaction: she couldn't do it all!

"Still raining," he commented. His eyes darting to the window, as if to check the veracity of his own statement, he murmured, "I got so used to hearing it, I thought it wasn't, you know?"

"We can still go, if you want to." She hoped he would decline.

"Naw, that's all right." He rolled over and stared at the ceiling. "Sometimes insects . . ." he drifted off, then came back with a jerk. Louder, he continued, "Sometimes insects are harder than jaguars."

Lawrence shifted, bringing her back closer to his chest. "Of course they are."

Jeffrey snaked an arm across her. "I mean, it's just *me*."

Lawrence could understand that. Hadn't she just been thinking it herself? They couldn't do it all, but, still, updating even a few gene maps was worthy, bringing her ever closer to the Cube. She had to believe in progress, that someday all would be known.

Jeffrey spoke softly. "I was thinking of trapping the big animals. This is so placid. I count my bugs, and you smell the flowers. I think I could live here forever."

Lawrence silently agreed, sensing a lazy tone, imagining him to be presently bored. Each day would be dedicated to the work, and one would pause only to cook. Lawrence suddenly envisioned the swinging pot of rice, though they had eaten native foods when she could figure out how to prepare them.

What a place, though! No screens, and a little boat they could sail to get through the jungle faster. It was freedom of some sort.

Forever, though. Daily the memories filled, and Lawrence longed to return to the Cube. After three months, she knew she would seize it eagerly, fresh to the task. *Let's have one day off,* she urged. *I practically must.*

Lawrence turned to Jeffrey, and she knew he was thinking the same thing. She cradled her head under his arm and sighed.

"We shouldn't get up until it's unbearable," murmured Jeffrey.

They slept, made love, and arose near noon. The rain still poured. They cooked half-heartedly, and ate even less enthusiastically. Washing the dishes was more exciting.

"Well, let's go," Jeffrey said as the last plate was put away. He turned to gather his tarpaulins.

Lawrence still stood near the sink. He looked at her curiously.

"What's the matter?"

Lawrence sprang toward him urgently. "Let's not wear them."

"Okay." He yanked himself free.

Lawrence pulled at his arm. "Let's just *go.*"

Jeffrey chuckled. "Yes." He released the door. "Well, what do you know? It's raining!"

Lawrence pushed him aside and walked straight into the wall of water. The inevitable path worn from their door led down to the river. The rain was blinding. Lawrence rubbed sheets of it off her face, veering off the path, therefore allowing Jeffrey to move ahead. Not noticing, she waited a while, then took a deep breath and plunged forward once more. Down a steep section she slid on the instant mud of the semi-eroded path, catching herself in the vines. Something red hovered in front of her; she watched as it froze. She glanced at it curiously. Oh, it was Jeffrey's mud-splattered back. Not hearing a thing, except her own slogging, she wondered if it were real. Jeffrey was back there, wasn't he? She put her fingers forth tentatively, feeling slick cotton cloth clinging to a warm back. Jeffrey looked around.

"Hey, what are you trying to do, push me in?"

They stood sheltered underneath a *Copernica cerifera*, so Lawrence could now see where they were. She came around him and stumbled, "Oh. We're already here." She stepped back to avoid the crumbling bank.

"Yes, we would have to be 'here,' wouldn't we?" Jeffrey asked cryptically, pulling off his shirt. "Go ahead. Push me in. Ready?" He grinned.

Lawrence looked at him slyly but kept her shirt on.

"Ah, come on."

Lawrence stepped even further back, up against the trunk, and looked at her bare feet.

195

Jeffrey squinted at the sky. "I see a crack," he announced. "It shouldn't be long."

"Hieeyahbo!" Lawrence ran and took a flying leap into the river.

"What was that?" Jeffrey yanked his pants off and sailed after her, making an even noisier splash.

Gasping, Lawrence forced herself under.

"Not too far," Jeffrey warned.

"I know." Lawrence spluttered, noticing a sudden slack in the rain. Now it only dotted her head. With hard strokes she came near a huge root at the bank and wrapped her arms around it to rest. Jeffrey swam, or attempted to, then came to lock his arm around her waist.

"Are you okay?" he murmured.

Lawrence nodded and buried her head into the moss. Jeffrey was quiet, floating next to her. He stroked her hair, moving it from her shoulder, then rested his head where it had lain.

The rain stopped totally. Lawrence pulled away to paddle toward the shore.

"I'm coming!"

They climbed up and flopped down, chests heaving.

"I can't believe it," Jeffrey panted. "I'm worn out from that current in ten feet. I'm glad we didn't go too far out." He glanced down at the river from underneath large lids. "It looks slow-moving. Sometimes at mid-day it looks stagnant, yet I stare at it, hoping . . . for a long time." He shook his head. "If I'm not careful, I could lose days like that."

"Or years," Lawrence answered eagerly. "Sometimes the years can weigh me down." Her voice lowered. "Contemplation, instead of action. Time, sneaking up on you. I don't feel as if . . ." She caught herself droning, and shook herself to say more brightly, "I've achieved anything."

"What's wrong with it? Contemplation, I mean. It sure beats force learning."

Lawrence hadn't seen that connection before. Maybe if she had had a chance to ask Kamela what it had been like. Tom had gotten it too early to ask him. "You know anybody like that? I mean, personally?"

"Yeah." Jeffrey wove his fingers into his hair to squeak out the water. It glistened in the new sun. "My ear's full." He leaned his head to start the water flowing out. "It's a concentration of so many years of education. A reduction of time. I don't know if that's useful. I'm in no hurry." He lay back into the vines, soporific heat waves haloing his naked form as the sun returned with full force, greatly reducing the effect of the rain.

Lawrence rubbed her shirt, front and back, and sighed. "We'll get back. I want to go back, but I can't help but feel like I can't get into another biome. We flew, we rode in the egg trucks. It was so separate."

"So what were you going to do? Walk here?" He threw his arm over his eyes.

Lawrence remembered all the walking she had done, especially recently. It wasn't like there was something strange every ten feet, although she did see new things often enough, it was the act of walking itself, being somewhere different every step, so that she had to keep going, anticipatorily, until she was forced to turn back, and that meant she could only go the same distance every day, in radii, and soon knew everything. She had to keep going. "Yeah. I'd like to. But I wouldn't aim for here. I'd just walk. This place, if I ever got to it, wouldn't seem so unreal. I am dreaming, ain't I?"

"No," he said heavily. "You're not. Plenty of people come here every year, adding to the banks. We're not special."

"It's not like I need the reassurance of a bunch of people to convince myself it's real, Jeffrey. I can live here, alone, or with you, and see it all. Just because we're alone . . ."

"We're not. We are surrounded by creatures." Jeffrey spoke assuredly.

Lawrence took a deep breath. Maybe Jeffrey was aware, in being of all, no separation, all alive. She wriggled forward and smacked him on the stomach. "It's easy for you?" Her heart lurched at the eager words that still came hard.

Jeffrey opened his eyes just a bit. "I guess you're better off in wet clothes." He stretched out his hand and pulled his pants to him. "Damp, but not much. This sun!" Idly he got up and pulled them on. "What are you talking about?"

Lawrence cast down. "Nothing."

"No." He yanked his muddy shirt loose and put his head into it. "What are you trying to say?" He crouched beside her and stroked her neck, talking gently. "The plants, the animals—you figure their genetic code is seizing them? People used to cradle the *names*, and that's never enough. Didn't they have enough imagination to choose at random?"

Lawrence, of course, with no knowledge of Latin or the history behind the common names given to species, thought they had. The names she had painstakingly learned were so bizarre that she couldn't even imagine a language at first. Gradually, however, she saw some patterns emerge. "They show the relationships. Like, similar animal, same genus."

"I had a lot of problems with that. Ick: this shirt!" He yanked it back off and eyed it scrupulously. "How'd it get so muddy? Anyway, it's important to see the relationships in action, not just study physical similarities. Besides, each individual is different. With your research, it might be possible for one of us to sit within the Cube and actually see how other life forms relate. And if you get it so that they're individuals, not some ideal genetic code, we'll see something!"

Lawrence nodded. Jeffrey left his crouch and settled beside her, shirt ready to spring into the air. "Are you aware of all that grows about you? That is what I was trying to ask."

Jeffrey flung the shirt up to the fronds, then stood to catch it. "Unbelievable," he muttered, staring down at her uneasy face with awe. "About five years ago, I had much the same idea in the woods of my region. There was a bear, far off, near the water. I sure ducked when I saw it, but it was so far off. I stood, seeing a bird fly past my head, red and golden brown, that I was not even aware of before. I decided I had to acknowledge it. The bird saw me, and took flight. The bear did not know of me, but then it turned. I looked upon its unknowing face. It knew. I had to know." He lost it. "Well, never mind. It's crazy."

197

"I want to be with them," Lawrence said, throat sore from held back tears.

"Of course," he said softly.

"It's just me," she continued.

"I'm going to go change. We shouldn't goof off anymore, now that the sun is here."

Lawrence shuddered. She took the plant, disintegrated it, read its genetic code, then took another plant . . ."Jeffrey," she began timidly. "To do what you ask, we'd have to disintegrate all life."

"Naw. You'll figure out some way to have it all. Regressive programs? You'll think of something." He smiled cheerfully at her. He immediately frowned. "We should forego the temptation to return to the hut. We've been everywhere around here. We've got to move on."

"The map's got all the huts marked. I guess we should avoid those." She considered. "It's hard for me to envision that map still. It's pretty much covered, isn't it?"

Jeffrey thought. "A blank corner to the northeast. We need a pilot, go beyond it."

Lawrence joined into his excitement. "Yeah! Maybe they don't even have a map for that region!"

With renewed vigor they climbed the hill to make first contact with the agricultural station.

Lawrence slumped up against the door and gasped, "I can't do it, Michael. Get it open for me."

Her comrade slung his gun back onto his shoulder and obliged. She stumbled into the dark room beyond. Michael hastily shut behind her.

"Gotta mattress?" she whispered.

"Yeah. Jo left this morning. This way."

Lawrence limped toward Mary's voice. "It's not that bad," she grunted. "Just a superficial wound. Give me a few days. I can help around here, then go straight back." She gingerly stretched out onto the moldy mattress. "It hurts, though. Damn."

Mary lit a lantern and peered at the wound. "Tore it up quite a bit, didn't it? I'm surprised you can still walk. Probably won't, neither. The surgeon's lost."

"Probably on the other side, now. I never trusted doctors," Bill E. groaned from the corner. "Hell, Lawrence, you learned a bit from her. Heal yourself." He wheeled over to be grazed by light.

Mary shook her head. "We've got nothing at all. Maybe a few bandages." She patted Lawrence's thigh. "Take your pants off."

Lawrence complied, than wrapped a ragged blanket around her middle. "Pretty cold," she commented.

Mary tightened a tourniquet high on her right leg. Her cold fingers felt light. She bit her lip. "Does it hurt?"

Lawrence shook her head. "Naw. It's like you numbed it."

Mary sighed. "I don't know what else to do." Again her fingers fluttered around the bond. "I guess I can let it stay, for now." She lifted the leg and stuffed a rotted sheet underneath Lawrence's knee. Dabbing at the blood, she whispered, "Must have done a good job out there. Most people lose a lot."

Lawrence rolled her eyes. "I know. I saw it." Her throat caught. So much blood.

Mary patted her shoulder and helped her pull the blanket down. Without another word, she slipped through the door.

Lawrence listened to her clatter. "She's got her gun," she muttered. She knew she would not come back.

Bill E. wheeled closer to the bed. Lawrence glanced up at his calm, sneering eyes. "You've quite a bloody revolution," he groaned.

"Who? Me?"

He nodded. "Yeah."

"Why?"

He straightened his army blanket around his broad shoulders. Lawrence waited for him to speak, then shot a glance at the covered window. The light seemed a bit brighter out there. Then she saw sparks, like lightning.

"It's coming," she said.

"I know." Bill E. rubbed his stumps. "I feel like running, you know?"

Lawrence felt her thick lips blabber, "We'll get you out of here, Bill E. Shit. We ain't gonna run off and leave you. You're the best strategist we got." Lawrence struggled to sit up, then she lifted her head. Bill E. looked a little like Charles, despite the crewcut. Lakota.

She could feel it flowing, and she wanted to close her eyes and slip through the gaps between the trees. Bill E.'s voice recaptured her.

"Why?" he finally said, an amused quirk around his eyes. "Maybe because of what they did to me. Maybe for what they're going to do." He stopped.

Lawrence leaned back, suddenly asweat. "Linda and her bloodless revolution."

"Still calling the shots, she is, up in the business world. When you think about it, nonviolence can incorporate a lot, like extortion, bribery, brainwashing, you name it." Bill E. nodded, firm in his belief.

Lawrence found her limited experience and made it relate. Pleasant smiles followed by intense misery, whether from a kick, or hunger, or just a snide remark. "Yeah."

"You need a drink?" To Lawrence's bleary sight he seemed a lot closer, magnified, aglow, except that that last was the effect of the brightness in the window, now overpowering the single candle. The light as it grew brought with it sound, and Lawrence cringed at the rumblings of the tanks and shouts. *I've been. I've done my share. I don't want to go back.*

Bill E. was here, though. She felt safe.

"Yeah," she finally said faintly.

Bill E. brought her the dipper, and she drank the warm water whose rancid taste reminded her of roaches.

Boom! What were they doing? Trying to tear down the building? Lawrence spun, trying to leap out of bed, but Bill E. caught her shoulders and pushed her down.

"You can have all sorts of revolutions. Sure, a lot of them are bloodless," he said calmly. "Which one are you gonna choose, Lawrence?"

Lawrence lurked in the outskirts of the city, kicking at the dust, peering out occasionally into the chirping forest. It was early. No one wanted to be out here; they were all heading for the courtyard as soon as their eyes could struggle open, long before the bells that shattered dreams. And Lawrence had to join them. The young students' eyes had been eager as they begged her to come. Even her co-workers had expressed interest. At nineteen, she felt awfully old.

"Blah!" She strode away from the precipice, ignoring the artists' camp of egg trucks below. Skipping, she left the edge of the city and crossed to its center.

In the courtyard Lawrence went and stood behind the walba, streaking electricity into its memory in preparation for the long beat. It whirred when she yanked the plug. Firmly her fingers reached into the currents of coated plasma, and she stroked out a slow and rhythmical melody in defiance of its mode of power.

Once she was sure she could keep it going unthinking, Lawrence glanced up to observe the already crowded courtyard. The sky was cloudy but bright. Though there was no wind, it was cool.

Lawrence stood across from the silent Center in the shade and rested her eyes on the patch of fluffy, blue-green grass that students strolled upon. Despite the traffic, the grass remained lush, if short.

Maricela burst her reverie. "Hey, Lawrence! I brought the water from the clinic!" She slapped the icy jugs onto the table next to the walba. "We'll need it, no matter what."

Lawrence's throat was already dry. "Hand me some now," she croaked.

Maricela looked down at her hands, deep in the current. "Uh, I guess I'll just feed it to you, okay?"

Lawrence lifted her head, mouth open. She jerked when the water hit her throat. "Crap," she grunted. "That stuff's cold!"

"Too much time in the jungle," Maricela surmised, "drinking it lukewarm. Or in the lab, too, probably."

Lawrence grinned sheepishly. "You're right."

"You work too hard, Lawrence. Just because you got a lab doesn't mean you have to live there. When was the last time you slept?"

Lawrence gazed happily up at the elm leaves above her. "I sleep normally . . . in the lab, and I ate . . . yesterday, some time. But look, the other musicians are joining in." Lawrence pointed her skull out at the eager students, already dancing on the green. She didn't even indicate the musicians beside her, just listened to their strains, and tried to lead.

Maricela didn't seem to notice this incongruity. She peered at the dancers. "I don't see those artists. It must have worked."

Lawrence chose not to comment right away. The artists *could* have ripped off their badges they had sewn on in alliance with the badge of the city and mingled in, with no one the wiser, but Lawrence couldn't see it. They wanted to stand out, just as she did, back when she had planned not to be at the holiday. She wanted to stand out now, even as she meekly played. *Why did the artists want to come? Did they want to communicate something? Will I?*

"What did the Center tell them?" she wondered.

"I don't know." Maricela tossed away all speculation with: "I just know it worked. Here." She brought out some hickory nuts. "I won't ask you to remove your hands and lose the mode."

"Thanks." Again Lawrence opened her mouth and was fed.

"I'm going to join the dancers. See ya." Maricela loosened her vest and stepped onto the grassy oval.

Lawrence watched the patterns shift and the clothes, a hindrance to their graces, come off. Lots of people were already naked. She shivered. That was okay, except for those breezes that came every once in a while. Maybe out there the dancing would warm them sufficiently. She watched Maricela leap high, grimace, then step out of her jeans.

A flutist stood to her left, waiting for her to notice him. He seemed hesitant to tap her arm, and stood well away from the walba.

"We're going to follow you, okay?" he blurted when her eyes met his.

Lawrence pretended to be modest. "I—Uh, why? My walba's big, but . . ."

"It's good! It's good!" he burst out. "You must have kept up with your practicing. All this studying . . ." He looked sadly down at his bamboo reed and kissed it passionately, eyes solemn. "I need some time to get back into it."

Lawrence considered the other musicians sympathetically as she timidly asked, "Do you think the artists wanted to teach us, or to help us smooth out?"

"Oh!" He looked delighted. "Eric said 'orchestrate.' Do you know Eric?"

Lawrence shook her head.

"Well, we're trying to do what he said. We're aiming for something coherent." He frowned down at the gentle walba. "Did you juice it loud enough?"

"No," Lawrence said honestly. "Why don't you add some?"

"Sure." He bent down and plugged it in, then pumped a few seconds. "Is it burning?"

"Not yet," Lawrence hastily said.

He pumped again. "These things." The flutist looked at the walba ruefully. "How do you know how much?"

"It's tingling now. Stop," she said tensely. More calmly, Lawrence answered, "I just do it until I feel like stopping."

"Oh! I could never do that. I start playing, and I never want to stop." He paused and poured himself a cup of water. "So, we'll follow you, okay?"

Lawrence nodded irritably, already carried on the rhythm she brought out.

Her crystalline extract passed by on a small tray. She examined it thoroughly until she was satisfied that it was hers. At this distance, it was hard to recognize, so many chemicals were around today. She blinked and went back to staring at Maricela, who had broken from a string of dancers and now stood on one of the ellipse's foci to the left, dancing slowly to Lawrence's beat, eyes closed, mouth gasping for breath.

Mostly braindead took any form of chemical enhancement, though the trouble of raising them was too much for most. Trade flourished as they sought to escape their sown memories. Once, when she had first come to the city, Lawrence had wanted to try one, why she couldn't remember, but never had. The Cube kept her busy.

Except for now. Her extract had been only one of the many things she had brought back from West/South continent. She of course hadn't known its potential until she had tested it in her lab. While waiting for approval to experiment in psych, she had slipped some to the great demand of the braindead. The results had been amazing.

"Hey!" A man veered into her vision. "I'm talking to you!"

Lawrence did what she always did lately when she came across someone acting abnormally: she studied his eyes. A bluish tint, characteristic of massive ingestion of her extract, had crept over his whites. She gulped and stood helplessly inside his hallucination to hear the nonsense that would flee his lips.

"Carnivals. Lousy time I'm having. Pass me a beer, will ya?" He dragged on his unlit, invisible cigarette and sighed. "And these girls—won't give you a thing. And I *tried*!" He pointed at the walba. "Whazzat?"

Lawrence kept silent, uncomfortable in her new guise, whatever it was. His fantasy fledged, so that he wasn't seeing her, but somebody more appropriate within a benighted past.

The man stared at her, then followed her gaze to the prancing Maricela. He leered, pointing. "Looks good, she does, up there on the stage. You think so, too, son. You like her, don't you?"

Lawrence stroked a higher beat. In her nervousness, she had lost track of her chore. The walba seized again, and soared.

"Yeah," he belched. "Where's that beer?" He churned some water into his mouth and spat. "She sure is nice. I wouldn't mind a bit of that pussy for myself." Thirstily he glugged a full cup of water. "Ah!" He smacked his lips, then wiped them on his forearm. "Good stuff!"

Lawrence peered at his sweaty face as his eyes grew calmer. The seizure was over. He shuffled away.

"I *love* her," she whispered. "All of her." But no one needed to hear.

Lawrence was the fox, and she leapt from the fence into the woods. The hounds madly followed her.

I know I can make it. I am young, fresh. I will reach my burrow. She gasped for breath easily. *Those stupid hounds. I am just a little thing. I should be free.*

She stumbled over some fresh dirt. *Wait a minute!* She dug frantically, her little white paws quickly becoming clogged with red clay. *Here is where my burrow lies. Where is it?*

The horns sounded, and Lawrence left off sniffing the earth to run again. She could see the brightly colored hunters on their shiny horses, and eventually felt fear.

I know where there is a wide stream. It's far, but I can make it. She turned to dash across the colorless tundra and enter the foggy woods.

Lawrence stopped with a lurch on the creek's bank. Though she could still hear the shouts and howls behind her, the hunters now stood on the other side of the glittery water, and even now they were urging their hounds across. The chase was on again.

Lawrence ran fast enough to pause rather early. *Here is a hole, under a root, or it used to be. It has been covered, too.*

Again she ran, but this time she was straining to make those leaps, pulling her legs in arcs that did not quite make the stretch. When next she paused, at a time which was not wise, but she had to, she could see out of her bleary eyes her own tongue lolling, the saliva running unchecked. *Now I look like those hounds.* Lawrence dragged her tongue and squeezed her eyes shut. *If I rest, so do they, right?* She tried to suck in a long good breath. *Unless they're stronger.*

Lawrence ran a little farther, then halted abruptly at a strange sight.

Before her was a large dirt mound, much taller and wider than she was, that shone golden in the morning sun. She watched the height rise, and disturbed particles flick over the edge. Someone must be digging a great hole behind it.

Lawrence blinked. It wasn't a dirt mound anymore. It was a full grown, majestic doe, shaking her head and stalking to come between the fox and the hunters. With each step she took, the sound of the hunters grew fainter. By the time she reached the thick pine tree, they were silenced. Lawrence looked nervously around. Would they reappear behind her?

The deer kicked her feet in a jig and pulled back her ears, and so rolled back every earthwork so that all the burrows and hollows reemerged.

Lawrence crept forward and sniffed at the closest hole, home to a platypus. Amiably the deer trotted up to her.

"You see it was not just for you alone. It is all places, all creatures."

Lawrence cocked her head. "Who are you?"

"Does it matter? Listen."

Lawrence plopped onto her haunches and took deep breaths. Only now did she remember that she was exhausted.

"In the summer where you live, the trees are full, so you cannot see the sun, or the next building, whatever it is you seek. In the winter, the trees are bare, the undergrowth has vanished, and all is visible."

Lawrence scratched behind her ear. "Don't know about that."

"I think you need to clear away what blinds you. You see too much. Take a familiar pattern. For instance, that one on your badge. If I were to draw an incomplete picture of your badge, couldn't you connect the dots and bring it back to completion? When something is that familiar to you, you see it complete whether it is or not."

Lawrence licked her paw quite thoroughly, taking her time.

"But you might be seeing what you want to see and ignoring what is already there. You've got a way out of the prison. The Cube is your model. You're in control. Am I right?" The deer straightened, becoming erect. Lawrence stared into the soft, free smile of the Shawicc.

"I guess so." Lawrence tucked her shirt in and stood. "You and Bill E. There's got to be something." She pointed into the woods. "Those hunters. My prison. Are you trying to tell me someone else is in control?"

"Stand back!" Venut ordered as he swung up the cutter and clamped it into place onto the front of the harvester.

Lawrence jumped a full three feet back at his shout, almost collapsing Mony, prevented only by Maricela and Shaste catching her arms on both sides.

Maricela giggled, her eyes half shut with glee. "Oh, Lawrence, you didn't have to jump back that hard!"

Venut came around the harvester, legs swathing the golden wheat, eyes anxious in a deeply tanned face. "What happened?"

Lawrence pretended not to notice him. She had been studying the machinery and had been more frightened by his shout than the possibility of getting her head chopped off.

Now he was looking at her leerily. "Are you all right?"

Mony said calmly, "You don't need to yell, Venut. We can hear you perfectly well. You aren't running the thing yet."

Venut dropped his eyes, suddenly sheepish. "All right. I'm just used to it, is all."

Lawrence edged closer to the harvester, watching Mony out of the corner of her eye. How had she known that it was the shout that had frightened Lawrence?

"Here." Venut ran to her side. "Here's how you climb aboard. Put your foot there. No, not that one."

"It feels more comfortable to start with that one," Lawrence insisted, her left knuckles white as she gripped the handrail, hoping that he wouldn't touch her.

"No, let me show you." He clambered aboard in no time flat, Lawrence absorbing his movements so that she was able to climb a lot faster when her turn came than she thought possible.

"Gorry! Born to it, she is!" chuckled Venut while Maricela more slowly followed Lawrence, getting a boost from Shaste when she stumbled. "What, are you coming, too?" He half stood to look sternly down at Maricela.

Maricela waited until her eyes topped the side so she could glare at him. "Yes. Lawrence is my guest, after all."

Lawrence paid no attention to their spat. She was too busy looking around. She was up high, above the grain, seeing long rolling hills of just wheat under a fluctuating sky. A cloud shadow, huge and dark, fled over the fields faster than she could think.

"Wow!" Eagerly she drank it in. "It's so weird! Just wheat as far as I can see!" She stretched out over the cutter, wanting to sink into the yellow waves.

Venut tugged her overalls and pulled her back sharply. "Watch it! You can't fly!"

Lawrence qualmed and meekly sat on the seat beside him. Immediately she tried to look bored. "Go ahead and get going, then."

Venut stared at her, eyes wide as he shook his head. "Never seen the like. Really." He started the machine, and Lawrence rode it all the way down a row and back. It did get quickly boring, and she could see no need for conversation at all. Why yell over all that muck? So she had time to think to herself, which was time that came rarely at this bustling commune. Since the artists' strike, people had had to help with harvest for the first time in their lives. Lawrence had come at the perfect time to use her latent talent, helped by being director of the lab, to organize workers. Some skilled farmers remained here in the prairie region, like Venut, who seemed to have great disgust for artists, but it wasn't enough. Lawrence found so much of her vacation spent explaining tactics to new farmers that she hadn't had time for Maricela. And now here they were, together, but on a noisy harvester in the fields, with no chance to talk.

When they had at last come back to their starting point, behind them only stubble and chaff, Venut stopped the motor and waved across at Mony and Shaste. "Go on, now. You've had your taste."

Lawrence courteously waited for Maricela to climb down before jumping partway to the ground, accompanied by Venut's "Gorry!"

Maricela and Lawrence picked their way over the dark ground to the fence. Maricela waved Mony and Shaste on. "Go on home. We'll follow. I need to talk to Lawrence."

While Venut's harvester grumbled behind them, they watched Mony smile and nod before turning to grasp the tiny Shaste around her shoulders so that her short black hair barely touched the pale arm. Tall Mony then followed the gesticulating Shaste back to the commune. Lawrence laughed. They were so lively that she sometimes forgot they were twice her age, and Maricela called them both "mother."

Maricela coughed. "Why do you always have to be such a showoff, Lawrence?"

Lawrence's grin faded. She kicked the wooden railing and answered tightly and sardonically, "If you mean me climbing that tractor, I watched him."

"Ha! I've watched them a million times. You just want to best me on my own home ground." Maricela sniffed and looked away, toward the ranch-style huts.

Lawrence wrapped her arms around a post and hugged it to her, rolling Maricela's words in her mind. It was not like her, to be so nasty about something like that. She knew Lawrence had meant nothing. To give herself time, Lawrence muttered, "Because that old fart bothered me. I had to show him I knew chit."

Maricela's eyes widened. "Who, Venut?"

Lawrence glanced at her. "Yeah."

Maricela answered haughtily, "He's my uncle."

"So?" Lawrence gulped. It couldn't get any worse than that, could it? Digging deeper into her own wild conjectures, she asked softly, "What? Is it Adelaide?"

"That's part of it."

Lawrence puzzled over this small hint. Maricela jealous? Of her? When they could both share Jeffrey? Impossible! Maricela had a lot of lovers; Lawrence was just something she tolerated, right? Because . . . oh, hell, who knows? "Adelaide is my brightest assistant. You should talk." There. That should bring it into perspective. After all, Maricela had Jan, Thelma, Urse, Fagui, just to name the few Lawrence was aware of.

"I don't want to talk about it," Maricela spurted in a pout.

Lawrence shrugged and let go of the post. Carefully she climbed the fence and hopped onto the dirt path on the other side. Slowly she walked to the commune.

Behind her, Maricela slid through the planks and followed. They did not speak until they reached Maricela's loft bedroom, which Lawrence could never enter without being amazed at the bright sunlight giving the room an Arctic look that matched its ambient temperature.

Tamis gave them a sleepy glance before tucking himself more snugly into Lawrence's pillow. Lawrence pointed at him. "Look at him! He thinks it's his bed!" She reached out to pat the huge gray and white cat.

Maricela characteristically flung herself onto her bed and gazed distractedly at the ceiling.

Lawrence glanced over at her and suddenly gulped. "You want to know why else I'm a showoff?" she said shakily. "I always try to do my best, and, while I'm here, I'm extra careful to shine. I want to impress your family. I want them to like me." She crumpled the linen bedspread with both fists, face buried into the lace. That had been harder to say than she had thought it would be.

Maricela continued to observe the ceiling. "Don't be silly," she said calmly. "They already like you, because you are my friend."

"It's not silly. I have to prove myself." Lawrence painstakingly curled her stomach around Tamis so that she just barely graced his curve. He lifted his head, looked at her, then, sighing, leaned his back into her and started to purr. Ever so gently she smoothed his rumpled fur, then moved her head to keep a tear from falling on him.

"Sheesh! What am I, a psychcomputer?" Maricela threw up her hands, then smiled at her. "Come here."

Lawrence gently released her little friend Tamis and jumped over to land on Maricela.

"Ugh! Get off! That's better. Yes. Right there. Thank you. Now."

"It's . . ." Lawrence began from her new place at her side.

"No. Let me say it. You got a reprimand. So what? You're still head of the lab, and you can still work on the Cube."

"Yeah, but it's what it was *for*. Not getting psych permission to pass a new drug. Who cares? They don't care about the harm it might have caused. They're just mad because I broke one of their stupid rules. And another thing: the reprimand had no effect, except to make some people jealous of my position snicker. That's so stupid! If I'm to be punished, go ahead and punish me." Lawrence kicked the footboard. "I can't stand it!"

Maricela was silent for a while. When she finally spoke, she still hesitated, as if she couldn't decide on what to say. "Listen. Can't you just be angry about being punished? Why do you have to be angry because you haven't received any more? If you're going to worry about principles, you're going to be one unhappy person."

"I don't care. What else is there besides principles?" Lawrence clamped her mouth shut. "Did you hear a knock?"

"Yes. Come in," Maricela shouted at the door.

Kiri peeked in. "There you are. I thought you two wanted to go to the meeting." She smiled warmly at Maricela, her freckled cheeks dimpling.

Lawrence studied her fluffy yellow hair loose from its customary braid and her soft pale blue eyes. This was the "matriarch" of Maricela's family, and she already loved her.

"Naw," Maricela said tiredly. "We're busy. Maybe next time."

Kiri seemed disappointed as she tilted her head toward Lawrence. "It's not going to be much of a meeting, but we were concerned with scheduling. Venut wants to see Lawrence."

Lawrence stood up. "Venut?" Instantly her mind started to track. Six hundred workers to do the cranberries alone, and he had asked about the cherries. She'd forgotten, but it had seemed to her that reducing cranberry in favor of cherry would be all right, except that the flooding of the bogs was so strenuous that . . .

Maricela squirmed. "Tell ol' Venut to wait his turn." Then she laughed. "Is he going to schedule appointments for folks to talk to Lawrence? If so, tell him to get busy."

Kiri pushed her hair back and considered. "You know," she said softly, "I might just have to do that. Being informal about the harvest could lead to disaster." She turned, pulling the door close behind her. "I'll be back later."

Maricela groaned. "Me and my big mouth. As if Venut could ever impress *you*."

"It's not what they say, it's how they say it. Everyone here is in love," Lawrence said innocently.

Maricela burst out laughing. "What is it with you? You mope around here starry-eyed for two whole days. You think I got a good deal in the gene toss?"

"Yes," Lawrence said fervently. "My family was horrible. I was so happy to go back to the nursery and school."

"Oh, you were only three. What could they have done that you can still remember it?" Maricela scoffed.

Lawrence was caught. "I don't know if I do remember, but the way I act, trying to please, trying not to get hurt . . . I do remember getting hit. Sometimes I remember sex, or something. Something rammed into my mouth, anyway. One time I ran away. I was older then, but I only ran to hide under the bushes near the waterspout, where a white wheel stood. I remember years later wondering why that wheel was put there. It wasn't a mill, and the pebbles near it scratched my face as I was dragged back. Their smell . . ." Lawrence shivered.

Maricela reached out to touch her arm. "Whatever happened to them? Were they ever punished? Did they ever get any more children to raise?"

"Not that I know of. Of course, I kept away from them from then on. After a while, it became natural to disappear when they entered the room. I don't remember even thinking about it, or planning it. It was like they had moved away." Lawrence rolled her eyes up to peer through her bangs. "As a matter of fact, I think they did, around my ninth year."

Maricela sat up to stroke her hair. "Go ahead and cry."

Lawrence shook her head. "No. I don't need to now." She kissed her lightly on the cheek and smiled a sloppy grin.

"I'm sorry I was mad at you, or jealous of you and Venut." She paused. "What am I saying? Venut ain't got nothing on me!"

"Well, he does look a little bit like my guardian, so I try to give him more attention. It's *not* him, because he's lived here all his life, and, besides, I checked. The male adult of my family went south. Besides, why should it matter to you?" Lawrence persisted. "You've got . . ."

"Oh, chit!" Maricela put her hands over her eyes. Tears squeezed through her fingers.

Lawrence gaped. "Hey, I didn't bring this up to make you stop being mad." She felt her throat closing up. "Ah, well, don't feel sorry for me."

"Oh, Lawrence!" She reached out and clutched her arms. "I could kill you! I would scream at you to stop being so absurd, if I didn't love you so much! I wanted to tell you something anyway. Maybe you'll leave me to dash to the screens, but they asked me for my egg before I left."

Lawrence felt a hot rush. It was like Kamela, when the doctor had implied that Lawrence's eggs would be a good thing to procure. Except they weren't! Kamela had wanted Lawrence for her reputation, for her brains, while Maricela . . . simply wanted nothing. *And I,* Lawrence thought. *And I seek nothing, too.*

"You're right," she finally said, "I would like to run some numbers, but I don't think I need to. I think they are going to increase our numbers." She clamped her mouth shut. *Okay, smartie, there's your theory. Now what?*

"But why?"

Lawrence tried to hypothesize as she had done with the Elaborynth, except that was too much like Maricela demanding something from her.

"I don't know. They must have calculated that it would be all right. Besides, they can take your egg, but they don't have to use it."

"Yeah." Maricela relaxed. "I'm not worried. I turned down their request, because I thought I'd ask you about it first."

"On the other hand, you're a One. Why not reproduce your superiority? Now that these memories are being released," Lawrence sucked in her breath, "maybe they found out a reason behind extra breeding."

Maricela slipped her arm about her waist. "I was thinking about you all that last week. You seemed so cold. I almost didn't invite you here, but then I thought I had to get you away from those morons in the city. I did wonder, though, who was more at fault, the authorities for blaming you for bypassing tests, or you for not caring that the inlaid got zapped. Or do you care? I need to know."

Lawrence gulped. "Well, at first, no. I'll admit that. But once I started to see the results, to talk to Tom—he's an inlaid from my commune, and he's with the artists in their camp—You cannot imagine my relief when I found out that the drug actually released them. I don't think I could do it again, though. I . . ." She scratched her head, face flushed.

"That's good," Maricela sighed. "I was seeing you as someone who would do anything for her project."

"Well, yeah, of course, I guess I used to be that way, because I've been living the thing for years, but it was all for you, and now . . ."

"What?" Maricela blinked. "I don't see it. The Cube is for me? But you first came up with it long before you met me. How does that relate to . . ."

"It doesn't," Lawrence hastily interrupted. "I admired you for coming out of your adversity so brilliantly, and . . ."

"What adversity?"

Lawrence grimaced. "Remember when you told me that you lived with your family? I imagined all sorts of evil things. I couldn't let you . . ."

Maricela's laugh rang out. "Would it have made you feel any better if I had told the truth? It's not even my family here! It's my friends!"

"Well, yeah, I see that now, but . . ."

"And you are my friend," she said solemnly. "It's something you have earned, but I was attracted to you because you seemed so startled, so naive, so hidden, so deep, yet not inlaid. I couldn't get over it." She traced her fingertips over Lawrence's breasts where the shirt had tightened when Lawrence had pulled her arms in close to her sides. "Even after four years, I wasn't going to see that rotten Adelaide seize your vision. Is it going to be for her?"

"I *told* you," Lawrence groaned. "If you can take sweet Unvil and spin him around . . ."

"That was just to get your attention."

"Don't use people like that. Now he's mooning around my laboratory, hoping you'll come by, so what good did that do, I'd like to know? When are you going to stop being so jealous? It doesn't make sense, coming from you, who have had everything . . . but, then again, maybe it does. I . . . I'm just now beginning to understand. Am I right? What's it all about?"

Maricela murmured, "Sometimes it seems like it's you who have everything, who will have everything, doesn't it? While I pretty much stagnate. Now I know better, but who will the Cube be for, then? Who's going to thank you for your gift?"

Lawrence hunched over. "I don't know."

"You could do it for yourself," Maricela said softly.

Lawrence started. The way she had had to say "gift." Vance had wanted her Elaborynth, and now she had to go on without showing her assignment? What the heck? What could she do then? It seemed so pointless, only something the . . . the *Center* wanted! That was it! They had given her support, both materials and labor, so they could get the Cube. It would be difficult to transfer that old tenderness for Maricela's sufferings to *them*, but apparently she must. *Do it for me? Ha!*

She leaned back and let Maricela finish unbuttoning her shirt, trembling under her hot breath as it inched down her belly. "You're right," she panted. "I'm going to do it for me!"

Lawrence snuggled deeply into the thin, musty quilts to the soothing sound of pouring rain. It was easy to sink back into her half-awake dream of Scott's hands, his tender pink lips on hers, his chest pressed close against her back as he reached to unzip her jeans, her back arching to tilt the nape of her neck into his mouth . . .

Lawrence squirmed, fully awakening. "Drat!" she muttered. She rubbed her aching crotch, her weak eyes looking across the sagging four poster. "Ain't nobody here. I knew that." She shifted. "Sure is getting lonely, here in the Cube."

Lawrence rocked back and forth. It wasn't true. Like Jeffrey had said, *I am surrounded by creatures, and, who knows? Maybe they have some effect on events here, too.*

Idly she pondered this, as much as she could with the rain coming in the hole in the roof and splattering in a big tin pot. With slight interest she glanced at it.

"When it fills a little more, it won't be so loud, I know." She climbed out of bed, chose one lavender quilt to wrap herself in, and went to sit on the floor next to the pot. Lawrence stroked the hand-carved cigar box on the stand next to the footed bathtub. "Pretty," she murmured. "Now I've got my own indoor waterfall."

Thunder boomed, but she couldn't remember the flash. She looked up through the hole, still dazed from sleep.

"I never had sex with Scott. I wonder . . ." She pointed at the hole. "Maybe this means something. Besides my reprimand, maybe they found another way to punish me."

That seemed right.

"Maybe all my memories are false. No," she answered slowly. "It's only this one with Scott I question. So only it must be false."

Lawrence stood up and pushed the tin pot closer to the center of the drip. "Yes, someone is in here messing with my mind. Somebody's been fucking with my Cube."

She shrugged and went to settle back under the quilts, went back to her dreams.

Lawrence walked out from her lab that morning mildly depressed. It was all she could do to make herself go to class. Graduation was coming up soon and she needed to be present at the lectures as much as possible. She didn't mind this as much as she would have if she hadn't come to a stopping point with the Cube. The gene maps were in place and all the patterns she could think of were programmed in. Lawrence felt as if she could do no more, even if it did feel as if it weren't yet complete. *Maybe I'll never finish it.* Lawrence flinched. *Either it's infinite or I just can't let it go.* Lawrence was so caught up with trying to resolve this dilemma that she didn't even notice until she had almost bumped into them that her classmates were clustered just outside the door with no intention of going in.

"What's going on here?" Lawrence blurted harshly, striding up to meet the most hesitant student.

"It's . . . all of us must go to the Center; class has been canceled," Eric squeaked, immediately placing himself at her command.

Lawrence glanced back and forth at all of them. It seemed pretty obvious that they were expecting her to lead them. "Okay, let's go. What are you waiting for?" She tossed her head and began walking rapidly to the Center, not pausing to let them catch up.

The auditorium was already packed; Lawrence was lucky to get a seat in the back. Up on the podium the lights seemed dim, but Lawrence still could not help but see Charles' nasty face up there, floating above a chair. She blinked. Now he had a body, in dark clothing, and his black eyes seemed to be staring right at her. She hurriedly sat down and tried to duck behind the shorter person in front of her.

When every seat had been filled, an older man came up to the stand. She recognized him as the renegade psych, or philosopher, as he called himself.

"Students, a new series of classes will be introduced to this generation. It will consist of political science, history, sociology, and anthropology. There will also be a study of arts and other cultures. Er . . ." He gulped. "A message will appear to each of you shortly concerning what these strange words mean. We will disseminate the new information in ways you can understand. Um . . ." With a shaky hand he took a water glass and sipped from it. "This is necessary because we've learned from our new sources that a segment of humanity does not live on Earth with us. They are above, in the wandering stars, in what we thought was simply space debris. We must learn of them. We cannot afford to continue to live in ignorance." He pointed at Charles. "This young artist, Charles, will continue the story."

Charles rose smoothly and replaced the philosopher at the lectern. He stood for a moment gazing down as if he were shy and had forgotten what he was going to say, but then he seized the small lectern and threw it from the table and onto the floor. A triumphant smirk highlighted his features as he gazed out into the restive audience. Lawrence again felt like he was looking straight at her, so to avoid his eyes she concentrated on the audience. At first she had been too stunned and aware of just what those "new sources" were—the dredged-up memories of the braindead—to notice the murmurings, the leanings forward. Beside her, a student breathed heavily.

Charles finally spoke. "I have reconstructed the Great Eviction upon our medium." He gestured angrily up at the wide screen above him. "The Great Eviction is a part of our history in which great masses of people were deported to the stars, the satellites that even now circle our Earth. To reconstruct this event, I used accounts from our new sources, using artistic license to bring forth its drama." Lawrence glanced around; she wondered if she were the only one who had caught the extra stress on the syllables "artist."

Charles continued smoothly and proudly, "Let us go immediately within the universe of my opus." He turned to release the images that would project onto the huge screen.

Students witnessed an overpopulated Earth. The more squeamish darted up to pass to the aisles and gasp for air. Lawrence herself felt tight, but she forced herself to remain seated and take deep breaths. The images were accompanied by some woodbine/carrion scent that Charles had stolen. Lawrence held her nose and deduced that he hoped to create the worst smell possible. With great effort she forced her fingers away from her nose and breathed in that stench. She felt obligated to completely experience Charles' opus.

Cacophony—Lawrence recognized it as several cranking tools and the clattering of wares, overlaid with human murmurings and shouts at an unbearable intensity. A strange, pulsating, loud rhythm beat onto Lawrence's face. It felt so alien that she was sure that Charles had recaptured it from the braindead's nightmares of the past. It took longer for her to rip her hands from her ears and endure the painful noise.

War was declared, and the birth rate dropped. Soon the crowds were reduced, but not by much. Disease then came, and famine, and only a small fraction of people were left in a world that Charles made gangrenous but quieter. The audience then witnessed a certain fraction of the population being herded into spaceships that would take them to their new homes in the satellites. Lawrence leaned forward. Charles had made collages of human features to create unique people. Lawrence felt a shiver climb up her spine and onto her scalp. Those people were definitely alien. Apparently the braindead had described them, but it hadn't been enough. Lawrence was fairly certain from her study of human genes that these sort of people couldn't exist, yet there they were. Her mind resisted the image while at the same time it tried to explain it. For the first time in her life she let go, observing mildly the images, certainly not as closely and carefully as she had always observed reality.

She saw the satellite dwellers beam energy down to the choked planet, saw it freshen and green while the satellites accepted in their turn enough supplies for a sustainable ecology. A new society was built on Earth, and Charles had to tone it down, because it was much as today. Lawrence saw the communes set up, the egg factories built, and she even glimpsed the banning of art, but only very subtly. The opus, aware of the paradox, had to end.

Lawrence sucked in a deep breath. It was over. She felt great relief. Around her, though, people were only now starting to rev up. She sat frozen as they engaged. Everyone everywhere was caressing and petting. Someone even lifted Lawrence's hair and nuzzled her neck. Just like at the dance, most people started taking their clothes off, but they were jerking at the rough fabric with a sad desperation. Right in front of her a woman yanked her pants off and veered the rich red triangle of fur her way. Lawrence calmly jerked her head away and stood. Even the people on the stage were joining in, except Charles, who had disappeared. Lawrence saw a quick route to the exit through the palpitating bodies, and she took it.

Outside it was quite dark. The cloud cover was heavy, yet the air was still. Lawrence took a few more deep breaths and stepped out into the abandoned city. She took one glance at the door, but no one had followed her.

A breeze came up, and she walked into it, trying to describe what she had felt upon seeing the new data.

Curiosity. Fear? A little. Desperation? No. A need for sudden comfort, like the others in the auditorium must have felt? No. Just curiosity, and a need to . . .

"Hey! Here you are!" Charles was suddenly there somehow. He grabbed her arm and tried to pull her to him.

She jabbed viciously at his belly.

"Ow!" He released her, then stood huffing. "I guess it didn't affect you like it did everybody else." He looked her up and down. "Why? Some ugly thing like you getting enough?"

Lawrence shrugged, puzzled enough by the reaction not to say anything nasty.

"Well?" He stood, bare chest out, so that Lawrence had to admire its smooth brown convexity. "How'd you like it?" he asked tauntingly.

Lawrence gulped. Charles *would* have to be the sanest person around to talk to at the moment. She pushed her hair out of her face, self-consciously straightening it in the back to rid herself of the eerie tingling left by the nuzzling and turned to him. "I must go up there!"

Charles instantly sobered. "Yeah. Somebody's got to."

It did seem strange, thinking that Charles would magically grant her a way to go. Lawrence decided not to say any more.

Charles, however, wavered. "Why you?" he asked suspiciously.

"What does it matter?" Lawrence spat. "We can't get up there anyway."

Charles snorted. "Yes, we can. The same way *they* got up there. We'll build floaters that can get up there. We must."

Lawrence shook her head. "We could just communicate. Tell them to come down here."

"Yeah," Charles admitted.

Lawrence walked out over the green, clutching at her suddenly aching heart. To be inside a metal shell, to not walk freely in the air. It was like the first time she had been locked in the closet with a cut on her finger. "Why did they do it?" she asked dully.

Charles crept up from behind her, his voice actually soft. "Forget all that now. What are we going to do about it?"

Lawrence flung her gaze at him and saw concern in his eyes. She tried to calm her own wild look, but she only grew more intense with saying, "I must see them!"

"Why?" Charles repeated, practically stroking her shoulder as he drew closer.

"I need their gene maps for my opus," Lawrence spluttered, prevaricating.

Charles stepped back, hardening to his usual self. "Ah, yes. Scott told me about that."

Lawrence ignored his sullen anger, seized by the greatness of it. Yes, build the Cube for them. Of course! And with their help!

"Put aside your stupid opus for a second and think this through! Chit!" Charles began.

He should talk! Why did he assault everybody just now with *his* precious opus, huh? Lawrence ached all over. It was like the Elaborynth all over again. She needed to draw, plan, contemplate, design the future, so that all would come out right. It wouldn't even hurt right now to have some of that nice white paper Vance had given her.

"Excuse me." She pushed Charles aside and ran back to the lab.

Lawrence brushed aside the Spanish moss and gazed in on the live oak dying beneath the strangler fig. Parasites upon parasites, like humans on the Earth, pulling the resources into space.

Charles strolled from beneath the fronds. "Hello."

Lawrence stared at him, tense. She had not wanted to meet him in the Cube, especially when seconds ago he was the angriest she had ever seen him.

"This Cube is beautiful," he announced.

"That's because it is the Earth," Lawrence answered readily.

"No, it's not. It is only a model of the earth, and an imperfect one at that. Don't you get it yet?" He squatted and unwrapped the Cube from the paisley cloth beneath his feet.

It was weird. A Cube within a Cube. An Elaborynth within an Elaborynth. Smaller and smaller, but less intricate. Lawrence felt dizzy.

"The Cube holds beauty because it is how *you* see the world. You have provided the beauty." He spoke in a lazy tone.

Lawrence remembered helping Angela etch patterns on glass in the lab once. Was all art communal?

"Charles, why did you show the satellite people as strange? I've seen them, and they are beautiful." She shook her head. "Not alien at all."

"Why can't something strange be beautiful? Strange *is* beautiful, to you, anyway," Charles answered. "Besides, I had a reason. I needed to shock everyone so that they might become more aware about an important issue."

Lawrence disagreed. "It was shocking enough, just to learn the news. You didn't have to . . . heighten it." She sank down beside him. "You made people frightened."

"They were already frightened," he insisted mildly. "The strange, the new, all changes frighten them."

Lawrence nodded. "Yeah, I guess people need some predictability, some comforting repetition . . ." She trailed off, remembering arbitrary commands from authority, some days praising her sins, other days punishing them.

"Yes," Charles quickly flicked his gaze at her excitedly, yet pleadingly. "That is why they need the Elaborynth, or the Cube."

"The simulations to test hypotheses are in place," Lawrence affirmed. "However, nothing is certain."

"One thing is certain," Charles quietly yet firmly intoned. "They need the Cube to plan political strategies in this new age of war."

Lawrence stood solemnly in her tiny dorm room and stared down at the jacket she had earned upon graduation. She had been staring at its small badge for several months now, and she had finally figured it out. A large, diffuse dot was surrounded by smaller dots that were separated by heavy lines. In the space to the right was an oddly shaped figure that overwhelmed the rest of the diagram. She traced the shape with her finger. It was beautiful, shimmery with many colors.

Over a routine lab duty it had come to her. The Center city, surrounded by its communes, separated by distance and distinctness, and the beautiful shape that could only remind Lawrence of a flower—it is what we are striving for. The words sounded rote to her ears, and it didn't make her feel any better to hear a braindead glibly tell how old it was and why it was created as a plan for all human activity. She didn't need that frap.

Lawrence shook herself from her reverie and neatly folded the jacket to be tucked into her personal drawer. It was time for her appointment at the Center.

The streets were empty, the students having left long ago. Lawrence had hung onto the lab and the reports that communication with the satellites had not yet been established. She passed the new shipyards, around which clustered the egg trucks of the artist/farmers, still on strike though harvest was ended. She paused to see the spaceships; they seemed complete as viewed from the outside. A thrill shot through her. *Somebody* would soon go, and the Cube, and the Earth, could be completed.

On time at the Center, she did not wait to be called in.

When she strode into the room, conversation ceased, with all fourteen attendants staring at her.

The little man of the first days coughed. "You are not wearing your badge."

"I'm off duty."

"We—uh—wanted to talk to you about—uh, please have a seat."

Lawrence gingerly chose the chair at the end of the table. By now, fourteen people didn't bother her anymore, but she didn't want them knowing that. She figured if she appeared timid, they'd feel more confident and thus more easily slip.

"Our records show that you were with the farmers a while. We were hoping that, as our employee, you would work with us and use your alliance with them to . . ."

"What alliance?" Lawrence demanded, all thought of appearing timid gone.

"Well, you seem to be on good terms with the fellow named Scott, and he seems to have some position with them."

"No. I am seeing no one." That was true, since graduation.

He shifted impatiently. Another attendant came to his rescue.

"What we would like you to do merely involves speaking with the artists. We need to know why they forsook harvest."

Lawrence forced herself to remain calm. "It's ludicrous!" didn't quite fit the moment, and she wasn't ready with anything else to say.

"Perhaps you are waiting for us to offer you something in return for your cooperation," the attendant stumbled.

Lawrence had to stare at her, amazed. That of course would never have occurred to her, yet, like Vance with his deal, the feeling was sweet. "Yes."

"What?"

Lawrence tried to hesitate, but couldn't. All of her sarcastic acting ability had seemed to fly out the window. "I must receive in whatever way possible the genetic records of the satellite dwellers."

"We'll do whatever we can." The little man shrugged.

"It would also be best for me to observe them and learn of their ways, so I can accurately represent them in the Cube," she rushed on, no longer satisfied with flat records. The Cube must live!

They paused, and Lawrence wondered at the look in their eyes that made them identical. She couldn't place it. "Whatever we can do," the attendant murmured at last.

Lawrence stood and bowed in her haste. It was difficult to contain her excitement. "Whatever they could do," when they could do everything! She left almost skipping with joy, until she figured out their expressions in a burst of insight.

They're scared!

It made her stop right there on the green. Lawrence knew all about fear. It was powerful, and she supposed it could make a powerful adult do a lot of really stupid things. It also meant that she mustn't expect too much from their promise, if they felt hindered in any way.

Frowning, Lawrence wrapped her arms tightly around herself and paced, almost running Maricela down.

"Hey!"

Lawrence jumped back a foot and took a full second to come to her senses enough to hug her.

"Have you seen Jeffrey?" she blurted. Seeing Maricela made her want all three back together again.

"Oh, no, no, I haven't! He's on the East/North continent, with elephants, tigers, and such," Maricela laughed.

"Oh." Lawrence tried to feel curiosity over the unvisited continent, but couldn't. "Maricela, I think the Cube should be for them." She pointed up at the sky.

Maricela only stared at her with concern; Lawrence felt like an invalid.

"I've got a chance to go up there. In fact, I'm certain I'll go up there, because otherwise I'll never finish the Cube. I need their gene maps, and I need you to get them for me. Will you go?" It all came out in a rush.

"Is that the only reason you want to go?" she asked quietly. "Remember? You came to me and said you would go meet my family as part of your psych research, when really you were going to protect me. There's more to you at all times besides your project."

Lawrence drew closer and lowered her voice. "Apparently, everybody's got a way of picturing those lone souls."

Maricela frowned, puzzled. "How can we not conjecture? We have the inlaid memories to produce a fairly accurate image of them."

Lawrence shook her head. "We've got to face up to the fact that they are alien. When the braindead—ack, I can't help it—the inlaid told us that we were a combination of races, instead of one pure one, we were stunned. How much more so when we learned of this. Listen. People are scared. I'm going to try not to be frightened. I'm not going to form any impressions of them until I meet them face to face. And then I'll observe with what I hope to be innocent eyes. Who knows? Maybe that's impossible. But I must go. I must learn how they feel. Are they scared like us? If so, then the future here will be highly uncertain. Are they angry? They have every right to be. And yet . . ."

"How they feel?" Maricela interrupted, stretching her hand out to grasp Lawrence's shoulder.

Lawrence wrapped an arm about her waist. "Yes," she answered intensely. "Can't you see that that's the most important question of all?"

Lawrence held Jeffrey close. "Oh, if you only knew how scared I am."

She pulled away only far enough to look into his friendly eyes full of lions, giraffes, and elephants, not the soil organisms he had sought for study. When he smiled, though, it was all right.

"Lawrence." He spoke her name as if from far away. She tried to focus. After all, he was right here, wasn't he? "Your Cube is flawed."

She pulled away rapidly. "Who are you?" she hissed.

His innocent eyes widened, and immediately she felt guilty. "Lawrence, they might have power, but they can't mess with the gene maps."

"Sure they can. Don't be ridiculous. We were all born in a laboratory, after all." Lawrence pushed him away. "And they can mess with our minds. Maybe they *can* create you here. A Jeffrey for their purposes. Anything is possible here."

"No," he answered quietly, letting her push away completely and stand up. He watched her silhouette in the sky, grass to her waist.

Lawrence blinked. For a second they had merged in beauty. She saw herself as Jeffrey saw her.

He continued, "You're unique, Lawrence. There's no denying that. But you're not that different from everyone else. Look." He gestured. "Getting back to *why* I said your Cube was flawed—it's pretty obvious, isn't it? You have the Flora, the Fauna, and the humans, but the humans are animals."

"I know, but the intent was—What am I saying? All I can be is human. I am a human being. All I can create must be from the human viewpoint." She squinted, those small dark eyes becoming a line of smudgy black. Her chartreuse shirt flapped idly. It was hard to see her as intense. She was a lax fluid, an open field.

Lawrence blinked. Again it had happened, and it must be from Jeffrey's eyes, his opinion of her. She wasn't even sure she liked it. "From my viewpoint," she finally muttered, knowing how absurd it sounded.

Jeffrey heaved himself up off the ground and came over to cradle her elbow. Lawrence shivered at the touch. She at once felt gentle, as if it were *she* cradling the elbow, yet at the same time, she felt touched, as herself.

"No," Jeffrey breathed. "I'll have to show you." In the field of spelt he pointed toward the buildings. "What meaning do those convey?"

Lawrence peered as if she had all the time in the world. Even her words came out slowly. "The silos? Security." She nodded. What else could they represent?

Jeffrey nodded. "Think back now. Remember the mother duck? How she reacted?" He brushed his hand over his eyes. "Uh, I'm sure there were others, but . . ."

Lawrence interrupted because, from where she was now, it was easier to think like Jeffrey, to be him. "I wasn't attacking the duck, but she interpreted me as a threat."

Off in the distance a zebra was caught in the act of kicking a hippopotamus.

"She was scared." Jeffrey's lips moved, or so she thought. She wasn't looking at him.

"Yes," she murmured.

"So she attacked."

"No, not really." Lawrence shrugged. "I didn't get hurt."

"But it worked, didn't it? She attacked, and you backed away. She was satisfied. How about you?"

Lawrence said nothing, fascinated by this new unique power that allowed her to see Jeffrey, the silos, the duck, the zebra, all at once, without moving her eyes, without even opening them.

"You were the fox. Remember that?"

Lawrence shuddered.

"Somebody rescued you, sure, but what did you want to do to those who were chasing you, frightening you, torturing you?" Jeffrey's voice droned on, even as she understood so well she no longer needed words, no longer needed . . . anything.

Lawrence could no longer see anything. No longer could she hear Jeffrey's voice that had begun to sound like Vance's. Vance as he had once been, in those days long ago when she had sat on the ground and he had droned on and on about his suspicions, his fears, his speculations.

She wanted to hug herself, but her fingers were numb, wedged into place.

"Jeffrey, why are you so serious?" she asked. "I'm sick of so many people lecturing me, when I'm in here to feel, to be . . ."

Lawrence felt a burst of nausea. "Except . . . I'm not."

She disappeared.

Lawrence held the Cube idly, not noticing or caring that two hours had passed in the dark while she sat alone with her creation.

The door popped open and the room flooded with light.

"Oh, I'm sorry. I . . . We thought you were . . ." Adelaide stuttered.

Lawrence solemnly watched as she and David came tiptoeing into her office guiltily, as if it had been they who had been caught doing something unusual.

"We just needed to log out. Is that okay?" David asked.

Lawrence smiled to herself. David was new to the lab; he couldn't disguise the awe in his voice at all. She straightened and tried to look scholarly, but it didn't work. She was too tired.

"Are you okay?" Adelaide asked softly, trying to pass behind Lawrence, who merely circled in her chair so that she was always facing her.

"No. Does it matter?" Lawrence didn't even look at Adelaide's face, the face that was five years older than hers, yet looked so young and fresh and inviting that Lawrence had readily accepted the invitation.

"I wanted to tell you," Adelaide whispered. "They're wondering if you're going to take all the credit."

Lawrence stared at her blankly. "No need to whisper." She fumbled in her lap. "For this?" She shook her head. "No. It wasn't me at all."

David snickered. "What does that mean?" Lawrence saw Adelaide turn sharply to glare at him. She saw his grin fade as he bit his lip and swallowed, but she didn't turn to look at him. "Uh—never mind. I better be going." He slunk out of the room after hitting the appropriate sequence on the keyboard.

Adelaide gulped. "I'm sorry, Lawrence." She put on a genuine smile and asked, "Now that it's finished, what are you going to do with it?"

"It will never be finished, but there comes a time when you have to just take it as it is." Like when Vance had thrown her into the Elaborynth. She hadn't been ready then, either. "I'm living, ain't I?" Lawrence tossed her head, then faced Adelaide. "I'm going to enter it."

Adelaide gasped.

"What else can I do?" Lawrence explained, but it was no use. Adelaide still looked shocked, wary, and . . . respectful. Lawrence stood up and tucked the Cube under her arm. "Like David, I must be going." She brushed Adelaide's hand away and walked outside.

Lawrence trudged into the circle of egg trucks, shielding her eyes momentarily from the glare of light panels that were oddly set right out in the middle of the clearing.

"She's come! At last!" came a breathy yell. Lawrence squinted, but now all she could see were dim shadows running back and forth, their rims haloed in the yellow light.

"Call Charles!" came a strong male voice.

Almost immediately Lawrence felt a hand grasp her shoulder. Before she could flinch away, a gentle voice said, "This way. It's all right. I know your eyes need time to adjust."

Lawrence blinked as she turned toward it. "Antem?"

It was she, and Rover wasn't far behind. While Antem eagerly nodded and grinned, Rover shouted, "Hey, welcome back!"

Lawrence tucked the Cube more tightly under her arm and shook her head at him. *I'm not here to side with you artists, idiot.* But the words wouldn't come out. Lawrence found herself linking her free arm to his. *Who cares? Let them think I've come to rejoin them.*

Antem came over to her right side and put her arm around her shoulders. Lawrence gulped. It was impossible for her not to feel trapped, surrounded on both sides like that. "Let's go down to the depot," Antem said. "We'll all meet there."

Lawrence was led to a storage building down near the road. Already her breathless audience had converged. Lawrence felt like before, at twelve, when she had longed to be a farmer. The artists sat in a circle, but Lawrence was not to join them. Instead, Antem gently pushed her to the center of the circle before sitting down herself. Lawrence put the Cube down on a wide, smooth, beautifully polished table that stood there amongst the bags of grain and beans. She decided not to be stunned by the contrast, but she did wonder how Charles had gotten it.

The crowd thickened. Lawrence shifted impatiently. Again she was waiting on Charles. She kept her eyes to the ground and kept a frown firmly on her face. She had to accede to Charles his power, because everyone else, even the Center, accepted it.

No! That was stupid! She would wait, but she didn't have to like it.

If she chose, she could look at Scott. She could see him now if she slid her eyes over. He stood near the door, by the lights. At her glance he would instantly brighten, that smile would come to stay, and Lawrence would feel . . .

She wasn't sure. Accepted? Loved?

She shook her head. Scott was too easy. It was better not to look at anyone, better to keep her focus, her self.

Charles had finally arrived. He strode right through the crowd up to Lawrence in her circle and put his hand on her arm.

"Hey!" Lawrence jerked her arm away and looked at him wildly. As always, his face was confident, but this time she saw something more, and it made her hesitate. She restrained herself from hitting him as she puzzled what it could be.

"Why have you come?" His voice was calm, almost gentle.

"They want to know why you've not held harvest. They want to know what you're trying to do." Lawrence spat the words out from behind gritted teeth.

Charles leaned back on his heels. He was *not* cocky. Lawrence frowned, her eyes furtively crawling over his face as she tried to see just what he was. "Did they tell you what the consequences of our inactivity will be?"

Lawrence shook her head, still intent on her study of him. "As if I needed to be told. It's simple. We'll all starve if you don't go back to distributing the food."

Charles laughed. "And what are you going to do about it?"

Lawrence jumped as his voice instantly snarled loudly. Not to be put off guard she shot back, "I . . ."

But Charles was back to his new self. He held up his hand loosely as he said tenderly, "No, not you, Lawrence. Who, then? They? Yes, this time it's they."

"Who's 'they?'" Lawrence replied irritably.

"For you, I'll explain it. The silos . . ."

"Silos?" Automatically she searched for a definition. "The . . . ships? The . . . spaceships?"

"No," he answered patiently. "Silos are storage buildings. They have enough to feed us for a while."

"Why do you use archaic words?" Lawrence looked around at the crowd. "What are you trying to prove? I *know* you're in league with the braindead."

Charles slapped her, but not very hard. "Don't call them that."

Out of the corner of her eye she saw Scott advance, and she shook her head. "Don't call . . . Hey, you're the one who introduced me to the term." Lawrence found herself ignoring the slap, at least for now. It surprised her, but she needed no distractions. Yes. That was it. New holy Charles could wait for his comeuppance.

Charles looked genuinely repentant. "Yes. I know. We all know. There's been a change, however, and I hope you're observant enough to notice it."

Lawrence hung her head. This was terrible, to be insulted and wonder what was behind it. No one could just do it out of spite, as she saw it.

"A ship is ready to go up tonight, Lawrence. Who do you think should pilot it?"

Her head shot up. Yes! She had seen the preparations, had known the time had come, yet hadn't known it.

"Congratulations on mastering the basics of flight, Lawrence," Charles said cheerily.

She nodded, shrugging away the memory of the electrodes. She hadn't needed them. Not with Scott and Tom helping her learn.

"The engineers built the ship. They are familiar with its workings."

Lawrence did not look over at Number Five, now Betan. She knew that spaceship. It had been she who had instructed all the student pilots, telling them the ship's capabilities.

"The inlaid have fragmented memories. They remember the necessary 'instinct' one must have to fly. They even remember flying spaceships during the Great Eviction."

Lawrence remembered the feel of the tractor, the ecstasy of first flight.

"Yet we artists fly planes. We have done so in our lifetimes. So . . ." Charles finally paused. "Who should it be?"

"I have passed your pilot project," Lawrence answered slowly. "I performed with flying colors. Tom gave me the highest rating." She blinked. Suddenly she saw everyone very clearly. She began to address them. "But that's not important. That's not the point."

Apparently what had just come out of her mouth was completely unexpected. Charles stuttered, "What . . . what do you mean?"

Lawrence still addressed everyone, and spoke conversationally. "The question here is not who would make the best pilot. You're just thinking of the journey, the trivial, primary schematics of the shift. That's better left to a mechanic. Besides, it's what's at the end of the journey that matters. The person to go on this expedition must be a diplomat!" She said the new word carefully, but they knew what she meant. "Sure, somebody can fly, somebody can take the gene maps, but somebody's got to go along to develop a peaceful relationship with these people." Lawrence nodded. She had thrown that bit about the gene maps in intentionally, making it clear where *her* priorities lay.

"Who?"

"I don't know!" Lawrence waved her hand. "I'm just a mere botanist. Just make sure it's someone with tact, someone who . . ."

"A psych?" Charles asked.

Lawrence instantly thought of Kamela, her fake friendliness and power trips. "Oh, no, we need sincerity. Someone who *cares*."

"A passive succor?"

Lawrence hid her surprise. "No. No missionaries." Now *that* new word had been very important during the years of the Great Eviction, so, again, they knew what she meant.

"A scientist?" he asked teasingly.

"Possibly," Lawrence admitted honestly. "Their occupation is not what matters. It's their personality."

"Do you suggest we test for . . . sincerity? I don't—"

"Ah, forget your stupid tests," Lawrence said wearily.

Charles burst out laughing. "Lawrence, we paused our harvest to make people realize how much they need us. And to get us a little power. It shouldn't have worked. There's enough food for all, and most everybody came back just fine from the fields."

Her mind instantly totaled harvests, births, and rations and knew he was right. And she had heard that an emergency had been declared, so practically everyone had worked, had brought in the fresh fruits, the nuts, everything. "Okay," she said quietly, even resignedly. "But what do you need power for?"

"The ships are ours. Transportation has always been ours. You got to visit Maricela while most every other student was stranded, thanks to you knowing us. They tried to take them away from us," Charles began.

"What's wrong with that?" Lawrence flared, recalling the time when the one who now stood before her had denied her access to the egg trucks. So what if he had graciously allowed her to *ride*?

"Because we are the only ones who know who should go," Charles continued mildly.

"Who?"

"Lawrence, you shall go. Probably the doctor, what's-her-name, should go, too."

"Maricela Rose."

"Yeah, but that's it. No one else."

"Who said it was your decision?" Lawrence bristled.

Betan snickered.

"Aw, come on, Lawrence. It's *your* opus," pleaded Scott.

She whirled to see Tom and him nodding. Furiously she pounded her fist on the table. "So what? That's probably why it *shouldn't* be me. I can't go barging up there and demand my data. I have to be delicate."

"You see?" Charles demanded.

She shook her head.

"Not that it's unprecedented, but you *think* that all you care about is your opus, when really . . ."

Lawrence interrupted, "Please stop calling it my opus."

Charles smiled ingratiatingly at her sharp tone. "Okay. When really you're worrying about these people. Most anybody else would look at their . . . project and see only it, no matter what. And what about my presentation?" He spoke louder, jumping up onto the table to gesticulate at her. "You're the only one who's seen it that hasn't fribbled. Even though these people were different, alien, you studied them dispassionately, and remained calm."

"That's not compassion," she complained. "And that wasn't anybody real to care about. That was just your construct."

"But you *do* have compassion," Tom said quietly.

Lawrence stared at him, then she remembered that twilight she had been sitting outside the laboratory, exulting inside over the brief half-darks each day brought, and Tom had come to thank her for freeing him. He had even touched her face. Yet she had felt foolish, because, after all, she had merely acted as a scientist would. She hadn't known that the drug would cause so much ecstasy.

While Lawrence cast her glance away, Charles folded his arms, still gazing imperially down at her. "Look. Not all of us is rarin' to go. I know *I* don't want to. It's too dangerous, if you ask me, to rely on the old technology that we didn't create ourselves."

"Who cares about you?" Lawrence pointed around. "Maybe someone else would like to go."

Charles passed his broad hand over the crowd in imitation of her own movement. Lawrence felt uncomfortable looking at his ropy muscles, knowing she was too soft to jump up on the table in one smooth leap. "No. They've all agreed that it has to be you."

Lawrence smirked suspiciously. She certainly didn't trust Charles to be that honest where desires were concerned. Suddenly she thought of something else she could say. "Who asked you all?"

Charles jumped off the table and backed away. Holding his hands like a frame, he just whispered, "Look."

Lawrence turned and saw the Cube on the table, solemn, alone. She gulped, seized by her possession.

"It's yours," Charles said, echoing her feeling from a mass of canyon walls.

She shook her head. "No. I mean yes. But that's why I can't go." She closed her eyes and turned away from the Cube. "When I meet these people, if I go, I will be wanting something from them. How can I show tact that way?"

Tom came into the circle. "They are going to be wanting something, too. They must want something. Presumably, they want to return. We think the satellites are in need of repair and they must return. Well, you want something, too. It's balanced."

Lawrence again remembered Vance's long ago deal. Yes, what Tom was explaining sounded all right. An exchange.

Tom continued, "If you didn't want something, they'd be suspicious."

Lawrence interrupted, "What? Why? How do you know?"

Tom blinked down at the ground, where a few grass stems grew, only slightly trampled and still green, as if coming out of a braindead trance. "Uh, I don't know. That's how it was, a long time ago. People figure you wouldn't be communicating or negotiating unless you want something. Yet you're beholden to them, because you need them to finish your Cube. So they'll feel powerful." A smile washed over his face as he warmed to his subject. "You want that. You want them to feel good, to think they have power, see? They'll be so happy about it they'll gladly help you. But then after they help you, they'd want you to help them."

"Good, Tom," Charles said carefully, noticing his rakish grin, sweaty forehead, and bulging eyes.

"And that's when you'll say, 'No!'" Tom screamed, making Lawrence leap backward and Charles come forward to grab him.

"No, Tom! Snap out of it!" Charles wrapped his arms around him while Scott ran forward with a bucket of water and a sponge. Charles seized the sponge, plunged it into the water, and wiped Tom's face.

Scott looked over at Lawrence ruefully. "That wasn't the end we wanted, but, it's clear what you must do, isn't it?" He seemed to be pleading.

Lawrence stepped aside, wanting to pace as she thought about what Tom had said. "Yeah, help them." It still seemed odd. "But, Scott, I can't understand it. I can't think like that. My demanding something gives them power?" She rapidly shook her head as if to clear it. "But if you all think it's okay . . ."

Scott dropped the bucket to approach her with arms spread. For a second there, Lawrence thought he was going to hug her. He stopped, though, about a foot away to say, "Listen, Love, you have an important opus." Lawrence blushed. His voice had come out even more tenderly than she had ever heard it. She smiled foolishly as he grasped both of her arms. "You have something."

Lawrence remained there a second staring into his eyes. The only thing she could compare it to was the Cube's beginnings. Everything seemed to be rushing toward a vortex as she tried to make sense of it all. One clear concept came through.

Eyes distracted, she pulled gently away from Scott and stumbled forward to take up the Cube. "Of all the people on the Earth who might go," she began hoarsely, "I have the Cube. When I go to deal with those people above, there could be sacrifices on both sides. As a matter of fact, I guess there will be, in the name of harmony." She sniffed, shaking her head. "And of all the people on this Earth, I have the most to lose." She raised the Cube with a nod toward Scott, who returned her nod with a grim smile.

"Come on, Bobby! I found it! It's over here, near the pine, like I said it would be!" Teri was smug as she waved her brother over to the tiny cave hole.

Bobby was so excited that after a half morning they had actually found ("rediscovered" was how Teri proudly put it) the place, he ignored her expression. He eyed the hole suspiciously. "That little ol' thing? What?" He scratched his head. "Can we even fit?"

Teri slapped his belly that protruded out slightly over his jeans. "*I* can. I don't know about you."

Bobby sighed. She had promised, since he'd never seen it, to let him go in first, but now he wavered. "Uh—maybe I'd get stuck."

"That's why you need to go first. So's I can pull you out," Teri said sensibly.

Bobby was only just now dimly thinking that maybe Teri had never gone in at all. Maybe she'd just made up all those stories about the shiny walls. "Gold," she had said matter-of-factly.

"Well, yeah," he finally said, "but you can go ahead. If I get stuck, you can *push* me out. Yeah. It'd be easier that way." He sneaked a look over at his older sister, who was now frowning. Not a good sign.

"Oh, Bobby," she moaned. "Don't tell me you're chicken. Go ahead and jump in with your flashlight. You're the one who wanted to see it. I've already seen it," she pointed out needlessly.

Bobby took a deep breath and pushed the tiny flashlight through his belt. He rushed the air out to try to flatten his stomach. "Okay." He squatted, then stuck his head into the hole. He scooted a little bit, then a little bit more. It was then he felt Teri lifting his feet to help push him in.

"Hey! Stop that!" He gurgled, feeling the rocks scrape his belly. "Ugh."

Bobby had now slithered in far enough that he could reach his flashlight. He yanked it from his belt and clicked it on.

He wasn't sure what happened next. All he could remember was hordes of screeching, furry things flying at him, making him drop his flashlight and scream.

"Help! Teri!" He screamed over and over. His feet, still outside, clawed at the rocky hillside.

The reddish brown bat crossed the blackberry bushes before turning sharply to float over near the fence. Once there, again it turned, this time to fly toward the duck house. There it hovered at about a meter and a half from the ground, but only for a second. Swiftly it crossed over the blackberry bushes again. The pattern was repeated, over and over. On the fifth circuit of identical movements, the human watching it chose to experiment.

"I shall stand right there near the duck house, right where it hovers at a few centimeters less than my height, and I'll see if it flies near my ear." More eagerly the human spoke. "I'll even see if it flies there more than once."

Only once.

Lawrence gripped the Cube, all eight kilograms of it, and stepped outside, gasping the crisp, moist air after the warmth inside the depot.

Near the road, she could peer up into the gap the trees made and gaze upon a perfect, clear, starry sky. Lawrence paused in the middle of the road to gaze upwards wide-mouthed.

That's where I'm going. The stars were brilliant; they seemed to swoop around her. Only later did she realize she was slowly spinning around, and she made herself stop. Stumbling on the wet grass, she almost dropped the Cube. Clutching it once more, she gulped as she saw the spaceship as a tiny black spot against the stars.

The depot's door banged. Lawrence jumped, peering to see who had come out. The bright lights had been shut down when she had entered the depot, and they wouldn't go on again until launch. She pulled out her light stick.

"Don't light that thing!" came Scott's voice. "You don't need to see me. Just this." He lit up a Scroll in his hand.

Lawrence leaned up against the nearest tree. The weight of the Cube had suddenly become too much for her. Dimly she heard Scott explain.

"We'll be sending a message along with you. It speaks of—"

"I don't care what it says," Lawrence answered sharply. "Just put it into the ship." The ship! "I—I guess I'd better go get Maricela, shouldn't I?" She took a big gulp, feeling her heart pound as she realized what she was getting into.

Scott looked at her puzzledly. "It's strange to want to face people without knowing what you've already told them through the Scroll."

"I don't care." Lawrence studied him. His dark eyes, their hollows prominent, frightened her. He tightened his fists. The starlight made it obvious. Her heart lurched. What a difference it made now to leave him, perhaps forever.

Tucking the Cube under one arm, she reached up to touch his cheek. Scott started, then merely shoved the Scroll into her hand and squeezed it tight. "Remember," he whispered.

Charles whistled from near the ship.

Scott nodded. "That's your signal. Now run." He pushed her toward the fields.

Lawrence took off, running as fast as she could carrying both the Cube and the Scroll. Clumsy as she was, she felt as if she were flying over the long, wet grass, no longer touching the pebbles underneath her rubber soles.

She neared the ship. Charles had lit up all the panels, so she could now clearly see Maricela running, too. How had she known to come? But there was no time to wonder. Her arms and lungs ached as she paused to let Maricela hug her.

There was the ship now, its glowing portal blasting their eyesight. The steel stairs that Lawrence tripped up, Maricela quiet behind her. The suits dangling, *their* suits, from the pilot project. Tom and the others suiting them up, the cotton lining coming into contact with her skin, the helmet sealing her off. Lawrence suppressed a gasp at being so isolated.

Maricela clumsy on board, Lawrence impatient. The Cube safe in its nonconducting alloy fence. The Scroll slipped into the broadcast slot. Then, the climax, the controls, the ship's controls, coming to her steady hands as if all she had been raised to do was fire that ship. As they had said during training, "Intense, brief, total concentration like no one else."

Lawrence nodded to Betan as she surged from underneath the vessel, running and signaling. The night sky rushing to meet her eyes even as she strapped in, Maricela doing the same. Screens alive, rapidly reviewing the sequence. Requisite memories playing out in her head, those of Tom and other braindead explaining the nuances as their haunted memories were seized. It was necessary for her to become those ancient pilots. Lawrence divorced herself momentarily.

They were aloft. Blanking all else except the most perfunctory motions, Lawrence remained calm at the controls.

No room at all for thoughts, for anticipation, for a plan to meet the new people. No hearkening to Charles' plans, the council's plans, everyone's expectations. No time even to think of the Cube and its gene maps.

The city, and Earth, was left far behind.

Spacer pilot Catherine Blintzsky stepped out onto the planet surface, handscan already tasting and sampling the air.

"We should be able to breathe it," her companion reassured her. "All readings showed a . . ."

"Quiet. Do you think I'm going to rely on ship's sensors? If you choose to trust things that aren't here, that haven't directly experienced this air, one day you might find yourself . . ." Her drone paused as she read the handscan. "Breathable." She glanced at her companion.

Renee pointed, laughing. "Do you think I'm going to trust *that* thing?"

Catherine smiled. "You're right. The only thing for us to do is to risk it." She tugged her helmet off and breathed deeply through her nose. Tossing her head, she commented, "Free." Her tone was delicious.

Renee followed suit, though she looked less ecstatic in the mild air. Together they cautiously looked around at the landscape.

"Where's the city?" Catherine strode around the small ship to peer in the other direction. "Did we land in the wrong place?"

Renee pointed. "It could be behind that hill." She chose the most ponderous.

Catherine spun to look, then snorted. "Not even a little village could hide behind that hill." She folded her arms. "And I guess that's all I should expect. The inhabitants of this planet are clearly primitive." She came back around the ship and spread her arms wide over the gently rolling grassy land. "Look at this place! It reminds me of the prairie." She peered down at the knee-high, spindly, black plants, pausing to break off a firm leaf. "No wildflowers, though," she murmured. When she straightened, her mouth was a tight line. First she placed the leaf in her sample pocket, then she turned to Renee. "Think they got our message?"

Renee shrugged. "There's no guarantee that they can understand our pictures." She lifted her handscan. "I sense . . . something . . . that way." She pointed vaguely toward the green-yellow sun.

"Be specific," Catherine ordered.

"It's heat, concentrated in a region about 10° off the sun path." Again she pointed. "It could be the city."

Catherine slapped her hands. "Shall we split up? You stay here and guard the ship, while I head over that way."

Renee hesitated. "We can come back to the ship."

Catherine paused. Of course the natives were harmless. There were no signs of advanced civilization, and, after all, *they* had not been the ones to make first contact. "All right."

The two women silently marched through the sparse vegetation, climbing the tallest hill. Right before their eyes could see beyond the crest, Catherine turned to Renee with a smile.

"It'd be a better hike if we could get out of our suits."

Renee nodded. "It's not far." She indicated the grass with a jerk of her head. "It looks continuous from a distance. I'm glad it grows so far apart in reality."

The city was unimpressive in the dim light. Though made of light-colored buildings that were intricately decorated, it did not glitter. Silence adorned it.

Catherine sniffed. "It sure is *small*," was her comment.

Renee was again studying her handscan. "I wish this thing were more accurate. I'm still receiving heat, but where are they?"

Catherine stepped out onto the road. Her feet, encased in boots, could not feel the abnormal warmth of the smooth, glassy surface. "They might have fled," she surmised.

Renee cautiously followed her out into the first range of buildings. "Or, they could be right here, hiding."

They stopped walking. As if on cue, the ground began to tremble. No, the planet wasn't undergoing a tremor. It was the road, the buildings, that shook.

"What the . . . ?"

The solid walls started to melt, flooding toward them, and the hard surface started to flow. Renee screamed.

"Shit!" Catherine screeched. "Run!"

Too late. The monster flexed, arching the tall buildings to wrap around the two women, finishing them off in one gulp.

Nathan Tucker paused, slipping his foot into a rock crevice before taking a sip from his canteen. "Maybe I should pull out my map and check where I am," he muttered vaguely, ignoring his own words as his eyes scanned the mountains.

He had seen the glittery light near the trees, he was certain. That's why at first he had only thought of it as a wide creek glinting in the sun. But when it still shone at night . . .

"Let me just get up on that ledge," he continued muttering. "It looks like a good place to stop."

He stepped out, immediately slipping on some loose dirt. Wildly he grabbed at the sloping rock. Maybe he shouldn't have been so eager to accept a crash course in rock climbing. Besides that, he, a beginner, shouldn't even be out alone.

But he had to check out those lights. It wasn't something you could tell other people. "Uh, Fred, how about coming out with me next weekend and hunt for UFO's?" Yeah, sure.

The ledge at last. Before yanking out the map, he squatted and peered up at the rest of his route. Yeah, it looked easy compared to what he had already climbed. He took a deep breath and nodded as he folded the map away. *I'm right on target.*

Underneath the trees it was cool and dark. Nathan blinked. Ruefully he considered his surveying skills. "I could have missed them by a mile." He shook his head.

At first he thought it was the sun peeking through a cut the lumberers had made, but the light was too blue for that. He fell to his knees.

They were beautiful. Tender smiles kissed his lips and drained his sorrow. "My wife," he sobbed. "How did you know about her?" Their haloes twinkled as they led him away from the anger, from the chasm, from the pain. "It wasn't her fault," he heard himself babble. "She wasn't drunk or anything, just mad. At me. Heck, she was already dead when they got through the wreck, and the guy she hit was just fine. It's 3 that's not okay. Me." He grabbed at their glowing robes. "But you . . . you have made me happy."

They floated him over to their wondrous starship. "For me?"

Maricela whispered, "I hate to bother you, but apparently their orbit is more erratic than we calculated. I can't find them."

Lawrence answered, "They could have some way to maneuver. In which case, they could run from us." The first words she had spoken since flight weren't that hard; still, she continued to give the controls her full attention.

"Ah," came Maricela's gentle whisper almost immediately. "I spoke too soon. There they are. I'll put it on your screen."

Lawrence saw a flashing rectangle in the top right corner of her screen. "Thanks," she said. Her faceplate faintly misted as she adjusted the controls to aim for the satellite. No time to get excited now. Still, her heart pounded.

"I'm . . . nervous," Maricela said needlessly.

Lawrence grinned. "We don't know." Vaguely she thought of being suffocated, as one of the folk had done for fun night after night with her pillow, then fought the feeling off. "We will just have to go in there and see what happens."

"Wow!" Maricela waited a second before explaining her outburst. "I just scanned it. It's huge!"

"Look at that!"

At about two kilometers from the satellite, portals and exterior lights began to glow. Within two seconds the gesture was completed, and the two women, Lawrence constantly glancing down at the controls, stared at the vast array of sparkles.

"It's just like the city," Lawrence breathed.

"Can we interpret this as a welcoming?" Maricela more pragmatically asked.

They decelerated gradually, Lawrence ready to swoop around it in case she miscalculated. Maricela leaned forward.

"I don't see what Tom called a 'dock.' No, wait. That could be it right there. Let me check." She flashed up a memory onto her screen. "It matches. Yes."

Lawrence passed her right hand down sharply. From their hastily designed system of silent communication, Maricela could understand that she was nervous. "It's straight on," she voiced her concern grudgingly as she positioned the shuttle to meet it.

"Maybe they were tracking us also," Maricela said brightly.

Lawrence nodded, teeth pressed against her lip. Tom had said that docking would be difficult. Her eyes judged, her mind calculated. The information on the dials in front of her merely confirmed her guesses. With care she aligned the shuttle to the door. When all appeared stable, she unstrapped and stood up slowly, smiling ruefully at an appropriate "Gorry!" that filled her mind. At that instant, she heard a thump.

Lawrence froze, staring into Maricela's terrified eyes. As the noises continued, she watched them gradually become calm.

"I think it's okay," Maricela whispered to the accompaniment of thumps and crankings. "They must be securing us."

Here was Lawrence priding herself on a good docking, when she should have remembered that there was no guarantee that the coupling could be exact. The designs were highly unlikely to match, no matter what histories they studied, because there might have been a different, unretrievable system in place, or, over time, the inhabitants of the satellite could have changed or removed it.

She went over and stood beside the door. Maricela waited until all was silent to unstrap herself. Still, at any minute they could go spinning. *Well, let it,* Lawrence thought irritably. *I don't want to be helped up.* She nodded at her.

"I want you next to me." She leaned over to pop open the door to see the interior of an air lock. Her heart lurched.

How am I supposed to act? I look with compassion upon the natives. What facial expression should I have on? What gestures should I use?

Together they crept into the air lock. Lawrence felt around for the inner door handle while the outer one slowly sealed.

I can't do it! It'd be a lie. I can't be fake-friendly, or anything else. They'll just have to take me as I am.

Maricela pulled out her light stick and beamed it at the door, catching Lawrence's face in the glow.

"What's the matter?" came over the radio.

"Nothing," Lawrence answered tiredly. She turned back to the door.

"Africa," Maricela read out loud carefully, as she had been told how to pronounce the early name of the East/South continent, pointing to the label just seconds before the door unsealed.

Maricela and Lawrence stepped out into a floating mass of people. Lawrence found herself accepting a ring that was attached to the wall. She gulped as a small person dashed past her to check the door. In a daze, she watched him pass an instrument over the seal. When he turned, he nodded.

"It's complete," she read his lips. "Start it."

Lawrence turned to see a tall figure in the back of the crowd nod and leave the small chamber. She turned to Maricela, who was shyly gazing at the people.

Lawrence decided to look, too. It should have been easier behind her faceplate, but it wasn't. *They look a lot like us. I suppose Maricela would know the exact differences.* Lawrence suddenly felt very isolated in her spacesuit. *I guess overall their skin is darker. The braindead kept emphasizing that. Why?*

A young woman, the only one in robes, used the rings to crawl over to Maricela. Lawrence watched the red folds float out behind her. Maricela shook her head when the woman spoke to her, and pointed to her ears. Lawrence almost giggled at the sight.

The woman now approached Lawrence. "Will you remain suited?" Lawrence again read her lips.

"No." Aggressively she yanked off her helmet. Maricela followed her instantly. "We brought oxygen for our needs," she blurted. Everybody on Earth had been insistent that Lawrence and Maricela should not expect to freeload, though when a visit to another commune was necessary, hospitality had always been easy. Scott had explained to her the method of supply and storage that guaranteed that. After a visitor, supplies could be replaced. There was no clue that the satellites could handle this, of course. Still, she felt weird having to say it. In fact, they had ended up bringing more than they needed for a first two-week visit.

The woman nodded. Lawrence tried not to stare. She was quite dark, even compared to the others, yet she had some of the facial features that Maricela had. Lawrence tried to think: *Did the egg labs interbreed us with them long ago, not just us? How?*

"Steady!" came a man's shout. "Be sure you two have a firm grip on those rings." Both women obediently wrapped their gloved hands tightly around the metal.

The room changed. That was the only way Lawrence could explain it. She let out a moan unintentionally and crawled to the floor, going hand over hand down the loops.

"What's wrong?" Maricela's eyes darted from Lawrence to the group, but she didn't move from her erect stance.

The woman bent down to speak slowly to Lawrence. "Don't worry. It's the artificial gravity. You'll adjust eventually. For right now, let us take you to the most comfortable part of the satellite. We'll worry about getting the oxygen later. Please." The young woman extended her arm out to Lawrence, who didn't feel like moving at all, who just wanted to lie down and perhaps vomit, but who also knew the importance of seizing that helping hand. She reached out.

Standing, it was actually not so bad, or at least she tried to tell herself that. Lawrence grasped the woman's waist and leaned quite heavily, though she tried not to squash her with her suited weight. The young woman bore under the burden bravely. Lawrence noticed, however, that her waist felt misshapen. Maybe that was why she was wearing robes.

Ahead in the curving corridor, Maricela was helped out of her suit. At a further point, Lawrence was stopped and assisted, also. During this lag, a young man, perhaps a teenager, eagerly spoke to Lawrence.

"Your little ship looks *exactly* like the old ones. What did you do? Renovate one? How could it have been in any shape to fly?"

"No," Lawrence said heavily, puzzling over exactly how to explain. "We built a new one from old memories."

The young woman frowned at the teenager, who hurriedly moved on. Lawrence stared after him vaguely, wondering what he expected. That particular technology had to stay stagnant, didn't it?

As Lawrence and Maricela stood there naked, they clasped hands. Let 'em look at the paler skin, though of course Maricela's wasn't so bad, but the man who had checked the air lock seal came up just then and handed them their clothing bags. Apparently he was getting in the oxygen, water, and food, too. Self-consciously they unzipped the bags and hauled out clothes as the young woman looked on wryly, but there was nothing else they could do. They dressed slowly, awkwardly, each leaning on the young woman through half of it, as the remainder of the group passed into another small chamber. Lawrence gave Maricela a sharp look. Another air lock?

When she was done dressing, the young woman finally released her. Maricela quickly stretched her arms out, but Lawrence shook her head.

"No, I'm fine now. It feels better here. More secure." They turned and followed the young woman into the small chamber, and the door was shut behind them. Lawrence gulped.

But there was an inner door which the young woman turned to unlatch as she announced proudly, "Now you will see our garden satellite."

Lawrence found herself leaning forward. What was a "garden"? It was in the best location. It must be precious. What was it?

The door opened into wilderness. Both Lawrence and Maricela stepped back. "What?" whispered Lawrence. A tin can full of trees!

"I was picturing a hospital myself," Maricela whispered back. Lawrence shrugged.

They all stepped into the trees. Tears trickled into Lawrence's eyes as she noticed a few diseased bushes. Still, they were all familiar; they must have passed into a temperate zone.

The young woman turned to explain. "We are going to the Old One."

Lawrence stroked ahead to be at her side, not noticing the worried glances several of the group gave each other as she did so. "I don't understand. Is this your garden?"

She stared straight ahead. "Yes. Do you not have gardens on Earth? Places where you plant lovely things and help them grow?"

Lawrence wondered about the new formality in her tone, and the way everyone else had neared her at her approach. After all that care, and her vulnerability, earlier, (No one else was naked, surprisingly.), what did she expect? She waved a mosquito away from her nose, again ignoring her less friendly tone. "Yes. I mean, I guess, no. We plant crops so we can eat. I guess they're lovely," she said awkwardly. "But this is just trees."

The group stopped walking. Lawrence lurched and fell back just to stay in place.

"*Just* trees?" At last Lawrence could hear a trace of anger. Her blatant curiosity that had thrust her into the conflict readily died down, leaving her to think quickly.

"I didn't mean it that way." It would be hard to explain what she meant. "Where we come from, they aren't tended, and they are so many that . . ."

"Here we must care for them."

Lawrence nodded. "They are precious." It still didn't clear the air.

"Your crops," the young woman continued mercilessly. "How are they handled? Do you have famine?"

Lawrence was about to enter confidently into a subject she knew a great deal about, but the last word stopped her. "Famine?"

"Hunger."

"No. Each year we calculate how much we need. Our food is rationed." Only now, despite Scott's concern, did the screen sessions with Charles when he had reluctantly asked for her mathematical skills seem odd.

"What about surplus?"

Lawrence could now detect in her voice an urgency that the young woman was desperately trying to hide. "There is surplus." She remembered Charles' recent emphasis on this very thing. "We're not allowed to use it." When the young woman did not change her expression, Lawrence uneasily continued, "I have worked on the farm."

"Don't we all?" the young woman murmured, and it was all over.

They came upon a field. Lawrence turned to see Maricela nod. It was warmer here, though how they did that was beyond her.

"Not quite prairie. More like savanna," she told Lawrence.

It was a lot like home, Lawrence told herself as she looked around. No animals were obviously apparent.

When they finally came to a stop, it was at a huge pine tree that dwarfed all the other growth in the forest that they had reentered. Apparently the temperate zones were not all together, though in her excitement she couldn't see a pattern yet. She looked up at it ecstatically, clearly part of the pride that emanated from all those around her upon looking at the giant.

"This is the Old One," the young woman said.

Lawrence nodded eagerly. "This is it." *This is where it shall be*, she exulted.

"Let us sit."

They crouched in a small circle, Lawrence still gazing up through the branches at the indeterminate ceiling.

"As I understand it, you have come to secure our gene maps."

Only then did Lawrence cringe at leaving the Cube behind in the ship, but she faced her fully. It had been the right thing to do, to introduce them to it gradually. "Yes. My project requires them so that the human record can be complete."

"I shall ask the Shawicc about it. She is currently considering all of its ramifications."

Lawrence bowed her head.

"We heard your message of peace. Of course we understand it, but we must move carefully on this. What is the situation on Earth?"

With her head down, Lawrence could listen to her tones better, and she could sense a switch to a more cautious, suspicious nature. "There are plenty of supplies—and plenty of room."

"What would happen if we were to renew our relationship with Earth? What would be your reaction? If we were to end this farce and land, how would you greet us? Would we be shot out of the sky? Sold into slavery? Brutalized? Exploited? What are your plans?"

Lawrence shifted uncomfortably underneath that inclusive "you." She gulped. "What do those words mean? Shot—do you mean destroy? Slavery? What do you mean?"

The patient, rich voice again developed an edge. "Will we be harmed in any way?"

Lawrence at first wanted to blurt out, "No!" but she had to think. "There is no guarantee that someone somewhere won't hurt you." She looked up at the impatient face.

"What kind of weapons do you have?" Before Lawrence could interrupt, she said sharply, "Things that harm!"

Lawrence leaned back. "Some people . . . can hurt." Maricela immediately grasped her hand, so that it didn't bother her as much, remembering. "I think most people are frightened . . ."

"What does your government plan to do?"

Now Lawrence had to try to remember what Tom and the other braindead had explained. Government was . . . No, it was too strange to really grasp. "I think control evolved from patterns set long ago. They think art is dangerous. They do not understand my project."

"What I envision is physical harm," the young woman said, slipping into Lawrence's vernacular.

"Oh. Ummm—We . . . we have knives. Fists. Tractors." Lawrence tightened her grip on Maricela's hand. "I don't know. I thought I was explaining." She looked up again at the young woman's blazing blue eyes.

They had finally softened and now appeared thoughtful. When she caught Lawrence staring at her intensely, however, they narrowed. She stood.

"It is time for me to report to the Shawicc. I do have one final question: Will you help us?"

Lawrence drew her knees up to her chest and placed her chin on them. "I am willing to help. I will do what I can."

Everyone stood then, and Lawrence watched as they canted so that she could view them all briefly, their bright clothing, soft mouths, shining teeth, brown eyes.

The young woman flashed a glance her way as they departed. "You will do," she tossed off casually over her shoulder. "I am Aratesht."

Nicole Garner pulled up her chair and tightened her grip on the mauve pencil.

"Where do you go after Ayres Rock, after all the sacred stone formations, after the revered waterfalls, caverns, and storms? Once you've protested the blasphemy in the name of others' religions, once you've demanded that the goddamn pervasive Americans leave off, if only for a brief century, so that some valuables survive, what is there left to do?

"Maybe it's time to look back at what you thought you were protecting. What do these sacred spaces have in common?

"Maybe it's time to look forward to what you thought you would accomplish. Does anyone really believe that saving one rock, albeit a huge one, for the sake of one conquered culture is going to save that culture?

"Maybe it's time to look inward, at the damaging, feeble squirmings of Western civilization, and learn what it is that *you* worship.

"Think about it. The only way you can see it is to observe the others' bounty, and only then will you see yourself, for you are so radically different from what had gone before.

"The groups that you call primitive worship that which, until now—and some say it will forever be so—has never been created by human mind or hands. They stand in awe of what is not themselves.

"We are different. Today we worship the Mona Lisa, the sonnets, the skyscrapers, the robots, the artificial intelligence. It is an effort, if not an impossibility, to acknowledge the power of nature. Oh, a couple of floods, tornadoes, maybe, things that jar us out of a somnolence brought on by comfort. But, over all, we have an unchecked admiration for what some might even call profane—ourselves."

Discomfort swelled into misery. She moaned, tongue lolling, dry, onto the leaves. Her swollen abdomen ached, but when she shifted, it scraped the branches above. Any action to ease pain was fruitless. Better to stay still; maybe then sleep would come with its blank comfort and stop the telltale moaning.

She had grown weaker, from a lively, lithe pup to this full monstrosity. The yet to be drained: the calcium, the nutrients, her very life from her cells. After birth, though, it would be the same. The helpless organisms would demand milk, protection, even her cleansing tongue, and she would give, give, give all she could, until they were strong and self-sufficient, and she, a mere husk, would begin her routine again.

Alone below the great spreading branches, the two visitors sat. Lawrence glanced wryly over at Maricela before leaning against the flaking trunk.

Maricela took a deep, shuddering breath and sighed, shaking her whole body in acquiescence as she lowered her head.

Lawrence jerked her gaze back over to her. "What's wrong?" She reached over to stroke Maricela's hand.

Maricela gave her an odd look. It was so penetrating and searching that Lawrence felt as if they had just met, and Maricela, unlike her usual outgoing self, was suspicious. Impossible, she would have thought just yesterday, but, here, in this strange place, she allowed herself to accept the scrutiny. She cleared her throat. Maricela looked away.

"It's nothing. I'm just nervous." Again she sighed.

"That woman—the one called Aratesht. I noticed something strange about her as we walked together. I think she's . . . gravid."

Maricela straightened and stared at her, horrorstruck.

"Her waist was swollen. You're the doctor. She seemed otherwise young and healthy, right? What else could it be?" Lawrence spoke mildly, curiously. Now that she could tell another, she could pretend to get over her initial shock.

Maricela drooped her shoulders. "Yes. Why shouldn't they be different? In so many ways they are different. We can tell that already. Why shouldn't they choose pregnancy, to be more like animals?"

"I'm not sure they chose it," Lawrence replied softly. "And they're not that different." She jerked her head to stare down the path.

A group of diverse people were passing through the trees. Lawrence glanced over at Maricela before peering at them calmly. At first she thought it could be the first group, or at least some of its members, but these were all new people who did not wear flowing robes. Most of them seemed to be in uniform, so Lawrence searched for a badge. None, so maybe they were limited in clothing choice. The group was led—no, not led, exactly—by the youth who had questioned her in the corridor. Lawrence timidly smiled when he caught her gaze defiantly, but inexplicably he immediately frowned and looked down at the ground, as if ashamed. Lawrence took a big gulp, then stood to greet them.

"What—?" Maricela hushed at a signal from Lawrence, the same sharp hand gesture they had used on the shuttle.

"Hello." Another youth in uniform greeted Lawrence, pointedly turning away from Maricela.

Lawrence merely squinted and nodded. His chubby, freckled face did not impress her with its innocence, since it was clear that he was deliberately ignoring her friend.

The youth seemed a little put out by her silence, but he smoothly began, "I am Wong. And these with me are my comrades." He spread his arms out wide in introduction, then dropped them suddenly. "We have come to learn of your purpose."

Lawrence shrugged. "It's not a big deal. We've come to secure your gene maps—"

Wong waved his hands rapidly to silence her. "Yes, yes, we know all that from rumors. You see . . ." He pointedly raised his chin to stare up into the branches above.

Lawrence followed his gaze, shifting her feet as she tried to keep her face calm. Would she have to go through the same boundless interrogation Aratesht had put her through?

"No, we don't see," interjected Maricela. "What are you getting at?"

Lawrence immediately confronted Wong's irritated grimace.

"You sit under the Old One," he explained.

"We were told to wait. This place is as good as any other," Lawrence answered.

Wong's eyes flew open wide. "My question, then, is do you really believe that?"

Maricela again spoke up, this time in a practical tone. "Yes. Why not? This is where we were led. It seems pointless to move. Besides, we might get lost."

"No," Lawrence said. Compared to Maricela, she sounded wondering, childlike. "I like the tree. It impresses me. Apparently it means a lot to your people."

"To some," Wong tossed off casually, "it is sacred."

Lawrence took a moment to read their faces, but all she saw was expectancy. What could she say except what she was going to say anyway? "I'm not sure what you mean by that. I hope you don't mean that it's off limits. I would like to use the tree for my project."

Wong stepped back; now all the faces looked blank, like they usually did in class. "Are you serious?" He blinked before grinning and clasping his hands together.

Lawrence folded her arms. Maricela was looking up at her with a wary, pleased expression. Mentally she shrugged. It was her Cube.

"Will you then work with us? No, I probably shouldn't ask that. Your actions speak for themselves. You are on our side already." Wong spoke rapidly, proudly.

Lawrence shook her head. "I am on no one's side. And I don't think I will ever be, no matter how much you appear to be . . . right. I mean—am I making myself clear?"

Wong waved down her protest. "No. Let *me* explain."

"No," interrupted the youth who had accosted her. "Let *us* explain." He glanced at Lawrence apologetically. "We come from two different worlds. It is quite possible that neither of us knows what we're talking about. What Wong represents is our disgust with tradition. Some of the people in this section, for example, are very pro-African."

"That means that they try to keep the old ceremonies, the rituals, the costumes." A young woman not in uniform, but wearing a simple pantsuit, continued his explanation. "Like those robes you saw. Don't you think they're highly impractical?"

Wong again took control. "We admire the tree for surviving, but we cannot see it as something to be worshipped. Er . . . we cannot see it as anything other than a robust specimen. After all, it is not greater than we are. We survived hard times, too."

Lawrence looked up into the branches and nodded. "Our society teaches us that there are no worthy traditions. We also have no history. I guess we also have no hierarchy. I for one accept the fact that one must adapt to different conditions. It is too dangerous to adhere strongly to a pattern that is ineffective. Of course, I'm assuming a person has a measure of choice."

"Exactly!" the youth exulted.

"Let me make it clear, however," Lawrence continued, "That I do not know if I am right. What if the tradition is neither effective nor ineffective? Why will it be abandoned if it makes no difference? Every culture has traditions, even mine. It might take an outsider, such as yourselves, to show us what ours are."

"But you have acknowledged the ideal. Maybe your people don't always live up to them, but they are there," the woman said.

Lawrence shrugged. "For what it's worth."

Wong grinned. "I am very excited about returning to Earth. It sounds just perfect."

"I don't know. From what I've seen so far, your people are okay. You've survived." Lawrence couldn't help but look admiringly at the group. After all, she'd never experienced a famine.

"Like the tree? Do you think it's an accomplishment to do what nature forces you to do?" The youth reached out to touch the tree's bark. "Maybe it is," he whispered.

Lawrence ignored him.

"Well," concluded Wong, "the Shawicc should be here shortly. We'd better be going."

"Goodbye," replied both Maricela and Lawrence.

Lawrence turned away at their departure to see a disturbed look on Maricela's face. "What's wrong?"

"I know it's kind of silly, but I'm angry that they didn't acknowledge my existence along with yours."

Lawrence leaned her head back. "Yeah. I guess it was all directed toward me. And, at first, at least, they seemed to want Wong to speak for all of them."

"I finally figured it out, but I'm still mad. Do you want to know why they acted that way?" Maricela stood up and stretched.

Lawrence darted a glance at her in irritation. "Of course I want to know. I need to know all I can about these people's ways."

Maricela bowed her head in concentration. "Okay. It's from Tom. We've got to remember that we're aliens here. Tom told me that the old joke was that the aliens always say, 'take us to your leader.' While I was mulling over that, he said that maybe the bits and pieces of what the inlaid remember is really the whole picture. Little phrases mean a lot. And I said, okay, but what does 'take us to your leader' mean? He said they're going to see a leader, even when there's not one. They've got to, or else they can't communicate. They home in on the strong. I'm not sure about why . . ."

"Nice theory, Maricela, but why me?" Lawrence interrupted from where she was studying a dead moss patch.

"Oh, come on, Lawrence. It's the way you act. Naturally you've noticed it. What am I saying? Yeah, of course you notice it, since it's obvious that you planned it all." Maricela twisted and strode over to where Lawrence was standing. "Look. It's you." She swung her arms in a big, all-encompassing circle around Lawrence's form. "I keep thinking it has something to do with the way you look at everything, the way you're so studious and so careful. Like when you climbed the harvester. You weren't going to mess up, because you took the time to learn it right.

240

The pilot trainers said it, didn't they? You know how to concentrate; you know how to respond. Sometimes, I've noticed, you lose yourself in contemplation, like you're not even with us. And yet . . . when you come into a room, everyone notices, everyone looks at you, while you're . . . yes, you've observed, perhaps you've seen it all already, yet you're inside, unreachable . . ."

Lawrence sighed. "What are you? A psychcomputer?" She drew closer to Maricela and traced her right hand over the bright hair and sultry brown cheek. Would it be sacrilege to fuck right now under the Old One? "You didn't like the way I look at you?" she said roughly.

Maricela glanced down at the hand that was now caressing her collarbone and shuddered, wrapping her arms around herself at the same time. "Yes, I do. Each time it's like you've never seen me before. It makes me feel important."

Lawrence grimaced. "Yeah. I used to think I was destined for great things." She drank in the curve of Maricela's waist as it met her hipbone. It was now like the first time she'd ever seen her, except of course this time she could lust with a sense of propriety. "I guess it was because I was always being singled out. I never could fit into any group."

"Well, you've done a great thing. You've created the Cube." Maricela relaxed under her hand, even leaning back a little so that when Lawrence's fingers touched her nipple, she could see it stiffen.

"Ah, that's nothing." Lawrence dropped her hand and crawled back under the tree to sit. "But now I see myself the way you see me. That could prove useful." Now she remembered the first time with Maricela, her clumsiness, and Maricela's laughter. It hadn't bothered her at the time.

"It's because of the Cube that they see you as the leader. You're the pilot. I'm just the auxiliary." Her voice came brightly, as if nothing had happened at all. Lawrence was simultaneously grateful and angry.

"So what?"

Maricela nodded her head to the path. "There are two coming."

Lawrence wrapped her arms around her knees and turned the other way. *I think those weird traits Maricela pointed out are products of fear. I'm cautious, careless. Can't figure it out.*

Aratesht was back, and with her walked a short, spindly, darker woman in a bright, multicolored robe. The pattern of the colors was not symmetrical; instead, it seemed to be painted on, not woven in. Lawrence noticed that, unlike all the others she had seen, this woman had gray hair that curled tightly around her head. She reached over and grabbed Maricela's arm.

"I meant to tell you earlier. I see a lot of features in these people that look familiar, like people I know. That woman—I guess she's the Shawicc—looks a little like you."

Maricela leaned forward a little more intently to peer. "Could be," she murmured. "Especially around the nose and mouth. How different are they from us?"

The two in robes stopped before the tree. Aratesht pointed at Maricela, giving her a haughty yet tolerant look. "Come with me. You may begin taking your samples now."

Lawrence nodded. "Okay." Maricela whipped around to glare at her. "It's all right, Maricela," she said gently. "I need to speak to the Shawicc."

Lawrence and the Shawicc as one bowed their heads and looked aside until the others had gone. When Lawrence next looked up, she found the Shawicc already staring at her intently, but she forced herself to remain calm.

"They told me about you, and I believed it. I knew you would be pale. Your friend, however, looks more like us. It is you who have the blue eyes, the golden hair. Is that common on Earth? Is your friend considered a freak?" While the Shawicc talked, her face showed no emotion. It was incredibly smooth and youthful, despite the gray hair.

"No." Lawrence shook her head and put on a woeful smile. "I'm more of a freak. I don't know anybody that looks like me. I know of one with green eyes, another who has red hair, but mostly the people of the Earth are dark. I see a lot who have brown eyes and brown hair. There is some variation, of course, just as you have here." Lawrence licked her dry lips and gulped. Did she sound *too* comforting?

The Shawicc tilted her head. "We have interbred. Those of Africa mingling with those of India, those of Latin America. You must have also interbred. I would say that you are North America and Europe."

Lawrence cautiously asked, "Are those . . . species? Were we once that different?"

"Those are old names of countries, and continents. The people of each region upon the earth were somewhat unique. They were isolated and could not mingle for a long time. But that does not mean we are of different species." The Shawicc glared at her suspiciously.

"I'm sorry. I know better than to call our differences special. We have been isolated for centuries, but we look less different now than we once did." Lawrence tried to look apologetic, but instead she merely sounded puzzled.

"That is because there were Africans and others like us in Europe and North America. As I said, we had begun to mingle. Enough so that when the races of people were combined, their traits survived." The Shawicc squatted neatly before her.

Now Lawrence regretted sending Maricela off. She needed to hear about how the human genes and characteristics had merged and diverged, or, at least, she wanted to. But the Shawicc had raised even more important questions in her mind. She began timidly, "Why, then, were you selected for exile? It was not due to color, or place . . ."

"Yes, it was exactly where one lived, how wealthy one was, that mattered. The planners of your world reduced the population by various methods, and removed the poorer peoples to these satellites. They taught us English—" Here she stopped, and glanced slyly over at Lawrence. "Did you just assume we would know your language?"

"No." Now Lawrence really regretted not having read Scott's Scroll, but she knew what he had done. Tom had explained that there had been other languages, now dead as the Language of Science, so Scott had put the message into however many the memories had dredged up,

242

as well as drawn pictures. "Our message of peace wasn't just in English. I'm sorry, but the convenience and thrill of just being able to talk to your people made me merely appreciate the English, not see it as strange. As a matter of fact," here she gulped, "I thought it made you seem more like us." She ended up smiling idiotically.

"The people who put us here were not racist, but they were ethnocentric," The Shawicc said heavily. "They took us as small children and taught us English before we had learned our native languages. They then trained us in technical disciplines so that we could live up here." She immediately raised her hands. "I know—you will ask me to explain further. And I shall, later. You will learn of the past, but I don't think you should take it that seriously. What's done is done. What we need to do now is consider the present. Aratesht said you had no weapons."

"That is true." Lawrence frowned, struck by a disturbing thought. "That doesn't mean they couldn't be recreated."

The Shawicc nodded. "Despite your people's obvious progress, there is still a chance that you will change. How do you feel about our return?"

"Me? I suppose it is necessary. This satellite, as I have already seen, is old and damaged. Even the garden satellite is dying. To survive, you must return to Earth." A bit of the lecturer's tone crept into her voice.

The Shawicc noticed. "Ah. Very pragmatic, just what I expected. What if this satellite were in perfect condition? What if we had no future crisis upon us? What then?"

Lawrence scrunched her head between her shoulders. "It would then be possible for you to return, but then we could also send some people up here so we could use your space research facilities." She let her excitement drip through her tone. "I'm indifferent, however." There. The paradox should flourish.

"Can you be?" The Shawicc asked calmly, not fooled at all.

She straightened. No point in giving much thought to that. "Yes. Whatever you want to do is fine with me. The Earth is so large."

"What if it were not?"

"Huh?"

"What if you told us that you hadn't brought extra supplies and oxygen along? What if you had no surplus on earth and no more room?"

Lawrence pulled herself in, letting the outside world fade as she thought. Immediately she could have argued that since that was not the case, it didn't matter, but that would not be a good idea. The Shawicc posed the question seriously, and that was how she must consider it. "The only solutions I can think of take time. We could reduce our population, grow more food, but all that takes time."

"Good. You considered it as if it were really in existence. But what I meant to imply is that it is quite possible that you could imagine insufficient supplies and fight to keep them, rather than share, despite the obvious fact that there is plenty." The Shawicc paused. Her face fluctuated, as if she had a tic. "Do you understand this?"

"I'm trying." Lawrence guessed that the tic was merely the Shawicc in her turn trying to believe that Lawrence was being honest. Again she hunkered down to think. It sounded so familiar . . . suddenly it became clear. Lawrence flashed a look at the Shawicc. "Of course." Kamela. She had not helped Kamela, though it would have been so easy, so painless.

"I think you do." The Shawicc was nodding slowly as her look seemed to penetrate Lawrence's face, and Lawrence couldn't help but feel that she knew everything about the incident. She blushed.

"Now. What will you do to our tree?" The Shawicc's voice was smooth, yet firm.

Lawrence started. How could she do that? How did she know? "I will do nothing to it. I wish to set up my project here and sit under the tree while I test it. Nothing will be permanently attached to the tree, and it will not be damaged."

The Shawicc put on a rueful grimace. "It is our tree."

"I know that. It's hard to explain. It's the fact that it is so strong, that you have a beautiful garden in the middle of a cruel vacuum. It wouldn't be the same on verdant Earth." Lawrence blinked at her own tone. She would plead. The project, okay, her opus, must be perfect. It must fit her vision.

The Shawicc stood and stretched her legs out, rubbing under her thighs in obvious pain. Lawrence could see her difficulty in rising, but she did not assist. She knew somehow that that was the last thing the Shawicc wanted her to do. In sympathy, however, she reached over and massaged each knee. As she did this, the Shawicc spoke. "I must accept your admiration . . . for our tree, and not too deeply question your apparent need. It must come from without. Perhaps it is your spiritual world crying for attention. I do not think you have chosen to act with malice. Let me tell you what I insist upon, however."

Lawrence nodded. Here it was, what they told her was negotiation. Leave it to Vance to prepare her for this moment. "Yes. I understand. You wish to grant me something, and in return I must do something for you." Again, as she had once before felt with Vance, a thrill shot through her. What would the Shawicc request?

"We will set up a ritual that shows us what has happened. Your visit with us is the greatest event we have ever experienced. Do you agree?" The Shawicc's eyes darted across Lawrence's face, and she had the sudden impression that the Shawicc was not being totally honest.

Lawrence thought about her life. She couldn't call it boring, exactly, because she always managed to have something to learn, to do, to think about. Still, actually meeting these people and having to consider the consequences of a strange new beginning was exciting. "Yes." What else could she say?

"To commemorate this event, we enter it into our history by using a reiterative ceremony," the Shawicc explained in a sing-song tone. "This rite is simple enough to be grasped, yet complex enough that it can grow. Through interaction with its elements, people change, yet they also change it." She took a deep breath and asked, "Will you participate in this ceremony?"

Lawrence waited a while before answering because she did not want to appear eager. "You want to record me onto some kind of program? That's fine with me."

The Shawicc's eyes flew open. When she spoke, however, she sounded calm. "No, a ceremony is much more than that. It is an activity. It is very important to us, probably more so than this tree, because we will create it."

Lawrence stuck out her hand as Tom had instructed her to do to signify agreement. "I will." Inside, she laughed. It sounded like fun.

"I do believe, colleague Karen, that your form of analysis is outdated. If you would merely deign to have read my treatise, humorously entitled 'Consumer Alert,' you would have learned of your error beforehand, before you, as one might say, made an ass out of yourself."

Colleague Karen interrupted, with some heat, as opposed to colleague James' cool expression, "Uh, colleague James, if I may. My expressive point of view is quite valid. Perhaps if you had read my groundbreaking, cutting edge, avant-garde treatise, or shall I say, clock-fiction, as it has been termed by those postmodern enough to recognize its true value, then you might understand that all stances have merit, and you wouldn't be so hasty as to bluntly impose your admittedly massive output upon what is commonly called (by Brusch, Kent, and others) freedom of choice."

"Colleague Karen, you ought to be ashamed of yourself. I am in no way imposing my opinion to the detriment of all else in the world. It is my job, as a cultural anthropologist (with deservedly achieved accolades in the field of literary analysis), however, to persuade. And I am a bit miffed, to say the least, that you remain unconvinced of my charitable correction of your, shall I say, absurd theories. To be quite frank with you, I announce them to be *ludicrous*!" He leaned back from his rapidly attained, yet briefly held position, which had been to breach colleague Karen's personal sphere and scream in her face.

"How so, colleague James?" colleague Karen asked mildly, apparently accustomed to such irrational, childish outbursts from well-respected old men. "My theory states that a social trend is chosen by members of a society. All cultural anthropological research is bent upon establishing what rituals have become accepted by the populace. How can one study cultures otherwise? An example, if you please: If the entertainers of some murky Hollywood are overpaid, then that means that such celebrities are deemed important by that society."

"Nonsense!" spluttered colleague James. "What you have failed to note is that there usually, at least during the early phases of enculturation, which is not something that can ever be taken lightly, is some form of training, and I will be the first to support Reighnal's theory that such training necessarily involves some limitations enforced by expectations. Now, during this time it is quite possible that a person will learn to desire certain things, but not necessarily. I believe that comes later, when the freedom of choice is banished. If I may present an example. Suppose only purple clocks were offered for sale. Market analysts therefore find their task simplified, because they will be pleased to announce that consumers must love purple clocks."

"But, colleague James, you can always choose to not purchase a clock," colleague Karen answered mildly, sipping lukewarm prune juice.

"What!? And forever be asking the time, thereby remaining dependent on those infernal purple clocks? Yes, I suppose you would have to make your own clock, or do without, but when, I ask you, is this type of minority ever noticed? Does your theory state that a significant minority of people detest the convention that supposedly talented celebrities get paid more in a year than they'll see in a lifetime?"

"As a matter of fact, yes."

"I see."

"Perhaps you do. I don't really care."

"That's as it should be. We can't go around understanding each other's massive brilliant output, much less read it all. Uh, what are you doing there?" Colleague James controlled his alarm while keeping a faint concerned tone as he beheld colleague Karen lift a large, newly pink eraser.

"I'm going to erase the Elaborynth." She slapped the eraser down onto the ragged sheet of paper that was once more tacked to the stump.

"Why, whatever for?" Colleague James noted with some satisfaction that colleague Karen hesitated before consigning the poor Elaborynth to the unknown. Perhaps she couldn't yet bear to lose that sense of comfort the Elaborynth invariably brought.

"Look. Haven't you read my article? If I may be modest, I'm referring to the one that was published (along with the requisite acclaim) while I was still a mere undergraduate. I proved that the modern practice of isolating newborns from anyone's touch was not a conspiracy aimed toward producing conformist, if psychotic, pardon me, I suppose now I should say, neurotic adults."

"Oh," colleague James almost whispered, "*that* one."

"Mock me if you will, but look." She whipped the Elaborynth off the stump to reveal a flagged expanse of rings.

Colleague James kept his gaze staring straight into colleague Karen's admittedly dark, intriguing eyes, not for a second glancing at the exposed stump. "What, then, is the reasoning behind isolating the babes?"

"Mere efficiency. No one knows for sure all of the results of a choice. The people who isolate the infants do so for short term effects only." Colleague Karen smiled. "Perhaps it is after all harmless."

"Hmm." Colleague James cast his eyes down. "Diversity is nice, but *chosen* diversity? And what kind of human being do you want to end up with? Why not have some studies point the way to a better world?"

"Better in what way? Look at the rings. Notice the distribution of the flags." Colleague Karen pointed toward the outer rings.

Colleague James peered to count the flags clustered there. "You seem to have emphasized the last twenty years. Is that significant? Why have you almost totally concentrated on Lawrence?"

"She is the product of your 'studies.' Plans that were made centuries ago for a better, self-sustaining, low population society have finally borne fruit." Colleague Karen leaned forward. "Such as we are."

"But I thought you said there was no conspiracy." Colleague James scratched his head. "I must admit that I am at a loss. Lawrence hasn't had much choice, you know."

"Wrong. She practiced freely all along, since she created the Cube." Colleague Karen folded her arms. "As you were saying?"

Colleague James gulped. "Nothing. Maybe now that Lawrence has had this experience, maybe . . ."

"What?" Colleague Karen again smoothed the Elaborynth onto the stump and lifted her eraser.

"Nothing."

Merrily colleague Karen ground the eraser firmly over the surface of the Elaborynth, smearing and obliterating the admittedly dark yet ineffective pencil strokes that a future child's hand had scribbled.

Daisy in the field. Daisy in my field.

"Come on, Daisy," Jared gasped from under the willow. "What next?"

Daisy, a suntanned child of about eight, instructed, "Nod your head three times, then kiss the pumpkin." She went back to counting leaf veins.

Jared hurriedly nodded, then bent to kiss the Halloween flashlight. "Is that it?"

Daisy looked over at him carelessly. "Yes. Now you are a member of Kikewa." She shivered. Every time she said that word, she shivered.

"Oh, boy! Wait until I tell Marc." Jared plunged out into the meadow, willow leaves flapping his bare shoulders. He ran up to where Daisy was sitting demurely on her bed of moss. Hesitating before disturbing her, he stuttered, "Uh, by the way, Daisy, what does 'Kikewa' mean?"

Daisy lifted her eyebrows. "Oh," she answered carelessly. "The sun club. That's all."

Jared nodded solemnly.

She once more bent her head after he had dashed away. She didn't bother telling him that the ritual changed at every initiation, as did the definition of Kikewa.

Lawrence jerked her arm away. "Cut it out," she grunted.

Maricela stepped back and gathered up her suit. "You're absolutely right. It makes no sense to give you a physical now. You were sick all along, and it was all in your mind. Don't think I'll be able to help you now." She stepped into the suit and sealed it before picking up her helmet. "You realize, of course, we're wasting suit time and oxygen by participating in this ceremony."

"It wouldn't be a ceremony unless there were some sacrifice," Lawrence murmured, giving her a dazed look.

Maricela paused, helmet half on. "What is it with you and the Shawicc anyway? You both seem so intent on this ridiculous ceremony." She slammed the helmet on and sealed it. When she spoke again, her voice was muffled. "You know, I can never tell about you anymore, either. I never know if you're being honest."

"You want honesty? The Shawicc and I are lovers." Lawrence also sealed her helmet.

Maricela turned on the radio link to grunt. "I figured that." Lawrence saw the helmet nod as Maricela adjusted her oxygen tube. "That doesn't explain it, however."

"No, I guess not. It wouldn't be too obvious at all to someone like you, who takes her relationships so casually." Lawrence spoke mildly with no effort, but it wouldn't have mattered anyway. The radio link masked strong emotion.

Maricela said nothing until Lawrence once more opened the door to Africa. "It's not you, is it? You're not really the collusive leader here, are you?"

Lawrence tried to make her voice sound hearty. "Maricela, I'm glad you understand that. Of course all of that was just an act."

"Then *why*? Why are we going through this again? Why must we take part in their ceremony?" Maricela's voice sounded hopeful, but Lawrence couldn't see her face.

"It's for the Cube. We bargained, the Shawicc and I, and this is our agreement. We, you and I, would consider their ritual to be as important as they would consider one of ours. Do you see?" Lawrence reached out her hand, then stopped. She wouldn't be able to feel anything past the suitskin anyway.

Maricela folded her arms. "I'm not a psychcomputer, but you certainly sound obsessed."

"I am," Lawrence answered readily. "Everything I have ever done was for this moment. I'm not going to let some silly ceremony get in my way."

Maricela coughed. "Yeah, you admit it's silly, but I have to admit some compassion for these people. What about you? Do you only care about them because you need their gene maps?" She shuddered. "I don't know if I can make you believe me, but the way you act around that Shawicc, as if you were just faking the affection to get what you want..."

Lawrence whipped around. "Chit!" she yelled so loud that the suit radio compensated by damping her voice. "No way," she gasped as the outburst cost her oxygen. "I figure you're just jealous."

"No," Maricela immediately replied gently. "That's what I thought you'd think, but believe me when I say that has nothing to do with it. I guess you're sincere, so can I ask you one more thing? After this Cube is finished, what then?"

Lawrence stepped forward to re-enter the satellite. "I don't know. I'll find out when I get there. Are you coming or not?" A wave of misery overwhelmed her, but she didn't have time to figure out if she had all along prized Maricela's jealousy, or if she had all along been fake friendly to survive, or whether it was just the danger she risked to enter the Cube.

Maricela stood behind her and put her hands on her shoulders. It calmed her immensely.

They entered the arena. For the first time they saw all the inhabitants together in one room. Besides Africa and India, they saw China, parts of Australia . . . Everyone in the tiers of seats around them, staring down . . . Lawrence grew dizzy. She took deep, steady breaths so as not to overload her suit system. Then she forced herself to look around. She remembered learning about these people. Some of the information was rather useless, she knew, because she couldn't seem to get a grasp on it. These people that she had observed had spoken quite a bit about their history, about events and traits that no longer applied. Lawrence ended up accepting all of it, yet she had to admit that she had finally encountered data that, at least for her, could not be simply transformed into a computer program. She gulped.

"Look." Maricela squeezed her hand. "Over there, near the door."

Since Maricela didn't point, Lawrence didn't turn her head to see Wong and the rest of the rebels lined up at the entrance, backs toward them. "It's all right," she murmured. "They're present, so they're still part of the ceremony."

Aratesht in a blue robe came in, passed between the ranks of protesters, and walked calmly across the arena to meet them. She bowed, then gestured. Suddenly a group surrounded Lawrence and Maricela, and again they de-suited. Aratesht led them to the side facing the door, where there was a recessed chamber. The whole group stepped down into it; now it was their turn to merely watch.

A long string of diverse members entered, each carrying a traditional instrument. The flutes were first. Each player strode to the exact center of the arena before lifting the flute to play. Lawrence blinked at the sound. She rubbed her fingers together needlessly. What she wouldn't do to have a rhythm board at hand! The acoustics probably were not the best in this hastily constructed arena. Since each player waited to get to the center before playing, each was slightly behind the one in front of them. As they crossed to meet the recessed audience, however, the music seemed to catch up. Lawrence stared into their solemn faces as they neared. The effect was impressive, even if she was simultaneously trying to calculate how they had done it.

At the edge, they took sharp right angles alternately right and left and eventually formed a circle. The several hundred players had to make a ring several people deep before the procession, and the music, halted.

The Shawicc entered, carrying the Cube. Lawrence eyed her with concentration. Even now she would not trust anybody with her creation. She did notice, however, that the Shawicc was holding it carefully, even reverently.

Behind her came perhaps a hundred adherents, each carrying some form of plant life. Most of them only carried rotten tree branches from the dying garden satellite. As the musicians had done, the plants strode to the edge before forming a circle.

Lawrence found herself backtracking as she tried to remember when the music had suddenly leaped, setting her heart to pounding. At the Shawicc's entrance, of course. Why, then, were the strains now sad and deep?

After the plants came the animals. Hastily put together costumes reflected Mammalia, Insecta, and all the other orders. One hundred adherents lumbered to the edge. Interestingly, after they had formed a circle, the animals all crouched, leaving the plants to waver above them.

The music climaxed. Huge drums pounded briefly, followed by a melody that mechanically ticked and hummed. Lawrence leaned forward to peer through the ranks, yet she knew they had no synthesizers.

Thirty masked inhabitants entered, accompanied by gasps and moans while Lawrence merely nodded. The masks were well done; the white skin looked realistic, and the hair was woven effectively, she thought. Led by a tall, muscular woman with long blonde hair, the Caucasian race stayed in a long, swaying line to the door.

The music now sounded delightful as it tripped through a scattering of melodies. Lawrence tapped her foot and eyed Maricela. What now?

The white people crouched to sit cross-legged on the floor. Alternately, they faced right and left. At a certain beat in the music, they lifted both their eyes and arms up to the audience. Lawrence pictured someone running to fill those gaping, straining arms, yet no one came. She gulped and drew her arms around herself. A glance at Maricela showed her doing the same.

Then, before Lawrence could moan, they came. Thirty members of the audience crept down the tiers, pushed through the ranks of musicians, plants, and animals, and ran to be gathered by those arms.

Lawrence felt all her breath whoosh out as the light brightened and the music stopped. Shaking herself, she stepped into the arena.

As she walked toward the Shawicc, she heard her intone: "Renewal of the Earth shall be accomplished in just this way."

The walk to the door where the Shawicc stood seemed to take too long. Lawrence's mouth was dry. Her hands trembled as she secured the Cube.

Several attendants seemingly flew past her to crack open the door to the garden satellite. Lawrence felt like a turtle surrounded by sparrows. Even the animals in their awkward costumes seemed to move faster than she.

Lawrence stepped up to the tree, taking a moment to stare up into the branches before leaning over to feed the Cube into the data box. *It's too soon for it to be all over,* a part of her mind wailed, instantly quenched by her rising excitement.

Maricela was there as she lay down to be hooked up. She saw her bite her lip before seizing her hand. Lawrence caressed her palm because it was already beginning to feel strange to her. Maricela then spoke, but Lawrence shook her head lightly. She couldn't hear her; sound must be going first.

The garden around her began to fade, and she blinked. Her brain itched. Nothing. She felt nothing. Lawrence could no longer hear the festivities, feel the couch underneath, or see the tree's branches above her. All was nothing.

Then it happened. She lurched as the patterns seized her to the exclusion of all else. Bound, she still felt a euphoric release, as if freed from existence. Eagerly her non-self sought it all.

"Where's John?" asked Carole, her wide smile betraying her thoughts as she tugged a short, black lock of hair off her forehead.

"What do you think? The dumb fool forgot the popcorn again," Kasturbai blurted. "I sent him to supply."

Umo put the readout onto the broad, rough table and murmured, "It's not like we *need* his popcorn."

"What have you got there?" Carole leaned forward to point at the readout. Her black eyes narrowed impishly as she grinned at Umo's apparent discomfiture. She reached over and cradled his large, chocolate-colored hand.

"It's just the log of the Cube's journey. It hasn't gone far in its 120 years." Umo stared at her. "Do you want me to chart it?"

"You're asking *me*?" Carole reclined, looking awed in mock appreciation.

"Yes, you should graph it, Umo," Kasturbai inserted firmly. "Or at least tell us where it is. These numbers don't tell us a thing."

"Not even up to Fomalhaut, in absolute distance. Of course, it's nowhere near that star, really. It's more near Auriga." Umo looked thoughtful. "I wonder what Lawrence was aiming for."

"Okay. I'm back," came a breathless voice as John banged the door open, scattering the candle flames and extinguishing five of them.

Kasturbai tightened her lips and pulled the big, globular lantern closer to the chart. "Relight those candles, Carole. I'm studying."

"Ooh! Black this time!" Carole ignored her as she gloated over John's small seeds of popcorn. Quietly Umo struck a match. "Give me some! Come on into the kitchen. I can't wait!" She jumped up and pulled at John.

Kasturbai sighed as she watched them head for the common room. "We're outside of the rings, but that doesn't mean . . ."

Umo waited a few seconds, then prompted, "What?"

"That we aren't out there with the rest of them," she murmured, then shook herself. "I just wonder some nights. My dreams . . ." She straightened, her sallow face glowing in the refired candlelight.

"Hi. What have you all been doing?" John grinned as he pushed back his reddish curls. Kasturbai gazed at his cheerful freckles solemnly.

Umo touched her arm. "I have dreams, too."

"Oh, those." John tossed his hand up and leaned back into the kitchen. "Hey, Carole, do you want to talk about *dreams*?" His emphasis caused Kasturbai to wince.

"Mmmm." Carole came to the door, mouth bulging with freshly made popcorn.

"Well, come on. Do you?" John grabbed the bowl.

"Hey!" Carole yanked the bowl back toward her, spilling a few fluffy kernels onto the chart. "This is *my* popcorn! Make your own."

John ignored her, lifting his hand to Kasturbai, thumb firmly pressed to the fingers. "Ah, beautiful one, do you really think that stupid Cube is affecting us back here on Earth? Or that we are affecting it? Make up your mind, now. Personally, my theory is that we don't exist because we are a paradox. We can't be in two different places at once, you know—here and in the Cube."

Umo spluttered, then forced his face to look solemnly disgusted. "I forget that it is best to ignore you, John."

He shrugged. "Suit yourself."

"Some do believe," Kasturbai said softly, "that we no longer belong here. We already exist in the Cube. Any other existence would be superfluous."

Umo accepted the bowl of popcorn from Carole. "I still think it's possible that everybody's consciousness can be in two different places at the same time, and, perhaps, because the Cube is now a lone wanderer in space, the experiences are diverging. That's why we get these crazy dreams. It's communication with our other, more adventurous selves."

Carole shook her head. "I take the easiest explanation. The Cube is identical to us, and, as it travels, it changes in exactly the same way as Earth. Everything was programmed to match all predilections on Earth. The Cube evolves as we do. If the Cube ever does get an observer, they will see the Earth as it is at that present moment. If we could somehow transport instantly to the Cube, we'd see ourselves."

Umo rolled his eyes. "You sound so confident, yet you have brought us back to the beginning. Your argument can be true, but what good is it? It doesn't answer any questions."

"Could you expect any more? In this place?" John jumped over to the door.

252

Kasturbai looked alarmed. Memories chased each other about the woods, each not willing to assume a future coherence. As their personalities began to flee, she asked, "Where are we?"

John opened to door to nothingness.

Grayness filled the blank void which curved to simulate a cavern. Moisture slid down the walls to spill over newly formed slime. Oceans crashed in the distance as prokaryotes formed, illuminated by the sky's lightning.

"Lawrence?"

She wiped away the drops of moisture that trickled into her eyes. "Yeah?"

"It's over. You've gone back to the beginning, we're almost out of energy, and it's time for you to leave."

Lawrence wrapped herself up into a little ball, wanting to be alone. That stupid voice! Why did it have to show up just now, when she'd finally caused the others to quit bothering her? "I'm not leaving."

"Then you will die."

She shrugged. "I thought I was already dead."

"Is that what you wanted?"

"I think so. The whole ceremony was a suicide pact. We made so many sacrifices that there is little left to live on." Lawrence tilted her head. "Are you listening to me?" Drat. Her voice came out as too wistful.

The voice paused, and Lawrence could feel it waiting, but then it spoke harshly: "It's best for you not to call me 'you.'"

Lawrence inched forward, curious, stretching her face out as if to see the speaker. It was such an effort to flip from the inside world that was inside her to the inside world that was the outside world of the Cube. "You are me? I don't understand."

"Yes, you do. Nobody else is in here, you know."

Lawrence chuckled. "Talking to myself — that's nothing new."

The voice felt nearer, warmer. "Yes. To create the listener is not hard. You could always create a dialogue out of nothing. What's hard is . . . Now listen to me. It's time to be yourself again."

"I don't think I ever knew what that meant." Lawrence gulped down her fear. Damn it, she felt alone, and yet was everyone else *still* in her? The voice was probably right. All her attempts to separate herself had failed, and she had probably wanted them to all along.

"Maybe not, but you will live past the Cube, and then you will be able to create yourself. It's hard, but you'll end up doing it, because you will have no choice. Or, rather, you will,

253

and to meet your goals, creating Lawrence will be the best way to go." The voice now became concerned, and Lawrence could feel it slithering around inside her.

She frowned. "Creating myself—is that art?"

"No. I've found that all art is but acting. Your true self is not art."

"Yeah, but you've got to understand why I must stay here. If I leave and return to Earth, I can never experience anything new ever again. If we, who are everything on Earth, return, everything will be boring. That's why I'm going to shoot the Cube off into space."

"No!" came the voice so that the mental caress became an odd ripping gash. "Give me my own identity. If you stay in here, it will be just as boring, because all you can do is repeat everything that just happened here. Your life cannot have any variations unless you leave. You must, as you have always done, strive toward new experiences, and the only way to do that is to leave me and go back to Earth. Besides," the voice chuckled, "how the heck are you going to toss me away into space unless you get out now, huh?"

Lawrence snickered, then burst out laughing. "Oh, that's a good one!" She glanced up at the roof of the cavern in alarm. "Besides, I'm not even sure I *can* get out. How do I stop all this?"

"Remember when you learned how to stop the screens?"

"I don't think that I can use the same method, but I see what I need to do." Lawrence nodded. It hadn't been the sequence of keyboard commands that had had any significance; it had been her attitude. So now all she had to do was kiss off the Cube and she could leave.

"Remember the hermit," the voice warned. "You'll need that for a while, but not forever."

Lawrence nodded. "Gotcha, but there are plenty of alternatives." She shifted eagerly, mind busy with trying to envision all the possibilities beyond just merely everything. It was no use. She couldn't just sit here anymore, so she jumped up. "Hey, look, Cube, I have to get going, you know. Goodbye."

No answer, of course.

EPILOGUE

Exiting the Cube

Maricela watched with concern as Lawrence opened her eyes. She hadn't known what to expect, so she had thought she would be ready for anything. Nothing could prepare her, however, for the oblique, flat stare Lawrence gave her, as if she didn't want to look, but had to. Maricela classified it as Lawrence's tendency to withdraw whenever human contact became too much, but the expression was all wrong. The only word for it was "transcended," and Maricela had to wonder briefly where she might have heard of such a vague, useless word. She awkwardly took her hand.

"How long?" Lawrence whispered.

"A little under three hours," she said in a normal tone. "Are you all right?"

Lawrence stared at her, then lifted her hand to touch her cheek. "It feels the same, as if I'm here and you're there," she said enigmatically. "Why?"

Maricela leaned forward to hide her face from the Shawicc, who was approaching fast. In a tight, urgent voice she said, "Quick, Lawrence, tell me what it was like." With a fast beating heart she reached out to stroke Lawrence's hands, which leapt and trembled in many shapes, some as if she were spinning dials, or combing hair.

"I'm a little more interested in what my condition is now," she answered mildly, and Maricela had to admit that she was touched by her amused tone. It raised her spirits; Lawrence couldn't be *that* bad off. Then she gasped as she felt her vulva throb. "Well," she heard herself say cheerfully, "first I have to give you a physical." She whipped out her medical bag, but was stopped by the Shawicc pulling it away.

"That can wait," the Shawicc said. Hastily she looked around, but no one was within hearing distance. Only a few were crouched under the dogwood trees in the dim light. "Lawrence, you have drained all but a few weeks' supply of power from this satellite. That gives us insufficient time to recharge." She paused, forming the next sentences carefully in that way she had to cultivate in order to advance to her position as political/spiritual leader. "As a matter of fact, it is doubtful we can recharge. I would like to point out that your shuttle is intact, so that you two can leave us to this fate. I do not want to wish death on anyone, so I shall not stop you if

255

you wish to return to Earth." The Shawicc inexplicably felt her confidence disappear as she now stumbled, "Will you do the humane act and stay with us?"

"What is so humane about that? It saves none of your lives," Lawrence answered softly, knowing without doubt that only the three could hear her. "When I bargained with you, I explained the need for a crisis that would energize everybody, causing them to react to an eminent danger."

The Shawicc watched as the attractive doctor whipped around to gape at Lawrence, who only grimaced tiredly. "And I agreed." The doctor then whipped around to glare at her, but she could feel a twinge of satisfaction that this ever-so-confident doctor had been kept in the dark. "I did not, however, want to sign some sort of suicide pact. I think it is quite obvious that we will not survive without some aid from Earth, aid that you have not yet guaranteed."

"Why didn't you pull me out once you saw the danger?" Lawrence asked.

The Shawicc gestured in frustration at the device still clamped to Lawrence's skull. "Yes, I did request that we disconnect the device, but you stopped breathing. Your friend here worried for your life, so we let it run. Now I wonder: should you have died so that we might live?"

The Shawicc waited as Lawrence looked away. "I wonder when that was," she whispered in puzzlement, then paused to search their memories. "Oh, yes, when I disappeared, or, really, when I became not. And that had been lovely, but then I was back again and everything was still the same, with the memories, and the inhabitants of the rings surging vignettes around me." She shut up and looked at both Maricela and the Shawicc. She even reached out both hands, but only Maricela took her left and placed it on her chest. "Please believe me when I tell you that I fiercely wanted you to kill me, but it is too late for that now." But the Shawicc *still* didn't believe her infatuation with suicide, nor did she trust her. She looked up as a shadow passed over her chair.

Wong heard these last words as he neared Lawrence. They spurred him on, and he felt it was perfect timing for his speech. "I have an announcement, if you please." The Shawicc swiftly gave him a glance of severe anger as jealousy and puzzlement swept over her, but he smiled serenely from the standpoint of historically verified truth. "Well, it's for Lawrence's ears only."

"Those are the only ones here," Lawrence replied in that new, exalted tone.

"Yes, you'd think so, wouldn't you?" And Lawrence smiled at him. He seemed to be the only one so far who knew what had happened. But did that mean that for some crazy reason *he* was her symbiote and no one else was? Either that, or he was more intelligent and perceptive than the rest, and there wasn't anything wrong with that, either. "You've been through a sacred ritual, and you went through a rite of passage, but one that is distinguished, because it was for you alone. If we were to cater to history with its hypocrisies, we should now bow down to the messiah, the newest evolution of humanity. But we won't. We wouldn't dare. Do you understand?" Wong frowned as he felt his heart fill with friendship for Lawrence, his newest powerful enemy.

"Yes, I do. And I am grateful for your lack of awe," she said meekly, and they smiled at each other. She leaned her head back. "Oh, Maricela, I am so dizzy. Right now, all I can do is get my Cube back and rest."

"Okay," Maricela said, standing. She darted a glance at the other two. "You heard her." She leaned over and popped the Cube out of its receptacle, then paused to stare at it in wonder. It was in her hands, our hands . . . She blinked as Lawrence leapt to take it from her. Seeing them unite was uncanny, but it was infinitely preferable to how she had felt when *she* held it. Maricela stared uneasily at Lawrence's blissful look. "I must take her to sickbay. When I deem her ready, we'll discuss how to get out of this mess."

Lawrence ducked her head, then muttered to her incoherently, "Maricela, take me to our shuttle first, please."

With that statement, the Shawicc lurched, yet she felt paralyzed, incapable of stopping her from what was obviously a desertion. She swallowed before lifting her shoulders with dignity. "You can't leave us to our doom," she said firmly. Her tone, however, no matter how much she had strived to make it commanding, had come out pleading. The Shawicc shook her head. She concluded that, despite Wong's belief, here was a person who had done something that had never before been attempted, something spectacular, yet every bit as dangerous. She therefore was a powerful creation, not something you could dismiss that easily. Instead, she needed to be handled carefully, controlled. The Shawicc watched helplessly as she limped off with her friend.

Goodbye

"I guessed you'd want to put the Cube up in here to be safe," Maricela babbled over the suit radio. "Remember, though, that our suits don't have much oxygen left, so please hurry up."

Lawrence slumped after feeding the Cube into its receptacle. Oddly, Maricela could only think it was because they had broken contact, and Lawrence was at last recovering from that odd symbiosis. "It's so hard," she murmured. She lifted her eyes to the ceiling. "Already."

Maricela reached over and took her hand. "Please," she urged. "Come on."

"In a minute." Her weakness apparently vanished, and she reached over to touch the controls.

Maricela hunched over her. "What are you doing? We can't go anywhere. Yes, we might be able to make it, but we just can't leave these people here." Maricela found that she could not raise her hands to stop Lawrence, while in contrast, Lawrence's hands leaped over the buttons as if in play, not at all like her cautious movements on the way up.

Lawrence bowed her head, then said, "Let's go."

Maricela hesitated over the active controls, then shook herself to follow Lawrence back into the satellite. Once inside, she was beckoned to the nearest porthole.

"Watch," whispered Lawrence.

The empty shuttle disengaged and floated off slowly, its rockets bursting forth briefly. Maricela's jaw dropped, and she swayed against Lawrence, who had again slumped against the wall. "Lawrence! Now we'll never get back! And the Cube!" In frustration she beat the wall, gasping madly until she ripped off her helmet and threw it to the floor.

"Yes," she said. "It's gone, at least in one of its forms." She also popped off her helmet, then slit the oxygen tube to let it bleed into the satellite's air.

Maricela paused over such a drastic action, then she saw the Shawicc behind Lawrence, and the satisfied look only made her want to hang onto her oxygen a little longer. But she also slit the tube, feeling tears reach her eyes. "Why?" was all she could utter.

Lawrence revived eagerly. "Didn't I tell you that it must go into space? That I needed to send it in the shuttle so it could reach escape velocity? It's all we are, and we must share us with those who are not us." Lawrence peered at her wild, bewildered look. "Never mind. I feel like I said it a million times already." Erratically she began tearing at the suit, unfastening the torso and clutching at the leggings before collapsing on the floor.

"*Now* it's time for sickbay," Maricela said sorrowfully, giving the Shawicc a wry shrug.

The Plan

The two left sickbay, Maricela anxiously stepping aside and motioning Lawrence ahead of her. Two days was not at all enough to completely cure her, but the committee couldn't wait much longer. Maricela could only sympathize with the weak patient, despite the danger they were all in.

"Are you sure you're okay? I could present your argument for you, of course."

Lawrence stiffened and lifted her chin. "Yes," she mused. "You could."

Maricela waited.

"No." was the final answer. "What then? You could not continue past their initial objections. And they need to see me. You mustn't underestimate the effect of my presence."

"I wasn't thinking of winning them over," Maricela interceded gently. "I just noticed that you seem more comfortable when you're by yourself. I thought you'd prefer to stay away."

Lawrence shrugged and started walking again. "Who cares about how I feel?"

Maricela opened her mouth, then shut it, nodding. They would not see Lawrence as anything other than the culprit, the literal scapegoat, certainly not as a human being, a wounded human being.

The table set up in the arena was much too big for the self-selected and Shawicc-approved arbitrators. Lawrence waited until Maricela was seated before she pulled a chair away to sit about three meters distant.

The Shawicc nodded at the two and began calmly. "Now it is time to hear some suggestions."

Wong leaned forward intensely. "What's so hard about it? All we have to do is sit tight, and those on Earth will rescue us."

"Forget it," Lawrence said immediately. "They don't have enough ships to evacuate all of us." She glanced at the Shawicc. "We counted 4561 gene maps; is that correct?" She shrugged. "Anyway, as I was saying, there is no way they can build enough in the few weeks we have remaining." She grimaced in apparent anticipation.

The retribution came. Wong whirled upon her. "Okay. What can we do then?"

"No communication with the mental patient, the *mudaboo*," the Shawicc commanded.

Lawrence shuddered. These satellite folk didn't know any ancient African languages. Sadly, the pro-African Shawicc had resorted to making up a word that to her Westernized ears *sounded* African. Through her pity at the pathetic attempt at multiculturalism, she could sense the Shawicc's shame.

"Why not?" Wong burst out. "She's the one who got us into this mess. Besides, she's not even wearing the signature."

"I will gladly wear the signature," Lawrence announced, and Maricela gulped at how much that bright, declarative submission had rippled in tight echoes in her mind, from so many—movies and whatnot. "Give it here."

Now it was Maricela's turn to complain to Lawrence, whose eyes glittered. "No, you don't." Rapidly she faced the Shawicc.

"No," she said firmly. "She's *my* patient, not yours, and I'm not going to see you put any of your silly, primitive marks on her."

"She has assented," the Shawicc answered simply, nodding to Aratesht, who stood, white cloak in hand. "Blanket her."

Lawrence stood and allowed her to place the cloak around her shoulders, to wrap her arms around her waist to tug the straps tightly, to tug on the forearms to ensure that the circulation hadn't been cut off. Maricela couldn't help gawking. Lawrence had never before been so indifferent to being touched. "Thank you," she whispered to Aratesht. "I won't wear it as I work," she explained. "It's too inhibiting."

The Shawicc said nothing.

"I think Wong has something," Maricela began timidly. "You can't get to Earth without cooperating with us. But that means that you have to listen to Lawrence. Even if you reject her plan because you think she's insane, you must listen first."

"If she has a viable plan, she may speak," Aratesht offered.

Maricela stared at her.

The Shawicc smiled. "I am not all-powerful, nor do I strive to always have the last word."

Maricela twitched, blinking. The room seemed different, as if catering to the echo of Lawrence's unspoken whisper. Everyone seemed to be straining to hear it.

Maricela heard an odd squeaking, rustling sound, so she moved her chair halfway around so she could watch Lawrence.

In the cloak, Lawrence creaked over to the shadows. "I know the way out. It may not work, even then, but it is the only plan we can try." Lawrence looked at each in turn. "We must prepare the arena for landing. How? At first it seems impossible, but once we acknowledge that the parts of the satellite that you have closed off are worthless, that there is only a small fraction of the intended population left . . ." Again she turned to the Shawicc. "How many was this colossus intended for? Was it 50,000?" She tightened her arms around her waist, straining the material but not popping a single buckle. "Anyway, since it has been proven that all of us can fit in the arena, we should concentrate there, using the rest of the mass as insulation." She paused, sagging against the straps. "We will need supplies from Earth," she gasped, "to make nets and such to protect ourselves in flight, but we can also salvage parts from the satellite's branches. Then, of course, we need retro-rockets to slow our descent, and Earth can supply those. If we all work together, with help and machines from Earth, I think we can get it done in a few weeks. Look at how much we have accomplished so far," she said vaguely. "Sending the prepared arena to a selected spot on Earth is the only way we will get there."

"And how will Earth learn that we need rockets and other things?" Wong asked.

Lawrence pointed to Maricela. "She will contact them, using our suit radios." For a second, she regretted not being able to send a mental message to those on Earth, whose thoughts of course she could read freely; the suit radios were not reliable.

"That is all very well," interrupted the Shawicc, "but you are forgetting the most important thing of all. What guarantee is there that Earth will deign to help us?"

Lawrence licked her lips. "What kind of guarantee do you need?" She sifted her new knowledge carefully. The artists were in control of all forms of space travel, of course, but she sensed a menace only just now passing. What to call it? Conflict? War? She spoke sincerely. "Currently, there is only one other shuttle, but three more will follow rapidly." She stumbled as she came toward the table into the light so that Maricela could see her red face and bulging eyes. "Listen: let Maricela contact Earth. Let's get started on preparing the arena. If they do not arrive when expected, we can come together again and devise another plan."

The Shawicc shrugged. "I grant you your request."

Wong sat quietly, stroking his chin. "It needs to have its details worked out, but I can see no other way at this time."

Lawrence leaned against the table and winced as everyone rose to leave. "I think it's time for my anti-mens shot," she muttered to Maricela, clutching at the belt of her smock. She knew from the satellite women's experiences what menstrual cramps were like.

"Okay," she muttered absently. "Though you know that if it's already started, we can't do anything about it. Keep track of it, remember?" Maricela kept her tone low as everyone else shuffled out, each looking rather eagerly at the Shawicc for more detailed instructions. "They acquiesced too soon, don't you think?"

"The Shawicc had already thought of something similar, but without Earth's help. Wong rejected all planning because his solutions relied too much on Earth rescuing us. I am the only one with the information necessary to come up with the cooperative plan, the only one who can calmly accept what is necessary. The Shawicc will go along with my plan, so that if it fails, she can die guiltless, and her approval is really the only one that matters." Lawrence spit it all out rapidly, then sat and closed her eyes. "Damn. If I'd only known how wonderful those anti-mens shots really are. You got any painkiller?"

Maricela opened her medical kit and nodded. "I have a drug that Aratesht said had worked against menstrual cramps in the past, and, boy, was she eager to get it after all these centuries! She didn't take all of it, though. Let me get it." Tugging at Lawrence's cloak, she said, "And you can tell me how you know all this. No one has been negotiating with you lately. And how do you know there is another complete shuttle? Furthermore, why must *I* contact Earth? Why can't you, since you know so much, and you know the artists?"

Lawrence opened her eyes blearily. "Maricela, the pattern of events seems to go on forever. An event happens, then it gets discussed, several times. It gets thought about. It gets recorded. Years later it is rediscovered." She sighed. "Do you see? It's so tiring, having to explain everything, when it's all so obvious to *me*."

"Well, you're going to have to," Maricela said grimly, passing her the water pack to swallow the medicine with. "Bear with us. It's your point to grab onto; it's your sanity."

"You have to contact Earth because the people here trust you more than they do me, obviously, and the people on Earth would rather hear from me. If they don't, they're going to be more alarmed than if they didn't hear from you. Sorry." She grimaced before continuing in a conversational tone, "I was thinking that maybe my drug discovery would help my condition, but it would only cause more misery, I'm sure. I have enough visions as it is. I keep seeing the garden satellite as an oasis in a desert. It has been my inspiration."

Maricela ducked her head. "I know . . . what am I saying? I *think*," she corrected herself, "that it's something you wouldn't understand, but I'm *scared*. This plan could mean all of our deaths, Lawrence."

Lawrence's eyes flew open and she reached over to touch Maricela's hand. "What can I say?" She pulled away and snapped, "Call Charles. Call Scott. Call Betan. They're with the second shuttle."

Breathing Space

Lawrence scraped the hoe in a flat arc toward herself and planted her chin on her rough hands that caressed the smooth plastic, consciously patterning her stance to an age-old remedy for tiredness. It felt good to rest so artistically, so that her mind could sense all those ancestors doing exactly the same thing in the quest for potatoes. They'd been painted enough.

As she stared down at the heavy green tops in their eternal rows, she could know that she was alone, still looking out at the stars, despite the presence of the other farm workers at the edge of the field. Lawrence did not watch as they passed the water dipper back and forth, its bright metal flashing. Instead of licking her lips in anticipation, what seized her mind was a glittery, magical image of the Big Dipper in a velvety dark sky.

Her. There. Flying through space. Free. Her heart beat at the strain.

A cough.

She used her knuckles as a child would, pushing her hair off her cheek. "Hello. I've been all over looking for you. I thought you'd be up in the sky, welding." Maricela's voice sounded brave, yet timid. She stepped forward, taking only a quick glance at Lawrence's white cloak that lay in the dirt beside her. "What's wrong? Has the flow ceased?"

Lawrence stretched out her hands vaguely, then stooped to pick up her hoe. "I didn't feel it fall," she whispered, "but, no, the flow persists. Aratesht told me—er—I found out that it can last up to eight days. Don't worry. I was—" She straightened. "I like to be alone."

That fact, so obvious to Maricela, felt like a slap. Didn't it occur to Lawrence that *Maricela* might not want to be alone? Until those from Earth arrived, she could forget any interaction with the satellite dwellers. "I know," she finally said gently, "but I think it might be better if you aren't." Maricela tilted her head toward the other workers. "And nobody else is willing to approach you, so all you have is me!" She stretched out her arms and smiled, then gulped to see Lawrence's eyes raking her. It could not be, that Lawrence could look at anything without interest, yet Maricela felt herself sinking into space, heading toward the unknown, the fresh, exhilarating unknown, but, no, she was here, flat on the ground, she would always be here, stripped of everything, confined, bound, teeth set for what she could never have, yet so achingly full that she must sink.

Maricela blinked.

Lawrence looked away.

"I—I wish I were a psychcomputer!"

Lawrence put her hoe down and squatted. "I did not love you for your compassion." She glanced over at the workers, who were coming closer. "Not that psychcomputers have any."

Maricela gulped, noticing the past tense all too well. It shouldn't hurt, because this odd creature wasn't the Lawrence she had known, and she was hard put to say that she still loved

262

her, either. But that was because she had changed, and maybe, in her typical honesty, she had admitted that therefore she couldn't love. "Tell me how it felt," she urged.

"Why?"

"Telling me would help you; plus, I'm curious, just as you were, as you would be, if . . ." She watched as Lawrence stiffened, but her voice, when it came, was mild enough.

"You'd have to experience it for yourself," Lawrence said, drawing a circle in the dust, a simple maze.

"I can't do that, as you know."

"All right," Lawrence sighed. "It felt like upholstery."

"I feel as if I'm getting somewhere." Maricela mulled it over, stretching her hands out over the potato leaves, rubbing her fingers together. "That's touch."

Lawrence interrupted. "I don't mean what we call upholstery, that belted cushionery we sit or lie on. I'm talking about upholstery as it once was done, in the factories. Can you imagine that?" she jeered. "In all its intimations? The workers, the springs, the soft wood and the possibility of leather or plastic?"

Maricela answered tightly, "What else, please? Sound?" There was, after all, the rhythm board. Lawrence had strewn *some* landmarks onto her path.

Lawrence watched her nimble hands. It was new; therefore, it could interest her. "Really. It felt like music."

"Like the rhythm board," Maricela supplied.

"No," Lawrence said crossly. "It's gone. It was sent off in the shuttle with the Cube."

"Oh." Maricela waited, then tilted her head, humming. "Music," she murmured.

Lawrence winced. "I've told you quite often that you are a dreadful, tuneless hummer. Besides . . ." She shifted. It was interesting, to tell it again, from her solitary perspective, the story. "It wasn't the sound of such music. It was more how music makes you feel."

"I can accept that," Maricela said eagerly, "because I expected it."

Lawrence scratched her arm, her eyes intense. "It's not how it felt. It's what it was." Lawrence remembered one theory she had run across during her journey through the Cube. "Do you think it's a brain? Is it the way a brain sees the world?"

Maricela shrugged.

Lawrence persisted. "Is it an encyclopedia? Pay attention. Is it?"

"Why? It's gone. What difference does it make what it was?" Maricela decided that she had asked partly just to get Lawrence to talk to her, and she now realized the futility of her initial question.

"No!" Lawrence pointed to her head. "It's still here. In me." She spread her hands. "What am *I*, then? Or does that not matter, either?" She bent to gather up the hoe again.

"Asking me to tell you doesn't make any sense!" Maricela yelled as Lawrence started hopping away, away from the approaching workers.

"Yes it does!" she yelled over her shoulder. "But never mind," she muttered. "Those braindead memories have given me the answer."

"Don't call them braindead," Maricela immediately said absently, rising to trail her.

Lawrence picked up her cloak, only to toss it ahead of her, then run after it and toss it again. In this manner she got to the side furthest from the workers, who successfully ignored her to belabor over the patch she had just cleared. "The Cube," she announced, "was like reading a novel."

Solitude

"No. Afraid not. I'm just the pilot. Betan here is the one you need to talk to." He jerked his thumb to his left, trying to smile, but ended up merely frowning. *I can't do it. These desperate faces won't get any hope from me.*

Betan crossed in front of him. "Yes. We can take six. With this ship, you will not need suits, either. However, you will be kept restrained throughout most of the flight. We need to take only people who understand this restriction. Very young children must be closely monitored. Any questions? Good. Now, we have some supplies that must be unloaded immediately. Any volunteers?"

Scott grimaced at her calm, pleasant tone. How could she do it? Yeah, she had to tell them what they wanted to know, but to do it so efficiently irked him. He was still gawking at these odd people, while Betan . . . Betan had already accepted them as equals? Maybe. She was an engineer. He looked out over the crowd, catching Maricela's eye as she came in. "Maricela!" He waved at her.

She had been looking as anxious as the rest, but when she approached him, her face became smooth. Scott gulped. What kind of hope was she pinning on him?

"Have you decided yet who's to go?"

Maricela nodded. "Yes. Aratesht is one." She indicated the woman beside her.

"And you?" Scott merely glanced down at the swelling abdomen and nodded. He had been warned several times about pregnancy; even Betan had told him on the way up that they would go first.

"No." Her smile was serene. "Lawrence has chosen to stay, and I must, also. I will be needed."

Scott didn't want to argue in front of the satellite dwellers; that could come later. "Sure." He peered around her immediate area. "Where *is* Lawrence?"

"I'll take you to her. Come on." Maricela turned back to him. "I'm *so* glad you're here, Scott!"

He stumbled, blathering, "Uh, it's all right, everything's going to be all right. We just need to get you out of here." He trailed off, gaping at Maricela's beatific smile. He rolled his eyes when she turned away. Whatever.

She led him to a forest built right into the metallic hull. He gaped. "What the—?"

"Come on," Maricela said impatiently. "I need to take you to the arena. This and the arena are all we have left."

Scott straightened and almost cursed. Oddity consisted of the unexpected, and what did he expect the people to do instead? Conjuring up scenarios, even after his history lessons, was best forgotten as the true reality sank in. He followed Maricela up through some kind of cafeteria and ducked his way through groups of people eating greedily off of plastic plates. He felt awkward having to stoop so low as to peer into their faces. Light panels brightened only a few spots. The suns were long dead.

Each face that saw him lost its universal anxiety at once and smiled timidly with hope. Stiffly he ignored them all, looking for the one familiar face.

Stupid. He should have known she wouldn't be in the crowd. Scott burst into a grin as he strode toward her, watching as her fork clattered onto the plastic plate, making a crosshatch in the gray potatoes.

Maricela explained softly, "The cloak is important."

Oh. He saw it now. "It's hard for me to see in dim light," he explained. "Always has been."

"They've declared her insane and dangerous," Maricela continued relentlessly.

Scott nodded. "Okay, that's society for you. Why isn't she tied up?" he asked flippantly, then squatted and turned his head, hoping she'd get the hint.

She did. As a matter of fact, she left rather *too* quickly, he thought. He waited until she could no longer be seen behind the diners, who were now rising and shifting toward the back of the arena, somewhere in the dark. "Well?" he blurted, facing Lawrence. "Was it worth it?"

"Yes," she answered bleakly.

Scott shifted. "Are you . . . hurting?" There. The way she winced as she moved might mean it was only a physical reaction to the Cube.

"Yes." Her hand darted out to caress his freckled hand.

Lust hit him like a wave. *What? Not now!* He found himself clutching her hand, gathering up her cloak, ready to rip it to shreds. His mouth watered as he moaned.

"I'm sorry." Lawrence fell out of his grip as he felt his hands inexplicably loosening and numbing. "I should have expected that."

"What? What happened?"

"I don't know. I wasn't really expecting *that* so much as some kind of feedback. I touch you and feel you touching me and me touching you and . . ." She shuddered. "Besides, I'm on my period now." She quickly added, "I'm menstruating."

"Damn," Scott muttered. "This satellite is something else." Lawrence continued, as if to herself. "Vance's 'wife' used to 'forget' her anti-mens shot all the time. Drove him crazy," she chuckled. "But back to the matter at hand," she said officiously. "I'm guessing it was partly your reaction, right?" Her voice sounded extraordinarily uninterested. "It's the Cube inside of me that I know all of you."

"But that's not me," he protested. "It's the Cube's interpretation of me. The Cube is art, a mere representation, not reality itself." But how to explain his instant conversion here, huh? He grimaced as he blushed, though he knew that Lawrence knew he would and she didn't care.

"Yes, you're right. It's probably not that accurate since it's . . . it *was*," she corrected, "how I saw the world." She paused. "What happened just now. You still interest me, while everyone else is bland. What is your secret?" She scraped up the rest of the greasy potatoes and shoved them into her mouth unselfconsciously.

Scott hesitated. "I know a place. It's a small cabin in the woods, up in that range of mountains that grows to the east of us. The Appalachians," he said carefully at the newly learned word. "I mean, east of our commune, our home. I've lived there myself recently, since she died."

"I know." Again she reached for him, then dropped her hand. "I'm sorry. I know *now*, is what I meant." Scott's girlfriend had not died so long ago not to be included in the gene maps, but since the map had been dormant by the time she had experienced it, she had gotten the information, plain and simple, from Scott's echo of sorrow.

Scott bowed his head. "Do you want to come now? I can take you and Maricela on this ship. I think it would be better that way. You could take off your cloak, run with me to the mountains . . ."

"How will it be better?" Lawrence smiled, then said, "Oh, you can ask Maricela if she wants to go, but I'm staying. One of us has to remain to convince these people that we are not abandoning them to certain death, and of course that person shall be me. I don't care if I die."

Scott turned away from her sudden desirous look. "Suicide? You? I can't . . ." When he looked back, unable to escape his concern for long, he encountered her eyes, those new eyes that looked so uncannily blank, despite ephemeral emotions she must have placed there with great effort, to look normal. "You're too valuable an asset to society to commit suicide. Look, I can stay here to convince these people that we of Earth are committed." He stared, suddenly hushed by her bemused look. He found himself babbling, "I fell in love with your eyes first. I spent some time making a piece of deep blue velvet, but I never gave it to you because there was no way it could look the same." He ducked his head.

Lawrence waited a few seconds before answering. "I can't believe you even give a chit about society, you who were always abandoning it. But I think I know what you were trying to say." She sighed and rubbed her neck. "You could ask Maricela, but I think you already know that I can love no one. I probably never have loved anyone . . . No, that's too absurd. Just accept the fact that I will no longer love, okay?"

Scott grabbed her arm. "I want to shake you, slap you to your senses, except that you are already too much so. What do you think? On the Earth, while you have been up here, plans have been made to kill these people, or, at the very least, make their lives miserable. They can't blast them out of the sky, not yet, anyway, and bringing them down only serves to bring the enemy within closer range. There is an old concept the braindead brought up—war. Even as we speak negotiations continue. It seems unreal to me, yet what do we do? It's important not to lose sight . . ."

Lawrence pulled her arm away and scrunched up. The knowledge was there, but she had kept pushing it off. She did seem to have some limited way of influencing others. Maricela had told her about the shock Lawrence had apparently given her in the shuttle, so that she wouldn't mess up her plan to launch the Cube, and of course there was Scott's passion, which might have simply been repressed all these years, though it was more likely to have been merely her desire that got in the way again. Still, it didn't seem possible that she could use this new talent to stop a war. She had to ask. "Where are the peacemakers?"

"Guess. Most of the farmers are back to work now that they've learned that these people will be helped to return to Earth. Some artists are still quite active, but most people seem to be indifferent, waiting to see what happens and what the Center decides before they act." Scott stood. "I have been to some of the meetings. I want peace, but you've got to admit that it would be very easy to feed upon the people's nervousness around crowds and around strangers, and their fear of what the strangers might do, of what they might eat or where they might live." Scott turned. "Well, I guess it doesn't matter, especially to you."

Lawrence looked up at him with an odd expression, as if she were analyzing some tricky math problem with horror. "To be by myself is sweet. The others, even you, can stay over the horizon. I must heal."

"Looks as if we all must heal," he said shortly.

As if called by a need for healing, Maricela was back, and she held out her hand to take Lawrence's dish. "It's my turn to wash," she explained.

Scott began walking away.

Maricela turned to obliquely face him. "Betan needs you."

He nodded and moved off.

"I saw it all," Maricela said slowly, "because I knew that he, of all people, would have an effect on you. What is it about Scott that relieves you? Is it—is it because he's from Earth? No," she answered herself, "that's stupid. You can feel them as much as us."

"You're close," Lawrence said dully. "He has been alone a lot. Anybody that is distant from society like that—they were only partially in the Cube, after all."

Maricela thought it over, then answered, "What happened there at the end, though? Is something wrong?" She blushed. Wasn't she the nosy one?

"Yes. He's beginning to think that being alone isn't so great after all, the asshole." Lawrence started to move away, furtively, this time, keeping her eyes on Maricela's face.

"But . . ." Maricela sighed and waved her hand. "Go on. Go wherever you have to. I have to gather up the dishes."

Reconciliation

"Why are they crying?" Lawrence asked callously as she stepped around yet another tiny pile of possessions heaped to the side of a large group of huddling people.

"Because they miss their friends and their family members who have already left for Earth," Wong answered in what he hoped to be a tolerant tone.

Lawrence shrugged. "I thought it was because they were cold," she said, rubbing her arms.

Wong led the way through the dim masses of people grouped in the arena—3321 at last count—at an unbearably slow rate. Lawrence shuddered. She could pick a path that avoided everyone immediately, but Wong's sharp eyes could better distinguish those lumps of personal items. He might as well lead.

Lawrence marveled at their tears. To be able to feel separate from others! To be an individual once more! She opened her mouth slightly and breathed through it as the wave of desire passed through her. *But, come to think of it, when was I ever like that? Vance left, Kamela left, Jeffrey left, I left . . . I can't remember ever caring. Ah, well.*

Wong pointed down at his feet. "This material, your foam, is very interesting. It feels like walking through mud, or quicksand," he muttered. "As a figure of speech, I mean." He paused. "Is that right? Is that what mud feels like?"

"No, but I suppose it's possible for a thick layer of mud to hinder motion." Lawrence thought a moment before continuing. "This doesn't cling to us. Why did you choose that expression?" She swallowed as the reality of what he was surged through her. He had never been on Earth. He had never seen a morning, an ocean, a breeze.

"I don't know. We learn a lot from our memories that have little to do with life up here." Wong ran his fingers through his straight, short hair. "Do you think we will be prepared for Earth?" He glanced at her shyly.

Lawrence halted. Still she was unsure what Wong was about. It took her a minute to let her mind take up where his persona was and follow it. She sighed. "Sure. Why not?" was what she ended up saying, and she couldn't be sure it was right even then. She glided to another topic. "When they bring up the webs—they weren't ready for last shipment—we can let everybody bolt themselves in and inspect each one."

"Protection is important," acceded Wong, "but getting out is even more so. Oh—I can't wait to see this beautiful Earth! The pictures I have seen are so incredible!"

Lawrence suddenly had a great urge to seize his hand, then both of them would be running through a meadow she knew of, in the crisp spring air, laughing. Oh, to be able to feel so much excitement—to see it as a child would, for the first time, except Wong would see more, being twenty years old as she was. She licked her lips. The whole image was strange and beautiful.

"We've got seven exits that are possible," Wong pointed. "Six on the sides. Er, I know those two lead out to other rooms, but after those are cut away, the doors will be feasible exits. The seventh one goes through the ceiling, but it leads to machinery." He frowned. "The problem is they're all on the same level, so there's a very good chance that if one is blocked, they'll all be blocked."

"Yes," said Lawrence, "but it's better to worry about that later. Maybe we'll land at an angle." She grimaced at her confident tone. More than likely, they'd simply die, was what she really meant, so who really needed to plan ahead?

Wong squatted near an exit and waited for her to awkwardly crouch down beside him. "I feel sometimes as if I am doing the wrong thing, completely siding with the Shawicc, but do you know what she has done?"

Lawrence guessed it was the old ploy of granting close followers some control over proceedings so as to appease them, while in the meantime the leader remained in power, but she shrugged. "I can't keep up with everything."

"She has allowed me control over the rockets," Wong said proudly. "I told her I was the most qualified engineer, and she agreed. Still . . ."

Lawrence lifted his chin and stared into his eyes. He blinked, staring at her soft smile. "I can't blame you. You acknowledge her because you must have the rockets, because you feel they control our flight, and you must control everything, even when it's only after all going to be chance that determines where we fall. You are acting on emotion, a feeling of insecurity and a terror of death, but who acts otherwise?"

Wong gulped. This sounded too much like the Shawicc at her best, but, at that moment, he found himself smiling. Lawrence was looking at him tenderly, with understanding, and he felt an odd sense of looking at himself in those eyes.

And maybe it was him at that moment. Later, of course, he was sure it wasn't.

Crash

Anxiously Wong tore his gaze from the screens and peered toward the Shawicc. "We're entering the thermosphere."

She nodded, removing her robe and placing it under her. Wong watched as she lay down and closed her eyes. He fired a few rockets half-heartedly in response to the readings that stated they were tilting too far to the left.

Left? What? Momentarily he was dazed, staring down at the screens with a sharp fear that he had interpreted them wrongly. His self-imposed direction sense in the absence of gravity only served now to confuse him. It could be fun, he mused, asking for instant death, for descent would be fast. He shut his eyes. Yes. He could see it now. The painstakingly built up layers of metal and insulation burning away, red-hot, glittering molecules of oxygen feeding, friction eating away, hungry fingers reaching in for him . . .

He gulped.

"You're doing fine," Lawrence whispered.

Wong opened his eyes to see another person's fingers in front of him, flashing the screens in an endless, rapid cycle, so they were practically a blur. Funny. He'd never noticed how short and stubby Lawrence's hands were. He looked up to see her eyes following the screens blandly.

"Just as I thought," she muttered. "Watch out for the mesosphere. It's — "

Wong wet his lips. "When will it get hot?" Then he felt absurd. She knew as much as he did, or did she?

"Temperature in here is 33°," she said, switching from her more familiar Kelvin to their Celsius. "but I don't think it'll get much higher. Probably be 65°, at the most." She drifted away.

Great. We'll just die from heatstroke, that's all. He shifted and went back to reading the screens, slowly. Then it hit him: *Damn. If Lawrence can read these screens so rapidly and not get disoriented, then obviously* she *should be the one chosen to guide them. Damn the Shawicc and her decision about the helplessness of the insane.*

Lawrence floated across to the Shawicc. Dispassionately she wavered above that calm face before pulling herself down. Taking hold of one of the loops attached to the floor, she strapped herself in, breathing heavily.

Maricela looked over at her wryly. "Everybody seems okay, so I'll just sit here until we land. I'm sure I'll have plenty to do then."

Lawrence saw it. Although they were moving quite fast, despite the retrorockets, time seemed slow, maybe because of the way most people forsook any bondage and floated free. In this slow dance, she felt calm, as if they would ever so gently float to Earth, be seized by its gravity, and drift off to sleep.

No! Her fingers scrabbled at the webbing. I'm falling! Help! I want to fly out to where I am, where I should be, to be waiting forever, never contacting anything ever again. Just me, alone, in space, adrift . . .

"Hey!" Maricela's yell caused her to jerk and her eyes to fly open. "If any of you hear us command you, or you feel any disturbance, you come down at once!" Lawrence watched as she put down the effective megaphone and grimaced at the Shawicc, who had opened her eyes at the shout.

"Good," was all she said as she shifted. "How hot is it?"

"It's 40°," Lawrence answered. "But it's best not to think about it."

Maricela frowned. "Oh, yes, Centigrade." She quickly translated to Kelvin, 314°, then shrugged.

"If we live," the Shawicc began in a firm tone, "how will we be treated? What do you do with strangers on your world?"

Lawrence quickly frowned and searched. They'd been through that so many times! Was the Shawicc losing oxygen?

"You've been with us, and other people from Earth, for quite some time," Maricela said hotly. "Why don't *you* tell *us* how we treat you?"

Lawrence leaned over toward both of them. "No," she whispered. "I think when the situation will be reversed, with *them* coming to *us*, it will be different. But I can tell you an analogy. We live in fairly large communes that are isolated from each other. I know there are highways, and egg trucks, and screens, but I felt isolated. A guest, a real live in person guest, was a big deal. They got everything, including my thrilled attention. So, I think, in our society, you will be considered a guest, at least for a while, and it will be all right." Lawrence pondered. It wasn't quite right, it was only how she would greet them, and Scott had warned her that naïveté was unbecoming in one who refused to face the truth.

"But we are not guests. It is our home, too." The Shawicc reminded her.

"I know." Lawrence shook her head over her last speech. What now? Nostalgia? Is that where she was heading? It wasn't as stupid as it seemed. "We will see you as guests at first, though. And when that fades, we will see you as friends."

The Shawicc grunted. "Do you not know of your history? All societies have a legend, a myth of their creation. What is yours?"

Lawrence hunched over and thought. The best answer was — "We had no conscious retelling of any events. I suppose, though, I should continue and tell you that a concerned group of people in the past saw the inequality, the overpopulation, the pollution, and the ignorance, and they decided to do something about it." Lawrence stopped at the look on Maricela's face. "What's the matter?"

The Shawicc answered, "She should hear this, too. You know we have pictures and records of these long ago days. We also have maps of your Earth's surface. We can see the ruins your routes never take you."

"What? What is this?" Maricela snorted. "We have scientific stations all over the world, and communes all over the West/North continent. There are no ruins."

Lawrence shrugged. Now she understood. The Shawicc wasn't suddenly cowering down and pretending to be Lawrence's friend at the last minute. She was simply preparing for war.

The Shawicc turned to her then. "How do you think you get your tools, your machines, your screens? Many a time your authorities must have headed to the ruins and salvaged what they could. You and your ideal society. Give me a break."

"Oh, Zenobia," Lawrence grumbled, then burst out laughing at Maricela's face at this inadvertent use of the Shawicc's name.

The Shawicc noticed Maricela's look of curiosity and said smugly, "Do you think your people would want to hear our stories? What about the guests who bore bad news? What did you do to them?"

"Lawrence, what about your benevolent creators?" Maricela stuck her head out over the Shawicc. "Were they responsible for the Great Eviction and the loss of contact with these people?" She tried to sound curious, but instead she jeered.

"No," the Shawicc replied. "We're fairly certain, though, that our removal was the atrocity that started the whole thing, and during the resultant conflict, all ships were destroyed, we think. And, of course, nobody knows who cut us off." She leaned back with a sigh. "That's history for you. Even we with our records don't know whom to blame. But it is not my place to put the blame on the people of the present day. I only wanted to warn you that I cannot believe your simple view of peace."

She could say no more, and Lawrence followed suit, leaning back as the ship began to shudder. Idly she watched groups hastily, or, really, very slowly, but panicking with flapping arms, climbing over or down to strap in, responding to the turbulence with no warning from Maricela.

"Hey," Maricela patted her arm from the side opposite the Shawicc.

Lawrence murmured tiredly, "How'd you get over there?"

"Listen: are you telling me there are ruins?"

"Sure." Lawrence rolled over and looked at her. "Apparently, they only showed you what you wanted to see. They had a set pattern of paths that even the planes followed. You've got to give them some credit—"

"No," Maricela said immediately. "That means that the transporters were in on it, also. It seems too unbelievable."

Lawrence shrugged and looked away. It took a while, kind of like noticing an ant in motion several feet away, but Lawrence finally saw a group of about ten people inching over to her, and she tried not to be prepared for what she knew would happen.

Their spokesperson was a short Indian hybrid with wide, black eyes and short black hair that clung slickly to her skull. "Can you predict the future?" Gill asked innocently.

"No," Lawrence said firmly, not even deigning to look at her.

"Stratosphere," reported Wong from his position behind her.

"There." Gill pointed at the wall to Lawrence's right. "Can't you see it?"

Lawrence refused to turn and look. "No."

"Temperature: 45°," came Wong's supernaturally calm voice.

"It glows. It's red hot. Can't you see it?" Again she pointed, this time stretching her arm out further, over Lawrence's head.

"No." Lawrence yawned. "We can know from past knowledge and scientific calculations that it burns *out there*, but in here there is no sign of it." In this heat, she found it easy to remain unconcerned. Only Wong, in his critical position, had a spritzer of ice water on hand to dash on his head and to drink.

"Temperature: 50°." Again Wong's calm voice came through.

"I'm hot! We will burn up! We'll die!" Gill clutched at her thin tunic, ripping it to free her throat.

"Perhaps," Lawrence said.

"Lawrence!" Wong at last raised an alarm. "Our velocity is increasing!"

"Naturally," she answered. She could feel the pressure now. She shifted. The heat was quickly becoming unbearable.

"Messiah! Show us a sign of our future. Will we live?" Gill moaned.

Lawrence finally sneaked a glance at the wall. No, *she* couldn't see any sign of redness, but it was hard not to superimpose Gill's vision over her own cool, clearheaded acceptance of a normal wall. She was hot, so hot that she could only distantly admire Wong at his controls, sweat held out of place by a hastily pulled on headband. She rolled her eyes slowly over at Maricela, who was staring, horrorstruck, at the wall.

"Oh, Lawrence! I see it! A hole will burn through and we'll die!"

Lawrence bundled her head into her arms. Mass hysteria. Great. So we all die. What difference did it make? But she kept herself in readiness to replace Wong, nevertheless, though it had been agreed that when the crisis came, it was highly unlikely that anyone would be able to do anything.

"Troposphere."

"Okay! Everybody strap in! Now!" The Shawicc's ringing, commanding tones were useless, because everybody was already hanging on for dear life as the ship battered them back and forth. All, that is, except the group of penitents crouched before Lawrence.

"Messiah!" they screeched, arms stretched toward her.

"Oh, all right, but I want you to cram everything about this Messiah chit after we land. I *have seen* the amazing future, and I see our beautiful garden ship, our beautiful tree, lying as a goodly oasis in an Earth desert. If that isn't a vision of hope, what is? Now shut up and strap in!" Lawrence gulped for air as she rolled right into the Shawicc, then just as quickly rolled over Gill, holding her down as Maricela pulled the straps.

Wong was there, too, near her head. "Oh, shit," he screamed. "Here it comes!"

What few lights there were blinked off, and several people screamed over the noise of the screeching. Lawrence let go, desperately holding on to only her sensations of great pressure as several bodies pummelled her to unconsciousness. Dreaming, she heard a large boom.

A Rose in Bloom

Murmurings. Groans. Heavy weights pressing on her. Gravity once more. A soft arm, flattening her ear. Lawrence opened her eyes.

She was back on Earth, and she was alive. Paralyzed by the bodies on top of her, she felt her heart seem to start up from nothing and begin to pump too rapidly. When she took a breath, it felt as if it were her first.

She knew. All she had to do was think a moment, and that hidden sense told her what she wanted to know, unlike that time long ago, when she had merely seen the kitten and sat in the field.

Some had been conscious a while; most were still unconscious. Had *she* been unconscious? Lawrence wasn't sure. She could tell that some were injured; no, all were injured in some way. Was *she* damaged? No. No? How? A coincidence? Lawrence lay there quietly a minute more, then reasoned, *I had those ten people clustered around me to cushion me. It's still odd, though.*

Time to get up. Slowly she moved an arm here, a leg there, selecting where she knew there was the least injury among the bodies moaning around her, and pulled herself free from the supplicants.

A groan. Lawrence nodded. Wong, whose water bottle was dripping on his head, was coming to.

It was still hot, but it couldn't be more than 314° again. Lawrence smiled wryly, remembering those Region 12—Georgian—summers and how she automatically took it easy during the rare, yet dreadful 314° days.

There was no one outside of the blistered shell to tell her through her new sense where they had landed or how they were to get out, yet they had to get out soon. And, of course, everyone here knew as much as she did. Even Wong, who had been watching the screens, had no idea where they were or how the vehicle had ended up. Lawrence pondered as she lit a light stick.

"Lawrence?"

"Yes, Maricela? Are you all right?" Might as well ask. "We need a doctor, that's for sure."

Maricela heard the slow, thumping voice and raised herself up. "Are *you* all right?"

"Yes. I am uninjured." She pointed the light stick at her. "And you?"

"I'm not sure. I can get up, though."

"You have several abrasions on your face and will probably need plastic surgery. Other than that, you're fine," Lawrence said dully. "You were also well-cushioned. I don't know where your medkit is, though. You'll have to find that for yourself."

"Why is it so . . . cold?" She had to smile at that. "I mean relatively, of course."

"I don't know. My guesses are we've been out a long time. It's night, we're under water. We landed in snow," she hazarded at the last moment, picturing an arctic waste and shivering delightfully. "I don't know," Lawrence repeated, savoring the wonder of being ignorant.

"How will we get out?" Maricela asked casually as she searched the floor for her kit.

"I don't know that, either. If someone was outside, then I could tell from what they were thinking how we landed." She straightened. "We were heading for the East/South continent at Wong's last reading. We could be in any type of region, I guess," she muttered. Did she have to climb all the way up to the ceiling? The most efficient way would be to find ground level and cut her way out there. But how? Gravity told her they were at an angle, but that could be the arena nestled in the outer material, not the ground.

"The Shawicc took it pretty badly," Maricela whispered. "Perhaps due to her age. I had hoped she'd be alive and alert during the greeting."

Lawrence walked away, stepping over bodies as she went. The Shawicc *was* alive, and was in fair condition, but how much longer would she live under these conditions? Maricela needed more than a simple medkit for a few of the cases, and, of course, they needed more than the few doctors here who were conscious and capable of practicing.

Trial and error. A thrill shot through her, yet her brain wasn't racing madly, searching for solutions. As a matter of fact, she felt like a moron. It must be the heat. She climbed over the seating and stepped up to the nearest exit. Hooking herself onto the welders' clasps, she grabbed the wheel and began tugging it clockwise. "Come on," she muttered to herself. "Don't be fused shut."

"Can I help?" A voice sounded from her right.

"Yes, Wong," she said tiredly. The ten supplicants with their cushioning had left her with some pretty predictable companions: whoever had been able to sit next to her.

As he moved to take a firm grip on the wheel, she whipped around. "See about that leg, first."

Wong stepped back, away from the wheel, and tested each leg separately. He looked at Lawrence puzzledly. "They're fine."

Lawrence frowned. *Could she be wrong? No.* "Just be careful, then. The left tibia is slightly cracked."

Wong resumed tugging at the wheel. Almost immediately it began to turn, and they had it open within three minutes. Wong shone his light stick onto the outer shell. "Just as I thought," he muttered. "The door's fused. We're going to have to cut through with a blowtorch." He turned to go fetch one from the storage case Scott had welded to the floor weeks ago, full of the few things they thought they would need: not food, not clothes, not even water, but lots of blowtorches, hammers, and ladders.

When he returned, Lawrence accepted it to cut a five centimeter hole at waist level. Sand trickled out as she cut. Wong fingered it excitedly.

"What is it? What does it mean?" he asked Lawrence.

"We're most likely in a desert. This is sand. Remember from your memory banks about the huge dunes of sand of the Africa? That could be where we are." After a few seconds the sand stopped. She stood there a full minute before it hit her, feeling quite grateful that almost everyone was still unconscious and therefore using less oxygen, because at the rate she and Wong were getting them out, he with his excitement and her with her lassitude, they'd run out pretty quickly if they were lively. "The heat fused it into glass. But it means we're below ground level. We'll have to move up."

Wong shined his light stick at each exit, aiming at their exact location instantly. "We still have the one at the top," he surmised, "but we are at an angle, and that's the highest side exit." He pointed toward the one slightly to their left on the other side of the arena.

"Okay," Lawrence grunted. She led him through the groaning people immediately, remembering to give Maricela a reassuring glance as she passed her, placing her face directly in Wong's light stick so she could be seen, but Maricela was already hard at work with a new patient, a surgeon who could help her with the broken bones once she treated her twisted ankle.

Again they were able to open the exit, and this time Wong cut a small hole in the outer shell. No sand appeared. Gingerly he slid his hand through the little circle of blackness and waved his fingers in the outdoor air. "This is it," he whispered, and the joy he felt made Lawrence plop down on the floor in a heap. It took a few seconds for her to mutter new instructions to him.

Together they cut a three meter wide hole, taking turns. It was a pain having to climb up and hold the blowtorch steady, while the other held the light at a safe distance, then to switch places frequently, but in the darkness Lawrence wasn't taking any chances. Wong had been able to poke the light stick out and see where the ground was, so they were able to match the bottom of the door with the level of the ground, roughly. At first Lawrence didn't even care, but then she remembered that not everyone would be able to climb, and the few people in best condition still shouldn't be forced to carry the injured.

"When they come," Wong said eagerly about halfway through, "how will they come?"

"Remember your pictures in your data bases? The first meeting they'll have to come in planes, because they don't live on this continent, and they tracked us pretty well, so it won't be long." Lawrence pulled up to take his place. Now, if she thought about it, she could sense the Westerners in the plane, and she could sense that they were less than an hour away from where they had landed in the East/South continent. *We are in Africa!* She thought some more, searching the minds above. *In the Sahara Desert!* Rats. Now she knew everything, except why deducing things was more fun than having them confirmed in a cheating manner.

It was night when they finally finished cutting the hole, so the fresh air blasting in was relatively cool, moist, and reviving. The outside of the dome was still very hot, and she was glad she had accepted the work gloves from Wong when he had returned with the asbestos pallet to lay over the rough edge of the door. Better warn everybody else not to touch it, though. Lawrence bent down to help Wong carry the cut-out away from the door when she sensed Maricela nearby, down on the floor below them.

"Watch out for the sand," Wong warned. "Some will sift in, no matter what we do."

"It's dark," Maricela said in a disappointed tone. "I was hoping to get more light in here. My eyes are dazzled from peering into these light sticks."

"Maybe some mechanics can be cared for next so they can raise the light panels for you," Wong suggested.

Lawrence smirked, looking out over the moaning mass of people. "Come on, Maricela. We're naked. You want us with lighter skin to burn in the sun? This is better."

Maricela ignored her and answered Wong. "That would help. However, I came to tell you that most people are safe to move outside. I think we can start moving them now. I wonder when they'll arrive."

Lawrence tore her gaze away from Wong's blissful look. The wind gradient was lifting his hair, rippling the tunic he had hastily grabbed from someone's pile of possessions when he had carried the blowtorch. Imagine looking like that at someplace new! She had been feeling quite superfluous during the brief conversation; now she could help. "Less than an hour, closer to a half-hour."

"Okay," Maricela said in a monotone, making Lawrence feel separate and alone. "Let's get to work."

When the planes flew overhead, only a few people were out on the sands. The planes' searchlights shone concomitantly down on them in swathes, and Lawrence stared at the vision of hundreds of bodies ghastly lit in sudden stripes before being wiped out in the darkness.

Wong had a tiny group of technicians over near the door setting up light panels. When Lawrence wandered back to assist a patient, he turned to her and grinned. "Did you see it?" He pointed to the north. "The garden ship, over there. It's cracked open. I can see the tree whenever the planes' lights brush over it."

Lawrence said nothing.

The planes landed as close as they safely could, and Lawrence could see from their lights small clusters of people racing toward her. She helped three other walkers gently place a patient down near Maricela, who was too busy to look up, and went to meet them. Maybe it was now they who needed her help.

"Lawrence! Hello!" It was Charles waving at her, but she didn't even notice his face in the glow of his light stick. Instead, she stared at his badge.

It was practically still the same, with the image of the Center surrounded by interconnecting, smaller communes, but the odd, yet beautiful construct was different. The tight, unusual bud had flowered.

"We're unloading paramedics and equipment," Charles explained. "We think we've got room for the most critical cases to be flown over."

Almost instantaneously Lawrence calculated his fifty-seven floaters with room for three patients, then compared that to the most severe injuries. No, she couldn't do it, because she wasn't able to assess, as a medic could, how many were really that serious: all she could really rate was their amount of pain. She tilted her head. "You'll have to speak to Maricela and the other doctors, not me. She's right there." She turned and pointed exactly at her position.

"Okay." Charles hesitated, squinting in that direction, then turned with a smirk to Lawrence. Looking her up and down, he taunted, "All buck naked, I see, and against our webbing, too? Didn't that hurt?" But then he shut up, and Lawrence had to see that same mixture of awe and curiosity she had seen on so many others' faces since she had come out of the Cube. "What—?"

"Go on," she answered, at the edge of her stamina, walking away, back to the edge of the seated crowd of arrivals.

The Shawicc was there. Maricela had brought her out first in a sling made from her robes, and somehow she had brought her to a weak consciousness. "Africa?" Lawrence overheard her murmur. Her joyous voice could not be described, nor could it match what Lawrence felt from her: a rich satisfaction and ecstasy. "We're in Africa?"

"Not for much longer, I'm afraid," Maricela said softly. "We need to take you back to our continent for treatment, but you'll come back someday."

"Africa!" she murmured.

Lawrence squatted alone. What had happened here? Why had the badge changed? Did it happen on its own? Wait. She wrapped her head in her arms. It was coming to her, and it had something to do with the Shawicc. Some old theory of warfare, in which somebody had once said that the main purpose was to wreak havoc upon the society, causing it to fall. If that was so, then the Shawicc had a very powerful weapon indeed.

She felt him coming as an enigma, someone she could not read, whose own memories had been so engulfed by the past conflicts that it was the same old inscrutable story. Still she waited until he had tapped her shoulder before muttering, "No."

An attendant she did not recognize from her past sat down next to her and peered at her face. "What will you do now? As I think you know, we've been doing a lot of planning during your leave, and we've decided not to punish you for leaving without our permission."

Lawrence sighed. Now she knew why she had suddenly crept with exhaustion to the edge of the people, when just minutes before she was physically hale and ready to continue hauling out the rest of the thousands of injured. She was tired. Tired of *them*, anyway. "No."

"Instead," he blithely continued, "we'd like to see you become one of us! Yes, you can now become an attendant! Won't that be fun! Oh," he tut-tutted, "there'll be the usual tests, the psychcomputers, all the necessary checks to make sure you're balanced, but, really, I think there's a place for you with us!" the attendant finished magnamiously.

"No." She grimaced. Damn it, what she didn't need right now was to try to explain all her careful analysis of human behavior, nice predictable human behavior, to this moron. Something urged her to try, though. "I realize that you are terrified of change, and that you think you must defend your way of life and material wealth against these space invaders, but you won't be able

278

to use me a weapon. My knowledge is useless to you, okay? If that's really all you want from me." She stood up. "I have to go."

The attendant casually mirrored her movements, shaking his head. "Well, then . . ."

And she could feel his excitement. In the glow from the light panels that just now came on, she could see his uniform, an odd motley green and brown relic his mind was proudly calling "camouflage." Is this how it was during the Rapacious Age? He only made her queasy, made her want to roll up into a ball, but she still felt like she had to stand there calmly and firmly, playing out the farce, and then go.

She felt the cold steel of a gun pressing against her temple. There was no way he could have fashioned one! Just like Vance's book, she couldn't yet see where the antique had come from.

He pressed her back against his front, and she could feel his hard penis pressing her, the cloth of his pants already soaked. "Oh, God," he rasped. "Look at you all! Naked and fornicating right here in front of our innocent souls. Thank goodness all the children were already safe on Earth before this atrocity, this orgy had to happen! Have you no shame? Wait! Don't I see a teenager over there?" He leaned his head to point it toward a young man hauling a stretcher. "Oh," he squealed, beginning to pump his penis harder and harder into her lower back, "this can't be! You hooligans, mating with the inferior, the breeders of other lands! And he's such a comely child, too!" He moaned, and Lawrence could feel the wet spot spread down his leggings.

"Morals!" he gasped. "We've got to teach morals! We've got to be civilized here! We've got to deny them in the name of national security! Where's the prison to hold so many deviants?" He hissed.

Lawrence interrupted. "Your tiny weapon there ain't nothing compared to what they can do. Go ahead and kill me. You know I am death and life and everything. My personal death means nothing to me. Yes, I'll bleed, but blood is universal. After you shoot me, not everyone will die, just me. So go ahead. I welcome it." Lawrence could feel her own excitement grow, overcoming his infantile symptoms and even compensating for her slimy back. Death of her mere organism would be new. Yes, she honestly did welcome it.

Charles was there, taking the gun away from the attendant's paralyzed hands. Lawrence came down from her euphoria and frowned. He couldn't shoot her, because . . . Hey, had she paralyzed him in her terror? Had her self-preservation kicked in after all? Dimly she heard Charles say, "Come on, man. That's not how it's going to be." He wrapped the attendant up in a tarp and tossed him to Scott, who had appeared suddenly, apparently unaware of what was going on. "Here. Take him to Tom. He'll know what to do with such hallucinations."

"Really?" Lawrence blurted, suppressing as hard as she could the sick, twisted braindead memories that had arisen from contact with the attendant.

Charles smiled as he pulled off his shirt. "Come here," he said silkily, and he began wiping around her buttocks. "He got you good."

"Oh, chit. I might get pregnant!" But then the old memories faded, and she could only stand there sheepishly as he cleaned her up.

"What?" he asked, truly puzzled.

"Never mind," she whispered. "Do you think there will be more of them? Do you think the Shawicc and the people of the satellite suspect that some of us have the old hatreds?"

Scott was back, wrapping his arm around her slumped shoulder. "Don't worry about the politics anymore, Lawrence. We'll take care of it." He smiled ruefully. "Are you okay? Do you need to hang around and get medical treatment, or can we just go? I brought my small floater. We can leave right now if you're ready."

Lawrence no longer felt superfluous. The attendants were the ones who were unnecessary, she suddenly decided. She nodded, leaning her head onto his shoulder. "I'm fine, and I can't wait to get there."

The two outcasts slowly turned around as one and headed for Scott's floater he had landed far away from the official planes. Luckily, in all the excitement, no one had noticed.

"I'm taking you to where I said I would. That cabin. It's only fair. None of us need suffer. Or something like that," Scott explained.

Lawrence said nothing, just smiled up at the tiny floater and took his hand.

Healing Takes a Long Time

Lawrence shifted under the moist quilts and murmured. Another dream, this time of Jeffrey at an open fire, calmly eating beans and looking up at the mountains. He would not come to the cabin, no one did, but he would stand there and ponder, wondering what had brought him here, wondering what was keeping him away.

She remembered another dream, of the endless negotiations between what seemed to be the Shawicc and everyone else, how she agreed to work in exchange for a new life in Africa someday, while the other satellite dwellers, some of them, mingled quite well, Wong and others like him, so eager to please in exchange for one more walk on the beach. Some, of course, wanted to see the ruins. Some were more ambitious, as they wandered from place to place, accepting food and work in exchange for the chance to tell stories, stories about the past and their own experiences in that can in the sky. She wanted to . . .

"Lawrence!"

The whisper beside her caused her to open her eyes to a tiny crack to see gray dawn out the windows. "What?"

Scott lifted his head from the pillow and grinned. "Why didn't you tell me the roof was leaking?"

"Oh. It's been leaking a long time. I forgot all about it." She didn't look at him, just kept staring out at the rain.

Scott sighed and rose to dress. "I've got a tarp," he muttered, "best I can do until it lets up."

"No, leave it alone. I like it." Lawrence sat up and wrapped the quilt around her.

Again Scott sighed as he left.

Lawrence got up and woozily went to her stool near the bucket. As if she were still in a dream she stared blindly at the dripping water and pulled out her little green notebook.

The door slamming didn't rouse her. "No way I can get up on that roof. It's about to cave in. I should have thought of that. I guess we're stuck." Scott squatted beside her. "What are you writing?"

"My autobiography." Lawrence looked down at the book and picked at the frayed cover. "Not really the events, as it's turned out. More like what makes what I am." She looked at him. "I think it helps."

Scott frowned. "While I was out, I noticed a small camp near the foot of the mountain. Who else has been up here?"

"Lots of people. But I don't go out to them. Still, they stand out there sometimes and look. I don't know why. Seems to me they have a lot of work to do as it is, without searching for me." Lawrence tucked away her book and pencil.

Scott hung his head. "I should have known this place wasn't completely hidden. They haven't been bothering you, have they?"

"No. I said they just stand there. And . . . I don't mind knowing them within. It's okay."

"It's strange," he muttered, then straightened. "Listen . . . has a year been enough time for you to get over acting like a hermit? Can you think now about what you want to do?"

Lawrence hitched herself over to the window to stare out at the garden. She'd finally got it going, and he wanted her to leave? What was wrong with staying here until the roof caved in? "I like to see myself flying in space, flying with the Cube," she found herself confiding. "I still dream about it. At the end of my journey, I come upon a pristine planet before any life has begun to form. No one is there. That world is blank. I'm at peace." Unconsciously she smoothed down a fresh sheet in the notebook. "It sometimes seems better than here."

Scott shifted impatiently. "But you couldn't *live* on such a world, don't you see? Besides, do you want *this world* to be like that? Forget it, it's not." He mused. "If it interests you, this last year, when I was alone, I thought about the final destiny of the Cube. I doubt it will ever fall into aliens' hands, and if it does, will it matter?" He chuckled self-consciously. "I mean, I came up with some pretty wild speculations. Like: if the aliens really cared, then they would have already manipulated the combinations and seen humanity."

Lawrence burst out laughing.

"No, no! Let me finish! And maybe we, maybe *you*, can do the same!"

She hushed to think it over. Excitement was quickly followed by severe nausea. "No," she sighed. "That's too much like the Elaborynth." For a long time she gazed upon his puzzled look.

281

"The precursor for the Cube," she explained. "It was on paper, like this notebook. I drew it for my Mentor in low-tech school, another outcast."

Scott shook his head. "Maricela told me about why I seem acceptable to you. It got me thinking. Wouldn't you like to see the other outcasts? You know, in person?" He shifted, regretful for having to add *that* in his eagerness, but then he rushed on gallantly: "Yes, let's go see *those* aliens that live in the mountains!"

Lawrence giggled. It would be fun, seeing Vance, and Kamela, and Cinda, and all those others that lived in Vance's "prison." Now that she knew about them, she was still faintly curious. Maybe they weren't as predictable as all the others. Maybe they could still surprise her, darting about those genetic precursors and slapping her with vivid, coursing originality. Yes. Why not? "It would be fun to go *see* that library buried underneath the mountain and take a look at Vance's books." She threw the quilt off and grabbed him around the waist. "Yes! Let's go now!"

He held her close, and, though he couldn't directly experience it, *he* could imagine the wounds healing, the heart opening.

Lawrence had finally shown up.